END'S BEGINNING

TOLATIN TESTAMENTS: BOOK ONE

KENDALIN BRIANNA

ISBN: 0-578-57577-9
ISBN-13: 978-0-578-57577-3

To Melissa Marie Iriene Burns (My Mib)

Mama,

You were and will always be a guiding light in this world for me. You were my biggest blessing, truest friend, confidant, and number one fan. I truly could not have done this without you. Even though you're gone you still helped make my dreams to come true just as you always did growing up. Although you didn't get to see the final product in person, you were the first to read these pages. Thank you for the hours you spent listening to this story and all my others. God made me a storyteller and I imagine raising a storyteller is no easy feat. But you created the environment in which that passion could flourish and thrive. Thank you for taking on the task with grace and love, just as you lived your whole life. You're forever my best friend. I miss you every day.

I love you with all my hearts,
Kendalin BriAnna

CHAPTER ONE

The world of Tolatin is a wondrous one: full of magic yet driven by consistency. And, like any good world, brimming with adventure and quite a bit of danger. Which, of course, makes this particular adventure of ours all the more intriguing.

Not that Gardeniyah knew much about that. Of course, she liked to think she did. She'd read every book available to her from the castle library, talked to as many elders in Eastern Tolatin as she could who would humor a human such as her. But the truth of the matter was that Gardeniyah knew very little about the world she claimed to understand. And our story begins on the very day she finally started to figure that out.

Five thousand four hundred and sixty-one. Gardeniyah stood in the closet behind the row of her and her sisters' clothes, tracing each line carved into the wood as she counted. *Five thousand four hundred and sixty-two.* She rubbed the blade of the knife with the thumb of her other hand as she counted. *Five thousand four hundred and sixty-three.* A lump formed in her throat as she retraced the same tally. *Five thousand four*

1

hundred and sixty-three. She closed her eyes tight, even though it was unnecessary in the darkness. She willed the number to be different, pressing her thumb too hard against the side of the blade.

"Fitting," she muttered as blood seeped from her finger, a gash in her flesh to match those on the wall. She pressed her bleeding thumb to the wood, then carved another tally on top of the bloody thumbprint.

Gardeniyah knelt down to feel the first ragged gash—her four-year-old self's first attempt at carving a mark into the wood. Breathing in deeply, she lit a match, illuminating the wall before her. Five thousand four hundred and sixty-four days gone by all etched into the wall. The new blood-soaked tally meant one thing: her time was up.

Gardeniyah's days had been numbered since her first in the East. The ignorance that comes with the last day of normalcy before your whole world changes is a gift. You treasure the memory for years to come regardless if the change is good or bad.

The problem for Gardeniyah and her sisters was that they never got that gift. Nor did they get to believe—even in the naivety of childhood—in the idea of permanence. Such a luxury is not something one gets to enjoy when your mother abandons you and your two sisters at the border of your race's enemy when you are four years old.

Knowing what the future holds is an odd and rather tragic way for anyone—let alone a child—to spend their life. But Gardeniyah passed her days this way, etching marks into the wall and memories of this place into her mind. Because she knew that, one day, she would have to leave and wouldn't be able to do either.

The match singed her already injured finger, snapping her out of her thoughts. She backed out of the closet and returned to her bedroom. She briefly considered lighting the lantern that was beside her on the dresser. But that would risk waking Lorella and Evanlee. So instead she grabbed a second match. She knew it wasn't the Eastern way to waste another. But Gardeniyah also knew—as any sensible person in any world does—that getting dressed in the dark is not wise when you are about to visit a castle.

Gardeniyah slipped on the simple green dress she had worn for her eighteenth birthday the year before. She couldn't help but smile, even amid the heaviness of the day, at the memories of one of her happiest days. But her smile faded as she looked over to her sister's bed. Lorella would never have that. Tomorrow was Lorella's eighteenth birthday, and though there would be a celebration, it wouldn't be a happy occasion for the three of them. Because, the day after, Gardeniyah, Lorella, and their youngest sister, Evanlee, would be banished from the East forever.

Gardeniyah shook her head, a desperate attempt to clear the thoughts swirling within. She crept from the darkness of their room and through the dimly lit living room illuminated only by the crackling fire to the front door. She swiftly pulled on her boots and then slipped just as quickly through the doorway. It was still too early for her venture, but Gardeniyah didn't care. She hadn't slept all night, and she couldn't stand the maddening silence or the slow ticking of the clock any longer.

When Gardeniyah had taken a few steps, she turned around to look at her home. The enormous evergreen tree loomed high above her. The front door was average in height, but in this light, it seemed tiny in comparison to the height and width of the tree. The smoke that eased out of the pipe in the side of the tree home was dark and ominous in the moonlight. Everything about it seemed more haunting than it did during the day. But, to Gardeniyah, it was, and would always be, the picture of peace and comfort.

3

She closed her eyes and breathed in the smell of smoke and fresh leaves in the early morning. Countless times, she had been awake late enough to witness the last day of the cyclical, to see spring end as the leaves shriveled and the flowers closed their petals. However, she wasn't often awake early enough to see the process of spring starting over, as it did every ten days in the East. Her lips twitched. It was not the worst final memory of their home she could have had.

But the idea of being in her last hours in the East sent an ache from her chest to the tips of her fingers. Gardeniyah took a deep breath—this time to muster the strength to turn from their home and continue onward.

It wasn't until she reached the meadow that lay between the evergreen tree home community and the capital city of Relis that she realized leaving had been a mistake. The meadow was dark. The dew had not yet gathered on the blades of grass and so the moon wasn't reflecting off it, illuminating the ground as it normally did in the morning. She had been counting on the dew light, which was why she had left the lantern on the dresser by her closet.

Regardless she couldn't go back now, or she would inevitably wake someone up. She would have to make do with the light the moon offered from the sky. Thankfully it was a cloudless night and so the light was enough to see a few feet ahead of her at a time—though truthfully all of these factors were a moot point. For Gardeniyah would have known the way regardless.

The castle at Relis stood tall in front of the Assana Falls. It was the second tallest waterfall in the East and a fitting backdrop for the intricate workmanship of the Easterners' hands. Some might argue that building the castle near the *tallest* waterfall in the East would have been even better. However, that location was a sacred place that few dared to venture.

Regardless, the castle at Relis was the crown jewel of the East's creations.

The castle beckoned to Gardeniyah. She walked slowly, fixated on it. The wet stone gleamed in the moonlight like the jewels that the dwarves mined in the East's northernmost mountains, just as it had every night for seven hundred and fifty years. Yet, despite its beauty, the night worked its charms, and the castle's four tall towers and grand entrance and gates were ever so slightly daunting in the moonlight.

A gust of cold wind cut through Gardeniyah's cotton dress. The wind whipped her brown hair around her. The thickness of it meant that there was plenty for the wind to abuse, which was the very reason she hardly ever left it down. But her mind had been too preoccupied to remember to tie her hair back in her usual braid. As she walked through the meadow, she shivered, more from her thoughts than from the breeze. *How will I survive in the North's winter if I think the East is cold?* she wondered.

Gardeniyah stopped suddenly and shook her head. She knew better than to think that way. The North was the only place for humans—despite humans believing otherwise. She felt she would have no choice but to adapt to the North's ever-present winter.

Though Gardeniyah wouldn't admit it, the idea of living in the West's perpetual autumn or the South's endless summer was much more appealing. But she wouldn't let herself entertain the idea of going anywhere but the North. To do so would be to venture down the slippery slope that had led man to disrupting the Divine Order in the first place.

Though the East's Grand Council didn't believe it, Gardeniyah and her sisters weren't like the average human. How could they be? They had been raised not just among the mystical creatures who were native to the East, but with beasts and monsters as well. They had been haunted every day by stories of the misery their own race had caused during the Great Wars, and they lived amongst the very creatures their own kind had displaced every day of their lives.

So, although Gardeniyah was a firm believer in the Divine Order and would never entertain the notion of going anywhere but the North, the council didn't trust her or her sisters. Mankind's assaults on the world made them believe doing so would put the East, the last protected corner of the world, in jeopardy.

Gardeniyah understood the Grand Council's reasoning. Still, she wished she could convince them to change their mind. She would do anything for the opportunity to remain in the East. Anything to prove to the beings she loved so dearly that her allegiance was not with man; it was with them.

Gardeniyah looked up to the moon. She bit her lip to hold back the tears threatening to escape. She wished at that moment (with a pure innocence the East didn't know she still possessed) for the chance to prove her loyalty.

In her naivety, she didn't know a wish such as that—made with one's purest desires—is one of the most powerful things in any land. Scholars in every world debate why this is. But, whether or not you believe it was magic, destiny, or the guiding force of fate's hand, that is of no consequence right now. The wish was made, and more importantly . . . it was *heard*.

Arriving in the capital city of Relis, the scent of bread, maple buns, and ebonycreme brewing met Gardeniyah's nose. The bakers were already awake, always the first to rise in the East. They kneaded their dough in the moonlight and their bread rose in their ovens in time with the rising sun so that the rest of Relis could start their day with their favorite morning drinks and food.

The familiar scents helped Gardeniyah estimate the time of day. Despite taking her time walking as slowly as she could, she was too early. The gates of the castle would still not be open by the time she arrived, so she decided to stop at her favorite bakery. Mib, their adoptive mother, had brought them maple buns from Gerald's bakery the first day she was given custody of the girls. So Gardeniyah and her sisters always begged Mib to go whenever they went into town early.

The bell over the door rang as Gardeniyah entered, cutting through the otherwise silent morning. The startled baker let out a cry and dropped the pan of bread he had just pulled out of the oven.

"I am so sorry, Gerald!" Gardeniyah said, rushing over to help.

"My goodness, Gardeniyah! What on earth are you doing here so early?" The elf's small hands picked up crumbs as Gardeniyah scooped up the larger pieces.

"I'm heading to the castle."

"What day is it? I thought that wasn't until tomorrow?" Concern flashed across his face.

"It's not." Gardeniyah paused. "I, uh, have some things I need to do."

"I see. You decided you needed one last Geraldian maple bun, yes?" The elf chuckled. "Well, here." He reached into the glass display case for a maple bun so fresh that steam fogged the container. "Take this," he said. She reached into her bag for some coins, but Gerald shook his head and waved his hand. "No, little lady. It's on me. A parting gift for my favorite customer. And here, take some ebonycreme too. If you're out so early, you'll need the energy."

Gardeniyah breathed in the sweet, oaky smell of the

maple and the bitter, sweet smell of the ebonycreme. The memories associated with the scents were enough to put a smile on her face. But the kind gesture from the elderly elf made her smile grow even wider. She thanked the little creature she had grown fond of over the years before venturing back out into the streets.

Walking slowly and enjoying Relis one last time was comforting, despite her eagerness to begin the day's list of things to do. She absorbed everything, from the sound of the bakers clanking their pans to the intricate designs of flowers and vines that were etched into each stone in the road. They mimicked the vines and flowers that grew on the buildings surrounding the path. It took the skilled hands and unique focus of a fairy to do such work. She was sure there would be no such designs on the Northern roads.

The castle gates were still closed when she arrived, despite her stop. Annoyed and desperate, she sneaked around to the eastern wall, pushed back a bush, and grinned. The secret passage she and her sisters had made years ago was still there.

Though she had used the tunnel hundreds of times throughout her life, her heart was racing as she eased into and through the courtyard. Typically, if anyone saw her, they wouldn't bother her. But she feared today would be different. The Easterners in the castle had been growing wary of her. They no longer hid their sideways glances or furrowed brows when she walked around unattended.

Their new attitudes didn't stop her. She knew she wasn't up to anything more or less than things she had always done. Yes, technically, sneaking into the castle was frowned upon. But if she had always been allowed to do it, she saw no good reason that she should stop now.

So, with new determination brought on by a slight bitterness, she walked to the window of the library. With a small nudge and a little shimmy, she pushed it open and climbed through. This lack of security was one of the great things about a castle that was built long, long before the East had started not to trust mankind.

Gardeniyah scanned the shelves for the maps and books she needed. The librarian would scold her if she were caught, but she ran her fingers against the dusty spines of the books anyway. She loved this room. There was something magical about the mixture of dust and aged papers and the flowers beyond the open window.

If she could have bottled the scent, she would have taken it with her wherever she went. And if she'd been allowed to stay in the East, she would have begged for a job in the library. Nothing would have made her happier than living among the books and the voices of the past.

Arms full of ancient information, she walked to her customary table. As she did so, she crossed in front of the glass case stationed in the middle of the library.

She had passed the case hundreds of times but had rarely stopped to read its contents. But suddenly, the paper rustled within the enclosed shelter. She stopped. As she stared at the sheet of paper, she couldn't help but feel something was different about it. *Perhaps it's a different piece of paper?* she wondered. But no, that was impossible. The letter had been locked inside that case for over twenty years. She studied the contents for longer than she cared to admit before eventually walking away. *Oh well, it doesn't matter. It's a letter to the Easterners, not to me.* But Gardeniyah was wrong on both accounts. There was nothing different about the letter, and it mattered far more to her than she could have imagined.

CHAPTER TWO

L orella stared out the window above the sink in the little kitchen of her tiny tree home wiping the same plate repeatedly in the soapy water. The world of the East was dancing before her. Nymphs were gathering in the meadow in front of their home. The sound of a beaver and a woodpecker making their respective homes out of and in neighboring trees seeped through the open window. She could hear Cordove the Gnome, who lived across the way, and Lucille, a rabbit who lived next door, arguing yet again. Cordove was always convinced that Lucille was responsible for any missing vegetables from his garden—a prejudice that Lucille did not appreciate.

Lorella didn't blame her. Lucille was a lovely rabbit. More personable than the others. But most rabbits were nervous creatures, and their nerves did often manifest itself in bouts of kleptomania. But not all gave in to such urges. Lorella knew firsthand how it felt to be held accountable for things others of your kind did.

She was tempted to march outside and give Cordove a piece of her mind. But just as she decided to do so, she noticed their neighbor Shorton the Faun walk out in front of her home. He was gathering firewood from the communal pile. He waved enthusiastically when he noticed Lorella staring in his direction.

The greeting snapped Lorella out of her trance, and she quickly made an effort to wave back. "Ow!" she yelled as the blade of a knife cut into the tip of her pointer finger and slid down to her knuckle.

The scream startled the already skittish faun. He dropped the firewood he had been holding and rushed toward her front door.

"Where is Gardeniyah?" Lorella muttered to herself. Gardeniyah had left early in the morning before anyone was awake—leaving Lorella and Evanlee with all the chores for the third day in a row. Mib had declared that morning that the girls needed to get their chores done regardless, and now Lorella's hands were raw and wounded.

It was unfair; it was her birthday tomorrow, after all, not Gardeniyah's. She should be the one skipping chores. The thought alone was enough to annoy Lorella. But as the soapy water crept into the cut on her bleeding, throbbing finger, Lorella's annoyance grew to anger.

Lorella was rinsing her hand and dabbing at her finger with a dishrag when Shorton rushed through the front door. He didn't knock—he hadn't in years. But his hooves on the wood floor announced his presence all the same.

"Little Lorella, are you all right?" Shorton's rhythmic voice called as he hurried through the sitting area and into the kitchen. A smirk crossed Lorella's face despite the pain in her hand. It was amusing to her that, after all this time, the faun still referred to her as "Little Lorella." He was rather short for a faun, but even if he weren't, she still would have outgrown him a few years after arriving as a toddler. He now barely stood as tall as her waist.

But it made sense he would still refer to her as little. He had been their neighbor since Mib had built the tree home. In fact, he had insisted on helping the new—and very strange —family build it despite never having met them before. And from that day on he had integrated himself as a part of their bizarre little family. And therefore was the only being in all of Tolatin who could get away with such a nickname for her.

"My dear girl," he said, cupping her hurt hand in his, "you must be more careful!"

"Don't," Lorella said, pulling her hand away from the faun's grip, "you'll get blood on your scarf." Lorella continued to dab the wound with the dishrag.

"Oh nonsense. That doesn't matter at all. And stop using that filthy rag! Do you want it to get infected?"

"What?" Lorella chuckled. "It's been in soap water!" she said, attempting to defend her decision—more to tease her friend than to win her case.

"Yes, soapy water and food particles and who knows what else!" The faun turned up his nose as he moved across the kitchen to retrieve a clean rag from the basket where they kept them. He rummaged through the basket. Taking a peculiar amount of time to select which of the old pieces of cloth would be acceptable for the job of stopping blood. Gardeniyah rolled her eyes at how long he took to select one, but couldn't help but smile at the care he showed.

The smile quickly left her face however when he muttered, "I mean, really! I know Mib has taught you things like this. I don't know what you are going to do out there without us." With those words, the faun froze in his bent-over position above the basket of rags. He let out a big sigh as he grabbed one and turned back toward her. "I'm sorry."

Lorella looked down at the floor, ignoring for a moment the pain in her finger and the blood that was dripping to the floor without a compress to stop it.

"I don't know why I said that," the faun said with a huff as he walked back toward Lorella ringing his hands in the fresh towel. "You hardly need us or the reminder that you won't have us any longer." He again placed Lorella's hand in his, this time pressing the clean compress to it.

"It's all right. It's on everyone's minds today. Mib is trying hard to act like everything is normal. That's why I'm doing these dishes. She complained this morning to Evanlee and me that no one had done them in days."

"Where is Gardeniyah?"

"Who knows? She snuck out before daylight. I think in the middle of the night."

"That's unlike her!"

"Well, this day is unlike any other too—no matter how badly Mib wants to pretend otherwise."

Shorton clicked his tongue in agreement. "After fifteen years of having you girls in the house, I'm not sure what Mib is going to do without you all here."

"Oh, she'll be all right. She went several hundred years without us before we showed up."

"That may be true. But ever since you three arrived, Mib has built a whole new life centered around you girls. She went from a fairy whose war gift made her the talk of the council to a simple watch guard. I remember watching her performing archery at Ranosa's coronation celebration. Fifty arrows in a row hit the bull's-eye. She stopped only because they ran out of time. It seemed to be all the Eastern-ers, especially the natives, wanted to talk about for months. Everyone was sure she was the next General Vadeed. Instead, when you arrived, she made a home and a life that revolved around caring for you three girls from the land of man."

He was right, of course, though Lorella hardly ever thought of Mib as a warrior on par with General Vadeed.

Mib never talked about her accomplishments or the life she'd given up.

It was the least they could do to play along with her charade of normalcy on the last day. Lorella, however, appeared to be the only abiding by Mib's wishes. She wasn't even sure why she was. It was her last day here, just like her sisters. Yet, here she was working. She was sure that her whimsical little sister was more likely than not sitting on her bed daydreaming—or maybe even crying and worrying— rather than cleaning like she was supposed to be doing.

And even though Lorella had no idea where Gardeniyah was, she knew precisely *what* Gardeniyah was doing. She was off plotting their journey. Gardeniyah was always more concerned about the future than the present, which made things at home fall on Lorella more often than Gardeniyah would ever admit.

Lorella nodded in response to the faun. "Well, anyway, I've had enough of these dishes."

"Yes, probably best you don't place your hands back in that water!"

"Evanlee! Come and finish these! I did half of them, and they aren't any more my job than yours, so I shouldn't have to do them all." Lorella strained to listen, but no response came from their bedroom.

"Evanlee!" Lorella withdrew her hands from the faun's but kept the now bloody rag pressed to her finger. She marched back to the room the three girls shared. "Evanlee, I know there is no way you didn't hear—" she began as she pushed open the door to an empty bedroom. "Of course she's not in here!"

CHAPTER THREE

The birds chirped in a rhythmic song, speaking through hypnotic hymns. One would call to the other, and from some unknown location, another would sing out. From the opposite side of the meadow, yet another would chime in, and from another the next. Then the first would call again, and the process would start over. In the second or two it took one of the birds to respond, the leaves would gently rustle in the tree. Every so often, the wind would catch between the forks in a branch, resulting in a soft whistle distinct from the bird chirps. It was the chorus of the East at its finest.

In the meadow about a mile from the house among the flowers and the long grass, Evanlee was lying in her favorite spot soaking up the sounds of the East. If she were still for long enough, the butterflies would come back, and she could watch them dance from flower to flower. It was sometimes hard to lie so still because the leaves on the flowers would tickle her face when the wind blew strongly. However, after years of patient practice, Evanlee had nearly perfected being still.

Evanlee blinked slowly and deeply breathed in the world around her. This was one of those perfect moments in life. The kind that, even as it is happening, you are confident you will always remember it because it's too perfect to forget. Evanlee wanted to always remember that in the East the air smelled like honey and flowers. She wanted, at any given moment, to be able to recall the way the sun shined in the cloudless sky and how its warm rays bathed her body. Yes, Evanlee never wanted to forget what it felt like. The way it looked. The way it smelled. Because she was quite certain she would die if she forgot even a single detail.

"What are you going to do out there, Ev?" The deep male voice cut through the silence.

Evanlee opened her eyes in time to see that the voice had sent vibrations through the air that caused the butterflies to scatter in a frenzy. Evanlee rolled to her side to look at her best friend, who was lying beside her. His broad shoulders and height made him seem intimidating to most. He was a good six inches taller than the average fairy or man. But he was not the least bit intimidating to Evanlee, even with her rather short stature for a human. What did frighten her was the look of concern she saw in his eyes.

"To be honest, Brashen, I don't know. I have left the planning to the other girls. I haven't wanted to; in fact, I've refused to think about it until the last day or two when it became too real to ignore. I just don't want to think about leaving this place, of leaving home, of leaving you . . ."

"Can't you stay? You're not eighteen yet! Let the others go."

"I'm not getting separated from my sisters," she said, shaking her head. "I don't know how I would find them again, and I'm not facing the outside world by myself. Besides, all three more years would do is make it harder to leave." The silence hung in the air between them for a while before Evanlee spoke again.

"Brashen, can I ask you something?"

"Anything."

"Do you think we"—she blushed—"not 'we' as in you and me, but I mean 'we' like my sisters and I . . . you know, humans. Well, you're a fairy...Ugh, I can't figure out how to say this . . ."

Evanlee saw Brashen's face shift from concern to confusion. She loved watching a fairy's face do that. Their ability— or inability, depending on how you looked at it—to feel more than one emotion at a time caused their entire faces to shift when their mood changed. Some had gotten better at hiding it, especially the older ones who had been around for hundreds of years. But Brashen was not even a hundred yet, an age considered still adolescence in fairy culture, so he hadn't even come close to mastering that skill.

"Let me try it this way. Do you think something snaps in us?"

"What are you talking about, Ev?" Brashen said with a laugh. He was amused with her, which she didn't like. She hated when people didn't take her seriously. Unfortunately for her, it happened quite a lot. Her sister Lorella was the worst offender. But Brashen usually made her feel very confident and secure. So him acting this way would have upset her in response to any given topic, but especially in this instance.

"Are we actually evil after eighteen? If I did stay three more years, would I suddenly be this terrible person after my birthday?"

"Oh." His face was no longer amused. He was almost grave and very stern.

"Well?"

"Well, what?"

17

"Come on, Brashen, don't dodge the question!"

"Fine." He sighed. "No. I mean, I don't know. But I don't think so. I see Gardeniyah all the time, and she's nineteen, and she doesn't seem to have snapped. I mean, honestly," he said, scratching his head nervously, "she has made a lot of fairies rethink some things." He glanced around them in every direction as if looking for someone. It was a strange behavior, since, in all the times they had come together, they had never seen anyone out here this time of day. "But all of that kind of talk is crazy for a fairy to say. All right?" he said as he placed his hands behind his head and closed his eyes.

"Thank you." She placed her hands on the soft grass and leaned over to kiss him on the cheek. He smiled. She loved that smile. She would miss it so much. She took another mental picture. She was also sure she would die if she ever forgot that detail. As she turned away from him, her heart sank. The sun was sinking into the evening sky. She had to go. She quickly stood up, brushed the dirt off her bright-yellow skirt, then turned and walked away.

"Aren't you going to say goodbye?" Brashen called after her.

"No," Evanlee yelled back and kept walking.

"Well, why not?"

Evanlee stopped, turned around, and shrugged her shoulders. Then she flashed her crooked smile and said, "'Cause it's not goodbye."

CHAPTER FOUR

All day the sisters and Mib had each been coping with the upcoming change alone. But like every family in the East, the evening was when they came together. Mib would return home about an hour or so before sunset, just as she had every day as long as the girls could remember.

Gardeniyah got back from the castle about an hour before Mib was set to be home. When she walked through the door, she heard the most normal thing she had heard all day: the sound of her two little sisters arguing.

"I'm back now! So what does it matter?" Evanlee's whine grew louder as Gardeniyah neared the bedroom door.

"It matters because I had to do everything myself!"

"You could have left some of it for us to do."

"Maybe I would have if anyone had bothered to tell me where they were going and when they would be back."

"Well, like I said, I'm back now, and I can help."

"Oh good. And with what exactly? I already did the dishes. Our room is clean. The entire house is spotless. Shorton had to help me because you couldn't be bothered to do your part."

Gardeniyah could tell from her spot behind the closed door that this argument was not going to go away on its own. They hardly ever did, and she often had to intervene. She pushed open the door and entered their room. She had intended to be overly chipper and appear oblivious to the quarrel. However, Lorella never gave her a chance.

"Oh, look who else finally shows up!" Lorella gestured in Gardeniyah's direction as she rolled her head to extend the impact of her eye roll further.

"Hey, sis!" Evanlee bounced off the bed and rushed to hug her eldest sister. Of course, this movement inspired another eye roll from Lorella.

Gardeniyah hugged Evanlee briefly and then tapped her back twice. Evanlee's cue to let go. Gardeniyah knew that Lorella always got infuriated when Evanlee showed any affection for Gardeniyah when the two of them argued. Gardeniyah wasn't sure why this was the case, but assumed it had something to do with feeling as though they were about to team up against her.

"So what are you two arguing about this time?" Gardeniyah said with as little emotion as she could.

"Oh, you can be in on it too, if you like. I was just telling Evanlee here how much I appreciated being left with all of our joint responsibilities today." The corners of Lorella's mouth curved up in the sarcastic smile she always loved to flash during an argument. "Something you contributed to as well. So thank you."

"I'm sorry," Gardeniyah said.

Lorella closed her eyes and sighed before muttering, "It's fine." She opened her eyes and pointed her still piercing gaze at Evanlee. "See, that's what you should have said. Instead of whining and making a bunch of excuses."

"I'm sorry, Lorella," Evanlee said. She flashed her large blue eyes up at her sister and blinked a few times. It was a trick that often made others believe she was fighting back tears. It never once fooled her sisters, but still she tried.

"Whatever."

Evanlee let out a whimper at her apology being discarded. But Lorella was unfazed by the sound either and continued to ignore her. "So what was so important for you two anyway?"

"I went to the library to figure out our best route and look up some other information about the North." Gardeniyah glanced away from her sister. She had also taken the time to reread parts of *The History of the Great Wars* the last couple of hours she was there. Time she could have spent helping Lorella.

"That's all you did? No rereading for fun?"

"Well . . . I . . . It was only for the last couple hours. But I shouldn't have done that. I should have come back and helped."

"At least most of that was productive." Lorella turned to look at Evanlee. "And what about you, princess?"

"I was in the meadow with Brashen. But it's our last day here, and I just really wanted to be out enjoying my spot. You know the one a few feet away from the big feloriya tree with the white and pink petals where all those birds like to sit. They make the prettiest sounds there, you know! And anyway, I don't know that Brashen can come tomorrow. And I was cleaning this morning! I promise I was, but then it looked so nice out. Then Brashen walked by, and I couldn't help but go. I just had to!"

Lorella shook her head and muttered, "Typical," as she walked out the bedroom door and headed for the kitchen.

"Try not to be too mad. You know how she is," Gardeniyah whispered as Lorella walked by.

Lorella felt her head might fall off from the amount of times she had shaken her head during this conversation. She wasn't one to snitch on her sisters about being gone all day. But a piece of her had hoped that they wouldn't be home in time, and Mib would find out on her own. Instead, they had both showed up just in time to take care of their last responsibility of cooking dinner. Thus giving the illusion that they had taken care of all of their chores.

~

Lorella didn't speak to her sisters as they helped make dinner. Gardeniyah and Evanlee were busy laughing and talking as they cut vegetables from their garden and stirred the broth for the stew. Lorella kept to herself and busied herself with cutting bread and setting the table.

Soon the door to their home opened up, and Mib came inside.

"There are my girls!" Mib said with a smile. Mib's smile was equally lovely and contagious. She was so kind and warm that seeing her smile made you immediately happy.

It was enough to snap Lorella out of her bad mood. They all smiled back, and it all felt normal—for a bittersweet moment, at least. Then, seemingly simultaneously, they all remembered the weight the evening held. All their eyes fell to the floor. Tonight would be the last night Mib would walk through the door like this with the girls there waiting. The last night they would hear the greeting they had heard every day for fifteen years.

Mib didn't want the evening spoiled. Her favorite and most precious things in life were her memories. Mib had always told the girls: "When you live for hundreds of years, and the world is constantly changing around you, all you have are memories. Memories of how things were. Good or bad. And those memories shape the world you create for yourself in the present. Memories are the one thing no one can take from you. But you have to have the will and the wisdom not to forget." It was evident by the way Mib perked right back up and continued to carry on as if nothing were at all wrong that she intended this night to be a happy memory.

"Smells amazing, girls. Oh! Is that ginger stew?"

"Yep!" Evanlee beamed. "We know it's your favorite. We were going to make buckleberry pie too. But we ran out of time."

Lorella nodded at the window above the sink. Evanlee turned and looked. Then her smile grew even wider as she clapped her hands together and hopped toward the pie. "Yay, Lorella!" Lorella couldn't help but smile at her sister's enthusiasm and praise. It almost made up for the fact that she hadn't been there to help like she should have been.

After they had eaten, they sat around the living area reading books and talking. They all stayed up far later than usual to spend a few more minutes with each other. This evening was the last time they expected to see Mib. Tomorrow when they woke up, she would already be gone. They would pack their belongings and go to the castle for the party in Lorella's honor, then they would spend their very last night in the East there, away from Mib. And so they all dreaded going to sleep.

Gardeniyah found it hard to sleep that night. She wanted to see Mib one last time before they left in the morning, but Mib was always so quiet when she got ready that she hardly ever woke them up. She would hover slightly off the ground in the loft above them in her room so they wouldn't be awakened by the thud of her heavy, military-issued boots on the wooden floor. She would opt to float down from her loft as opposed to using the ladder and, while this may be assumed to be for the same reason, truthfully she would have floated down regardless. The ladder was there solely for the benefit of the three girls so they could climb up to her room should they need her in the middle of the night.

Gardeniyah always liked to see Mib float down, but not as much as Evanlee did. At three years old Evanlee had decided that she wanted to be like Mib. The nuances of the differences between fairies and humans were not completely understood by the young girl. So while Gardeniyah was busy reading and Lorella was busy outside practicing sword fighting by hitting their house with a stick, Evanlee had jumped down from the loft above. She of course did not have her expected result and instead of gaining the ability to fly, she got a broken leg.

Gardeniyah had quickly run to get Shorton. As she did, she yelled over her shoulder to Lorella that Evanlee was hurt. When Gardeniyah and Shorton had arrived they found Lorella tying a piece of firewood to Evanlee's leg with a scarf. At the time it wasn't very funny, but now looking back at Lorella's makeshift splint, Gardeniyah chuckled.

Luckily for the girls the incident had sparked Lorella's interest in field medicine. It wasn't often that Lorella would be caught reading, but when she was, it was always something about how to care for wounds and injuries when proper techniques and tools weren't available.

Gardeniyah always found those sorts of books boring. She had tried over the last several months to read a few of them so she could be better prepared for their journey, but every time she tried, she fell asleep.

Which was what she knew that she needed to be doing now. She needed to take advantage of the last night she would be in her familiar bed. She never slept soundly anywhere else. Even at the castle she slept much lighter. So she knew that she would have a hard time sleeping on the ground on their five-day journey to the first town in the

North. In fact, she knew until she adjusted to whatever permanent home they found, she wouldn't sleep well at all.

She thought about grabbing whatever book Lorella had on her bedside table and reading until she fell asleep. But, while she knew it was important to get her rest, she couldn't forsake the chance to see Mib one last time. No amount of sleep was worth that. Mib meant more to Gardeniyah than she even knew or understood at the time. But still, she wasn't sure how she would live without Mib. If she was honest, she wasn't sure she could. But she also knew that her family was looking for her to be strong, so she had to try.

At first Gardeniyah was surprised when she heard footsteps on the ladder, but then she smiled. Mib wanted her to wake up. Gardeniyah eased out of bed so as to not wake the others and slipped through their bedroom door.

As soon as she stepped out into the sitting room Mib looked over her shoulder from where she was boiling water for some tea.

"Good," Mib said with a smile, "it worked. I was hoping it would be enough to wake you." Mib turned completely away from the stove and faced Gardeniyah as she leaned against the counter, waiting for Gardeniyah to make her way to the kitchen. As soon as she was close enough, Mib reached out and stroked Gardeniyah's cheek. Mib looked at Gardeniyah's eyes and then clicked her tongue and said, "Never mind it didn't wake you. You never slept, did you?"

Gardeniyah shook her head and then said, "I didn't want to miss the chance to see you."

"I wouldn't have let that happen."

"Really? You don't usually wake us up."

"Well this isn't a normal morning." Mib turned away from Gardeniyah and grabbed two teacups from the shelf above the sink. She then scooped some tea mix from one of her many tea canisters on the shelf and put it in two little cloth tea bags. Mib didn't drink ebonycreme like most. Instead she harvested herbal leaves and flowers to make varying teas. She seemed to have a tea for every ailment.

"The usual tea this morning, Mib?" Gardeniyah asked as Mib poured the boiling water over the mix.

"Yes, no need to change that. Sadness is one ailment I don't have a tea for."

Mib took the two cups and walked over to the table and sat down; she placed one in front of Gardeniyah's usual seat and one in front of her own. Mib stared down at the tea as Gardeniyah walked over to join her. After a moment Mib muttered, "The world would be a much better place if tea could cure a broken heart."

She said it so softly that Gardeniyah was sure Mib hadn't meant to say it out loud. So instead of addressing the comment she just looked at Mib. She wanted to take in every detail she could. She loved Mib's hazel eyes. Her wavy, brown hair had subtle streaks of blonde from the time she spent out in the sun on guard. Her skin was darker than any of the sisters'. It was both a combination of her natural skin tone and, like her hair, her time outside. But unlike a human's, her skin was still very smooth despite her age and exposure to the elements.

Mib and Gardeniyah hardly looked like mother and daughter now. She looked more like the eldest sister than their mother. But despite neither looking like it, nor biologically it being the case, Mib was their mother.

They sat in silence for several minutes. The quiet was the comfortable kind that comes with being at total ease with someone. Because her sisters were so different, she could do most anything with at least one of them. Whatever she wanted to do, it was likely at least one would join. But Mib was the only one that Gardeniyah could do nothing with. She was the only one that a deep conversation and sitting quietly while drinking tea was equally as enjoyable.

Gardeniyah could feel the lump in her throat forming as she fought back the tears that were forming in her eyes. She wanted to enjoy this time. She didn't want to be sad during the last few moments she had with Mib. Gardeniyah coughed slightly to clear her throat.

When she did, Mib looked up. Her eyes were glassy from tears as well. She gave Gardeniyah what many would consider a weak smile, but to Gardeniyah it was the strongest smile she had ever seen. Mib had put a lot of effort into learning how to do that. For Mib, smiling when she was in pain was no easy feat. Her emotions were so strong for her that to train herself to display a different emotion than the one she was feeling took quite a lot of willpower.

With the forced smile still on her face Mib said, "I have something for you."

She quickly sipped the last of her tea and then got up from the table and floated up to her room. This time when she came back down she didn't use the ladder, she even waited till she was in the kitchen to step on the floor again.

"I didn't want the others to wake up before I gave you this. You know I always try to be fair. I don't like to give one of you something if I can't give all three of you something. And it seemed especially wrong to not have something for Lorella since it's her birthday. But I only have one of these, and nothing I could come up with could match it."

Gardeniyah looked at Mib's hands. She was holding something that was wrapped in a blue piece of fabric with stars embroidered on it. "What is it?" Gardeniyah asked.

"See for yourself," Mib said, as she handed Gardeniyah the gift.

Gardeniyah held the object in one hand and carefully pulled back the blue cloth with the other to reveal a golden compass on a long, silver chain necklace. It looked much like a pocket watch and she would have thought it was one if the gold plate on the front didn't have the rosary of the compass inside etched on the cover along with vines and flowers. Gardeniyah picked it up and held it by the chain. The light from the lantern on the table reflected as it spun slowly around. "It's beautiful," Gardeniyah whispered.

"It's been in my family for generations. We always pass it on to the oldest when they begin their life away from the family. It was, of course, a practical gift, but also symbolic. That's why those words are written on the back."

Gardeniyah stopped letting the compass spin in the air and placed it back in her hand so she could see what Mib was referring to. Etched delicately and deeply into the golden compass were six words.

"In the seeking we are found," Gardeniyah whispered and then looked up at Mib.

Mib nodded and said, "It is one of the truest statements I have ever known. You'll feel the same way once you find where you are meant to be. It's then you will see that you became who you needed to be along the way. Not once you arrived. But until you get there, the compass will help."

"Thank you," Gardeniyah mouthed. The lump in her throat had grown exponentially and she was physically and mentally at a loss for words.

Mib pulled her in for a hug and whispered in her ear, "Wherever you go and whatever you do, know I believe in you, in the good in you, in the strength in you, and most importantly, in the courage in you."

"I don't feel very courageous." Her voice cracked as the tears she had been holding back began to pour down her face.

"Good. You shouldn't feel courageous," Mib said as she let go of Gardeniyah.

Gardeniyah frowned and cocked her head to the side. "What?" she asked.

"You shouldn't feel courageous," Mib repeated as she stared intently at Gardeniyah. Mib wiped a tear from Gardeniyah's cheek and then took her by the hands and said, "Courage isn't an emotion—it's a choice. You can choose to be courageous when you feel scared. You can choose to be courageous when your whole world is falling apart.

"True courage isn't being fearless, it's facing your worst nightmare and not letting your heart fall, never letting the circumstances change you into something you're not. That's why people think warriors are courageous. It's not because any of us expect them to be fearless, it's because they choose courage despite being afraid. When the Easterners aided in the Great Wars, we were filled with fear. If we weren't, we wouldn't have been there."

Gardeniyah hung her head at the mention of the Great Wars, but Mib put her finger on Gardeniyah's chin and pushed it upward so she could make eye contact with her again before she continued, "It was our worst nightmare to see the humans invade the beasts and monsters. If we had acted strictly on our emotions—all the fear, all the anger— it would have made us something we weren't. It would have made us use our war gifts to do horrible things based on revenge instead of just doing what needed to be done.

"The knowledge of justice in the mercy gift would have been skewed to just seek out repercussions for their actions; and the healing gift would have been used to hurt people instead, because if you know how to heal, then you know how to harm in ways that can't be healed.

"But, we didn't do any of that. We didn't let our hearts fall. In the wake of our worst nightmare, we didn't become a version of ourselves that we couldn't live with once the nightmare was over. If courage was an emotion, we wouldn't have been able to resist the urges to do those things, because we would have been angry *or* courageous, we could not have been both. But we were both. Which means courage, though it masks itself as a feeling, is not an emotion. "You choose whether or not to be courageous, and I believe in your capacity to do that. I believe in you, Gardeniyah. I always will."

Mib let go of Gardeniyah's hands and grabbed her bag from where it hung on the back of her chair in the sitting room. She then walked toward the front door. Right before she opened it, she stopped and looked back at Gardeniyah. A half smile flickered onto her face as she said, "Don't believe what they say about you. Don't listen to the other mystics, the council, or even other humans. A predisposition is just the capacity to do something. All men have the capacity to let greed overtake them, but they also have the ability to control that. They chose not to. You will choose differently. I know it." The half smile became a whole smile as she nodded at Gardeniyah and walked out the door without another word.

CHAPTER FIVE

"This is dumb." Lorella stared at herself in the castle's overly large and ornate mirror.

"No, it's not, it's absolutely wonderful, Lorella!" Evanlee disagreed dreamily.

"This dress is hideous," Lorella insisted as she gazed in the mirror at the puffy metallic skirt and bright-pink bodice that drowned her entire figure. She was thin and athletic, and this dress didn't help accentuate her assets.

"You look simply enchanting! And I'm Evanlee, our resident sisterly expert on all beautiful things, so you have to trust me," she said in her sassy way that was endearing to most but just annoying to Lorella.

"I trust your taste about as much as I would trust an ari—arimapus?—around my treasure!"

"A what?" Evanlee huffed as she put her hands on her hips.

"You know, those one-eyed beings that steal gold to put in their hair!" Lorella replied spitefully.

Lorella didn't hear Gardeniyah come into their room at

the palace. But her presence was announced when she corrected Lorella in her usual fashion.

"They are called arimaspians, Lorella, and there is no reason to be hateful to Evanlee. She was merely complimenting you. You should apologize."

"And you shouldn't be such a know-it-all," she said with a scowl they all knew was insincere. Lorella had the sort of humor that challenged you above all else. She was constantly in a game of wits with you, without ever having told you the rules or even waiting for you to agree to play, for that matter.

"That's my job. I'm the oldest," Gardeniyah said. Lorella crossed her arms; she looked disappointed in Gardeniyah's lack of creativity in her comeback. "Besides, you would know what they were called to if you had listened in history. But that doesn't matter now. You will never have to sit through another lecture again. You are eighteen years old today, my sweet little sister." Gardeniyah wrapped her arm around her sister and whispered in Lorella's ear as she continued. "Which is why you are in this hideous dress going to this dumb party. Now let's get you changed," Gardeniyah said with a wink. With that, Lorella smiled, and they walked away from an oblivious Evanlee.

~

The party was soon underway. Gardeniyah, Lorella, and Evanlee stood at the door greeting each guest. Though it was technically a birthday celebration for Lorella, they all knew it was a thinly veiled farewell party. That didn't stop Evanlee from thoroughly enjoying the evening, though.

How can Lorella find these things a drag? They are absolutely wonderful! Evanlee thought.

Gardeniyah was making the rounds in Grandeur Hall, engaging in small talk with every guest. She looked stunning in her green dress. As Gardeniyah walked, the yellow flowers embroidered along the sleeves, collar, and down the center of the dress danced like the flowers in the wind Evanlee had watched yesterday. With the blue curtains blowing gently near the open windows and the light of the candles in the chandeliers, she looked like a painting in the library that had come to life. Evanlee thought she was perfection, despite the fact that, with each step Gardeniyah took, her long, thick brown hair that she had tied up in a loose bun halfway up her head fell ever so slightly. By the end of the night, her hair would be more down than up. But to Evanlee, she would still be perfect.

Evanlee stopped by the food table and plucked a few berries off the plate of assorted fruits from around the East. She glanced quickly over her shoulder to make sure Gardeniyah was still engaged with other guests. Her sister would have thoroughly scolded her if she saw her do such a thing without using a plate. But Evanlee didn't want to be bothered with a plate as she walked around the crowded room looking for Queen Ranosa.

It was easy to spot the fairy who Evanlee considered to be the most elegant fairy in the East. Evanlee was sure she was the most captivating fairy there had ever been, despite what others said about the former queen. Tonight the queen wore a champagne-colored gown that flowed easily to the ground despite its obvious weight. The gold embroidery that swayed as she walked around competed for attention only with the gold cape that was tied around her neck and draped over her tall, slender frame. The red jewel that served as decoration over the clasp of the cape was almost as capti-vating as the fairy herself. It was the same type of jewel that was featured in the delicate crown on her head. It wasn't a large crown nor Evanlee's favorite of the queen's collection. But the queen never wore an elaborate crown when the function wasn't about her. While everyone knew she did so to avoid drawing attention to herself when she felt it was unwarranted, eyes always found themselves wandering to her.

The queen was exceptionally tall, even for a fairy, which made many wonder how she had managed to hide in the shadows behind the former queen as her unseen advisor for so long. The only thing about her that would have blended easily into the shadows was her dark curly hair, which was tied back loosely in a bun at the nape of her neck like she often wore it. Evanlee had tried to copy the queen's signature hairstyle many times. But her lack of curls often left her very defeated in her attempt to look like the queen she admired so much.

When Ranosa saw her coming, the refined smile she wore as she nodded at any guest widened. She reached out the hands that had been folded in front of her ever so slightly to grasp Evanlee's as she approached.

"Hello there, sweet girl." Her voice was soft and smooth as she greeted the girl with a kiss on the cheek. Though Ranosa was aware such a display of affection by a queen would normally be frowned upon, the council had long ago given up reprimanding her for it. The three girls were as close of a thing as she had to offspring. They knew that, if things were different, the queen would have formally adopted them herself. Instead, she had been the girls' godmother of sorts and ensured, from a distance, that they had the best education—the best of everything, actually. She was always careful never to overstep Mib's role as the children's guardian, but a conflict had never arisen about it. The two had worked together seamlessly to raise the three young women.

"Good evening, Your Majesty!" Evanlee said with such excitement it was obvious she was stopping herself from throwing her arms around the queen like she had when she was younger and such an action would receive chuckles instead of horrified glances.

"Are you enjoying the party, my dear?"

"Oh yes! Everyone looks so beautiful tonight." Evanlee admired the way fairies, especially those on the council, always looked so elegant. In fact, all the members of the council and the Representatives who made up the Grand Council looked refined. She was sure it took a special skill for an ogre or a cyclops to look handsome, but somehow, on nights like tonight, dressed in their best, they managed.

"Yes, especially you and your sisters."

"Well, thank you." Evanlee beamed at the compliment for a moment before her face fell and became very serious and inquisitive. "Do you like Lorella's dress?" After she asked the question, she leaned toward the queen and whispered, as if she were about to share a very scandalous secret, "She wouldn't wear the one that was laid out for her. She made one of your handmaidens get another one from the collection. I liked it, though. I don't know why she changed."

"Yes. I like the one she chose. I never saw the other." To any onlooker, it would have been obvious that Ranosa was very amused by Evanlee's ramblings about the dress. But Evanlee was utterly oblivious. She was very passionate about beauty and fashion and assumed everyone except Lorella took it as seriously as she did.

Evanlee's posture eased at the queen's approval of her sister's attire. "Well, I think she looked prettier in the other one. She wouldn't listen to me, though. She never does." She sighed deeply but then perked right back up. "But Gardeniyah did! She let me pick out her dress. Doesn't she look gorgeous?" Evanlee brought her hands to her heart as if at any moment it may stop beating at the sight of her sister's beauty.

"Yes, she does. In fact, when I spoke with our former

queen Sanora long ago, the description she gave of King Madeous's wife, Queen Levena, matches her almost perfectly."

Evanlee had never thought of her sister like that. Like a historical figure born again. But she realized she thought the same. After all, that was who the paintings in the library were of. And she could absolutely see it now that she had heard the queen compare her to one of the few humans the East respected.

Gardeniyah's posture said she took care of things. And if you knew her, you knew she especially did so with anything that concerned those she loved. But not in the way it would for most humans. The way the East spoke of humans Evanlee was sure that most of humanity found caring for those they love a burden. Whether that was true or not, Gardeniyah saw the responsibilities in which she was entrusted as an honor, and therefore she had a sense of dignity and grace about it.

She even had that softness to her that one expects from a queen. Her face was always calm, and the corners of her mouth were always turned up in a refined smile, even if her vibrant green eyes were clouded or sad, much like they were at the moment.

The queen's attention was soon taken elsewhere, and Evanlee stood off to the side soaking in the splendor of the evening. She wanted to remember every detail, just as she had made a point to do in the meadow. She loved the way the swaying blue curtains, which were sewn together with thread made with silver from the dwarves' mines, glimmered from the flames of the chandelier. She closed her eyes for only a moment so she could pay closer attention to the accent of the Easterners. She breathed in the smell of the assortment of Tolatin delicacies from the East, West, and South—or rather what could be replanted from the South and West and survive in the East climate.

Evanlee quickly brushed the thought away and instead focused very hard on the way the smell of the food mixed with the flowery night air that came through the open windows of Grandeur Hall. But above the scents, the accents, and the dazzling details of the furniture and décor, Evanlee loved the way every Easterner appeared as if there was nowhere else they wanted to be.

The only person in the room who did not seem to be having the time of their life was Lorella. She sat on the sill of one of the large, open windows staring off into the night, engaging in her thoughts rather than her guests.

Lorella was so different than Gardeniyah. Gardeniyah had the dignity and poise of a queen. Lorella had the steam and stamina of a general. Rather than taking after Ranosa or the former queen Levena, like Gardeniyah did, Lorella had always been more apt to act like General Vadeed. Lorella had a hot temper that flared profusely when anyone crossed her (which, to Evanlee's dismay, she often did).

Lorella was an odd mix of rationale and passion. It was quite difficult to gauge whether a decision she made stemmed from careful planning and strategic maneuvering or was a rash act caused by a gut feeling that she would never explain even if you asked her. She had first exhibited this when the girls played hide-and-seek on the castle grounds. Lorella had always won against Evanlee and half the time against Gardeniyah. Evanlee was frustrated by this. And while Gardeniyah had assured her she only lost because she was the youngest, Lorella had taken the opportunity to chastise Evanlee, reminding her that the point of the game was to hide the best, not to find the prettiest place to hide.

Either way, all who met them agreed that if Lorella and Gardeniyah had been born fairies, they would have had the makings of the finest leaders the East had known aside from

Sanora herself. They no doubt would have been asked to join the ever-growing Grand Council of the East.

As far as her appearance, Lorella's could be described in one word: striking. Her jaw was pointed and her cheekbones high. Her skin was dark from the hours she spent in the sun secretly training with General Vadeed. Her narrow eyes, like Gardeniyah's and Evanlee's, conveyed her emotions easily. Tonight, as Lorella sat off to the side in her dark-purple and black dress, arms crossed and her black hair with its tight curls pulled back securely on top of her head in a small bun, her ordinarily golden-brown eyes were settling into the color of the South's setting sun, a dark gold flecked with red.

Evanlee began to wonder what people thought of *her* when they saw her. Mib said she had the most classic of beauty. But she wasn't sure what that meant.

She didn't realize that, while everyone else was done up elegantly, and well beyond their everyday look, tonight Evanlee seemed quite the same as ever. That's not to say she didn't look lovely. Evanlee just looked this way almost every day. Her golden-blonde hair had streaks of near white from the hours she spent lying out in the sun in the meadow. She wore a pale-pink dress that was made of mounds of see-through material with a white slip underneath that showed through down the front. White lace bordered the cuffs and the high collar of the dress. The dress was as dainty and lovely as the girl wearing it.

Evanlee's love for beauty made her appreciate the details and the serenity of the world more than most. She had a laugh that bubbled up so lightly that it was contagious. Her walk was less defined than Lorella's sturdy steps, and she didn't glide like Gardeniyah either; she almost sprang when she stepped. It was as if the bubbliness inside of her was bursting through her toes and making her feet leap off of the ground. She had an inner beauty that spread to the world around her with every smile. And she could brighten up an entire room with one playful look from her sky-blue eyes.

Her social skills were a force to be reckoned with. She could have anyone—besides her sisters, who were immune to her charms—believing that her ideas were brilliant, even if they had disagreed with her moments before. Give her half an hour, and she could have anyone convinced it was their own idea from the start. She was, perhaps, the most liked of her sisters, simply because it was somewhat challenging to find a blemish in her personality. She treated everyone like they were the most important person in the world to her, and in return, they treated her the same way.

CHAPTER SIX

The night carried on splendidly for hours. Had Lorella been an ordinary girl who found parties in her honor an exciting thing, it would have been her fantasy night. Instead, any outsider observing the evening would have thought the party was for Evanlee, who had everyone billowing with laughter the entirety of the evening. Evanlee noticed the pleased look on Gardeniyah's face when she looked over at her. Gardeniyah wanted to ensure that the sisters seemed proper hostesses despite their feelings about the night. She wished to guarantee that the fairies, as well as all the other Easterners in attendance, remembered them fondly.

Deep down, it wasn't with the purest intentions that Gardeniyah wished to make sure of this. A piece of her wanted their hearts to ache when any Easterners thought of the young women. After all, it was their fault that they would miss them. The sisters would never choose to leave the East. It was their home. The Easterners were more their people than the humans could ever be, and now they were being thrown out on the theory that corruption came with age.

Gardeniyah had been living in the East for a year as an adult. She had never even considered taking a hostile action toward the East or anyone in it.

Gardeniyah understood why the greed of man was so feared, whether she felt it pertained to her or not. Her people —though referring to a group of people she had never had any interaction with besides her own blood seemed awfully senseless—had in fact betrayed every law founded at the start of the Divine Order. She supposed she would hate humans, too, if she were a true Easterner. In fact, hating mankind made her even more sure that she was an Easterner in the most meaningful ways.

The party ended a little after midnight. The girls lingered, making sure to bid every guest a good night. If everyone in this group missed them like Gardeniyah planned, then their absence would be felt all across the East. It seemed as though a representative from every group had been in attendance, from Solido the Centaur—who, like all of his kind, was well respected among the people of the capital—to Baroque the Bear—who was considered a shifty fellow and had only been invited because he had once saved Lorella from the Jordana River when a rapid had caught her off guard and caused her to hit her head. The girls received many well-wishes. Since the girls were not fairies, they easily masked the many emotions that swirled within them with an expression of gratitude for the regards. The girls were exhausted—more from keeping a smile on their faces during the difficult good-byes than the party itself.

As the last guest left the girls, four guards walked toward them.

"It's time to retire for the evening, my ladies," the tallest of the four guards said.

"We were already planning on that. You didn't need to come and get us," Lorella said, her eyes cutting through the facade of curtesy that the male fairies escorting them away from the castle door were attempting.

Evanlee smiled genuinely at the soldiers. She didn't realize that the guards were escorting her and her sisters to their room out of fear and not out of respect. Although Gardeniyah was fuming internally, she attempted to hide that fact from her youngest sister.

"Who ordered this?" Lorella whispered to Gardeniyah. Contempt was all over her face as she eyed the guards up and down.

"It must have been the council. I can't see Ranosa doing this to us," Gardeniyah responded.

The exchange between the two eldest sisters shed light on the situation for Evanlee. She now realized that the escort was not an honorary one. Gardeniyah would have preferred her sister had stayed in the dark. She had a feeling that she was only beginning to experience not being able to shield her sister from harsh realities, something she had managed to do for so long.

"I can," Lorella huffed.

"How can you say that?" Evanlee said, as she let out a barely audible gasp and her hand flew to her heart.

"The queen is kicking us out because I turned a year older and you honestly think her ordering an escort is so out of the question?"

"She isn't kicking us out, the council is," Evanlee said. Her hand was no longer over her heart and instead was slowly balling into a fist at her side.

"She's the queen. A queen can do anything she wants. We can't even begin to imagine that power. But I know I would have done something good with it. Like fight for us."

"She did fight for us."

"That's what she says. All I know is she has the power to stop it. She didn't. That's all the matters."

With that comment, Gardeniyah couldn't help but join back in on the conversation. It was one thing for them to disagree about the integrity of the queen. None of them could know the intentions or motivations of the queen, so she let them argue their points. However, when history and facts came into play in a skewed manner, Gardeniyah had to step in.

"She doesn't have the power, Lorella. Sanora, she would have had the power. Ranosa gave most of the monarchy's authority to the council. She's more of a figurehead than anything."

With that, the conversation fell silent. Evanlee felt Gardeniyah had sided with her and that her role model was vindicated. Lorella felt her older sister was just acting like her typical know-it-all self, and she was over the whole discussion anyway. And Gardeniyah felt the entire conversation had been a waste of time, and though she knew she had only temporarily paused a discussion that would rear its ugly head again, at least for now her sisters weren't arguing anymore.

They were almost to their room when General Vadeed approached the three girls and their armed escorts. General Vadeed had been as much a part of their lives as Ranosa and Mib. He had been there from the first day that the girls entered the East, and he had been a protecting fatherlike figure in their lives since.

He was especially integral in Lorella's and Gardeniyah's lives. He had made sure to begin their training on self-defense in secret ever since their sixteenth birthdays. Lorella had taken to it especially well.

He had been so proud of how quickly she caught on that he had been secretly training Lorella for months in hand-to-hand combat. He told her it was an "early birthday present," but Lorella knew it was more out of concern for her approaching exile. It was comforting to Lorella that the one fairy she admired trusted her enough to teach her how to fight back. It hurt, though, that he didn't stand up for her right to learn it publicly.

She felt it was unfair that the East expected them to go out into a world they viewed as unbelievably cruel with no training. But he hadn't. Instead, he had trained her twice a week on the plateau above the waterfall the castle sat on whenever he was supposed to be stationed there to observe the trainees. Lorella would dress in the Eastern military trainee uniform and stand alongside them as they trained, always careful to keep her back to only Vadeed so they wouldn't notice her lack of wings.

"I'll take it from here," the head general of the Eastern military said to his subordinates.

Evanlee smiled. The general was the queen's right hand. So she assumed if he was coming to take over their escort, then she had been right. Ranosa hadn't been the one to order them to be walked to their rooms like foreign prisoners. She shot Lorella a mocking grin. Lorella crossed her arms and looked away from her little sister, which made Evanlee feel very accomplished.

The fairy soldiers responded to the general's command with an emphatic, "Yes, sir!" in unison before taking their leave. General Vadeed's shoulders were tense as he waited until the soldiers disappeared into the dark hallway they had come from before he addressed the girls or let his eyes break contact from the forms of the guards.

"Let's go," he said in a hushed tone, still not looking away from the now empty hall.

"Are you walking us to our rooms, sir?" Evanlee said in a loud volume that in no way matched the one in which the general had just addressed them.

"No. Just follow me," he said as he turned away from the

girls and the direction of their room. "And do so quietly," he muttered as he cast a warning glance over his shoulder at Evanlee. This time, it was Lorella's turn to smirk. Evanlee felt her cheeks growing hot as her face flushed.

The girls walked in obedient silence toward the grand staircase. Memories flashed through Gardeniyah's mind. Tournaments to see who could race down the steps the quickest without falling. The time that Lorella had attempted to slide down the banister, which left her with a broken arm and a poor excuse for it. Horrified looks of fairy council members and their spouses as the girls hid beneath the stairs and played hide-and-seek with the other castle children.

The four of them stopped when they reached the bottom of the stairs as General Vadeed looked around to ensure no one was coming or going. They were alone. Everyone else had turned in for the night so they would be ready for the first break of light the next day. The emptiness pleased Vadeed, and he began to walk up the flight of stairs and motioned for the girls to follow him.

At first, it had been difficult to heed the order for silence. The sisters were all curious as to why General Vadeed was acting so peculiar. However, the questions and the nerve to talk all disappeared when they reached the second landing. They turned to the right and began to walk toward the staircase they always went up. But Vadeed stepped in front of them and shook his head, then he walked to the flight of stairs to their left.

Time slowed with every step they took. The air grew colder as they walked higher and higher. The handrails had once had visible flowers carved into the wood, but now dust covered every inch. The stairway was as frozen in time as the girls' ability to speak.

Finally, they reached the top of the stairs. The only thing before them was a giant wooden door. They stood breathless before the ancient door. Their inability to take in the adequate amount of oxygen was from reverence rather than the climb up the stairs. Pictures of the formation of Tolatin were carved into the door with extraordinary detail: One of the ancient pairs of king and queen standing with a light beaming around them. A map of the world before the Great Wars with every mountain range, river, and town etched into the wood. There were countless other pictures that Gardeniyah didn't have time to take in before Vadeed opened the door.

If they had been walking to any of the other three towers, then being escorted by the general and the thick air that lingered between him and the sisters as they walked would have seemed odd. However, once they had begun ascending this wing, all questions as to why the general was acting so strangely disappeared. This was the wing that no one ever visited. This wing of the castle was left fully intact and undisturbed like a shrine. This wing and this tower where they now stood for the first time in their lives was Sanora's wing.

CHAPTER SEVEN

W hen the sisters walked through the door behind General Vadeed, they saw Ranosa standing in front of a window that stretched from the floor to the twelve-foot-high ceilings. As soon as the girls entered the room, the view mesmerized them, as it would any sensible person.

This was the tallest of the castle's four towers. So the window had the absolute best view of the East and the capital city. Gardeniyah was positive it had the best view in the whole world. She was wrong, but it was the best sight any human alive had ever seen. In fact, few beings of any race had seen better. One of the few that had was Sanora, the fairy who owned the room they were standing in.

Sanora was one of the founders of the Divine Order. And until about twenty years prior, she had been the first and only queen of the East. She was a fairy unlike any other. She possessed all the three of the gifts—war, mercy, and healing —whereas all other fairies only possessed one. Her abilities allowed her to rule fairly and even-keeled, despite fairies' emotional restrictions.

Then one night, she'd disappeared. No one knew where

she went. And no one in the East would ever lay a hand on Sanora. Everyone loved and adored her. Of course the immediate assumption was that it was a plot by man, and that they had killed or kidnapped the beloved queen. Luckily for the three human girls who would show up at the border five years later, while searching her room a few members of the council—who were merely advisors and representatives of the Southerners and Westerners and not yet the Grand Council—found a letter Sanora had left on the bedside table of her room. In it, Sanora put Ranosa in charge. And all speculation of foul play was nullified.

The day Sanora left, Ranosa took only what she needed from this wing and then she sealed it up. The room had not been entered since. It lay in wait for the return of the true queen.

Whenever the sisters came to visit the castle, they were given free rein, except for this wing. Of course, some of the now "Grand" council members who lived in the castle didn't agree with Ranosa's decision to let the girls roam around. It seemed far too risky to let the girls learn the ins and outs of the castle. Easterners didn't want them to know of the hidden hallways, back entrances, and everything else that comes with any decent ancient castle. Luckily for the three very curious girls, this castle was far superior to anything that would be labeled a decent castle, and even more luckily, Ranosa didn't listen to the council on this one matter.

Instead, Ranosa openly disagreed with the council, and never shied away from saying so. This made the girls feel special when they could have felt very distrusted by the beings they loved most. It was one of the many reasons the girls adored the queen. And so, although it utterly terrified the members of the council who felt sure the young girls would turn into women who could not be trusted, the girls had, in fact, learned every nook and cranny of the castle at

Relis. But even Ranosa had made this area off-limits. Until now.

Gardeniyah wouldn't have thought it were possible before now, but Ranosa looked even more magnificent than the first time she'd seen her fifteen years ago. The large window let the light of the stars and the glow from King's Mountain illuminate her tall but slender frame. The light from the candle on the desk reflected off her otherwise translucent wings that lay flat against her back. But it wasn't just this or her eternal youth that made her so magnificent; it was her poise. Her presence filled a room no matter how large it was. It didn't matter if she was standing before an adoring crowd or debating with the members of the Grand Council—as she had many times on behalf of the three human girls—her demeanor commanded respect with the meekness required to instill affection.

Ranosa's back was to the sisters. She hadn't even turned around to see them bow. She hadn't said a word. Her silence was unlike her, and the extended pause did not quite fit with the urgency with which General Vadeed had ushered them up here.

Gardeniyah's shortness of breath was too hard to ignore. But it was only when their footsteps stopped and only the stillness of the ancient room hung in the air that she could hear her heart's pulsing in her ears.

Etiquette dictated that Gardeniyah's gaze would have to remain fixed on the queen once she finally turned to speak to them, so she took the opportunity to scan the room. It was more unbelievable than she had ever imagined—and she had imagined it to be quite the sight.

Floor-to-ceiling bookcases lined every wall, interrupted only by the window that Ranosa stood before. The window was large and clear with a balcony on the other side. The handle was made of crystal that blended in almost seamlessly with the window so as to not interrupt the view. The sides of the windows had ornate stained glass that depicted the four regions of Tolatin. The golden orange and vibrant purples of the West paired with icy blues and grays of the North on the left. The pinks and greens of the East paired with the sky blues and yellows of the South.

An enormous and clearly ancient wooden desk sat in front of the window. It was said that a nymph had grown the large tree that the desk was made out of especially for Sanora to commemorate her three hundredth anniversary of ruling the East. It featured carvings that matched the ones on the door.

On top of the desk, a pen lay outside of its inkwell, hardened by time and with dust on the feathers. The room smelled like the Evergreen Forest and another scent that was light and lovely. She couldn't place it, as she had never smelled it before. It was Sanora's scent still contained within the untouched room. Gardeniyah loved it instantly, almost more than the smell of the library.

Finally, Ranosa turned around. Her eyes were glassy. She was not as poised as she had been an hour before at the party. Gardeniyah felt her heart sink to her stomach at the sight. She desperately wanted to know what could be making the most powerful and composed being she knew so distraught.

Time passed infuriatingly slowly in those moments. After what seemed like ages, Ranosa addressed them.

"My sweet children . . . No, I suppose you aren't children anymore, are you? That is, after all, why it has come to this."

Gardeniyah glanced to either side of her to see how her sisters were reacting to the statement. Lorella shifted her balance and closed her hand into a tight fist. Lorella always did that when she was fighting off an emotion she didn't want to feel—which to Gardeniyah's dismay, were most of the emotions known to man, fairies, mystics, beasts, and monsters. Lorella had always envied the fairies' abilities to feel only one emotion at a time. Though, truthfully, if Lorella had her way, she would often opt to have no feelings at all.

On the opposite end of the spectrum, her youngest sister let out a barely audible whine. Evanlee always felt far more emotions than were necessary for any given situation.

Gardeniyah simply didn't react. She nodded, but that was all she did to acknowledge the words. The words were a fact. That was all there was to it. Moreover, she knew full well that this was merely the beginning of whatever Ranosa had to say that was troubling her so. Therefore she couldn't let herself get upset already.

"I know the three of you do not wish to leave the East, or at least would like the option to come back," Ranosa said. "As of right now, I am sure you have accepted this can never be the case. However, there was a time during the Divine Order, before man and their greed infiltrated every corner of this world but ours, that people traveled and visited each other in every quadrant."

"We know all that. Why exactly did you call us here?" Lorella said. Although Gardeniyah didn't approve of the stern manner in which Lorella spoke to the queen, she had to admit, as much as she loved hearing about the past, this wasn't the sort of history lesson she was in the mood for either.

Ranosa seemed unfazed by Lorella's question. She had the same calm look on her face as she continued to speak. It was evident she rehearsed this.

"We, meaning General Vadeed and I, believe that there is a way that we can once again restore order to the world. If it is successful, we could reinstate our old border policy. Perhaps, with the blessing of the council, you could even come back for good."

"Wait, what? If this was an option, why haven't you all already done it?" Lorella demanded. "And when exactly do you think you can be bothered to get around to it, before or after we are dead?"

"Lorella, enough!" Gardeniyah said. Lorella shot her sister a glare that would have withered the spirit of most men and creatures, but she fell silent as she waited for Ranosa to continue.

"The reason we have not already conducted this mission, so to speak, is because it is not ours to complete. It is yours."

The girls could do nothing but stare at each other.

"I'm sorry, what? What do you mean it's for us to do?" Lorella's scowled, and every emotion was passing across her eyes at once. Even she couldn't hide how she was feeling in a moment like this.

"The night of the stars encircling the moon, when Sanora left, she left a note."

"Yeah, yeah, and she left you in charge," Lorella said, interrupting the queen once more. This was a time in which a fairy's inability to have multiple emotions worked in the human girl's favor. Had Ranosa been a human, she would have been very annoyed with Lorella and her gall by now. Instead, Ranosa continued in her serious manner barely responding to the fact that Lorella had said anything at all.

"Yes, she did. However, she spoke of a couple of other matters in this letter as well. One, she didn't want her people to lose hope. Two, the world needed to be made right again—back to the way it was during the Divine Order when man ruled the North, beasts ruled the West, and monsters ruled the South. Before the Great Wars when mankind broke the covenant and all groups but man were forced to relocate to the East."

Lorella began tapping her foot as she muttered to herself: "Clearly the queen is not going to accept that we don't want a bedtime story consisting of our race's mistakes." Lorella knew saying such a thing with Gardeniyah within earshot was a risk. But she felt validated when she saw even her ever-poised sister close her eyes and draw in her breath as Ranosa continued to speak.

"For some reason," Ranosa continued, oblivious to the sisters' frustrations, "she couldn't be around for the process. Even Sanora, the best of our kind, couldn't show man the error of their ways well enough to convince them to right their wrongs. Man needs to be the one to try to put things right. Since man can't be convinced, there is a spell that the Founders created with the Omniscient's blessing and powers. It acts as a fail-safe. If the world ever came to what it is now, the spell would put things right again. We aren't sure how. Sanora didn't clarify that to us—we assume for the security of the spell—but we know that it is supposed to make things right. If this happened, we could once again open the borders."

The words hung in the air alone as no one else spoke. Gardeniyah knew she should say something, but she couldn't. All she could do was stare past Ranosa out the grand window behind her. She saw the East and all its beauty. For the first time, she could even see as far as the border and, vaguely in the distance, the beginning of the North and its snowy mountains. She could see the Mountains of Man in the dark of night. It was strange to see lights in the middle of the darkness and at such an hour. The dots of light made it look as if the stars were cascading down in a waterfall from the sky. However, she knew it was really just a beacon of the humans' very different lifestyle.

She could have stayed looking at the view from Sanora's room all night, daydreaming about the very different lives the humans in the North led. But her daydreams were interrupted by the voice of General Vadeed, who until now had been standing off to the side of the room.

He stepped forward as he spoke. "I know this is a lot to take in and to ask, but we believe the errand and the effort must come from a human. You three are the only hope we have."

"He's right," Ranosa continued. "We didn't want to ask this of you. It will be a long and hard journey. I wanted only for you to be happy and continue on with your lives. But I think, for you, that being happy means being able to see the East and the people you grew up with again."

Gardeniyah was coherent enough at that point to acknowledge the truth in that statement with a nod. A few moments later, she was able to speak. "So, what's the spell? We will do it."

"It's not that simple."

"Of course it isn't," Lorella muttered as she stiffened her back and refolded her arms. Gardeniyah wanted to scold her for the impertinent statement. But it would have been hypocritical, as she had thought the same thing.

"The spell is in Sanora's book."

"Sanora's book?"

"Yes, she kept a journal—well, more accurately, it was much more than a journal. It was a historical account of every major event in the history of Tolatin, mixed in with various things in her life. When the Founders and the Omniscient created the fail-safe, they wrote it down in only one place, Sanora's book. Since she was the only one among them who would never die, it was the easiest way to ensure that this spell, and whatever other spells the book may contain, never fell into the wrong hands."

"Let me guess. We lost the book?" Lorella's haughty attitude was growing exponentially with every detail.

This time, Gardeniyah did give her a correcting glance.

Lorella was always forward and blunt. That's who she was. However, she had never been disrespectful like this to the queen before.

Lorella only rolled her eyes at her condemning look. In the middle of an eye roll, she noticed General Vadeed squint his eyes at her in disapproval. It was only then that she looked down repentantly. Gardeniyah had always favored Mib. Evanlee preferred the queen, and Lorella favored General Vadeed. So receiving a look of disapproval from him during one of their last few moments together stung.

"Well, we didn't lose the book, but we don't have it either. Sanora hid the book when she left. Somewhere in the world, it's out there. We think part of the effort she wants a member of the human race to put in is to find the book and then execute the spell. Or perhaps she just wanted to make sure it didn't fall into the hands of the wrong member of humanity in her absence."

"Do we have any idea where it might be?" Gardeniyah asked.

"No. We do know someone who may be able to help, though. He might have a clue as to where Sanora hid the book. His name is Methuselah. He's a human historian who was friends with Sanora for many years. He was alive before man took over the South. She trusted him and often visited with him. He knew about parts of her life even I didn't know. As a historian, she often shared things with him to help him write a historical account of and for man."

"Do you think he may have the book?"

"It's possible I suppose, but doubtful. No matter how much Sanora trusted Methuselah, I don't think she would have left such a valuable book with a man who would eventually pass away. He is, however, your best bet of getting in her mind, so to speak."

"Okay, we were planning on going to the North to live. If

he supports the Divine Order, he probably lives there and not the South, right? We can find him when we get there."

"I'm afraid not, my sweet children—I mean, sweet women. If you choose to do this, your plans are gone. He doesn't live in the North. He lives in Zaraneth."

The already thick air in the room became almost suffocating to the girls. Going to Zaraneth was not something the girls had planned. No one intentionally went to Zaraneth. It was the hive of corruption in Tolatin. The worst of the scum and traitors lived in Zaraneth.

"Why would he be in Zaraneth?" Lorella questioned, with pure curiosity and no edge this time, to Gardeniyah's relief.

"I assume he was banished there, or perhaps he's hiding there. Either way, his reasons for being there are no different than those of the other people who live there. Man does not want him. Being a supporter of the Divine Order isn't something celebrated in the rest of the world." Gardeniyah and her sisters, even never having been exposed to the outside world, knew that was an understatement. They just didn't know then how much of one it was.

Gardeniyah glanced over to her left when she saw Ranosa look at Evanlee with motherly concern. The young girl was shaking ever so slightly and had tears rolling down her face.

"You don't have to do this. We just wanted to offer it to you. We don't know any other humans who would help us. Perhaps Methuselah would have if he was younger, but he is a very old man. We can wait and hope to find someone else to ask. However, we don't want to. We want the world restored. We believe you can do it."

CHAPTER EIGHT

When Lorella woke up the next morning, she was unaware of precisely when she had fallen asleep. She supposed it was in a lull between the quiet sobs that Evanlee attempted to muffle in her pillow and the continual rustling of the silky sheets on Gardeniyah's bed as she tossed and turned. Lorella had alternated every few minutes between being annoyed with her sisters for so outwardly conveying their distress while she was trying to sleep and a sense of compassion that came with knowing all too well what they were feeling.

Lorella had just wanted to sleep. Tossing and turning while ramming her mind with incessant questions or crying herself to sleep was not going to solve anything. Sleeping, though, would make her forget about it all for a few hours. However, her sisters had made it somewhat difficult to execute her plan.

So Lorella climbed out of bed groggy, annoyed, and sleep deprived. A rather appropriate way to start off what she knew would be the worst day of her life. At least so far. As she glanced around the room, she noticed three things. Her bag was already repacked, as was Evanlee's, and the curtains were drawn back and tied in a neat little bow off to each side. That indicated to Lorella, before she even looked in the direction of Gardeniyah's bed, that her sister was already awake. The next thing she noticed was the view out the window. Not that there was anything particularly peculiar about the way the streets below looked. The view was the same as every other time she had stayed at the castle—which was exactly the thing that caught her attention. The world of the East was carrying on like today was just any other day.

The sun was up, so the shops in Relis were open. None of the shops were open much before sunrise or after dusk because the East didn't believe in wasting the resources it would take to power the city. Lorella had never seen the point in that. After all, Relis ran on water from the waterfall that it sat on. Still, the Easterners said that it was gluttonous to disturb nature more than necessary.

She never paid attention to the reasoning after the first time she had heard it. All she knew was that it was something about how the mill disrupted the flow of the waterfall's natural course when it was on and therefore, out of respect, it shouldn't be used all the time. Lorella felt that the water would end up back in the stream, so she didn't see what the problem was or why everything had to close. She supposed that was the "greed of man" in her because man had long ago found ways to work past the sun. Their technological advances had cost them their resources—which was one of the main reasons they began the Great Wars. She of course didn't want the East to end up like the rest of the world, but she felt that there surely had to be something in between mass destruction and being stuck in time with no technological advancements.

Despite believing it was a somewhat archaic lifestyle, Lorella had to admit there was a charm about the Easterners' way of life. Every morning, the bakeries were the first things to open. The delightful scent that the bread produced in the stillness of the morning spread through the city and signaled all those who lived around it that the day was about to begin. Then the sky awoke and, with it, the antiquated city.

The Easterners would make the most of every ounce of daylight. They worked incessantly but cheerfully—to the point of annoyance for Lorella on some of her especially grumpy days—until dusk started creeping into the skyline, at which point, they would head home for the evening to eat dinner with their families before turning in early so they could begin their day promptly at the next sunrise.

The city itself was as ancient as its lifestyle, and as equally gorgeous as old. Much of the city's structures were still the originals from when the East was first founded, dating back a thousand years. The aged stone buildings were faded to a light gray, but they still had the meticulous craftsmanship that had first gone into the intricate stonework.

The non-native Easterners had settled into the East's way of life too. Relis had a few beasts and monsters, but for the most part, the capital was filled with natives. It wasn't that they weren't welcome—far from it. Relis was the most diverse area of the East with all the different species of the East being represented and living together. The council even expanded to include non-native Easterners to ensure they felt included, valued, and a part of the East.

However, the groups had mostly split up and lived among themselves in their own unique cultures. There was no animosity between the groups. They were just trying to preserve what little they had left that man hadn't taken from them. Everyone, however, enjoyed coming together for festivals like Founders Day and the Solstice Soirée, where they celebrated the longest day of the year with a three-day festival.

Those sorts of holidays had always been the sisters' favorites, but, of course, as I'm sure you can guess by now, for very different reasons. Gardeniyah liked to see all the different species come together to celebrate. She would always seek out the elders of the groups and sit and talk about their lives for hours on end. Some species lived for hundreds of years, and so they recounted what life was like back in their home regions. She would listen and question them until festivities broke them away, after which she would find a new counterpart and begin again the process of discovering everything she could about the world.

Lorella loved to watch everyone interact. She would find a place out of view of others where she could see everything. One year, when she was twelve, she had found a tree ideally situated in the heart of the festivities and climbed it. She'd hid in the tree for hours and heard far too much for any little girl. Many of the secrets still either made her laugh or made her slightly uncomfortable when she saw the individual. In recent years, she no longer climbed trees to hide. Even though she was still rather slim, she wasn't nearly as small and would surely be noticed now. Instead, she usually opted for a table at the edge of a Clewberry Winery tent. She would sit, order a cup of braisonberry tea so she could be clear of mind, and listen and watch for hours.

Of course, some people on such holidays would get a little loud and overly enthusiastic under the influence of the warm, sweet clewberry drink, which could sometimes make it hard to hear the beings in the street. However, those same individuals often divulged many secrets as well in what they wrongly believed to be hushed tones. So a much older Lorella still learned far too much, and she thoroughly enjoyed it.

While her sisters were enjoying watching and talking to all those that had gathered, Evanlee just enjoyed the moment she was in and the festivities themselves. She loved seeing the fashions from all the cities of the East. She adored hearing the accents of the land. She reveled in the smell of the food from the Western and Southern lands mixed with that of the East's. And she loved the feeling of the electricity that the chatter and constant movement sent through the atmosphere.

Time stood still on those days. Even when night arrived, no one seemed to notice. They were consumed by each other's company. They were enjoying the games and the music. Of the three sisters, Evanlee was, in fact, the most like the Easterners in every way, including being present only in the moment that was upon them. For a day or three, Evanlee and the Easterners didn't care about anything except being there and enjoying every minute of it.

That was the sort of thing Lorella would miss. On those days, they burned candles all night so that the festivities didn't have to stop. They kept going and going until everyone was tired and went home again.

Yes, Lorella would miss those moments. But Lorella thought the rest of the Easterner way of life was a complete nuisance in its charm. She supposed, at some point in the future, she would miss even that aspect of living in the East. She knew there were plenty of things about the East she would miss the instant they left today, but she didn't think that waking up at the first glimpse of dawn to ensure you got everything you needed to be done would be one of them.

Lorella slowly eased out of bed. The fire had been on all night in their room, just as it was in every home to maintain the heat. So she didn't hesitate as she wiggled her toes and placed them on the floor. The warm stone sent a tingly feeling through her body. Her nightgown danced along to the rhythm of her feet as she made her way to Evanlee's bed to wake her up.

Evanlee always woke up beautiful. It was something Lorella very much resented about her. A hair or two might be out of place, but always endearingly so, and her eyes sparkled from the moment she woke up to the moment she closed her eyes again at night. Beauty was indeed Evanlee's gift to the world.

This morning, Lorella almost didn't recognize the girl who turned to face her when she placed her hand on the warm body. Evanlee's eyes only glimmered for half of a second and then clouded over. Lorella noticed how puffy they were. Her face was pale and tear stained, a far cry from the usual glow she had about her skin.

Lorella jerked her hand back from Evanlee's shoulder. She had no idea what to say to explain her reaction to Evanlee. At the same moment she pulled her hand away, a lump jumped into her throat, leaving her mouth feeling very dry. Lorella stood there, hand in the air, with a dumbfounded look on her face.

Lorella's odd position and expression caused Evanlee to give her a puzzled look.

Before Lorella had to come up with some way to explain herself, the door to their sleeping quarters opened and Gardeniyah reentered the room. There was something about Gardeniyah's being there that reassured Lorella. Though she would never admit it to her sister in a million lifetimes, her sister's presence often brought out a certain strength in her.

"You look how we all feel," Lorella said, bolstered from the bout of confidence she had gotten. Then she turned to Gardeniyah as Evanlee silently got up from the bed and smoothed her hair out as she walked toward the washbasin.

"You two are already at each other's throats, I see," Gardeniyah flatly stated as she scanned the tense air between her two sisters.

"If you expected anything less, then you're delusional. We

have accepted that we will always argue. Why can't you?" As Lorella said the words, she realized they had come out much harsher than she'd intended. She meant to say it in a joking manner, not in the spiteful way.

"I never thought that, but maybe I should. You are rather hopeless to get along with." Evanlee's words were so dry and unemotional, it took Lorella a second to realize what she had said.

Spiteful comments like this were unlike Evanlee. If Lorella was truthful with herself, she'd admit that most of their arguments were rather one-sided: Evanlee tirelessly defending whatever anecdote Lorella was picking on at that moment, and Lorella continuing to do so until Evanlee left in a huff.

Lorella wasn't sure why seeing Gardeniyah, as shocked as she was at Evanlee's snide remark, reassured her. Lorella was perhaps one of the few people in any world who could be simultaneously resentful of you and grateful for you, which was how she often felt about Gardeniyah. Lorella was sure this was yet another reason she didn't belong in the East, and, while she was sad to be leaving, she figured it was most likely for the best. The East was full of peace and joy. While most people would be happy to live in a place like this, Lorella felt isolated and restricted.

The Easterners were nearly always happy. It was easy for them to be. With their isolation from the rest of the world, and, as of today, their last influence from the outside world exiled, they would undoubtedly continue this peaceful life until the end of the world. It was an endless cycle of peace and life, just like the eternal spring that existed in the East. Lorella's musings over the East were interrupted by Gardeniyah's matter-of-fact tone she used when she needed her sisters to hone in on what she was saying.

"Well, all I see going on right now is that the two of you

are lashing out at each other so you don't have to deal with the actual pain you are feeling. Normally, I let you two bicker and try to understand that it's a symptom of your differences. Today, though, you both need to put that aside and act like the sisters we are, and the ones you could be toward each other if you tried." Lorella folded her arms as Gardeniyah spoke. She hated Gardeniyah's lectures, but she didn't interrupt. She didn't feel like fighting with her. Since her sisters had disrupted so much of her sleep, she didn't have the energy.

"Today will come with a lot of pain and new experiences, and with both of those will come fear. I am not immune to this just because I am older. I am hesitant to admit this to you both because I always try to be a source of comfort and strength to you. Even when you don't need it"—as she said the last sentence, she glanced at Evanlee, who then smiled meekly—"and when you don't want it." With those words, she glanced at Lorella, who returned the look with more of a smirk than a smile.

"Because of this," Gardeniyah continued, "we need to be each other's safe place for the time being, and that means the two of you as well. Leave the childish squabbles here. Your banter can be amusing, so continue that for a sense of normalcy if you must. But leave the hate-filled comments to yourselves." The two youngest siblings nodded. Then they gave each other apologetic glances—more to appease Gardeniyah than because they genuinely meant it.

"Now," Gardeniyah continued, "we need to talk about Ranosa and Vadeed's request. I think it was good that she suggested we sleep on it. But we need to decide. We have to leave soon. Honestly, I'm not so sure if we should do this. I want to help the East, of course. However, I also need to keep you safe."

With that statement, Gardeniyah saw Lorella's forehead

furrow; then her eyes sparked, and the corner of her mouth curled up in a sly, haphazard smile.

"What's life without a little danger?" The challenge came from Lorella and her mischievous smile. She emphasized the remark with a wink toward Gardeniyah. Lorella knew deep down that, beyond her feeling of familial responsibility and obligation, her sister craved an abnormal life as much as she did.

"Long." The meek voice belonging to Evanlee chimed in from the other side of the room.

It was the first thing she had said on the matter since their meeting with Ranosa. When they had first heard the quest, it had seemed like a rather straightforward and simple plan. Now, however, they realized that wasn't the case. Once they left these walls, they could head in one of two directions. They could go to the North, where they had always intended to go, or North and then West toward Zaraneth, the center of Tolatin and the roughest place in the land. All of this to try to find a spell.

Even if they did find it, they didn't know what the spell would be. If it were powerful enough magic to undo all the atrocities humans had inflicted on Tolatin for hundreds of years, then the spell would not be simple by any means. Furthermore, it would most likely require sacrifice and danger, as any good spell did. A fact that Evanlee, based on her last comment, was not too keen on.

"Long," Evanlee repeated, firmer this time. "Life without danger is long."

Gardeniyah and Lorella looked at each other and smiled at the innocence of the statement, as well as its blatant truth. But mostly they smiled at one another because it was so evident that Evanlee belonged here in the East, where it was peaceful and life was long. And they needed to do whatever it took to get her to be able to come back here.

Even if that meant scouring the entirety of a world they had barely seen a fourth of for a book that Sanora had hidden when she'd disappeared. However, the fact that it was a risky plan couldn't be ignored. It was far more logical to go about their lives and accept that they were humans and belonged in the North.

"Well, too long if you ask me," Lorella countered. "All right, big sis, it's a tied vote. What's it going to be?"

CHAPTER NINE

Gardeniyah looked from one sister to the other. Lorella had her arms crossed and a crooked smile on her face. Her eyes were begging for an adventure. Evanlee's eyes widened and begged for normalcy. Gardeniyah turned away from them and ran her fingers through her hair. She felt torn in pieces. She desperately wanted to give everyone what they wanted. *I can't give Evanlee what she wants no matter what I do. But I can give Lorella, and Vadeed and the queen, what they want if we do this.* Gardeniyah breathed in deeply and turned around to face her sister and the decision that would change the course of their lives forever.

She looked straight at Lorella when she spoke. She knew if she looked at Evanlee, she might say something other than what she knew was right because of the fear shadowing the young girl's eyes. So she focused on Lorella and took another deep breath. For the rest of her life, Gardeniyah would wish she had said something more profound at that moment than she did. But regardless of the lackluster thing and the way she said it, the words were still enough to change everything.

"All right. We'll do it."

It would have been much easier to decide if her baby sister had the same sense of adventure that she and Lorella shared. But regardless, this felt bigger than them. The look in Ranosa's eyes seemed much more grave than that of a life-long friend wishing to one day reunite with loved ones. Her gaze was pleading. Gardeniyah knew there was something she wasn't telling them, but she didn't know what.

She was familiar with the note of Sanora's that Ranosa had referenced. It was housed in a case in the library she had felt so drawn to the other day. She suddenly was overcome with the feeling that she had to read it once again.

"I'm going to go check on the food preparations. We need to see if we can bring more now," Gardeniyah said as she walked toward the door.

"I'll come with you," Evanlee offered sweetly.

"No."

"Why? I can help."

"No. No, you stay here and try to relax a little. It's going to be a very long day."

Gardeniyah didn't leave time for a rebuttal as she slipped out the door. She was glad no windows faced out into the hall from their room so that her sisters didn't see her turn right toward the library and not left toward the kitchen.

She was thankful for the excuse to visit the library one more time. As she walked through the doors, she disregarded the fact that she was running out of time. She paused a moment to breathe in the smell of leather, dust, and aged paper. She looked around at the towering rows of bookcases she had spent so many afternoons between. She would miss this room, among the hundred other things she hated to leave behind.

As the days grew closer to their departure, she had wondered if the North had any libraries like this one. Was literature something they even cared about? She had been sort of looking forward to learning about the people like her out in the rest of the world. But now she would be among only the vilest of men. She couldn't picture them caring much about having beautiful libraries.

After her moment of appreciation for a place that had taken up much of her childhood, she refocused on the task at hand. She walked to the case in the middle of the room, the one that had seemed to be calling to her only two days before. She stepped up to the glass encasement with more apprehension than ever before. The note read:

My dear people,

I know my course of action will be baffling to you and know to myself it is as well. If I had a choice, I would not have chosen to leave you all. I hope that is quite clear to you. The night of the bitter chill when the stars encircled the moon, I met with the Omniscient for the first time in many human lifetimes. The news he had for me was not that which I wished to hear.

He told me the end is imminent for our world unless things are made right. He also said I must leave you all so as not to interfere with what must happen. I have left Ranosa in charge so you all won't be entirely alone. I have had her work by my side, but in the shadows, for years. Trust her, and she will be a substitute for me. If all is made right and the prophecy comes true, I shall once again be able to return to you. If not, so starts the beginning of the end. Here is the prophecy I leave with you. Be wise, be just, and try in all you do to make sure it comes true:

"The descendants of the one who started it all
Shall stop mankind's bitter fall.
All the names shall have their stain
But they will free the world of her pain.
They must reconcile the present and past
For the forthcoming end comes fast."

Good faith to you, all my people, never falter and you shall not fail. Be open minded, and you will prevail.

—Sanora

Gardeniyah suddenly couldn't remember if she had ever read the letter before. She found it unlikely that she never had in all the times she had been to the library. But still, the words felt new to her. Gardeniyah would never have dreamed this letter had anything to do with her and her sisters. She reread the words "the forthcoming end comes fast." They sent a shiver down her spine, just as they had every time she had stopped to read them.

What end is it referring to? As Gardeniyah left the library and walked to the kitchen to make good on what she had told her sisters, the words replayed in her mind over and over. She now had more questions than answers. While she was glad she hadn't opted out, the weight of the task she had been carrying now intensified.

She decided right then that it would be best to keep that part of the prophecy to herself. The three of them would commit to Ranosa to try. As of now, they were all on board, so she felt no need to add any extra pressure to the situation. She would reassess the situation should that change.

She knew the journey would most likely be dangerous, and she knew she might not be able to protect her sisters from everything. Having to accept that realization was already eating away at her. She could, however, protect them from the weight of those words that she knew would haunt her from now until they found the book.

CHAPTER TEN

I n the time it took to talk among themselves and come to a decision and then tell Ranosa what they had decided, the few hours they had left in the East had disappeared. The sisters knew the guards would soon come to get them from their room.

The streets outside settled. The clanging of the ironsmith stopped. The laughter mixed with the occasional argument over a raised price, and the overall bustle of the market halted. Gardeniyah knew that the Easterners intended the silence to show respect and reverence toward the sisters. But to her, it felt eerie and made the still air seem too thick for her lungs.

Mib met them at the doorway of their room. Seeing her was a shock to all three of the girls. Mib rarely came with them on their monthly visits to see Ranosa, as she'd never been very fond of the castle. She was humble in all ways, and she didn't feel like she fit in with the "castle types," as she called them. That's why, even though raising the girls in the castle would have given Mib access to more help than she could ever need, Mib had politely refused Ranosa's offer to live in the castle at Relis. She had conjured up a reason that would be acceptable to the council. She knew they would not be fond of the idea that the girls would live where they couldn't keep an eye on them. So she'd said that she felt the simplicity of farm life and the meager earnings of a night guard would be better suited to stifle the greed that may grow in the girls. This reasoning, of course, did the trick and made the council agree with her wholeheartedly.

She later confessed to Gardeniyah that this really had nothing to do with her decision. Everyone at the castle had an agenda. To Mib, that wasn't life in the East. And a peaceful, happy life was what the sisters' mother had pleaded for them to have here. Mib felt it was the only real way to raise them and honor their mother.

The lump that was already in Gardeniyah's throat grew to suffocating size as she thought about how incredible her surrogate mother was. She always sacrificed her desires for others. For three hundred years prior to the girls' arrival, she had worked to advance in the ranks of the guard. That had changed when the sisters came to the East. She'd abandoned her dream in order to take care of them. And she had forgone the luxury and splendor of living in the castle at Relis to honor their mother's wishes—her decision based solely on the earnestness of the plea in the woman's eyes.

Gardeniyah and her sisters would miss very different things about the East and all that they were leaving behind. Gardeniyah wanted to ask her sisters what they would miss the most. But she knew she would take on their load as well if she did. For once, Gardeniyah couldn't take that on; she couldn't ease this for her sisters because the pain of leaving Mib was much more painful than Gardeniyah ever imagined it would be, and she had imagined it to be absolutely dreadful.

Mib grabbed all three of them the moment they walked

through the door and hugged each of them. Gardeniyah's tense shoulders eased as she sank into the hug. She felt more relaxed in that moment than she had at any point in the last day, and more so than she would feel for a very long time.

While she had them in close, Mib told them how much she loved them all. This was because Mib didn't want them to see her upset. She didn't want to add to how difficult this day would be for them. Gardeniyah was who she was, the protector of her loved ones, because of Mib and the example she had set for her. And as Gardeniyah held on to Mib tighter than she had since she was eight years old and had the worst nightmare of her life, she felt a tear slide from Mib's face and hit her shoulder. Mib stiffened when she realized she hadn't been able to stifle one. But this only made Gardeniyah cling to her tighter.

Mib didn't pull away until she was able to switch to a different emotion, though how she did so and what emotion she switched to, Gardeniyah couldn't figure out. Regardless, when she pulled away, she looked at the girls with a broad but obviously forced smile on her face. Mib proceeded to fix something about each of their outfits. She had refused the invitation to the ball the night before. Had she gone, though, she would have found it amusing how different they all looked today. They had traded their heels and dresses for formfitting pants that were easy to maneuver in and black boots that rose up past their knees to protect against the cold.

The colors were the standard of the Eastern military: tan pants and black combat boots. But that's where the similarities in their appearance stopped.

Evanlee wore a pale-yellow shirt that flowed about her still-developing frame and fell off her shoulders on both sides. Her hair was down despite Gardeniyah's and Lorella's efforts to convey how impractical that was for their journey.

Lorella's hair contrasted Evanlee's. She tied it back in a tight bun so it was out of the way and unmoving. Just how she liked it. Her black long-sleeved shirt hugged her petite frame. It was tucked into her pants, which were secured with the military belt that Vadeed had given her on her sixteenth birthday. She didn't have a weapon on there now, as weapons weren't allowed in the castle, but as soon as they left the gates, the dagger she had been making in secret for months with the help of Shorton would hang from the belt.

Gardeniyah wore a brown sleeveless top that hugged her body like Lorella's and a thick black jacket. While her sisters had packed their jackets away, Gardeniyah wanted to be able to layer clothing wherever she went so she had opted to wear the jacket so she could fit a sweater of Mib's in her satchel. However, the sweater was only partially practical and majorly sentimental.

It was Mib's favorite sweater. It was large and heavy and she wore it every time the East had even the slightest cold front. When Gardeniyah was little she had often swiped the sweater from Mib's drawers and cuddled up in front of the fire as she fell asleep on the rug. When Gardeniyah would wake the next morning she would be in her bed, but the sweater would still be on. No matter how chilly the night had been and how much Mib most likely would have liked to have had it herself. So although Gardeniyah knew Mib may miss the sweater the next time she reached for it, Gardeniyah knew she would smile and know exactly who had once again swiped it.

Her sisters also had a few additional clothing items in the bags they had slung across their shoulders. Lorella had strictly practical clothing. And Gardeniyah could tell based on her sister's bulging bag that Evanlee had slipped a few more things into her bag. Most likely the same things

Gardeniyah had taken out earlier that morning as she repacked her sisters' bags.

Gardeniyah carried an additional large bag on her back filled with the food and supplies that they had been slowly gathering for months. Landiel, the castle's cook, had always been fond of the sisters. The girls had always been very hungry after long, boring dinners they had attended with Ranosa in honor of some council member or new law. So once they had been dismissed, they always made their way to the kitchen where extra portions of soup, bread, and dessert were waiting for them.

So when Gardeniyah approached Landiel after her venture to the library, she managed to convince him to supply them with a few more provisions without having to explain anything. In fact, she was surprised with just how much he had offered her. Leathered fruit, dried herbs, nuts, and the soups that made him famous—and had secured his job at the castle—were all waiting for them to enjoy. It would all taste much better than the canned vegetables she had packed before. She would have to make sure her sisters alternated between Landiel's goods and their own.

Mib adjusted the shoulders of Evanlee's shirt to make them fall to an even length on both sides. She tightened the strap on Lorella's satchel. She tucked a piece of hair into Gardeniyah's braid that had fallen out. Then she stood back and, with a smile, said, "You guys are going to love it out there. There are adventures and romance and so many things to see, not like this boring old place. You'll love it so much more than here!"

Mib was trying. She was trying incredibly hard. The girls knew she didn't believe her words, just as they knew Mib didn't believe their enthusiastic nods of agreement. But it was all the four of them could do, all they could say.

The four of them walked down the halls to the main door

of the castle. The hallways had never seemed so short or so empty to Evanlee. Every detail of the large glass windows and the stone floors jumped out at her. *Have the stones always had so many shades of gray in them? Have the curtains on the windows always been so purple?* She suddenly felt ashamed of how many times she had walked these halls and been oblivious to such details. *How could I have let myself take all of this for granted? I knew this day would come.*

The air tasted bitter to Evanlee. But it wasn't actually the air at all. It was the tear she hadn't managed to subdue that had rolled down her face and onto her lips. This place was her home. Now she was an outcast. And her only hope of ever coming back again was to wander around the world looking for an ancient book to cast some spell to change everything. She loved how peaceful the East was and knew there would be nothing peaceful about the next portion of her life.

To Lorella, the halls had never seemed longer. She couldn't wait to get out of the castle. To be done with this awful day. She couldn't run or hide from the pain today. It was everywhere she looked. In everyone's eyes. In the silence of the capital. Everywhere. The sooner she could leave, the sooner she could forget.

Lorella didn't plan on letting herself miss anything. Yes, she was going to help her sisters find the book. They needed her. But she had no intention of ever coming back to the East. She wanted nothing to do with the people casting her out just because of the number of years she had been alive.

The East's bright sun blinded the girls as the double doors of the main gate to the castle opened. They all covered their faces and blinked back the ironically cheery rays to see what was in front of them.

They hadn't expected what they saw. The streets had fallen silent because everyone they had ever known, except the most skeptical council members, stood lining the streets. They had come to say goodbye. They didn't know about the journey the girls were about to embark on and the importance of their task. They came only to say goodbye and pay their respects.

The girls walked the streets in silence, nodding and making eye contact with as many beings as they could. They smiled when they could muster it and grabbed a hand or two each along the way. Some faces were dearer than others. Hothem, the guard who had been with Mib the day they were found, was there. His posture made him look as strong as ever despite his eyes showing the sadness he felt. Brashen was there too. He was the only hand that Evanlee grabbed. She wasn't able to fight off any tears as she said, "You're not getting a goodbye from me." She squeezed his hand tighter. His hand lingered in hers longer than was acceptable in public. His eyes and face showed the world he wasn't feeling any emotion but pain. And, in this moment, a human's expression matched a fairy's.

Other beings they had grown up around, whom they had cared about and loved, flanked the walkways. And now they had to accept the reality that if they failed they would never see any of them again. But the fact that there was even a chance gave Evanlee and Gardeniyah a little twinge of hope.

Despite this act of kindness, the idea of not seeing them again was still okay with Lorella. It didn't change the fact that none of them believed in her ability for good. Nor the fact that the Easterners further believed in her inherent evil. They were so wrapped up in the fear that she would betray them that they didn't realize they were betraying her. She was being punished for a crime she didn't commit. In fact, she was going on to do the opposite. She was setting out to save them. *No, one small gesture of kindness doesn't outweigh their betrayal*, she thought. *I'll help them because it's for the betterment of the world and for my sisters. But I'm done with them. Today will be the last time I will see them, and I wouldn't have it any other way.*

On the contrary, this moment was the definition of devastating for Evanlee. Her heart welled up with the type of pain that clutches at the entirety of your chest. It squeezes and pulls your stomach and heart down with it until the pain shows itself in the sobs between the breaths you are fighting to take. She had needed to cry like this for days, but she had been fighting it. Every deep breath she had taken, she felt her lungs catch and a sob begin to creep up on her, squeezing her lungs and begging to escape. But she had pushed it down. She had tried to be as brave as her sisters. She didn't bother to try to look tough now. All her strength was going into walking and breathing, in merely existing. Besides, she knew her sisters looked poised enough for all of them. Lorella so poised she appeared apathetic, and Gardeniyah poised to the point you could tell it was a facade.

For Gardeniyah, this moment brought on a new determination beneath that facade. She loved it here; more importantly, she loved these people. She knew she had to find that book. Not just because she wanted to be able to see each of them again, but because she had to make sure that whatever end was drawing in on these people stopped before it even started—if it hadn't already begun.

CHAPTER ELEVEN

No one had said a word for hours. The only sound was the wind in the trees and the occasional stick snapping beneath their feet. It was a difficult silence brought on by the lack of words that seemed adequate in the situation. Each girl walked alone with her thoughts. This silence gave them each time to sort out their feelings about the day and their new mission.

Evanlee had begun to say something several times by the time the sun started to dip down ahead of them. Each time, she had stopped herself. Twice, it was because she had immediately thought of at least three snarky remarks Lorella would be able to make in response, and she hadn't felt like dealing with them. Once was because she knew the question, "How do we know what to expect of Zaraneth?" had no answer.

They couldn't know what to expect. So Evanlee reasoned that there was no point in asking. Every other time she had opted not to speak, it was because the silence had gone on for so long that she felt that whatever broke the silence needed to be significant. None of her anecdotes about flowers, the annoying bee that kept following them, or the way her feet hurt in the new boots that were supposed to be good for this sort of thing (and in fact were excellent for it, but she hadn't taken the time to break them in like she was told) seemed appropriate. So she waited for someone else to disrupt the now overbearing silence.

She had been bored as they walked for the first hour or two through the Evergreen Forest she had grown up in. To her, every tall evergreen looked the same; their large trunks and thick branches looming high overhead were mundane after miles and miles of them. The only thing that made them unique were the homes that Easterners of all sorts, from fauns to pixies and fairies, had built inside them. But those had ended miles ago. They now had to walk through the trees that were waiting for future generations of homes to be built but were currently as boring as a blank canvas.

Thankfully, they had just left the large Evergreen Forest and were now in Nymph's Haven, Evanlee's favorite area to visit. It was a large, open space where all the best festivals of the East were held, much like the meadow she loved so much by their house. The trees here were small and delicate like the nymphs that lived inside them. Every time a gust of wind blew, Evanlee's heart leaped with anticipation. She hoped it was a nymph who had decided to make an appearance. She loved the feeling of the soft wind brushing against her when they did. She stopped frequently to see if the flowers would fall off a nearby tree and swirl into a flowered form of a human or fairylike being.

It was apparent why the nymphs chose to inhabit this part of the East. It was so far from everything. They could go about their nymph lifestyle without any interruptions, isolated from worries and surrounded by stunning nature. To witness nymphs playing and interacting was considered one of the most beautiful sights in the East. Nymph's Haven was, by all accounts, not just the nymphs' haven but Evanlee's as well.

Evanlee had not gotten to visit except during festivals. But when she did, she treasured it. If given a choice to be any creature in Tolatin, Evanlee would have chosen to be a nymph. She adored them and their culture. Her only regret was that she had not gotten to associate with them much. Some decided to uproot themselves and grow near Relis, but not many. Just like any other group, there were always a few representatives living in Relis, but the capital was mainly the fairies' area. If you wanted to see the other Easterners in all their natural glory, you needed to go to their areas of the East.

To Evanlee's right, barely within eyesight, the flat meadow gave way to rolling hills. The hills reminded her of the Centaurs who made their home on the plateaus somewhere beyond them. *I wish we would have had to go through the Centaur country. It's so beautiful there.* Centaurs lived even simpler lives than the fairies. They dwelled in little villages atop the plateaus and spent their time meditating and doing the minimal to survive. They were regarded as the wisest creatures in Tolatin because of this. *It probably would have been a good idea to go through there and ask for advice. They study the stars and the past and predict the future. Maybe it would have helped us.*

Evanlee almost suggested to her sisters that they change their course and head toward the Centaurs. However, as quickly as the suggestion formed, she shut it down, for she was confident that was precisely what her sisters would also do, and she could easily see their annoyance in her mind. *Besides,* she thought, *even if they think it's a good idea, it's too late now. The Centaurs live miles and miles away from where we are now.*

Unfortunately for the group, Evanlee had always

daydreamed during her lessons on geography and had no real inkling as to exactly how far they were from the closest Centaurian Plateau—which was, in this case, a shame, because they were not nearly as far away as she assumed. In fact, they were rather close.

Had she made the suggestion, Gardeniyah would have known that the nearest Centaur village could have been easily reached by first walking two miles to their right. There they would have followed the river that fed into the pond in the rolling hills for about three miles. After which, directly in front of them would have stood a waterfall and the plateau of the Great Centaur Chief Moonsire.

Knowing this information, there was a good chance Gardeniyah would have taken the risk of potentially angering the fairy guards who were watching them to ensure they made it out of the East by nightfall. Evanlee had no idea about the prophecy that was weighing on Gardeniyah's mind at that very moment. And so, she had no clue how much Gardeniyah would have valued the insight of the Centaurs, especially one with Moonsire's reputation. Evanlee would never have guessed the value of the insight he may have been able to give her on what it all meant for the world and for the three sisters. So instead of voicing this valuable opportunity, Evanlee let the silence linger.

"We're only about another three miles or so from the river border of the North and the East," Gardeniyah said from up ahead. Evanlee breathed a deep sigh of relief at the silence finally being broken. "Even though it's warmer on this side of the border and it would be ideal to make camp here, we have to be out of the East by nightfall. So we will cross over and make camp on the other side. Then we will follow the river down to Zaraneth."

"We agreed to do this crazy task for them, and they can't even trust us to stay in the East a couple more weeks as we walk down to Zaraneth so we can be warmer? How delightful of them," Evanlee heard Lorella grumble next to her.

For perhaps one of the few times in her life that she could recall, Evanlee agreed with Lorella. The fact that the people she loved so much could distrust them to such an extreme stung like the healing masters' alcohol in an open wound. She couldn't figure out what they thought she and her sister would do if they stayed in the East a little longer. If it was merely for the principle, surely they could have altered their views a bit when the sisters had agreed to take on such a huge request.

"The people aren't aware of Ranosa's request, remember? The council doesn't even know. So we can't stay. They have the guards watching at the border to make sure we cross it. It's just how it is and how it has to be," Gardeniyah remarked in that reprimanding way of hers that Evanlee knew Lorella hated more than almost anything.

"Well, seems to me she could have solved that pretty easily by telling everyone about asking for our help."

Evanlee noticed the way Gardeniyah's lips pursed and her eyes narrowed. Evanlee wondered why Gardeniyah thought it was such a bad idea to tell everyone. To Evanlee, and apparently Lorella too, it appeared to be the rather obvious choice.

She glanced at Lorella in time to notice that she, too, had seen the face Gardeniyah had made. Lorella's brow was furrowed as she made eye contact with Evanlee, but just as Evanlee opened her mouth to question Gardeniyah about it, Lorella reached out and grabbed Evanlee's arm and shook her head. Evanlee pulled her arm away and opened her mouth again. This time Lorella stepped in front of Evanlee, shook her head, and mouthed, "Not now. Wait." Evanlee rolled her eyes and huffed, but she obeyed.

They walked along the banks of the river in the direction of Zaraneth until the sun began to set. Then they quickly crossed.

The water was strange. With each step they took as they waded into the water, the temperature of both the air and the water dropped a couple degrees. By the time they were in the middle, they could no longer touch the bottom, nor would they have wanted to. Near the surface as they swam, the water was now cold enough to feel as though needles were piercing their skin with every stroke they took. Evanlee was sure she had never been so cold in her life, and she was right. She was also sure she would never be so cold again, and in that regard, she was terribly wrong.

CHAPTER TWELVE

It turned out to be a mistake to have waited so long to cross the river. Gardeniyah and her sisters wanted to stay on the warmer side for as long as possible. But now the suns had set long before their clothing had time to dry thoroughly. This meant they had to change into new clothing before their first day was even complete.

"We should probably bundle up the best we can. Maybe put on more than one shirt and our coats," Gardeniyah said. She did her best to hide the edge in her voice because she knew it had nothing to do with either of her sisters. She was annoyed at herself for already making such a blunder. She was thankful she had, at the very least, taken off her jacket. Though realizing she thought to take that off but had not thought to have them take off the rest only served to make her more frustrated with herself. If they had crossed earlier, or if she had thought to tell them to take off at least their outer clothes and put them in their bags, which they had held over their heads while crossing the river, they would have had more clothing to wear. Which would have been even more valuable than she could have guessed, as the weather was a great deal colder than she'd expected. But she hadn't, and now it would be very difficult to get warm.

They set up a rather pathetic camp. They had only a flimsy tent for a shelter from the wind and cold. It was designed for Eastern festivals, and so it was made of thin material that easily—and to the girls' dismay, continually—gave way to the harsh Northern wind. Worse, the only thing separating each of them from the frozen ground was a thin sleeping mat meant for falling asleep on the banks of the lakes of the East, not for the icy earth beneath them.

The fire the girls built didn't do much to keep them warm. And the blankets, like the sleeping mats and the tent, were made for the cool, breezy nights of the East, not the bitter cold Northern night. Gardeniyah began making a mental list of all the things she needed to take care of as soon as they got to a town. As the wind cut at her skin and sent another chill straight into her bones, getting a thicker blanket to keep her and her sisters warm at night jumped straight to the top.

What she hated more, though, was the reminder that came with every bite of the frozen air: she was no longer home and she wasn't prepared for this new world. In her old world, she was always so on top of things. She'd had her lists, her routines, and her plans. She had been good at living in the East. Every day, she had moved from one task to the next with ease because she knew her world, and so she knew how to operate in it and how to be ready for any situation.

She had a reputation for being prepared. Her sisters trusted her to handle situations for them. Mib had put her in charge of many tasks in their home at a young age. Most of all, Ranosa had entrusted the girls with this task, and Gardeniyah had felt a bit of pride in the fact that the queen had thought she could handle it.

Here, however, all she felt was cold and overwhelmed.

Her thoughts swirled fuzzily around her mind like the flurries of snow that kept coming every so often. She was out of her element, and she hated it. She started to very much doubt her ability to protect her sisters. *How can I protect them when I didn't even have the foresight to commission a thicker blanket to be made for us before we left?* She was quite literally ill-equipped to take care of them. Her heart fell to the depths of her stomach as she realized this may be the first of many nights she felt this way. Alone, overwhelmed, and ill-prepared. Those had been her antonyms before, but now they were her reality.

CHAPTER THIRTEEN

T he second day went by slower than the first. It was an endless sea of white. The new world that surrounded them was eerie to three girls accustomed to the vibrancy of the East and its many colors.

To anyone else, the sight would have been a marvelous one. The North had snow-covered hills as far as the eye could see. Beyond the snowy hills, one could see the outline of the Mountains of Man. In the center and rising high above all the rest was King's Mountain.

Gardeniyah couldn't see the castle that was built into King's Mountain, nor could she see any of the villages built into the sides or foothills of any of the other mountains. But she knew they were there. The citizens of the North were reliant on the mountains. They needed them for shelter from the wind and for the resources housed within. Almost all the cities of the North were built into the sides and foothills of those mountains except for residents of a few of the more rural areas who had made their homes in the hills.

Gardeniyah's initial plan, before the queen's request, had been for them to make it to the closest village. According to the maps in the castle's library, the nearest one was a three-day walk directly North of the border outpost they had left from. When she had calculated the time it would take to get there, it had seemed like a long way. Now when she thought about the journey ahead of them to Zaraneth, she longed for the shorter journey of their original plan.

Instead of crossing the river and continuing into the North, they were headed west. Gardeniyah decided that they would stay close to the river for as long as possible. She knew that following its winding banks wasn't the most direct route. In Gardeniyah's mind, it was, however, the safest. The four rivers that divided the world naturally at the northeast, northwest, southeast, and southwest all flowed to the center of Tolatin and directly into the Middle Sea, which held the island of Zaraneth. If they followed the river, they didn't risk getting lost in a snowstorm. Though, as she correctly estimated, it would add a day or two to their journey.

If Gardeniyah were being honest, as she always tried to be —but in this case, had you asked her, self-preservation would have made her deny it—she would have admitted that if she had ventured here before now, she would have enjoyed the sights in the North. Gardeniyah wasn't like Evanlee. She didn't need a grand assortment of colors or extravagant details to find something lovely.

Gardeniyah found the smell of old books enchanting. She found the scent of Mib's "garden dumpling stew," as she called it, to be the second-best smell in the world—second only to the smell of the soap they all used that they made out of the sweet pink elerieberries and yellow and purple lily-ackas that grew by the river. And unlike Evanlee, Gardeniyah didn't believe extravagant parties and beautiful outfits were the best sights. She thought that the best thing to see in the East was the little creek a few miles from their house. And though it was no more than three feet wide, when the morning light reflected off the ripples of the water between the rocks, it seemed larger than life. Her favorite sounds in the entire world were the sounds of their regular evenings at home. Through the always open window in the kitchen, she could hear the owls and the crickets competing for the prime spot in the nighttime symphony. And while they battled, the fire crackled in tune with the rustling pages of the books they were all reading. And to Gardeniyah, these things beat out any band at the Solstice Soirée festival.

So if any of the sisters would have, under different circumstances, actually enjoyed the unique beauty of the North, it would have been Gardeniyah and her taste for simple things. She would have noticed that the trees bordering the river were beautiful in their own unpretentious way. They weren't green and flowering like the East's trees. Instead, from their branches hung dainty icicles that were formed by the war between the two lands' winds. For, you see, whenever a warm Eastern breeze made its way across the river and melted snow from the branches, the North's wind would fight back and freeze it to icicles of all sizes. And thus the trees' charms were formed.

And when the wind got caught in a hole in an icicle, it let out the sweetest of whistles. The kind of sound that Shorton would make as he chopped wood behind their house. And in the morning when the Northern Light peeked out above the Mountains of Man for the first time that day and made a brief appearance from behind the ever-present gray clouds, those same icicles would create a kaleidoscope-like rainbow on the ground beneath the trees.

However, because of the nature of their venture, Gardeniyah noticed none of this. In fact, she found the wilderness of the North far less than appealing. Gardeniyah soon realized she hadn't accounted for the fact that the two quadrants' weather would be at war with each other here.

With every step toward Zaraneth, the heaviness of the air grew. And the fog that was ever present at the northeastern border of the world began to cloud their vision, leaving them with the inability to see beyond a few feet in front of them.

The weather only grew worse with each step they took toward the center of the world. Gardeniyah realized she had forgotten this was the case in every part of the world. That was why so many monsters had settled so close to the center on the southeastern part of the border. The harsher conditions led to a climate as closely associated with their home in the South as they could find. It was also why she hadn't wanted to walk along that border. The Easterners' feelings toward man were mild compared to the hatred the monsters felt. They hadn't adapted as well to the East as many of the beasts had. And worse, their pride had been severely wounded when they'd lost their Great War. And few things in any world are as terrifying as a monster with a wounded ego.

Gardeniyah realized now that her plan to follow directly along the river had to be altered. They had to move northward. Until now, the East's forests had stood visibly in the corner of their range of vision. It had been both tormenting and reassuring to see their old home as they walked.

"We should stop here for the night. The weather is getting worse."

"Can't we walk a little farther?" Lorella's face scrunched. She didn't like the idea of ending the day while there was still so much light left.

"Yeah, if we walk longer, we will get to Zaraneth sooner!" Evanlee said. An agreement between the two was so rare that it startled even them. They looked at each other with sideways glances, both questioning if they could possibly be right if the other agreed with them.

"No. We need to stop. We don't know what this weather

is like. What I do know is that the wind is picking up and the temperature is dropping. I don't trust it."

"I'm sorry, but it's two against one. We want to keep going." Lorella crossed her arms over her chest.

"Well, I am sorry that you both wish to continue. I can understand that. But until we know this weather better, we can't take any risks. We are stopping. End of discussion."

Lorella's face grew hot. Her breathing both deepened and quickened as she walked past where Gardeniyah was now kneeling and beginning to unpack her bag.

"Lorella, where are you going?" Evanlee's voice, which grated on Lorella's nerves at the moment—even though she had just agreed with her—called out after her.

"I said I wanted to keep walking. You are welcome to come, pipsqueak."

"Lorella!" Gardeniyah's voice rang out loud and clear in a warning tone that Lorella had never heard before and which caused her to stop dead in her tracks despite herself. Lorella stared at her feet, watching the snow that had just begun to accumulate on her shoes as she stood unwillingly frozen in her tracks. "That's enough now, Lorella." Gardeniyah's volume was lower, but her tone was the same disturbingly stern one she had used moments before.

Lorella was angry with her sister for speaking to her like that and with herself for obeying. Lorella turned around and came back to the camp that was now in full swing of being set up by an equally angry Gardeniyah and a highly intimidated Evanlee. It wasn't often that Gardeniyah and Lorella argued. Gardeniyah hardly argued with anyone—which was rather good for most people, because, as in this instance, she usually won, even at the sake of the relationship.

CHAPTER FOURTEEN

The night ended as the Northern Light rose over the top of King's Mountain. It lit the day in the shades of gray that covered the North. The sisters' attempts at sleeping were more grueling than restful. But all the same, the third day of their journey began. The hours went by quickly as Evanlee and Gardeniyah spent the time talking about all sorts of things. One conversation involved what they should expect from the new land.

"I wonder what Zaraneth is like?" Evanlee asked. Though she had opted not to ask the question earlier in the week, today the mood seemed lighter—despite Lorella still fuming from the argument with Gardeniyah the night before. They were all beginning to get a bit more acclimated to their surroundings, and Evanlee felt there was a good chance she could ask the burning question without *too* much annoyance from her sisters.

Lorella, to Evanlee's surprise, was the first to answer her question. Even if Lorella hadn't been excluding herself from conversations all day, it would have surprised Evanlee to hear Lorella chime in. It wasn't often that Lorella chose to engage in any topic of discussion that Evanlee chose. And so she was, at first, thoroughly delighted that Lorella had decided to contribute. That is until Lorella said, "I remember reading about how the worst of everything is there. Even the worst of the weather."

"Yeah, I remember reading that too. I wonder what it's like in a place with all four seasons. I think that's the craziest part," Gardeniyah added in an attempt to lighten the tone of the conversation as to not let Evanlee get too scared. The comment didn't necessarily help the conversation any, but it did end it. With their limited knowledge of Zaraneth, there wasn't anything further they could say on the matter, and they all knew it.

A little while later, Evanlee started to lag behind her sisters. She was caught up in thinking about everything except keeping pace with her older and taller sisters. But she quickly caught up as Gardeniyah tossed her a question that she couldn't refuse.

"So what are you looking forward to the most about going back to the East one day, Evanlee?"

"The Easterners!" Evanlee responded without hesitation as she jogged to catch back up to her sisters. She kicked the snow playfully as she reached Gardeniyah. The snow hit the back of Lorella's leg. Lorella huffed but didn't respond. For now, there would be no further arguing.

"I'm thinking a certain Easterner especially?" Gardeniyah winked, nudging Evanlee with her elbow.

Evanlee blushed at the comment and looked down at the ground before replying, "I have no idea what you're talking about." But the curve of her lips and the twitch in their corners gave her away.

"Oh no? Well, then I'll be sure to tell him you forgot all

about him when we get back. That he must move on and get over you because you had forgotten all about him before the second day out of the East was over."

"You wouldn't dare!"

Gardeniyah simply winked at her again in response. The two thought this conversation was over, as well. It had served Gardeniyah's purpose of getting her little sister to catch up so she could keep an eye on her easily. But they were surprised once again by Lorella joining the conversation. She turned around to face them, risking falling as she walked backward. "Would you have married him?"

Evanlee blushed deeper and looked down at the ground once again as she said, "Maybe. I would have liked to. Not that that's ever been heard of."

"Would have been an aunt to little nephalimas." She pursed her lips as she turned back around. "That would have been interesting."

"Little what?" Evanlee asked as she cocked her head.

"I hadn't thought about them being nephalimas." Gardeniyah nodded her head with a slight smile. "I would've loved to have seen that."

"Really would have been cool to say we were aunts to them, huh?" Lorella said more thoughtfully.

"Definitely!" Gardeniyah's nod was bigger this time.

"Wait. What's a nephalima?"

"You don't remember?" Gardeniyah asked. Her sisters usually didn't remember stories from their history lectures, but she was surprised Evanlee didn't remember a folk story.

"Should I?"

"Seems like something you, especially, would remember," Lorella said as she picked up her pace a little. Whether she was done with the conversation because she had lost interest or just her patience with Evanlee was unclear.

"Nephalimas were part fairy, part man," Gardeniyah answered. "They were said to have existed shortly after the formation of Tolatin, long, long before fairies and men had their separation of ideals. Before their civilizations were even really in order." Evanlee's mouth dropped open as Gardeniyah continued in the distinct voice she used whenever she told a story. It always captivated Evanlee. Even Lorella enjoyed it most of the time. "They were said to be the most stoic creatures anyone ever knew. But inwardly, they were tormented. Souls that felt all the emotions known to man at odds with a mind that only wanted to feel one."

Evanlee gasped in delight and suddenly stopped. "Do you think we could be nephalimas?"

"Evanlee," Lorella said over her shoulder without stopping, "you are the farthest thing from stoic I have ever seen. You, my excitable little sister, are definitely *not* a nephalima."

Gardeniyah chuckled. But Evanlee would not have the idea cast aside so easily. "Well, maybe I'm just a happier nephalima. After all, you two are pretty stoic. I mean, it would explain why we always felt so at home in the East. And why they let us in! And why our mother left us at the East! Oh, and why we're named after things in the East!"

Gardeniyah could tell the more Evanlee thought about it, the more convinced she was that she was a nephalima. She was right. Gardeniyah always thought it odd that they were named after Eastern things. Most people assumed Mib had named them. But she hadn't. For whatever reason, their mother had named Gardeniyah after a city that bordered the North. It had been one of the East's most thriving cities before it quit trading with man. Lorella was named after the river that fed into the waterfall that the castle at Relis stood on. And Evanlee was named after the East's most famous flower. It had once been used all around Tolatin a symbol of wealth. No banquet, coronation, or wedding of a well-to-do individual was complete without bouquets of the blue flowers that were flecked with pink and had purple centers. *Perhaps because she always planned to abandon us.* Gardeniyah shook the thought out of her head.

"If you're basing it off of us all feeling at home in the East, you can forget your theory. Unless I'm not actually related to you, which would make more sense than you being a nephalima," Lorella mumbled so only Gardeniyah could hear. Gardeniyah saw Lorella getting increasingly annoyed as Evanlee continued to ramble on about how much sense it would make if they were, in fact, nephalimas. Lorella shot Gardeniyah a warning glance to shut Evanlee up. But she didn't wait for Gardeniyah to do so before shouting, "Evanlee, shut up already! We aren't nephalimas!"

"Well, we could be! Oh, I hope we are! How would we prove such a thing? We should try to find out. Then maybe if we fail, they will let us back in. They'd have to if we were part fairy, right? Oh yes, we must find out! Then we wouldn't even have to do this stupid quest!"

Gardeniyah's shoulders tensed at the remark. It had only been a few days. She didn't want to have to tell her sisters about the prophecy yet. Evanlee needed to let this go before she really began to believe it. Gardeniyah was equal parts flustered, scared, and irritated, which was why when she said, "It's just legends, Evanlee. Nonsense and stories for little ones, like mermaids!" it came out much harsher than she'd intended. So much so that Lorella stopped walking and turned around, suddenly interested in the conversation again.

But Evanlee was not going to be shut down. Her mind and heart had already latched on to the idea. "Oh, come on," she said, waving her hand to dismiss Gardeniyah's comment. "Mermaids aren't real. Half human, half beast? Powers of a mystic but dangerous like a monster? That's ridiculous! But half human, half fairy? That could happen! After all, like you said, if I had stayed, I would have married Brashen. We loved each other. If it could happen with us, who's to say it hasn't happened before?"

Gardeniyah knew that Evanlee's logic actually worked quite well. It was obvious she and Brashen did care for one another. Whether it was a love fitting for marriage or young love wasn't relevant. It had happened. And if that had happened when they lived in the East, it very well could have occurred when man and fairies had cared for—not resented —one another. But that line of thinking was going to distract Evanlee from the task at hand. Gardeniyah couldn't allow that.

"You're right," Gardeniyah said. And for a moment Evanlee looked like she had won a prize and Lorella looked as though she had eaten a bitter herb. But their expressions switched as Gardeniyah continued. "Mermaids don't exist. And neither do nephalimas. We have to do what Ranosa asked if we want to go back. Don't let fantasies of alternatives dance in your mind. That's a dangerous game to play."

Evanlee looked down at her feet, ringing her hands as tears brimmed the edges of her eyes. "I don't think so," she said. "I think it's called having hope."

Lorella shook her head as she condemned her little sister's statement. "Hoping you aren't what you are and that you are something else isn't hope. It's foolishness."

Though Gardeniyah agreed with Lorella, she hated to see Evanlee like this. A conversation that was meant to lighten her heart and her steps had broken both her heart and their pace.

"Evanlee, we have hope. That's what this quest of ours is. We were never going to be able to go home again, but then we got this chance. Focus on the hope we have, okay?"

Evanlee nodded and even smiled for a moment. Then a

cold wind struck them so hard that Evanlee was knocked off-balance. Gardeniyah reached out to steady her. And with the gust of wind, they were snapped back to the task at hand. The North was not about to let them forget where they were or that they needed to keep moving.

CHAPTER FIFTEEN

While her sisters went on to discuss more things that Lorella found to have very little value or purpose, Lorella couldn't help but continue thinking about the night before. Gardeniyah had turned out to be correct about the weather. That bothered Lorella almost as much as the fact that she had obeyed her sister like an obedient hound being scolded for something it knew better than to do. The wind had picked up considerably, and the snow came down harder than it had since they had come to the North. It hadn't been a full-scale blizzard; they were too close to the border for that. It had, however, unbeknownst to them, been the outer rim of one.

Had they tried to continue walking like Lorella had insisted on, they would have gotten lost. A fact that made Lorella exceedingly irritated the entirety of the day. So much so that she snapped at both of her siblings on quite a few occasions. She snapped at Evanlee the most, of course, only daring to challenge Gardeniyah once when she bumped into her in an effort to take the lead that Lorella had been occupying since their discussion earlier.

"Watch it!" Lorella fussed.

"It was an accident. Calm down, Lorella."

"Oh, like I believe that. Why are you taking the lead anyway?"

Gardeniyah didn't react to the charge that she had purposely bumped her sister. Instead, she only acknowledged the question. "Because we are changing directions. We need to head more northward."

"I thought we were going to stay close to the river?" Evanlee asked, casting a pleading glance across the river to their former home.

"We were. But the wind here is too strong with the two regions always competing as they are. So we need to move more north. I figured out the problem yesterday, but I was stalling. I don't want to leave the river either."

"And how exactly do you know that it will be any better there?"

"It's an educated assumption, Lorella."

"Don't talk to me like that."

"Like what?"

"You know what. Like you're smarter than me. You're not."

"That may be, but I did pay more attention in our lessons. I did spend countless hours in the library the last few months researching the North. And I did think this through."

"And that may be," Lorella said, imitating her older sister's words and tone, "but I don't remember agreeing to let you make all the decisions for us."

"Lorella, is this really how it's going to be?"

"What do you mean?"

"Are you going to challenge everything I say, do, or decide, just because I am saying it, doing it, or deciding it?"

"That depends, are you going to act like you are the only one with any intelligence or opinions out here?"

Gardeniyah took a deep breath and closed her eyes. She knew they didn't have time for this argument. They needed to keep moving. They were losing daylight. She had made the call to stop the night before, and she didn't regret it. But the needed to make that time up. Time wasn't just theirs now; people were depending on them. She needed her sister to stop the nonsense. She needed Lorella to trust her. She wanted to tell her she didn't understand. A part of her wanted desperately at that moment to say exactly why she didn't want to waste time consulting with Lorella on choices she knew would lead to the same decision when she could just make them herself.

"I wish you would just listen to me like Evanlee."

"Well, I'm sorry I'm not your blind little personal puppet like her!"

"Hey!" the previously silent bystander yelled from a few feet away at the insult. However, they both ignored her and continued their argument.

"I don't want you or her to be a puppet. But come on, Lorella, why can't you just trust me?"

"And why can't you trust me enough to have a say?"

Gardeniyah took another deep breath, as she always did when she needed to calm down, and then looked into her sister's eyes with a clear mind. Lorella's eyes were pleading with Gardeniyah for respect. She was placing her value in having a say out here. Gardeniyah knew now they would waste more time always arguing with each other than if she just humored the girl and asked her opinion.

"I do trust you, Lorella. I was just trying to save time. I'm sorry, I didn't mean to offend you."

Lorella's icy and defiant demeanor melted like the icicles on the trees at the bank of the river when an Eastern wind made its way across. She unfolded her arms and gave a knowing nod.

"So we are heading north, then?" Lorella said with a slightly—almost but not entirely—apologetic smile.

"I think it's best."

"All right. Let's go, then."

The girls walked in silence for a long while. It didn't take long for the river to fade out of sight. And with the disappearance of the river, the girls' journey turned into a true adventure. For any good adventure has more than just decisions and quests—it has danger. Up until now, the river had been an emotional and—although they didn't know it at the time—physical safety net.

CHAPTER SIXTEEN

As they walked north, the world around them grew darker. They were under the misconception that time must be passing quicker. In truth, the world was just darker the farther north you went. In the land of man, especially in the mountains where most of them lived, that daylight only made an appearance for a few hours a day.

The temperature dropped as the Northern Light grew dimmer, and the wind was stronger than before. Thankfully, the wind didn't feel as cold here—it wasn't wet like near the river. However, its strength, coupled with the much deeper and less compact snow, made walking a more difficult task.

Due to the lack of daylight, the girls were able to cover less ground each day, and they had to stop much sooner than they would have liked. Gardeniyah made sure to consult Lorella before deciding to stop for the day. Lorella had readily agreed and was actually relieved when her sister suggested it. Her whole body ached from the effort it took to walk through the deep snow.

They made camp and were sitting around the fire eating dinner when a sound pierced the air. All three of them jumped off their mats. Since they hadn't heard any sounds besides their own voices and the howling of the wind in some time, the cooing of a dove or the meow of kitten would have caused the same sort of reaction. However, Gardeniyah, Lorella, and Evanlee were not fortunate enough for this to be such an innocent sound.

"What was that?" Evanlee asked with a quake in her voice.

"I, uh, I don't know," Lorella said, looking all around and trying to figure out what the noise was and where it had come from.

"It sounded like a wolf," Gardeniyah said.

Evanlee perked up. A smile spread across her face. "A wolf? I didn't know the North had beasts!"

"Neither did I," Lorella said. She turned to make eye contact with Gardeniyah. Lorella didn't like the look on Gardeniyah's face. "I thought all the beasts live in East," she whispered so that only her older sister could hear her.

Gardeniyah nodded as her gaze looked beyond Lorella, into the distant night in the direction she felt the noise had come from.

"Then why would there be one here?" Lorella said softly. She was trying very hard to keep her voice hushed. She didn't want to alarm Evanlee if it wasn't necessary. She hated how her younger sister got when she was flustered. However, Evanlee was so preoccupied with scanning the night that she wasn't listening to them anyway.

"I don't know. It shouldn't be."

Evanlee got off her mat. She picked up a branch from the fire and held it in the air in search of the owner of the sound.

"Do you think the sound could have come from the Eastern bank?" Evanlee asked over her shoulder. "Maybe it's just a very loud wolf." Her eyes flickered with disappointment.

Gardeniyah shook her head. "No. We are way too far away for that. It's close. Whatever it is."

"But it can't be a wolf. They all left," Lorella said as she shook her head.

"There are stories that suggest otherwise. Not many, but a few."

"What sort of stories?"

"Of defectors among the beasts."

"I've never heard any of these stories," Lorella whispered, her quiet tone now an attempt to control the quiver in her voice.

"It's not something the wolves, or anyone in the East really, like to discuss. Pokes some holes in the theory of man being the only corrupt thing in this world."

"How did you hear about it, then?"

"Two Solstice Soirée festivals ago, I met a wolf named Welshire. He had consumed a bit too much clewberry wine and was talking a lot. He was the oldest wolf I've ever met. Apparently, his great-uncle Gladire defected during the Great Wars. Gladire said it was clear that man was going to win. So he made a deal with them. He and a number of other wolves would work for them as hunters and spies, as long as the king of men promised to allow them to stay. The king wouldn't let them remain in the West for fear that they knew the land too well and may revolt down the road. So instead, he allowed them free range of the North where they could be more easily monitored."

"Why didn't you tell us this before now? Why would you keep something from us? Especially something like this?" Lorella asked.

Gardeniyah felt like Lorella had just punched her in the stomach. That was far from the most important thing she was keeping from her sisters. In fact, this omission hadn't even been intentional. Or, at least, she hadn't consciously left them in the dark about it, as she had about the prophecy.

"I had forgotten about it until now. Gladire didn't have many defectors join him. Wilshire assumed that Gladire and his clan had died out long ago."

Another howl rang out in the still air.

"Well, I think Wilshire was wrong."

Minutes passed and silence hung in the air between them. Evanlee soon gave up scanning the darkness. She placed her torch back in the fire and sat on her mat, slumped over as she ate the rest of her dinner. They had all nearly resolved that whatever it was had gone away when the noise shattered the silence again. This time, it was even louder than before.

Evanlee hopped up again and grabbed her makeshift torch. She walked a few steps toward where it was now evident the sound was coming from. As she did so, she illuminated the night enough to see two glowing eyes inching toward the sisters' camp.

"It is a wolf!" Evanlee cried and whipped around to look at her sisters, grinning from ear to ear and pointing frantically in the direction of the beast. "Look, right there!"

"Evanlee, come here," Gardeniyah said as she stood up.

"What?" Evanlee looked back and forth between the wolf and her sisters. "Why?"

"Because he looks aggressive, Evanlee. Just listen to Gardeniyah." Still, Evanlee didn't move. "Evanlee, back up!" The wolf's head was down. His eyes were glowing. Whether it was from anger or Evanlee's flame, neither of the older sisters knew nor cared. He didn't look friendly in the least.

"He's just scared. I mean, can you imagine? The beasts back home barely trusted us. He probably thinks we are horrible like the other humans." Evanlee turned away from her sisters once more and back toward the wolf. Gardeniyah moved closer to her sister. It was obvious Evanlee was not going to listen to them. "Hello, Mister Wolf! No need to walk like that. We mean you no harm. We are friends of the East." The wolf continued toward her with no change in his body language. "Mister Wolf, truly, I understand your concern with us," Evanlee said as she put her hand over her heart, "but, please, don't keep walking like that. It's making my sisters uneasy."

Gardeniyah was now standing right beside Evanlee, and whispered, "Ev, please." Gardeniyah grabbed her sister's arm. "Back up." Gardeniyah attempted to move her back.

"Stop it!" Evanlee said as she pulled her arm away. "You're going to insult him. I am trying to get him to trust us. He won't trust us if we don't trust him."

"I don't trust him, Ev. Look, he's still stalking toward us. He's either ignoring you, or he doesn't understand you. Either way, you need to back up!"

Evanlee whipped her head toward Gardeniyah and shouted, "No!" The wolf was only a few feet away from them now. The moment Evanlee looked away from him, he leaped into the air toward her.

Gardeniyah jumped in front of her sister, pushing her out of the way. Gardeniyah fell into the snow. Evanlee stumbled and fell into snow, screaming. Lorella rushed to try to help, but the wolf and Gardeniyah were rolling in the snow, kicking up the white powder everywhere. Lorella couldn't tell what was her sister and what was the wolf. Time seemed to stand still as the sisters helplessly waited for the results of the fight between their sister and the beast.

All at once, the snow settled. There was no movement. The fight was over. The victor was unclear.

The wolf lay in the snow. Gardeniyah was nowhere to be seen. The snow around became red as blood seeped out from beneath wolf and spread across the snow.

Suddenly, the wolf's shoulders moved. One, then the

other. His body slowly rose from the ground inch by inch. Lorella stepped in front of Evanlee and readied herself for the next attack as the wolf appeared to regain his strength and stand. Then, the body fell to the side. In his chest was a knife. From beneath where the wolf's body had been, Gardeniyah rose weakly from the deep snow.

Her face was bloody. Her shirt was ripped across her stomach, gashes and blood where fabric should have been. She was gripping one arm with her other hand. It was barely visible through the blood.

Gardeniyah fell to her knees as Lorella rushed to help her sister. She tried to wrap Gardeniyah's arm around her shoulders, but Gardeniyah wouldn't let go of her own arm. Lorella grabbed Gardeniyah's arms and placed them both around her neck. Gardeniyah nearly choked her as she shifted her weight to bring her sister onto her back. She wobbled for a second. It was challenging to balance her sister while walking through the deep snow.

"We need to stop the blood!" Lorella yelled to Evanlee. She laid Gardeniyah down on her mat and dragged it closer to the fire. Evanlee rushed to them with a piece of cloth from her bag. Just as Evanlee reached out to place the wrap on her sister's arm, Lorella remembered the faun's words after she had cut herself. "No!" she yelled. "We can't wrap it in that, or it'll get infected. Quick, clean a food tin. Boil some snow over the fire and put a rag in it!" Lorella shouted.

Gardeniyah had lessened her grip on her arm. Lorella knew she couldn't wait for the clean cloth before putting pressure on the wound. So as she waited for Evanlee to return, she pressed her hand hard against her sister's open wound. Gardeniyah let out a scream, and then her body went limp in Lorella's arms.

CHAPTER SEVENTEEN

Gardeniyah didn't regain consciousness that night. It terrified Evanlee to see Gardeniyah so still. She hadn't even so much as stirred for what felt like hours. Lorella assured her that Gardeniyah's heart was beating and that she would be okay—she was merely weak from the loss of blood. Evanlee was drained emotionally from the whole ordeal, and she gave in to sleep only an hour after Gardeniyah passed out. But Lorella stayed awake the entire night and watched over her sister.

The next morning, well after daylight, Gardeniyah finally awoke.

"Good, you're awake," Lorella said. "We need to clean those cuts again and put a new bandage on that bite wound, but I didn't want to disturb you."

Gardeniyah didn't say anything, but she nodded. Lorella pulled the rag from the boiling water that she had kept ready for when her sister woke up.

"How are you feeling?"

"Tired."

"I'm sure. You lost a lot of blood by the time we bandaged up all the cuts."

"We should probably get going."

"Oh no. We aren't going anywhere today. You need to rest. Zaraneth can wait."

"No. No, it can't. It's important." Gardeniyah's words were labored and delivered slowly between each breath.

"Gardeniyah, you can hardly talk. You can't walk right now."

"We have to. The end." Gardeniyah reached up to her forehead and pressed her hand to her head.

"Hey. Shh. It's okay. You need to rest."

"No. No. You—we—" Gardeniyah pressed her hand harder against her head. "You don't understand. The end. We have to."

"What is she talking about?" said Evanlee, who had been sitting across from them unable to look at her injured sister, finally glancing up from the ground.

"I have no idea. Gardeniyah, what are you talking about? What 'end'?"

Gardeniyah's eyes suddenly grew wide. She shook her head frantically before gripping at her head in pain with both hands from the quick movement. "Nothing. I'm just, I, nothing. Nothing. You're right. I'm going to lay back down."

"Well, I need to finish cleaning this. But then you can. Okay?"

"Yeah. Okay."

Gardeniyah didn't speak again, and once Lorella finished, she lay back down.

"What do you think that was all about?" Lorella asked Evanlee once her sister was sleeping deeply.

"I don't know. I don't know anything."

"Yeah, that's pretty obvious."

Evanlee looked down at the ground. Lorella knew her sister wanted her to comfort her. Lorella wanted her to tell her it wasn't her fault that Gardeniyah was hurt, but she couldn't. It was Evanlee's fault. If she had just used some common sense, she would have guessed the wolf wasn't friendly. If she had only listened to them, it never would have happened.

They didn't speak for the rest of the day. Lorella didn't have anything to say to Evanlee. And Evanlee didn't feel much like talking, especially to Lorella. So they sat in silence. All the while, Lorella closely monitored Gardeniyah and Evanlee sulked in her self-pity.

Gardeniyah woke up on and off throughout the day, each time with a little more of her wits about her and a bit more strength. She never explained her peculiar words to Lorella, no matter how many times Lorella asked. She merely excused them as the ramblings of blood loss. So Lorella let it go. The next morning came, and Gardeniyah insisted that they continue with their walk.

"Are you sure we shouldn't wait another day?" Lorella asked.

"No, really. Let's at least walk for a little while. I promise we will stop if I need to."

"All right. But I'm carrying the big bag. You just worry about yours."

"I won't argue with that."

Evanlee remained quiet as they packed up the camp. Gardeniyah noticed her sister's demeanor and made her way toward her.

"You all right?"

"I should be asking you that," Evanlee responded, not able to make eye contact with either sister.

"I've been better," Gardeniyah said with a chuckle, "but I will be okay." Evanlee still didn't look up. She was pretending to be reorganizing her bag. "Ev, look at me." Evanlee closed her eyes instead. "Ev, come on, look at me." When her sister finally did, there were tears in her eyes.

"I'm so sorry," she said, her voice quaking.

"It's not your fault," Gardeniyah said as she pulled her sister into her with her good arm.

"Don't tell her that! It is her fault," Lorella said as she slung the heavier pack across her back.

"Lorella!" Gardeniyah began to chastise.

"No, she's right. It is my fault. If I had listened to you . . ."

"Even if you had," Gardeniyah said, cutting her off, "we don't know what would have happened. He probably still would have attacked. Try not to be too hard on yourself."

Lorella shook her head. Up until this point, she had had nothing but sympathy for Gardeniyah. She had been brave and had protected their baby sister. That protection had been noble and necessary. But this protection was not. It was precisely the kind of coddling that had made Evanlee trust a ferocious-looking wolf in a land they knew nothing about.

CHAPTER EIGHTEEN

Gardeniyah was weak for several days following the wolf attack. The first day back on their journey, they'd only walked for two hours before she needed to stop. By the fifth day, Gardeniyah was nearly back to her old self, and they were able to continue in the manner in which they had before.

Sympathy between siblings in any world only lasts so long. It is rather easy to forget how frightened you were of losing a loved one. And forgetting often happens disturbingly fast. It occurs especially quickly when you are miserable in your own right. And the three sisters were all very much miserable at this point.

And so by the sixth day, all relationships were back to business as usual—each sister fuming about how their misery was, in fact, superior. Lorella had to deal with an incompetent sister and another sister who encouraged the incompetence.

Gardeniyah was in almost constant pain but felt unable to voice it. She had to be strong for her sisters. If they knew she was in pain, one would insist they stop and the other would spiral into self-contempt. And she did not have the energy to fight with either sister about continuing on physically with their journey or moving on emotionally from the attack. So she fought through the pain instead.

Evanlee had to deal with the constant guilt over causing said pain. It didn't matter whether her sister voiced her complaints or not, because, for a sensitive soul like Evanlee, just knowing her sister had been in pain at one point because of her was enough to cause her to be utterly despondent.

It was enough to cause tension between the sisters. However, each night at camp, they had to eat as little as possible to stretch their limited recourses as far as they could. They only had so much money, so the fewer provisions they had to buy when they got to Zaraneth, the better —the delay the attack caused only made the situation worse.

The mood at their nightly stops to camp was growing increasingly tense with each passing day. By halfway through the second week, they were at the point where it was hostile every time they spoke. The last night of the second week was no different.

"Will you please stop scraping at that can? The food is gone!" Lorella yelled.

Evanlee glared as she continued to scrape the tin loudly, staring at Lorella the whole time she did so. Lorella responded by hitting the can out of Evanlee's hand. After a scream of outrage from Evanlee, Gardeniyah got involved.

"Are you two kidding me with this nonsense? You are both so childish."

The statement didn't exactly defuse the situation; it just gave the two of them a common target.

"Oh really, we are childish? Well, at least we aren't a bossy know-it-all like you!" Lorella said.

"Yeah, Gardeniyah, why do you have to get involved in everything?" Evanlee asked. "You aren't our mom or Mib, so just stop. If it weren't for you and your stupid rule about how much we can eat, I wouldn't even be scraping a can trying to get everything out to begin with!"

"Fine, tear each other's heads off. Eat all the food you want." She dropped the provisions bag, which was growing smaller by the day, down in front of Evanlee. "I don't care anymore."

Gardeniyah did care. And her sisters knew that. They also knew they had crossed a line. But she didn't give them a chance to apologize. Gardeniyah lay down and rolled over so her back was facing them.

Gardeniyah drifted off to sleep after the argument with surprising ease. Even though her mind was reeling with thoughts until the very last moment before she slipped from the conscious world, it didn't take her long to do so. Her mind's constant activity continued even as she slept. It found no rest and barraged itself with its demons for the entirety of the night.

Suddenly, she was four years old again. The magna trees, the East's largest trees, which the residents had groomed for height and width over the last hundred and some odd years as a defense mechanism, stood before the long-lost version of herself. The air was hot and thick around her. Every so often, a voice yelled from behind her.

She turned around and saw the silhouette of her mother. Time had stolen nearly all of Gardeniyah's memories of her mother, but her mind in dreams had not forgotten a thing—her mother's face, her voice, the way she smelled, the touch of her hand, all perfectly preserved in her subconscious. A piece of her was in every daughter. Her hair was brown and wavy like Gardeniyah's, but it was frizzy and damaged from time in the sun. Her eyes were blue like Evanlee's, but they didn't look like hers, for though they were beautiful, they were sad. Her cheekbones were high like Lorella's, but her face was too thin. She was lovely, but she was haunted.

Gardeniyah's mother kept looking behind her shoulder and would yell louder each time she turned back around. The sun began to set. She started yelling more frantically. Gardeniyah stared up at her. What was her name? Why was she so scared?

Suddenly, a figure appeared at the top of the magna trees. Then three more. At first, Gardeniyah couldn't see their faces. But when they landed in front of her, she could see who they were: Ranosa, Vadeed, Hothem, and Mib.

Gardeniyah's heart started racing when she saw Mib. She tried to run to her, but she couldn't move. She started yelling for Mib, but no one could hear her. She was acutely aware of everything the future held. She knew who these fairies were; she knew who they would be in her life. A mother, mentors, friends, confidants . . . family.

But she was confined to the choices that her four-year-old self had made. She hadn't known them. She had run over to her mother and clung to her. So, although Gardeniyah loved Mib more than she had ever loved the woman she clung to, she couldn't go to her. She was frozen in the fear she had so naively felt that day.

"Please, help me. My children, they aren't safe here."

"We have a strict border policy, woman," Vadeed said.

"I know. I know. Believe me, I understand. I just have no other choice. They can't be safe or happy here. They are in danger. I can't protect them. Please!"

Mib was staring at Gardeniyah. She was calling to Mib. Mib couldn't hear her, but still, she smiled. Mib always smiled like that at Gardeniyah.

All at once, everything went black. When light again appeared, sets of large doors were opening in front of her. Gardeniyah was in a room. A large room. It was too bright to see anything. She could hear yelling and arguing, but she couldn't make out any of the words. She strained her eyes to focus.

When they did, she knew where she was. She was in Grandeur Hall in the castle of Relis. And she was standing in the middle of the room with all eyes on her. Easterners flanked her on every side in rows of benches around the hall. Not a soul's eyes left her and her sisters, even as they murmured among themselves. She was holding Evanlee in her lap as she sat on the floor of the enormous room. Lorella's hand clung to hers. She glanced down to see her hand was turning white and her fingers purple from the strength of her little sister's grip. She didn't tell her to stop holding on so hard. She had known even then that Lorella needed her. That from that moment on, she had to protect Lorella and Evanlee.

Queen Ranosa was sitting on her throne at the head of the twelve elders. Gardeniyah's heart was racing, but she didn't understand why. The elders were a scary sight then. Ranosa's Grand Council was made up of six Eastern elders, each representing a group native to the East: a dwarf, a faun, a nymph, an elf, a Centaur, and two fairies—one of which was General Vadeed. There were also three elders from the West and three from the South.

The Southern monsters had terrified her. Madelle was a hollingoth, who have notorious tempers. She had the form of a woman, but her skin was green and scaly. Her eyes were that of a snake's, and her fingers were twice as long as any human's. Her smile revealed fangs with venom potent enough to kill any man. But her greatest weapon would also kill her in one bite. She was perhaps the kindest hollingoth you would ever meet, which why Ranosa had chosen Madelle for the position. Gardeniyah, of course, didn't know that at the time. So she felt the fear her younger self had suffered at the sight of her.

Snordin was a giant. He stood over twelve feet tall. His eyes were eerily small and his nose too big for his large face. His eyebrows, ears, and mouth were the only things proportional to his face. His face had confused her back then. She hadn't liked it at all. She had no idea she would eventually light up every time she saw his peculiar face.

The last council member from the South was a cyclops. Of course, for a young human girl, a creature larger than any man she had ever seen before, who was pure muscle, would be scary enough. But take away an eye and make the remaining one enormous, and take away his nose and give him two small holes flat against his face—you will have a very terrified little girl.

The Western animals had only been slightly better. Lastinger the Lion was large and imposing. Harland the Gorilla sat intimidatingly tall. Only Warring the Wolf was less scary, simply because she liked how fluffy he was.

Staring at all of them had petrified her, so she had fixated her eyes on Ranosa. The queen was listening and watching the girls as the council argued. No one on the council wanted them here. Even her younger self understood that. Ranosa did not engage in the yelling. She had merely stared back at Gardeniyah, her expression soft but stern.

Finally, Ranosa broke her gaze and looked away from the girls and held up a sheet of paper. She read it out loud. Since Gardeniyah was so young, she had not understood what was said, so her mind could not replay it now.

Her mind did, however, remember how the atmosphere in the room had shifted. Everyone in the hall sat quietly. After a silence that had seemed eternal to a girl so young, a voice called out from somewhere on the council.

"So, what do we do with them if we let them stay?"

More arguing began. Then a voice cut through all the maddening ruckus. A voice Gardeniyah loved.

"I'll take them!"

Mib. Mib was going to save her. Mib had always saved her.

The world went black again. This time, it stayed dark for some time. Her little self was crying. Deep, heaving breaths and sobs shook her whole body. She tried to tell herself to calm down, but her body wouldn't listen. Because it hadn't back then.

After some time, a light came from far off and grew closer and closer. At last, the light was nearing. Gardeniyah could see in the glow of the light the outline of Mib's face. She was smiling at her.

"Shh. Shh, dear, it's okay." Mib picked her up and sat down on the bed Gardeniyah had been lying in and began to rock her back and forth. "You're safe now. I'll protect you. I know it was a scary day. It's over now. I'm going to take care of you."

The rest of her night's sleep was filled with episodes of memories like that. Memories of birthdays, story times, tea parties, lectures about schoolwork, lectures about chores. Moments from her life over the past fifteen years flashed through her mind. There was no rhyme or reason to the memories. Some were important and life changing; others were seemingly insignificant. All except the first few left a smile on Gardeniyah's face as she slept.

That is until the last memory came into her mind. Then, even in her sleep, her smile faded quickly. Standing before her was Mib. They were in the castle.

She was reliving their goodbye. She felt Mib's arms around her again. She longed to stay in that moment. In the safe embrace of her adoptive mother—her true mother. But then she let go, and once again Mib was gone.

Gardeniyah's eyes shot open when she felt something wet touch her lip. She opened her eyes but couldn't see anything until she blinked a few times. Something wet hit her lip again. She wiped at her face. They were tears.

She wiped at her face again to make sure they were all gone. She didn't want her sisters to see her crying. The sky was a light gray now. They could begin their day. So she sat up and started to pack up their little camp.

She hoped dreams like that would not be so taxing again. The night had drained her before the day had even begun. She wouldn't be able to handle it often.

CHAPTER NINETEEN

None of them had had the energy or the desire the night before to make up. So the two younger sisters had followed Gardeniyah and then gone to sleep just as the newest flurries had started coming down around them. Evanlee hated that the three of them were going to sleep fighting like this. A month ago, they would never have gone to bed not speaking. Well, truthfully, it would have been no shock for Evanlee and Lorella to do so, but it was quite a different matter for Gardeniyah to be involved in a feud and allow it to go on. So it was even stranger now that they didn't just sleep with their anger but that they carried it into the next day, content in their displeasure and happy to let those they loved most in the world brood because they were too tired to care about mending things. Evanlee already hated this place and this journey. Now she hated it all the more for what it was doing to them.

They continued on like this for days. No one made amends. They barely spoke. The life they had known was gone. What they knew about each other seemed gone as well.

Their personalities were different. *Everything* was so different than just a month ago.

Memory and time are funny things. Not only can time fade a memory, but if you do any one thing for a considerable amount of time, suddenly it's all you can remember ever doing. Day after day of this monotonous journey had left Evanlee with a void in her memory. She didn't notice much else besides dreary days that seemed endless until the gray skies grew dark and left behind a black sky and flurries of snow with wind that nipped at her skin until she fell asleep shivering.

She hated the North. It all looked the same. Blankets of white covering any life that may have lived. Smothered before it began. Never achieving its potential—if it ever saw the light of day in the first place.

Occasionally, they passed a tree. More specifically, they passed a practically dead tree. They were all grayish brown with no life to their limbs. To Evanlee, they were ugly compared to the always flowering trees of the East. No dainty and beautiful nymphs lived in them. They were lifeless and pale. She hated them.

Evanlee's hatred for this place and the misery she slowly let control her every waking moment for the next two weeks left her heart as cold and numb as the rest of her body. She was so miserable and had been staring at the ground in front of her for so long that she missed the moment when Zaraneth first came into view. It wasn't until she heard Gardeniyah and Lorella discussing if they should skip making a camp that she realized she had missed something.

"Well, I don't know about you, but I'd rather brave an hour or two of that nighttime wind and fall asleep in a warm bed for the first time in a month than spend another night out here," Lorella said.

Evanlee felt a flush of anger at her sisters for discussing

what to do without her, as if her opinion wasn't relevant. The good thing was that it was the warmest her face had felt in weeks.

"I feel the same way," Gardeniyah said. "My only concern is that we have a limited amount of money. I don't know that it's worth it to spend the money for an entire night's sleep when we'll only get half a night, and only if we are lucky and make good time."

"Fair enough. Guess I was being a little shortsighted," Lorella responded.

"Believe me, I understand. Glad we agree, though, and can settle it. Now we just have to mentally prepare to see those lights and know we are close and yet so far."

Evanlee could feel her face growing hotter and her heart palpitating in her chest as her two sisters finished the discussion without so much as a glance her way. "Oh, and I suppose since it's all so settled, my opinion is just irrelevant! You know, Lorella, you threw a huge fit when we first left about how unfair it is to be excluded from decisions, and yet you two always do the same to me! Do you ever ask me what I think? Why? Oh right, I remember! Because I'm just Gardeniyah's puppet, right, Lorella? You never take me seriously, ever!"

Her sisters, who had been walking side by side a few steps ahead, stopped dead in their tracks at the sound of Evanlee's voice. When they both turned around, it wasn't annoyance or anger she saw on their faces as she had suspected. It was shock.

"Evanlee!" Gardeniyah exclaimed as she rushed toward her sister and grabbed her hands.

"So your vocal cords aren't frozen. Good to know, kid," Lorella said, and smirked before turning back around and continuing to walk. Gardeniyah took the cue and grabbed Evanlee's hand in hers and began to walk as well. Evanlee followed her sisters' lead but was rather confused by their responses.

"What are you two talking about?" she questioned.

"Evanlee, sweetie, you haven't spoken in three days. We've tried to get you to talk or even look at us, but you would just stare off into the distance or down at the ground. It was like you didn't even hear us."

Evanlee was sure they were wrong and were exaggerating in an attempt to make her seem dramatic. But as she began to try to remember conversations between them, she realized she couldn't. She may have recalled some murmuring here and there, but they were right. She hadn't heard them. She tried to think of an excuse to give them as to why she hadn't responded so that Gardeniyah didn't worry and Lorella didn't find her weak. But her mind just felt like the flurries that had started up again. So she just fell silent. Gardeniyah didn't let go of her hand. They walked in silence with Lorella's figure leading the way through the snow toward the light in the distance.

CHAPTER TWENTY

Hope is a funny thing. It's a timid beast that comes and goes as the world around you changes. When you haven't had it for a while and then experience it again, it's like seeing an old friend. It is deep, bolstering, and lovely. More than you ever thought it would be, and even more so if you thought you might never see it again.

Gardeniyah liked waking up to the feeling of hopefulness again. She felt it as soon as her eyes opened. She had fallen asleep facing the lights so that she would see them as soon as she awoke. But she hadn't accounted for the daylight. So a moment of panic flooded her when she opened her eyes and didn't see them. But the timid beast returned all the same when she saw the outline of the buildings behind the dark-gray early-morning fog. They were a mere half a day's walk to civilization after a month of a vast nothing.

The sun had only started to light up the sky to charcoal, not the smoke color it usually was by midmorning. It was still early. But once again, the pounding in Gardeniyah's chest was faster than the ticking of any clock. So the minutes dragged on.

She hadn't asked her sisters if they wanted to leave earlier than usual. But she assumed they wouldn't mind. They wanted to get to Zaraneth as much as she did. Lorella stirred as she heard Gardeniyah packing up. Gardeniyah felt a little sorry for waking her before it was necessary. But not bad enough to tell her to go back to sleep.

Lorella just sat up and stretched the crick out of her back without a word. She gave Gardeniyah a half smile when they made eye contact. Then she began packing up her stuff as well.

The journey had done some good for Gardeniyah and Lorella's relationship ever since Evanlee had mentally checked out, which had taken away most of the things they argued about. Respect had grown between the two older sisters. Gardeniyah taking on a wolf was something Lorella admired. And the fact that her sister had possessed the foresight to swipe a knife from the kitchen to keep in her boot impressed her even more.

Lorella knew it had been hard for Gardeniyah to kill the wolf. Gardeniyah had always had the utmost respect for the beasts. And aside from Mib, her favorite Easterners were those that seemed to be both mystical and beasts, like the Centaurs and the fauns.

Lorella didn't quite understand the attachment. She could clearly differentiate that wolf from the residents of the East that she had called friends. But perhaps it was easier simply because Lorella had never really liked wolves. She found them to be quite a cocky species. They were always challenging other species to competitions—but only ones they knew they would win.

"Can you wake Evanlee up, please?" Gardeniyah said from across the camp. She was bent over the dwindling fire attempting to restore it. She was doing it wrong, but Lorella knew Gardeniyah didn't like being told so.

"Yeah. Hopefully, the only snapping she does today is out of her funk. This journey has been hard on all of us. She doesn't need to act like the only victim around here." Lorella hadn't expected it, but Gardeniyah's mouth twitched into a half smile.

Lorella had tried to understand her youngest sister's mood. She hadn't reacted the night before when Evanlee had lashed out. Lorella usually didn't take being snapped at so well. And she wasn't about to let Evanlee think that it was a habit she would get away with. She would put the little girl in her place if it happened again—which of course would mean that Gardeniyah would chastise her for doing so. No doubt it would all escalate into a fight.

That's why Lorella had, for years, had the firm belief that Evanlee was the problem in their sisterhood. She was the weakest link. "Her softness," as Gardeniyah put it, got in the way so often. Gardeniyah always pitied her for it and coddled her over it, just as she had done during the wolf attack. Lorella just resented Evanlee for it, and when she didn't make any concessions for the little girl, she got scolded by her older sister.

The fact that you resent your little sister is not the best thing to be thinking about after you are told to wake up said sibling. Lorella realized this as she began to nudge her sister with her snow-covered boot on her shoulder, which was bare from Evanlee's too-big shirt sliding off in her sleep. Lorella tried to tell herself she hadn't intentionally aimed for the only piece of bare skin exposed on her sister's body, but deep down she was pretty sure she had.

"What is wrong with you, Lorella?" Evanlee yelled after the squeal she let out as the icy boot touched her body.

"Oh look, she speaks," Lorella said as she pointed to her little sister and glanced over at Gardeniyah with fake enthusiasm. "Apparently only to yell. But she does speak."

"I swear, you are the meanest, rudest sister anyone has ever been cursed with."

"Evanlee, calm down," Gardeniyah reprimanded from across the camp where she was pulling out food for breakfast. It was strange to Lorella to hear Gardeniyah getting on to Evanlee the way she usually got on to her.

"No, no, don't worry, sis. Cursed? Thank you, you little ray of sunshine! Cursed makes me sound pretty cool. I like it," she replied and then proceeded to kick snow onto Evanlee, who was still sitting on her blanket. "Now get up."

Evanlee shrieked again. It was louder this time, fueled by anger rather than surprise.

"Lorella, was that necessary?" Gardeniyah said, shaking her head as she rolled her eyes.

"Yep," Lorella said with a nod and a crooked smile. Lorella expected Gardeniyah to defend Evanlee and to get a lecture. Instead, Gardeniyah just shook her head again and started mumbling.

"I can't wait to get to Zaraneth to have a few minutes away from you two."

Lorella wasn't sure there was ever a moment prior, or would ever be a moment again, where they all agreed so fervently.

They all ate breakfast and packed up their things hurriedly, with varying degrees of neatness. No one spoke. Sometimes with great anticipation comes a reverence for silence. Because sometimes, when there is so much to say, we often find ourselves without any words that seem good enough—but in this case, they were just all rather sick of each other.

CHAPTER TWENTY-ONE

The girls walked in silence, each of them fixating on the scene before them. The lights of Zaraneth grew closer, and the vague outlines of buildings began to be filled in with details of windows, balconies, and stonework. With each new feature added to the once ambiguous puzzle, the girls' anticipation grew. They couldn't wait to be out of the desolate and cold wilderness and in a town again.

Companionship and hospitality had been so nonexistent for the last weeks, and Evanlee couldn't wait to be a part of a community again, even if only for a few days before they continued on to wherever Methuselah told them to go.

It was midday when they finally reached the edge of the sea. The only way to the island was to cross over the rickety rope bridge before them. To say the girls were hesitant to walk on the bridge would be an understatement. Evanlee was petrified and considered refusing to cross. And she even opened her mouth to say so. But then came to the sudden realization that doing so would make her have to stay by herself in the Northern wasteland she hated so much, and so she quickly shut her mouth again.

The bridge must have been rather lovely in its prime, but now every few feet, a plank was missing. It was a wobbly venture to cross. The rope bridge was tied every mile or so to a new dock. But the docks looked as unsteady as the rope itself. It wasn't important to mankind to maintain the bridge. They didn't care about anyone who was crossing it.

Gardeniyah let Lorella lead the way across so that she could quickly act should either sister fall. Though she was trying to devote all her attention to the task at hand, she couldn't help but wonder if all four bridges that led into Zaraneth were in such bad shape. But there were only three bridges still standing that led to Zaraneth.

When the last of the Great Wars ended, and man had taken over the South and forced the monsters to move to the East, all beings except for man then resided in the East. Sanora knew they needed to take every precaution to keep man out. So the East had closed their borders to man for good. They'd built patrol posts in the trees along the northeast and southeast borders. The final step in isolation was to cut themselves off from Zaraneth.

Legend said that in the dark of night, Sanora herself, along with General Vadeed, went to the Eastern Bridge and lit it on fire. All the beings still alive to remember the event would swear on their lives that the bridge burned for three days and three nights. They said Sanora did it at night on purpose so that man would see the flames and know that the bridge between them and the East was forever burned.

Gardeniyah was busy picturing the burning bridge when she was jostled back into reality. The bridge was swaying more intensely.

"There's no plank." Lorella's voice was loud amid the wind that had picked up speed.

"What do you mean there's no plank?"

"What could I mean besides the obvious? There's no

131

plank!" Lorella leaned slightly to the left. The bridge swayed with her. Gardeniyah peered over her right shoulder.

She was right. The next plank was at least ten feet in front of Lorella. Lorella was athletic, and, on solid ground, she could have jumped it. With a running start, Gardeniyah may have been able to as well. But, in any condition, Evanlee wouldn't have been able to.

Gardeniyah felt Evanlee's hand press against her shoulder as she steadied herself and looked over Gardeniyah's shoulder. Evanlee gasped.

"We could swim it?" Lorella said. "It's not far."

"It'll be so cold!" Evanlee said.

Gardeniyah shook her head as she looked at the waves lapping the sides of the bridge. "The current would be too strong."

"Maybe not, if we hold on to the rope as we swim."

"What if we walk across the rope? We can hold on to the top and use the bottom one to walk." Evanlee pushed on the rope with her boot. The tension of the rest of the logs kept it from dipping into the water.

"That could work." Gardeniyah nodded.

"How is tightrope walking safer than swimming? The wind is as strong as the currents."

"You're right. It's not," Gardeniyah said as she looked up to the sky. Darker clouds were moving in. "I think it's going to rain. We can't cross. We will have to go back."

"Go back? I thought you were set on this quest?" Lorella said. Her voice was growing louder as the wind grew even stronger.

Gardeniyah looked down at the swaying bridge. It was getting wilder by the minute. She had to get her sisters to safety. Lorella was right. She was. But she wouldn't lose them.

"I am! But we can't cross here. We will have to go back."

"We came all this way for nothing?" Evanlee said. Gardeniyah winced and slumped her shoulders at the defeat in her sister's voice.

It was then that Gardeniyah once again remembered something about the bridges. Her shoulders straightened, and her head perked back up. "No! The Western Bridge. We can go to the West and cross the Western Bridge."

"And what if it's like this one?" Lorella said, gesturing to the hole.

Gardeniyah shrugged. "Then we walk to the Southern Bridge."

"And if it's like this too?" Lorella was yelling at this point to be heard over the wind.

"I don't know, I guess we will deal with that when it comes. We might be able to swim that one. The water will be warmer."

"They have hurricanes. The currents will be stronger."

Gardeniyah began to reply, but a flash lit the sky above them. It burned the sky in hues of gray and gold. A beam of gold light hit a building in the distance, and the entire building began to glow. The lightning was followed by thunder directly overhead. The vibrations caused the bridge to sway wildly.

"I'm not walking around the world to possibly face the same situation again and again." Lorella turned back toward Zaraneth.

"Lorella, no!" Gardeniyah yelled. But before she could stop her, Lorella jumped into the water.

Gardeniyah scanned the water as Evanlee screamed their sister's name. "Ev, stay here. Hold on to the bridge," she yelled.

"Deni, don't go, please!"

Gardeniyah looked at her sister's face. It was wet. She told herself it was from the rain. But she knew it wasn't.

Gardeniyah grabbed her face and gave her a kiss on the cheek.

Then she grabbed the bottom rope and eased herself quickly into the water. As soon as she made contact with the icy water, she heard Evanlee yell again.

"There! There! She's over there!"

Gardeniyah looked to where her sister was pointing frantically. A few yards away, Lorella's body floated. If Gardeniyah tried to swim that far, she knew she would be pulled away by the current. She held on to the rope and pulled herself farther along the bridge. All the while, the current dragged her feet farther to the sea.

Finally, she reached the other side of the gap in the bridge. She pulled herself up. When she was halfway out of the water, her hand slipped and her face smacked against the wood. Blood dripped down into her eyes. She wiped the blood from her face. Salt from the water on her hands stung the wound. She winced as she pulled herself the rest of the way out of the water.

She slipped twice more as she tried to run across the slick wood. Each time she stood, Lorella was floating a few feet farther away.

Finally, Lorella was parallel to her. Gardeniyah jumped into the water once more and swam hard. Thankfully, she was good at it. Mib had taken them to the river once every few cyclicals. While Lorella had pretended sticks were swords and Evanlee had played with flowers, Gardeniyah had swum. Lorella had hated it ever since nearly drowning on one of their first trips. This would not make her enjoy the water any more.

Gardeniyah reached her sister. She grabbed the pack that was across her shoulder. Gardeniyah winced as an icy wave slashed against the cuts on her stomach. She swam back toward the bridge, now fighting the current with the added weight of her unconscious sister. She wasn't sure how she would get Lorella up onto the bridge. If she let go, she might drop her. But she wasn't strong enough to pull them both up with one arm; it was hard enough to swim with one arm as she pulled her with the other.

Gardeniyah finally made it to the bridge. She struggled to keep a grip on the ropes as the water pulled at Lorella. Gardeniyah's muscles were growing weak. The icy water made it harder to breathe with each second that passed. She tried to kick her feet to help ease the strain on her arm, but she could no longer feel her legs. The world grew darker as her eyelids became heavier.

Suddenly, a hand reached out for hers. She grabbed it and looked up. Evanlee.

CHAPTER TWENTY-TWO

Evanlee pulled hard and tumbled back as her sister landed on top of her. Gardeniyah rolled over to the side to pull Lorella and her pack up.

When Lorella was on the bridge, Gardeniyah rolled her over. Lorella coughed up some water. She shook as the icy wind hit her soaked skin and clothes. It was enough to wake her up.

Gardeniyah and Evanlee helped Lorella stand and assisted her for the first few feet. The wind whipped at them as they walked the rest of the way to Zaraneth.

By midafternoon, the girls were off the bridge and in the outskirts of the city of Zaraneth. They sat down on the bank of the sea. The ground looked as though it was once covered in grass, but now only a few patches of weeds grew. The air was warmer, and the storm had stopped. They could rest.

"Are you all right, Lor?" Gardeniyah asked as she put her arm around her sister.

"Yeah. When I jumped in, I was fine, then the current swept me away. I was doing okay, but then I'm not sure what happened. I blacked out."

"It was the water. It was too cold. The same thing was happening to me when Evanlee showed up."

"Evanlee?"

"Yep." Gardeniyah smiled at her youngest sister, who returned the smile with a sheepish one of her own.

"How did you do that? You froze when Gardeniyah got attacked."

"I know," Evanlee said. She looked down at her hands and wrung them several times. "But I wasn't going to do that again. Gardeniyah told me to stay there. And I did for a second. But I thought she might need me. So I did what I saw Gardeniyah do. I grabbed the rope and eased down. Then I got to where I saw Gardeniyah jump in the water, and I waited. I wanted to jump in, but I didn't think three of us in the water would do much good."

"I think this is the only time you will ever hear me say this, but thanks for not listening to me," Gardeniyah said with a slight chuckle.

Evanlee smiled. She looked to Lorella. Lorella didn't say anything, but she tipped her head toward Evanlee and grinned slightly. It was enough. After a few more moments of rest, the girls stood and walked once more toward the city gates.

The girls had expected to be questioned as to why they were there when they reached the gate. Gardeniyah had a story ready to go. She had worked on it for the better half of their journey here.

She knew telling people she was after information on a secret book, the spell it contained and, ideally, the fairy who wrote it—so she could save the world from mankind— wouldn't evoke good reactions from these strangers. They would either think she was a traitor or that she was mad. Neither of which was ideal. However, her carefully thought out lie would go to waste.

Not a person stopped them.

Just past the gate was an open courtyard. The area, like the bridge, had been beautiful during its glory days. Flowerbeds surrounded every bench, but inside was only weeds and dirt. And to cap it off, an ornate fountain stood in the center—but by the looks of it, water hadn't run through the fountain in lifetimes.

Gardeniyah noticed as she looked around how the air felt different now. At first, she thought it was just warmer air compared to the bitter wind near the sea. But that wasn't it. The atmosphere and air were thick, which made it difficult to breathe.

Gardeniyah didn't want to risk not checking in with someone. Their mission and their lack of any sort of knowledge about this place was already putting them at risk. She didn't need to add being in the city illegally to the list of reasons she needed to be worried.

She looked around the courtyard for anyone approachable but didn't see anyone suitable. Everyone she made eye contact with gave her a glaring side-eye, or a smile so insincere and disturbing she quickly broke eye contact. So, since no one looked appealing, she chose instead to approach the nearest group of people and be done with it.

Unfortunately, that was a rather large and unattractive man, in the sense that his body spoke of his vile lifestyle. He had teeth missing from one too many fights and scars all over him. The man had two women hanging off of him. The women were clearly not in their right or stable minds, and the man seemed to be taking advantage of this. The display made Gardeniyah uncomfortable. And no matter how badly she did not want to go anywhere near the nefarious man, Gardeniyah wanted to get the information she needed as soon as possible so she could get her sisters out of this courtyard.

"Excuse me. I hate to, um, interrupt you, um, three, but I was just wondering if there is a censory we need to sign in with before we go into the city."

"Ha!" A slurred laugh came from the man. His breath reeked, and the bitterness burned Gardeniyah's eyes when he blurted out his reply. The rest of what he said was incoherent, and Gardeniyah eventually nodded and began to back away, careful not to turn her back on the man. As she did so, a woman called out to her from an open doorway.

The woman looked nothing like anyone she had ever seen before. Her shirt opened up farther down than Gardeniyah would have ever dreamed, and her skirt had a slit that went well up her thigh. Though she was sure the slit made it easier to walk, she highly doubted that was what it was for. A few more inches and one good rip, and the two openings in the attire would surely meet. She leaned in the doorway in a way that Gardeniyah was sure was meant to be alluring to any man walking by but just made Gardeniyah feel uncomfortable. She felt her face blush when she looked at her. Gardeniyah had never seen anyone dressed like that before, but she had a suspicion it would not be the last time in this city.

"Honey, you don't have to sign in with a censory. We don't have any here," she said and then turned to walk away further into the city.

"Wait!" Gardeniyah called out to her. The woman stopped and turned back around. "Why don't you have any census offices here? Don't they need to know who comes and goes?"

"Sweetheart, do you know where you are right now?"

"Yes." Gardeniyah's face grew warm. "Zaraneth."

"Exactly."

Gardeniyah knew she had a blank look on her face as she stared at the woman in confusion. She hated to feel ignorant.

The lady's face indicated she should not have to explain this to Gardeniyah.

The woman rolled her eyes before continuing. "Where on earth have you been your whole life? Under a rock? You only come to Zaraneth for one of three reasons: no one cares where you are, you don't want to be found, or you're not welcome wherever you want to be." The woman then looked the sisters up and down. "And based on the fact that you didn't know that, I think you should just walk right on back out of that gate." She tilted her head toward the massive iron gate that suddenly looked very welcoming compared to the atmosphere of this place. Still, Gardeniyah knew she didn't have a choice. They had to be here.

"We can't. We are looking for someone."

"What did I just tell you?" The woman was shaking her head. "This is the place people come when they don't want to be found. If you are looking for someone and you think they are here, well, then I sure hope they ain't important. You probably aren't gonna find them."

"He is very important." The annoyance between the two women was mutual at this point, and Gardeniyah didn't bother to try to hide it from her face or her voice. But the woman appeared unfazed. She merely huffed and continued.

"Fine," she said, waving her hand in a way that was as dismissive as it was demeaning. "If you're determined to look for your 'oh-so-important' man—though I don't see how he could be important if he lives in this land of rejects and outlaws—the best advice I have for you is to go to Osmond's Tavern. It's that way," she said, pointing toward the alleyway behind her. "It's basically the center of this part of Zaraneth. Everyone has been in there at some point. He might know your guy. He has some rooms too. Do what you got to do and then get out of here. This is no place for girls like you."

She turned away again. This time, Gardeniyah didn't go

after her. After the woman had gotten about twenty feet away, she turned back toward them, spread her arms out wide and said, "Oh! And welcome to the Land of the Filth. May your stay be short, so your life isn't!" And with that, she disappeared into a crowd.

Gardeniyah stared into the mass of people. Her jaw was set and her hands clenched.

"I like her." Lorella's amused voice came from behind and snapped Gardeniyah out of the trance the woman had left her in. She turned abruptly to face her sisters.

"She wasn't my favorite person," Gardeniyah muttered, "but she was certainly helpful. We should head to the tavern she mentioned. If a local says it's our best bet at finding Methuselah, we better listen."

"Yeah, if he's not dead."

Gardeniyah wanted to argue with Lorella. To tell her there was no way he was dead. However, the only reason she was so sure he was alive was that she had only ever grown up around fairies who didn't die unless killed.

But this man was no fairy. He was a human who Sanora had known and trusted, so he was indeed old even before she disappeared twenty years ago. She couldn't imagine an old man would last in this place very long.

So Gardeniyah didn't reply to her sister. Instead, she nodded, then turned around and began to walk into the city that she was already loathing.

The atmosphere didn't change as they walked. Gardeniyah had hoped that the courtyard they'd entered when they'd first arrived was the worst part. She quickly came to realize it was the best.

Unfortunately, Osmond's Tavern was toward the center of Zaraneth and quite a distance away from the Northern Gate. So they got the unpleasant experience of seeing much of what Zaraneth had to offer.

The city was an assault on one's senses. Gardeniyah's stomach lurched as her eyes burned from the putrid smells. The air smelled of poor hygiene, bodily fluids and alcohol that was either rotten or strong—and more often than not, it was both. The East only used alcohol that strong for medicinal purposes.

People all around them stumbled in and out of doorways. Gardeniyah was quite convinced these humans had never learned how to walk correctly. Of course, they had, but their motor skills were the first thing to go when drinking nonmedicinal alcohol. The streets were also incredibly and irritatingly loud. Yelling seemed to be the only way Zaranethians spoke. The screaming mixed with the fast-paced music that came from every tavern doorway.

What do these people do for work? she wondered to herself as she rubbed her temples. It was the middle of the day, and the whole town seemed to be out of their right minds. The only people who were working were the women serving the others in the taverns and the large, muscular men who threw out any man who didn't have the money to pay for their drink. She figured that there had to be some kind of work being done somewhere in the city. Some sort of trade or craft being honed. Or even a good being produced. Something. But if there was, she had seen no evidence of it yet.

Zaraneth was a far cry from the civilization she had been looking forward to. She had wanted laughter, but here it sounded sinister, as if whatever was being laughed about should not have been funny. And while people stopped in the streets to talk, they were always yelling. More often than not, one of them swung at the other, and a fight broke out.

The streets were muddy—despite the fact that it didn't appear to have rained in this area recently. The ground was soggy from spilled drinks of stumbling men and the bodily functions of those who weren't thinking coherently.

The buildings were on their last legs. They weren't particularly old but were so ill-maintained that they looked as if they might collapse should the wind blow too hard in their direction. Most of the windows were boarded up, with only a sliver of space between a board in the middle so the person inside could see out. If, by some chance, there were curtains on a window instead of boards, they were moth eaten and dingy. While Gardeniyah gave those individuals credit for trying, she would eventually figure out that if there was a window treatment in a window in Zaraneth, it was not a thing of beauty. It was a thing of secrecy. Whoever or whatever was happening behind that window was to be hidden from any onlooker in the street.

All of this made it evident to Gardeniyah that these people took very little pride in themselves or their part of the world. The crowds of people staggered around without a care in the world. The only things that most of the inhabitants of Zaraneth cared about were hiding in plain sight, their next drink, and their next pleasure.

CHAPTER TWENTY-THREE

Gardeniyah felt a flood of relief when a sign that read "Osmond's Tavern" finally came into view. The building stood alone, disconnected from either side of the road, and served as a fork to two different directions. It was a rather large building. Exceptionally large compared to all the hole-in-the-wall taverns that they had been walking by for the last hour or so.

All Gardeniyah could think about was getting inside. She didn't care what it looked like. Her hope that this place would be anything but dreadful had diminished about a mile and a half before.

They were about fifty feet away from the door when a familiar shriek came from behind her. Gardeniyah whipped around in time to see a large man grabbing both of Evanlee's wrists in one oversized hand, and with his other hand, he covered her mouth to muffle her screams. He dragged her away quickly with each giant step he took backward.

As if coordinated by the man, a wave of people stumbled out of the tavern to their right, and soon the giant man was barely visible. Gardeniyah and Lorella sprinted as best they could toward where the man had disappeared—but they were slowed by the crowd.

Gardeniyah had never thought herself to be short, but at the moment, she had never felt so small. She could hardly see over anyone in the street. She was swimming blindly through a sea of fabric and sweat.

In moments like these, time slows down. Every movement is either incredibly easy or unbelievably difficult. One hopes in a situation in which your loved one is in peril that your movements will be smooth and precise. That you will be swift and graceful like the brave and valiant hero in any good tale. But rarely is this the case. And it was not so for Gardeniyah or Lorella.

Gardeniyah's heart felt like it would beat out of her chest. Her movements felt sluggish as she pushed through the crowd of people, but they barely budged as she shoved. *How can I not be pushing through them? They can barely stand up, they are so intoxicated!*

She pushed harder into the crowd. *We haven't even been in Zaraneth a day, and I've already lost her. I've failed her.* Gardeniyah got angry at the realization. In her bought of anger, she shoved a man so hard he fell to the ground. He was immediately trampled by the group—who didn't notice or care about their fallen comrade. Neither did Gardeniyah, who stepped on the man's hand as she pushed farther in. *Why did I let her walk behind us? That was stupid. So stupid!* She shoved another man to the ground.

She was so focused on pushing people out of the way that she didn't notice the man who was already on the ground. She stumbled over him but caught herself by grabbing on to the sleeve of a man close by. He grinned at her and placed his hand on hers. She pulled her hand away and shouldered past him.

Her mistake was about cost her sister her life. She tried to shove another man out of the way, but the man pushed her back and she fell to the ground. Luckily, Gardeniyah's fate was not the same as the unconscious people she had pushed to the ground. Lorella was right behind her and quickly pulled her sister to her feet.

Pain shot through Gardeniyah's arm where Lorella gripped the still healing wound the wolf had inflicted. *I saved her then. I can save her again. I can.* But Gardeniyah knew that she had been prepared then. She had been alert. But now, she had failed Evanlee.

Lorella was now in front, effortlessly leading the way through what remained of the crowd. Gardeniyah was both thankful and resentful of her ability to do so.

They finally emerged from the crowd. She saw the abductor lying motionless on the ground. Whether he was knocked out or dead, Gardeniyah wasn't sure, but she didn't care. Evanlee was sitting on the ground twenty feet away rubbing her wrists and sobbing.

Lorella and Gardeniyah ran to her. Gardeniyah swooped her into a hug that Evanlee gladly fell into. Lorella looked around and stayed alert. Lorella knew Gardeniyah had not taken the warning of the woman by the gates seriously enough. She wouldn't let them make that mistake again.

"Come on, let's get into the tavern," Lorella said to her sisters.

Gardeniyah and Evanlee got up and began walking toward the tavern. It was an unusual feeling for Lorella to be in charge. The only other time it had happened, Gardeniyah hadn't been conscious. Lorella wouldn't admit it, given the circumstances, but she rather enjoyed having her sisters following her instructions.

"How did you get the man on the ground, Ev?" Gardeniyah asked once Evanlee had stopped sobbing and had started to shake less.

"I didn't. Another man did. It all happened so fast. I don't know how he did it, but he did. Then he picked me up, brought me away from the man and then disappeared again."

"If you recognize him, you tell me. I want to thank him."

Lorella huffed and turned around to face them as soon as they were standing in front of the tavern. "I think if he wanted to be thanked, he would have stuck around until we got to her."

Gardeniyah didn't respond. What Lorella said made complete sense. It was also an entirely obvious fact. She shouldn't have needed to be told that. Situations were leaving her speechless and feeling inadequate. Gardeniyah was beginning to feel as though she was a completely different person outside of the East. One who was far less adept at life.

In time with her doubts rising, the sun was setting. She was ready to enter the tavern and get a room. She needed to rest for a while before going down later to question the patrons about Methuselah.

They walked through the door quickly. Gardeniyah didn't even bother to look around the tavern. She walked straight to one of the women standing behind the bar and requested a room. She told them the cost. Normally, Gardeniyah would have been wondering if it was worth it to stay there or if they should search somewhere else to make their money last longer. But not this evening. In fact, if you had asked Gardeniyah even thirty seconds after the exchange what price the woman had said, she wouldn't have been able to tell you. She didn't care. She hurriedly handed the woman the money, then followed the woman as she brought them up a staircase located at the back of the busy tavern.

CHAPTER TWENTY-FOUR

I t's funny the things one takes for granted so often in everyday life. A pillow was one such thing that, before this journey, Lorella never realized she would miss. The mattress felt glorious on her back as she relaxed on the bed in their room. But it was when her head hit the pillow that she felt her whole body relax, as if every muscle in her body was slowly being unwound.

The peculiar thing was that neither the bed nor the pillow was anything grand. Far from it in fact. The pillow was lumpy in all the wrong places from so many heads resting on it and an equal number of arms hugging it into various contorted forms. The mattress was even worse. Springs jabbed up here and there, and the softness, if there ever was any softness to the bed, had long ago been worn away.

Had she slept in that bed or laid her head on that pillow a day or two after leaving the East, she would have complained constantly the whole night and most likely into the next day. But after weeks of just a thin mat separating her from the frozen ground and only her arm or a lumpy satchel as a pillow, she would have sworn to you that the bed and pillow she was currently falling asleep on—in this dingy tavern in the crummiest, dirtiest part of the world—was just as nice as the ones she slept on in the castle at Relis.

Lorella woke up in the now completely dark room. She had no idea when she'd fallen asleep, but she knew she had been asleep for at least a couple of hours. The nap had felt good. But she could have slept a full day and would have probably still felt drained.

She stretched and bumped a body beside her. She looked over and saw Evanlee curled up and breathing deeply. The bump had not fazed her in the slightest. Lorella lifted her head and looked to the other side of Evanlee, expecting to see Gardeniyah sound asleep as well. However, Gardeniyah was not there. In fact, it didn't appear she had slept there at all.

Lorella looked around the room for her sister and to take in the surroundings that she hadn't paid much attention to when they first got to the room. There was a chair in the far corner of the room, a washbasin and table next to it. A chest was sitting against the wall near the chair. No pictures or artwork hung on any of the wooden walls. The room was dull and utilitarian. It was meant for people passing through, not for anyone to linger in.

Gardeniyah was nowhere in the room. Lorella knew that her sister was down in the tavern trying to gain information when the most people would be there. A smart move in and of itself. The part that made the plan idiotic was that Gardeniyah had gone by herself, even after what had happened earlier that day to Evanlee.

Despite still being tired and shaken, Lorella couldn't leave her sister down in a tavern all alone. So she sat up and rubbed her eyes, then pulled her hair back into a low pony-tail at the nape of her neck. She walked to the washbasin and splashed some water on her face. The water smelled foul and the smell of it served to wake her up more than anything. She quickly grabbed the towel next to her and wiped her face. The towel was rough and scratched at her skin. Although the water and the towel had been unpleasant, they did serve the purpose of waking her up. So Lorella quickly went in search for her sister and the answers she knew her sister was after.

Lorella walked to the doorway of their room and stepped out into the hall. When her foot touched the floorboard, it creaked loudly. Lorella jumped. A floor had never made such an awful sound beneath her feet before. The floors of the East were made of stone, the ground beneath, or out of a hollowed tree. They had always securely held the weight of anyone who walked on them.

Lorella tentatively took another step. The plank yet again creaked under the pressure of her foot, but it didn't give way. With each step she took, the floor protested. She was sure that everyone could hear her coming by the time she arrived at the stairs and began to descend the narrow staircase into the tavern.

Lorella couldn't wait to get out of the tiny staircase and into the main room of the tavern. But when she emerged, she instantly felt even more smothered.

A room can feel terribly dense and almost suffocating when you know you don't belong with the other people in it. The atmosphere feels tight. The light in the room seems only to illuminate the differences between you and the people around you. Every word out of the crowd's mouth serves to convince you that you are, in fact, the most awkward individual in the room and that everyone is keenly aware that you are out of place.

Lorella spotted her sister quickly. Gardeniyah looked as out of place as Lorella felt. Gardeniyah had changed out of her traveling clothes into one of the two dresses she had brought, no doubt in an effort to blend in with the women around her. But the vibrant green dress she wore looked nothing like those around her. Most of the women wore faded red, brown, or cream dresses. The neckline of Gardeniyah's dress wasn't nearly as low, and her hair didn't have fake curls tied up in all manner of ways like the other women's. Instead, Gardeniyah's wavy hair was secured in a loose braid that hung down to the middle of her back—similar in style to the one she had worn on their journey here but not quite as tight. She had tied a ribbon to the end. Lorella knew Gardeniyah must have gotten that out of Evan-lee's bag. She wouldn't have wasted time or space to bring that.

Lorella hadn't thought to change into the dress she had brought. So, although her sister hardly blended in, she knew she stood out even more. She was thankful she didn't have to feel awkward and alone for very long, though. She cut through the crowd as quickly as she could and sat down next to her sister.

The air didn't feel as thick once she was near Gardeniyah. But it did smell. A rather odd smell, like fermented wheat and spoiled cheese—a far cry from the bakeries and sweet shops in the East that smelled of liliyack honey, sugar, and maple syrup. Lorella's stomach lurched back and forth between being famished and feeling like it may jump out of her throat from the smell.

Gardeniyah didn't address Lorella when she walked up or when she sat down. She was in a rather intense-looking conversation with an elderly man. *Maybe she has found the owner,* Lorella thought. She hoped so. She also hoped the owner knew where to find Methuselah so that he could help them find the book. Which would help them find Sanora, the next person they were looking for, so she could help them with the spell.

Lorella's train of thought made her start to doubt that this was going to be the adventure she had hoped for. It seemed more like a wild-goose chase. One in which they would spend their lives chasing person after person who may or may not be able to help them find someone else—a vicious cycle she had no desire to join in on. And yet here she was.

"All right, so there is no way we can get around having to talk to him?" Gardeniyah asked.

"Nope," the man responded. "It will be a miracle if you get an audience with him at all. He keeps to himself because he would scare off customers. I heard he's as big as two average men. That's why this place never gets robbed. No one wants to mess with Osmond."

After some time, Gardeniyah ended the conversation with the older man and turned to Lorella.

"I take it that wasn't the owner?" Lorella asked.

"No, that was Sawl. He's a regular here. He did tell me where he might be and he does think that the owner, Osmond, could help us."

"Of course," Lorella mumbled, "because it would have been too easy and too direct if it had been him."

Gardeniyah didn't notice Lorella's complaint, or at least she didn't acknowledge it. She was far too occupied with scanning the room. After she didn't find what she was looking for, Gardeniyah turned back to Lorella and said, "Sawl said to find the barkeep. He runs the place. He would know almost as much as the owner. There's no way we can talk to Osmond without telling the barkeep our business and him deciding to let us talk to the guy."

"Is it really a good idea to be broadcasting our story to these people?" Lorella eyed the people around. They were eyeing them in the same way.

Gardeniyah frowned. It was the sort of intense frown that tells you before the person speaks that they are both highly annoyed and confused as to why you would ask them that.

"I'm sure there are arguably safer ways." She paused for a moment, then her frown deepened as she crossed her arms and leaned against the back of the chair. "But when we have no idea where we are, who anyone in this forsaken city is, or where to find who we are looking for, I don't see as we have any other option."

Lorella was always taken aback when Gardeniyah was curt with her. It was so rare. Of course, things are more effective when they are rare. Lorella and Evanlee argued all the time, so they hardly batted an eyelash anymore or lost a minute of sleep if either of them yelled or was angry with the other. However, if Lorella even slightly got into it with Gardeniyah, or even merely annoyed her like she had just done, she would feel the overwhelming need to fix it.

"You're right."

Gardeniyah nodded. "Anyway, we will only annoy the barkeep if we interrupt him right now when they are so busy. It appears to be peak hour."

"Seems like, in this crack in the world, every hour is the prime time for tavern dwelling." Lorella snorted.

"Perhaps." Gardeniyah chuckled. Lorella was glad to hear Gardeniyah laugh. Gardeniyah wasn't annoyed with her anymore, so Lorella relaxed again. "Regardless," Gardeniyah continued, "I heard they close for a time in the early morning. There's no sense in waiting down here and being uncomfortable with all this noise."

"And the smells." Lorella scrunched her nose. "Don't forget the smells."

"Right. We might as well rest a bit up in our room. We'll be able to hear them call for everyone to leave from there."

CHAPTER TWENTY-FIVE

The girls left the table and walked across the room to the stairs. They were both aware of their surroundings this time. They could feel the eyes of the locals on their every move. Gardeniyah had never been so thankful to see stairs enclosed behind a wall.

Gardeniyah slept fitfully that night. Though insomnia was nothing new to her, it was extra fatiguing right now. The last couple of hours had brought nothing but racing thoughts, her mind swinging like a monkey of the Western lands from one thought to the next.

She played out nearly every version of how the interaction with the barkeep and Osmond may go. Everything from and between the two of them physically throwing the girls out of the tavern to them knowing not only where the historian was but also where Sanora's book was and leading them right to both. Her logical mind knew both extremes were equally unlikely. However, her current mental state was not nearly as helpful at eliminating outrageous thoughts. Instead, it entertained them all like an overzealous host.

By the time she heard them call for last rounds of anglo-juice—the drink that Gardeniyah was now aware was the source of the smell and the constant intoxication of its fans—she was quite confident she was more tired than she had been before she lay down. There was no way that her eyes would have felt that heavy, or her mind that weary, if she had stayed downstairs and waited.

Due to her state, she was rather disgruntled when she woke her sisters up a few hours later. But the sight of a refreshed Evanlee warmed her spirits. Evanlee rubbed the sleepiness from her eyes. Her hair was adorably out of place, and she easily fixed it with a rustle of her hands through her hair. It was the expression in her eyes, though, that caught Gardeniyah's attention. It didn't last long, but for a moment when Evanlee first saw Gardeniyah, she had the old familiar glimmer in her eye. Gardeniyah had been so afraid that that glimmer was gone forever.

"How are you feeling, Ev?" Gardeniyah asked as she walked to the other side of the bed to wake Lorella.

Evanlee looked down at her wrists and rubbed each one. She swallowed hard, then looked at her sister, nodded, and said, "I'm all right."

"Are you sure? You don't have to come with us. I just didn't want to exclude you if you wanted to be a part of it when we talked to the barkeep," Gardeniyah said as she shook Lorella's shoulder to wake her up.

"Yeah. I'm sure. I want to come talk to—wait, barkeep? I thought we were going to talk to the Osmond guy?"

"We are. We have to talk to the barkeep before we can, though."

Evanlee let out a dramatic and exasperated sigh at the newest development. Gardeniyah turned away and walked toward the pitcher of water on the dresser so they wouldn't see her roll her eyes. Her sisters were both acting like talking to one extra person was the worst thing in the world.

155

Gardeniyah and Evanlee waited for Lorella to wake up and get dressed. Once she was ready, they all ventured down the steps. During their descent, Gardeniyah could tell the atmosphere would be much different at the bottom of the steps than last night.

No loud tavern music filled the air. No voices to drown out your thoughts before they could form. When they reached the bottom, they saw the only people present were barmaids and bussers. The lone noises were the clanking of glasses onto trays and the rhythmic sweeping of a broom attempting to sweep away a layer of grime that had long since become one with the wood floors.

Gardeniyah got lost in the calmness of the moment. It was the most stillness she had encountered since getting to Zaraneth. She was reveling in the change of pace so much that the voice that cut through the air made Gardeniyah nearly jump out of her skin.

The voice was deep. Gardeniyah was sure it was the deepest voice she had ever heard in her life. Truth be told, it wasn't any deeper than Brashen's or Vadeed's, the voice was just far sterner and stronger. Which was why, given the way the voice commanded attention, Gardeniyah was surprised when she realized she hadn't actually comprehended what the man had said.

"I said we're closed. We already said last call. So just turn around and go back up those stairs, ladies."

It wasn't until the man repeated himself that Gardeniyah looked to where the voice had come from. A tall man with broad shoulders, a trimmed beard, and shaggy hair slicked slightly back stood behind the counter counting money.

It was instantly clear that he was the barkeep they were after. Maybe it was his demeanor and his voice, or perhaps it was the fact that he had ordered the girls back up the stairs like children awake in the middle of the night being scolded by their father. It also could also have been none of these, and just the fact that he was the one handling money while the others cleaned. Regardless of how she knew, she was certain.

Now that they had found their man, Gardeniyah just needed to find the words to speak to him. Gardeniyah had spoken before the Grand Council of the East on more than one occasion, she had hosted parties and balls alongside the queen of the East, and yet she had never been so intimidated in all her life.

Her mind went completely blank. All she could do was stare at this man. She felt her face growing hot. *Get it together, Gardeniyah!* she scolded herself. *You have to be able to talk to this man. He's a barkeep, not a king.*

Since she was able to scold herself, at least she knew her brain was back to forming coherent thoughts. Her dry mouth managed to stutter out a few words.

"Um. We aren't here for a drink."

Well done, Gardeniyah, she thought. *You managed to finally speak, and it was the least important of the things you needed to say.*

"Well, if you're here to hang out, we are closed for that too." The barkeep picked up a box and turned away from the three girls, then returned to his previous position facing them only a few moments later. She could tell they were irritating him. He had things to do.

"No. We aren't—well, we aren't here for that either. We are here to talk to you."

Finally, her mind was coming back to her. The barkeep's eyebrows furrowed together. His bright-green eyes narrowed to take them in more carefully. His jaw set as he straightened up and spoke. "Well, I'm not open for that either. Especially since I don't know you. I get off in an hour, and the only socializing I have any interest in is with people in my dreams." He turned his back to them once more and began placing dishes in another crate.

"I see. Would there be a better time to speak with you, then?"

He paused to look at the girls briefly, then replied, "Nope!" as he swung the crate out in front of him and carried it behind a set of doors.

"Well, that went splendidly," Lorella said dryly. "Oh so glad we woke up in the middle of the night to try to be considerate of him."

"Hush, he can probably hear you," Gardeniyah said.

"Like I care. It's not like he was a ray of sunshine himself."

"Lorella, if you aren't going to be helpful, just go back up to the room."

"You know"—the deep voice cut into the air again as he came back out through the doors with a now empty crate—"I think that sounds like an excellent idea. How about all three of you do that."

"Please just hear us out." The plea came from Evanlee, who was standing behind Gardeniyah peering out from behind her like a scared child.

"We really won't take much of your time, we swear," Gardeniyah added. Her sister's plea had been so innocent. On some audiences, that would work. But this man hadn't even stopped to see which of them had said it. He was thoroughly disinterested in them and their request. And he had no qualms about showing it as he continued about his evening duties as if he weren't even having a conversation with them.

They had tried being polite. They had, thanks to Evanlee, tried begging. Nothing. So Gardeniyah figured it best to switch tactics.

"Quite frankly, we have nowhere to be and nothing to lose. So getting rid of us will be pretty hard. In fact, we can work out a shift system real quick so that one of us is always here. You know, so when you finally do decide to give us a moment of your time, we will be ready."

Her sarcasm and annoyance were successfully conveyed to the man. He raised his eyebrows. Gardeniyah heard Evanlee let out a little gasp at the way she had spoken to the man. Gardeniyah held eye contact with the barkeep, and ever so slightly she raised one corner of her mouth and one eyebrow. After a moment, he pursed his lips before they eased into a half smirk that lasted for a brief moment.

"All right. Give me ten minutes."

"Perfect. We will wait right here."

That declaration received a roll of the eyes. But the man had agreed, and that was what mattered. His reluctance to speak with them was further illustrated as the night wore on and he hadn't returned—and the night did go on, and on, and on.

Gardeniyah wasn't one to assume the worst of people. She had tried to consider that perhaps he just got busy. However, as an hour rolled by and turned into two, she became convinced that he was playing some sort of waiting game with them. He wanted them to give up and leave. But he didn't know who he was playing his little game against. Gardeniyah was stubborn to a fault. She would wait there until this time tomorrow before she would give in to this man.

Despite being willing to do whatever it took to win, Gardeniyah was thankful when a voice rang out once more: "Oh good, you're still here." The monotone declaration announced the barkeep's reappearance in the doorway. He leaned his shoulder against the frame of the door as he sighed and shook his head.

"Of course," Gardeniyah said with a smile she knew was obviously fake and filled with annoyance.

He left the doorway and sat at the table that the sisters had moved to about twenty-five minutes into waiting for him.

"All right, what is it you could possibly want to speak to me about?"

"We are looking for someone, and we heard if you're looking for someone here, that Osmond's Tavern is the place to ask around. Specifically, to ask Osmond. I've also heard that you control who gets to see Osmond."

"Well, haven't you heard a lot," he said, rolling his eyes once more at Gardeniyah. She was tempted to tell him that they might develop a tick if he continued to do that, but he continued on: "I guess you didn't happen to hear this in all your talks with folks: here, if you don't know where someone is, then they probably like it that way—and more importantly want it to stay that way."

"Yeah, I've heard that too," Gardeniyah said through a forced smile. "We just can't accept that."

The man leaned back in his chair and folded his arms. His eyes narrowed for a second. His body language thus far told Gardeniyah that he had to be the most skeptical individual she had ever met in her life. After a moment, he bit the left-hand corner of his lip and cocked his head in the same direction. For the first time, he seemed to really be contemplating what she was saying.

"Where are you from? I don't know your accent."

"Not important."

"I think I'm the one with all the cards here. You need me to help you. I need to want to. So if you want me to talk to you, you should probably answer my question."

"Fine. We are from the East."

"I don't want some bogus answer. Where are you from? No one is from the East."

"We are."

He sat up straight in his chair. Folding his hands on the table and squinting his eyes as he leaned toward Gardeniyah, he said, "Look, I'm about to get annoyed."

"So am I," Gardeniyah replied as she mimicked his movements. It was risky to imitate him. She could see out of the corner of her eye how startled Evanlee was by it. She could also see how thoroughly amused Lorella was.

She knew it would seem unlike her. They were surely thinking they were seeing her lose her temper with someone outside their family for the first time in their lives. That was not the case. There was a reason why Queen Ranosa and the rest of the council had admired her aptitude and potential for political prowess from the time she was a teenager. Gardeniyah knew how to work her audience. Furthermore, it didn't take much time for her to figure her audience out. She could easily and, more importantly, quickly transition into a version of herself acceptable to whomever she was addressing.

This man distrusted sweetness. She understood why. Every compliment she had overheard in this town had been loaded with dishonesty and hidden agendas.

Begging didn't faze him. He ran a business in a shady town. If he were affected by sob stories, he would have run this business into the soiled ground by now.

This wasn't the way she would have chosen to speak to him, but it was the way she needed to. And if she was honest with herself, as she would be at a later time, it felt good and more like herself than she realized then.

"Look. You told me to answer your question, and I did. We are from the East. We were raised there. We want to go back but we can't. That's why we need to find the man we are looking for."

"Wait. Wait. Wait," he said, waving his hand. "How are you from the East? You're human, right? I've never seen a fairy, but you don't look like one, I don't think." He leaned to the left, peering around them, trying to spy any wings he may have missed.

"Oh, we do. All humans look like fairies except for the whole wing business, but those aren't very noticeable," Evanlee piped up for the first time. She wouldn't miss an opportunity to talk about the East or explain just how similar she felt she actually was to a fairy.

Gardeniyah sighed as the man leaned back into his defensive posture. The unnecessary explanation had thrown off the tempo of the conversation.

"Yes, we are human." She cut her eyes at her sister. Evanlee shrunk down in her seat. Seeing her little sister get silently reprimanded by Gardeniyah caused an already amused Lorella to let out a small chuckle. The man looked confused as to why she was laughing.

Thanks to the ever-growing distraction her sisters were creating, Gardeniyah knew she was losing her audience—and fast. "We were left there as babies. Look"—Gardeniyah leaned back in her own chair, again imitating the man—"it's a rather long story." She tossed her head back in fake nonchalance. "We will need to tell Osmond the same one. And to be honest, I'd rather not tell it twice. So if you think you are going to let us speak with him, it would be great if we could just tell you both at the same time."

"Hold on."

He got up and went behind the same set of doors as before. This time he appeared only minutes later. He nodded for them to come back. "He said he will talk to you." When Gardeniyah was in front of him, he leaned toward her and whispered, "You're lucky I want to hear this story."

CHAPTER TWENTY-SIX

When Gardeniyah heard about a man who knew where to find people in this city, she pictured a man who exuded power. The person that the old man in the tavern described had fit her assumption.

As they walked back behind the doors that the barkeep had been frequenting throughout the night, she braced herself for such a man. He would surely put the intimidation that she had felt when she met the barkeep to shame. The hallway behind the swinging doors was not as long as she'd expected. The majority of the building was the tavern itself and storage.

Still, as they stood in front of the door located at the end of the short hallway, she expected to see an office like the ones she had read about in the East. The kind that the old crime lords of the North who ran all the illegal trades between the lands had. An office filled with leather furniture and rich wood finishing on everything. Velvet-lined walls, gold lamps, and lavish rugs. And, of course, Osmond in all his intimidating power would be sitting behind the desk, feet up, wearing a big fur coat.

She shuddered at the idea of seeing a fur coat. She'd never seen one. During the time of the Divine Order, they were illegal and so had been a symbol of power in the underworld. Now they were rampant in the North. Though, of course, the East had never allowed them. It would be terribly distasteful to wear a mink coat when your neighbor could be one.

But her mental preparation wasn't necessary. She didn't see a fur coat. In fact, she didn't see anything she expected.

The room wasn't elegant—or even functional, for that matter. Instead of the room smelling like leather, it smelled like the trash heap below the open window. Osmond's desk —if you choose to call a bunch of crates with a piece of wood on top a desk—was crammed into the corner by the window. An obstacle of boxes stood between the sisters and the short, overweight, balding, and unintimidating man who sat behind the makeshift desk. Instead of sitting confidently, he was slumped over on a barstool. The stool, unfortunately, had one leg shorter than the others, and so it rocked annoyingly on the hardwood floor every time he fidgeted. Which, due to Osmond's jumpy nature, was quite often.

"Osmond, these are the ladies with the story," the barkeep said.

Osmond looked up from his pile of papers. He straightened a few of them and then began to look around for something. He didn't find whatever it was. He huffed a time or two in the process of continuing to look for the missing object. Gardeniyah noticed Osmond shake his head ever so slightly one of the many times he looked behind him to the windowsill. He patted the pockets that were on either side of his checkered shirt four times, then leaned toward the floor and scanned it a time or two. After this had gone on for a couple of minutes without so much as a word from the man who was growing more and more peculiar by the second, the barkeep finally spoke out.

"Osmond." The little man nearly jumped off of his stool at the sound of the barkeep's voice. "They are on your head."

Osmond patted the top of his head and nearly smashed the pair of glasses into his skull. He grunted and quickly dropped them to the bridge of his nose. Only then did he address the girls standing before him.

"Hello, come in. Come in. Terribly sorry. I can't see a thing these days without my glasses. What were your names again?"

"I'm Gardeniyah, and these are my sisters, Lorella and Evanlee." Evanlee began to bow, but Lorella grabbed her arm and shook her head.

"Ezer says you claim to be from the East."

So that's his name, Gardeniyah thought as she glanced over at the man who had now moved to the side of them, standing like a bodyguard between Osmond and the sisters.

"We are."

"Well, please, do tell me the story. I am quite fascinated with how you could be from the East."

"We were very young when our mother came to the southeastern border and called out to speak with someone in charge. The queen came and, for whatever reason, compassion, I suppose, agreed that the East would take us in. As I'm sure you know, the East doesn't exactly trust humans." The man nodded knowingly. "So when we became adults, they felt we couldn't be trusted any longer and we were cast out. But not before we were told a way for us to go back. There is a prophecy that states that the world can be put back in order. The way it was supposed to be. But it has to be fulfilled by the race of man, so the fairies can't do it. We want to be able to go home to the East. But until this prophecy comes true, the border will remain closed to all humans, even us. The thing is, we don't know how to do that. There's apparently a spell or something—who knows—in a book we are trying to find. The author of the book disappeared over twenty years ago, and her book went with her, or she hid it or something. Anyway, we have to at least find the book before we can figure out our next step."

Lorella smiled. The man would think it was her being friendly. It wasn't. She had little interest in the man. She was impressed with the way Gardeniyah was telling their story. She was leaving out certain details and downplaying others. Her sister got on her last nerve sometimes. She was controlling and stubborn. She liked to act like she knew everything, which was frustrating, to say the least. But moments like these showed Lorella just how much her sister really did know.

"So where do I come in?"

"Well, we are looking for the only living person who may know where the author hid the book. A historian named Methuselah. He got banished from the land of man because he stood up to the Northern King about breaking the rules of the Divine Order. The author of the book respected him for it, though, and they became friends. Apparently, she would come and visit him here in Zaraneth. We just don't know where he lives. We were hoping you knew him."

"A historian in Zaraneth?" Osmond leaned back on his barstool, rubbed his scraggly stubble of a beard, and thought for a few minutes before continuing. "Honestly, dearie, I have never once heard of a historian in these parts. I'm not so sure your information is correct. Even if he did live here, I doubt that sorta man would ever come to a tavern. If he had the clout to mouth off to a king, well, then I doubt he'd hang out in a place like this."

The girls did a poor job at hiding the disappointment on their faces.

"Osmond, come on," Ezer said from his stationed position. "You seem to know something about everything. You know nothing?"

"I truly don't. I tell ya what, though, dearies, I like a challenge. Give me a few days. I'll do some checking around for ya. See if I can get a scent on the man."

"You can keep staying in the room you have," Ezer added. "Four nights for the price of one. Go up and get some sleep now. I'll make sure to give you any information as he gets it."

With that, the girls nodded, thanked them, and left the room.

"Four nights for the price of one? Feeling a little generous, are we?" Osmond asked after they'd left.

"Take it out of my pay," Ezer said.

"Mighty, mighty generous. Why? Other than the fact that they are pretty. Doubt that their looks are enough to compensate much."

"They've had a rough time. They are in a land they know nothing about. They aren't doing too well on their own. It's better they stay here. They will be safer."

"How do you know they aren't doing well here? It's mighty rude of ya to judge based on the fact that they're women, if that's the case."

"I'm not judging it based on that." He flicked his hand to dismiss the comments. "I just know they aren't."

Osmond squinted his eyes. "One of them is the girl you saved earlier, isn't it?"

Ezer shifted from one foot to the other and looked away from his boss.

"How'd you know about that?"

"A couple of the barmaids were talking about it outside the door there earlier. One of them saw you save someone." Ezer didn't respond. "Ha! It is! Do they know that?"

"No, and don't tell them either. Just see what you can find out, all right?" Ezer said as he walked out of the room. He heard Osmond chuckling as he closed the door behind him. He wasn't sure what was so funny to the little man, and he didn't really care. He was done with all human interaction for the night. He had been done with it before the girls had thrown off his night.

CHAPTER TWENTY-SEVEN

A whole day had passed since Osmond had promised to help them find out about the guy that the girls were after. Ezer had grown amused by their presence. They clearly had three very different temperaments. *How can three girls be so different yet all be from the same family? Then again, I'm not exactly an expert on families. So as far as I know, siblings that seem as different as the four regions could be completely normal.*

As far as family, Ezer had grown up with only a father. His mother had died during childbirth. His heartbroken father had never gotten over it and so had never remarried.

Ezer was sure his mother had had a shady past before meeting his father, but his father had never spoken of anything except her kind heart and his genuine belief in the good of every man. So that's all Ezer chose to dwell on, especially after his father died when he was fifteen. Ezer had decided to cling to the man he knew and his father's memory of his mother.

Maybe that was why he sympathized with the girls. It had been hard enough those first few months on his own, and *he* had been trying to survive in a land he knew all the nooks and crannies of. These girls had no idea about where they'd actually come from—about the world they were in.

The girls weren't fond of receiving help. He liked that about them. But at the same time, they weren't stupid. He liked that about them just as much. They obviously had a limited source of funds. So after he'd offered the room to them at a discount, they hadn't once offered to pay the full price.

What they had offered was to work in exchange for their lodgings. So all morning, the girls had been deep cleaning the tavern—since before Ezer had even arrived. The place had never been more spotless.

He had tried to dissuade them at first. "Cleaning this place so much is like shining an earthworm," he had told Gardeniyah.

"Well, I'm sure that's true," she'd replied, "but we don't know how to serve in a tavern. We are fast learners, but it would take the few days we are here to catch on. So we would just be underfoot. Cleaning, though, we know how to do."

"There really is no point to it," he had half-heartedly tried to insist.

She just nodded. "Well, we have to do something useful to repay you. If you think of anything else, please don't hesitate to tell us." With that, she had gone back to her task and worked the rest of the morning just as hard as before.

She was stubborn. They all were. That was the only thing the sisters seemed to have in common.

So Ezer wasn't the least bit surprised the next day when he came in to see them back at it. Cleaning away at things that had never not been covered in grime since their first week in the tavern.

Respecting these girls came easy, especially the oldest. She was always working the hardest. Cleaning counters like the Northern Queen was coming to eat dinner there. She reorganized glassware, putting the pieces in a more logical place—completely ignoring the rather likely fact that they would just be put back in the original spot that night when the crew was in a hurry to get home.

Despite always working, she had a soothing presence. When Ezer walked by her, she seemed to radiate a peaceful presence that made him want to linger near her. But, of course, he never did.

Osmond had been right that they were all beautiful. And he was also right that their looks weren't why Ezer wanted to help them. It wasn't like him to get involved in other people's affairs. He had survived this long in Zaraneth by doing quite the opposite. He hardly talked to people beyond giving and taking orders. He surely didn't help them out in any way.

You never knew what was going to happen if you helped someone in Zaraneth. Most people who were in trouble were in that situation for a reason. Helping them would only get you into similar trouble with whoever was after them. So Ezer had kept to himself since he was fifteen, and it had been working quite well for him the last twelve years.

Yet, here he was breaking every one of his personal rules and helping complete strangers who were basically on the run. Strangers who were looking to upset the entire order of the world. Moreover, strangers who were either going to spend their whole lives chasing ghosts, or find the ones they were looking for and cause mass chaos and have many people out for their heads. He wasn't sure which was worse. Even more so, he wasn't sure why not being a part of this didn't seem like an option.

It's probably because they seem so helpless, he reasoned. *Like in the stories where sea creatures help drowning humans. The pathetic-looking humans so out of their element spark the nurturing instincts of those more skilled in the territory. So that's all I'm doing. Helping some drowning girls from losing their lives in this place.*

It was hard to forget how displaced they were. Every time Ezer saw the youngest, he replayed the scene of the first moment he had seen them. He could still see her frightened eyes and trembling body. Whenever he heard her voice, he heard the echoes of muffled screams. He closed his eyes as a shiver went down his spine when he thought about what would have happened to the little girl if he hadn't been there. He knew all too well exactly what could happen.

Ezer looked down at his arm and traced the scar that ran from the palm of his hand up to his elbow on his forearm. There had been a girl in his life once, Jetta. She had been his best friend—truthfully, his only friend for his entire life. He didn't remember meeting her; she had just always been there. She was an orphan around his age. When Ezer's father died, she was all he had. Until, not long after, he didn't have her either.

He had told her not to go. It had been too late at night. The worst of the worst were out.

"I'll be okay. You worry too much," she had said, winking at him and then sliding down the clothesline hanging from the rooftop he had called his home at the time. He hadn't wanted to be right. But he was. Only moments later, he'd heard the scream that still haunted his dreams.

When he ran to the edge of the roof, he'd seen his friend slung over the shoulder of a large man. He'd flung himself off the roof. He hadn't even bothered to try to catch the clothesline to ride down and execute a graceful landing as his friend had just done and as he usually did. Instead, he'd just jumped. He'd landed on a pile of crates below.

The crates had busted with the impact of the fifteen-year-old boy's body. A nail from one of the destroyed crates had caught his skin and pierced deep into his arm that day. He hadn't cared; truthfully, he hadn't even noticed how bad it was in the moment. His adrenaline had allowed him to ignore the pain and chase after the man.

But he was too late. He ran frantically for hours up and down every street searching for his friend. Eventually, due to exhaustion and loss of blood, he collapsed in an alleyway.

When he awoke the next morning, he knew she was gone. *I'll never see her again,* he had thought as he sulked back to his rooftop home. He had been wrong. He would see her again. He would just never see her alive again.

A mutual friend of theirs came to him later that day. "Come with me," was all he said. But his face told Ezer far more. The friend led him to an alley half a mile south toward The Center. There he saw her lying in the alley like a rag doll, her limbs in positions they could never have naturally been in. Her throat was caked in blood.

Every time he looked at Evanlee and remembered how terrified she'd looked that day, he thought of Jetta. He knew she had to have looked the same way. But Jetta had fought. Her face was bruised. Her hands were bloodied. She had lost, but she had fought.

Evanlee would not have been able to fight back. None of them would.

They need to learn to fight. *That will be a better use of their time than cleaning this dump,* he thought, but he didn't quite know how to tell them that. They were all so stubborn. *Will they even take my help?* It didn't matter. He knew he had to try.

Ezer cleared his throat. "Gardeniyah, can you come here?" Gardeniyah looked up from the table she was scrubbing and nodded.

"Got something else you want me to clean, boss?" she said, wiping her hands on a rag.

"No. But there is something I want you to do instead."

"What is it?"

"I want you to let me teach you and your sisters to fight."

"What? Why?" she said as she tilted her head.

"Because you need to know how."

"How do you know we don't already know?"

She's trying to act like they already know, he thought. *Great. Now how do I get her to agree without insulting her? If I do that, she won't let me teach them.*

"I just know."

"Why, because we are women?"

"No! This has nothing to do with that. Why does everyone always assume that?"

She was scowling now. Partly from confusion and partly from annoyance. Gardeniyah shook her head and began to walk away.

Ezer huffed. He knew he had to tell her. He leaned his head back. Then he closed his eyes and rolled his neck before calling out to her.

"Wait."

She turned around as he ran his fingers through his hair and pivoted his balance from one foot to another.

Again, he shook his head. "Look, I know you don't know how to fight because your sister didn't fight back."

"Excuse me?" she said. Her eyes flamed. "What do you mean my sister didn't fight back?"

"Calm down! I'm not saying I did anything to her. The other day with the man that took her. She didn't fight back because she didn't know how."

"If you saw her, why didn't you do anything? Why didn't you help her?"

Ezer looked at the ceiling again, and let out a sigh as he said, "I did."

Gardeniyah's hands flew to her mouth. "It was you," she said in a muffled voice. Ezer looked away from her. He was startled when a hand grabbed his. He looked to see

Gardeniyah's hand in his, and when he glanced up to meet her gaze, he saw her eyes were misty. "Thank you," she whispered.

Ezer cleared his throat and said, "Don't tell the others."

Her eyebrows furrowed, but she nodded and said, "I think those fighting lessons would be a good idea."

CHAPTER TWENTY-EIGHT

"Every muscle I have hurts," Evanlee whined as they walked through the door to their room.

"Of course you're sore. We just practiced fighting for four hours straight," Lorella said, jabbing Evanlee in the side and then pushing past her.

Evanlee hobbled to the bed and flopped down with little effort toward grace and a lot of effort toward dramatics. "I never want to do that again!" She moaned as she thrust her hand to her forehead.

"Well, you are," Gardeniyah said as she sat down on what little space of the bed her youngest sister wasn't occupying with her body and her dramatics.

"What? Why? When?"

"Because we need to learn how to defend ourselves, Evanlee. The only one of us who's any good is Lorella. We need to be able to protect ourselves. We have someone willing to show us, and we need to take advantage of that while we are here."

"Well, if it was so important to learn, why didn't we learn when we were in the East like Lorella?"

"Evanlee, come on. Think about it," Lorella said. "They didn't teach you two for the same reason Vadeed had to hide that he was teaching me. They didn't trust us. They didn't want us knowing how to fight."

Gardeniyah could feel her youngest sister's eyes boring down on her. She wanted Gardeniyah to tell her what Lorella was saying wasn't true. That they didn't distrust them that much. Gardeniyah just stared at the floor. She couldn't tell Evanlee what she wanted to hear.

"Even Mib?" Evanlee's voice quaked a bit as she questioned her sisters.

Her sisters looked at each other. In all honesty, they had no way of knowing. They had no reason to think Mib didn't trust them, but she had also never offered to teach them anything about defending themselves either. Gardeniyah had never thought about it, but now that she was, it did seem a little strange that Mib had ensured they were trained and educated on nearly everything else. *Surely, she just overlooked this,* Gardeniyah insisted to herself. *But it does seem like a rather important thing to forget to teach us.*

Gardeniyah hated lying to Evanlee, but she didn't know how to answer honestly. She looked to Lorella for assistance, but Lorella just threw her hands up and shook her head as she walked over to the chair in the corner.

"Well," Gardeniyah began, "Mib was really only trained in sword combat. I'm sure she knew that wouldn't do us any good out here since we don't have swords. So she probably just didn't see the point in teaching us."

"But, that's what Vadeed taught Lorella, right?" Evanlee wasn't satisfied.

"Yes." Gardeniyah cleared her throat. "But that was a gift to Lorella. Not because he thought it would be helpful. He just knew she liked it. Right, Lorella?"

"Uhm. Yeah. Right."

"I guess that makes sense." To Gardeniyah's relief she was satisfied with that answer. "I still don't want to do it again."

"Too bad," Lorella said from her seat across the room. "You still have to."

Evanlee rolled her eyes and then turned to her side on the bed and quickly fell asleep.

"You have to quit coddling her from the truth like that, Deni."

Gardeniyah was surprised to hear her sister use her childhood nickname. Lorella hadn't called her that in years. She was always so different when Evanlee wasn't around, even if it was just because she was asleep.

Hearing the name reminded Gardeniyah of simpler times. When she and Lorella were seven and six, they had loved spending time together. Nearly every night while Mib cleaned the kitchen from dinner with Evanlee at her side, she and Lorella would lie on the rug by the fire. Gardeniyah would read aloud whatever new book she was fascinated with, and Lorella would draw pictures of the story Gardeniyah was telling. Those were the days when they called each other "Deni" and "Lor." She hadn't realized just how much she'd missed that kind relationship with her sister.

"I know, Lor." Gardeniyah was happy to see a small smile creep across her sister's mouth at the mention of her own nickname. "I just feel like there's not much I can do for her out here. I mean, look at the other day. I already failed her once."

"Why do you think it's your job to protect her from everything?"

"Who else is going to do it?"

"No one. That's the point. No one protected us."

"Mib did."

"Not when we were Evanlee's age."

178

Gardeniyah sighed as she nodded. "I know. But her innocence and her love of the world and how she sees the possibilities in everything"—she glanced over at her sister, who was peacefully sleeping—"those are the best things about her. I hate watching her lose that. And it's dying so quickly out here."

"That's just part of growing up."

"Yeah, I know. But she's fifteen. She doesn't need to do three years of growing up in a month."

"Deni, come on. We both remember being dumped by our mother. But Evanlee was too young to remember, so she has gotten to stay naive for a lot longer than either of us. We never even got that. She has had fifteen years of it."

"Maybe so. But she's going to grow up in a much more brutal way. We already knew that the world isn't a great place before we left the East. We've always been expecting the worst. Anything less than that is good. Yet, this place has surprised even me. So imagine being her. Expecting the best and getting this."

"I get that. But one day, something is going to happen that you won't be able to shield her from seeing or experiencing. I just think maybe it's best she's eased into it a bit."

"Didn't that already happen?"

"What, the man the other day?"

"Yeah."

"Sure, that was scary, and I'm sure it shook her up a bit. It shook us all up. But nothing happened to her."

"Nothing that scary has happened to either of us."

"Gardeniyah, you got attacked by a wolf!"

"Yeah." Gardeniyah looked down at the now scabbed and scarring mark on her forearm. "But I'm okay. I was prepared. She's only okay because—" She started to say Ezer's name, but she stopped herself. The man who had saved her sister's life had only one request, and she would honor it. No matter how strange she thought it was. "Only because someone was there to save her. Someone won't always be there."

"Exactly." Lorella got up from her chair and walked over to her sister and placed her hand on Gardeniyah's shoulder as she looked her in the eyes. "And one day you won't be there either, or if you are, you won't be able to stop it."

Lorella didn't say anything else. She lay down on the bed and went to sleep next to Evanlee. Gardeniyah stayed at the foot of their bed and listened to the nightlife of Zaraneth begin. She could hear the sinister laughs seep through the floorboards. The chaos below them was as constant as the snow had been in the North.

Gardeniyah knew Lorella was right. One day she might not be there to take care of them. Either of them. Protecting them was all she felt she was good for. It's all she had ever done. She didn't know who she was outside of that one mission.

She had been willing to sacrifice everything for them. Her sisters didn't know, but after Ranosa's first attempt to allow them another year in the East had failed, Gardeniyah had gone before the council with Ranosa.

Gardeniyah at eighteen had tried to bargain with the East's Grand Council for Evanlee. She had tried to convince them that "their" baby, as they often fondly referred to her, had never known anything but the East. She had no memory of anyone but the loving family that was the Easterners, and therefore she had no inherent "man" qualities in her. Thus, she should be allowed to stay even after Gardeniyah and Lorella, who had known the outside, needed to leave.

It was on that day that Gardeniyah learned how deeply the hatred for man and the fear of their greed ran in the veins of the fairies and the rest of the races represented by the council. They believed that, eventually, even a human they had called their own would turn on them. They had denied her appeal. It was this desperate plea of sacrificial love, and Gardeniyah's apparent ability to forgo her own desire to keep the only family she had together, that convinced the council that her own natural greed had not surfaced. So they granted them one more year until Lorella also turned eighteen.

Gardeniyah couldn't imagine not forgoing everything to protect them. Lorella was right. One day she wouldn't be able to protect Evanlee—or Lorella, for that matter— anymore. But it wasn't now. For now, it was all she knew to do.

CHAPTER TWENTY-NINE

Ezer worked with the girls for the next three days. The first two days, they were already up and waiting for him—and had been for quite some time. So on the fourth day, he woke up extra early and hurried to the tavern first thing in the morning. But when he opened the tavern door, there they were.

"Do you three ever sleep?" he said as he eyed the girls, who were already not just awake but practicing the fighting techniques he showed them the previous day.

"Easterners rise with the sun!" Evanlee responded in a voice that was far too chipper for Zaraneth at any time of day, but especially at that hour.

"Yeah, it's true," Lorella said, shaking her head. "I always hated it. Thought I'd give in to the way the rest of the world lives. It turns out a fifteen-year habit is a lot harder to break than I thought."

Evanlee noticed a stray thread on the black shirt she had borrowed from Lorella. Evanlee had quickly learned her shirts weren't practical for practicing combat when she ripped a hole in the sleeve of her favorite blouse. So she had insisted on wearing Lorella's. She was frustrated by their lack of detail or design—and how it didn't bother Lorella that each one had fraying pieces. With Evanlee fixated on trying to remove the thread, Lorella punched her in the arm.

"Ow!" Evanlee exclaimed. "Why would you do that?"

"Always have to be paying attention, Ev." Her words said she was teaching her sister a lesson. Her face said she was merely amusing herself. Either way, Ezer couldn't help but chuckle as he began their lessons for the day.

The lessons were going well. Lorella was advanced, and he soon learned that he had been wrong in at least one of his assumptions and that she didn't need very much of his instruction. Instead, he had her spar with Gardeniyah. He had initially suggested she spar with Evanlee, but Gardeniyah had quickly informed him that it would not be a good idea to pair her younger sisters. At first, he had questioned her as to why. But as he did, he saw the mischievous smile on Lorella's face. And though he felt a little twinge of disappointment he didn't understand, he had quickly agreed.

Lorella and Gardeniyah's pairing worked well. They fed off each other. Whenever Gardeniyah seemed ready to give up and let Lorella win the fight, Lorella would urge her on. Once, Gardeniyah had swung a little too hard in what was supposed to be a fake punch. Lorella hadn't been blocking at full force, and so Gardeniyah's punch landed squarely on her jaw. It had been loud enough to stop Ezer and Evanlee's far-less-intense sparring match. Instead of getting upset, Lorella smiled. She touched her jaw and moved it slowly back and forth, then said, "That's gonna leave a mark." Gardeniyah had apologized profusely, but Lorella had merely told her, "Good job" and they had gone right back to sparring.

Ezer liked the girls more and more as he got to know them. But he craved to have his normalcy back. His life had structure, and he liked it. He liked to be in charge of things and ensure they worked properly. The girls would be gone soon, and so would his compulsion to help them. More importantly, he'd get his normal life back. So when Osmond came out of his office that day and asked for the girls and Ezer to join him in one of the booths in the tavern, Ezer felt a flood of relief come over him.

When they were all seated, Osmond began.

"First of all, I want it known, lassies, that I put a lot of effort into finding this Methuselah that you are looking for."

Ezer looked over at the girls, who were eagerly fixated on Osmond. He could tell that the girls felt like this was the lead-up to the big reveal. Ezer knew it was the beginning of one of Osmond's excuses—Ezer had heard a lot of them over the last ten years.

"Your fella did a swell job there hiding himself. I told you if you come here, you don't want to be found. Did I not?"

This time when Ezer looked at the girls, only Evanlee was still looking at Osmond eagerly. Gardeniyah's eyes now looked weary, and Lorella's eyes looked distant—as if she had left the conversation altogether. He couldn't take dealing with hearing the prologue to the letdown anymore.

"Look, Osmond," Ezer interjected, "whether or not you found the guy, the girls don't have a lot of time. So get on with it."

Osmond glared at him. Ezer knew by the look he needed to watch what he was saying. It was easy for him to forget that this cowardly, manipulative man was his boss.

"I couldn't find your guy. I—"

Osmond was interrupted by Lorella banging her hands down on the table and then abruptly standing up and walking upstairs without a word. Evanlee put her head in her hands and began to cry. Gardeniyah had the most controlled reaction. She leaned her head against the back of the booth and ran her hands through the top of her hair and shook the roots a bit. She took a deep breath and then leaned forward and placed her forehead in her hand.

"Do you even have a lead for us?" she asked. Her eyes pleaded for the answer her frown said she knew she wouldn't get.

"Any lead I had, I explored. I assure you."

"Evanlee, go check on Lorella," Gardeniyah said. Evanlee complied without a word and went upstairs.

Without saying anything else, Gardeniyah got up slowly and headed straight for the door. The idea of her going outside upset made Ezer uneasy, but he knew she wouldn't let him follow her. His heart began to quicken as the door slammed shut behind her.

Osmond quickly got up to lock the door. The tavern didn't open for another hour. But he wouldn't risk any early birds ruining the mystique he had built.

"You have no leads at all for them?" Ezer asked as Osmond walked toward the door to the hallway leading to his office.

"I already told the girl no."

"I just find it hard to believe you have nothing."

"Well, this time I don't." Osmond's small eyes squinted almost closed. His nostrils flared with an invitation to question him further. "Besides, it's probably best I couldn't help them."

"And why is that?" Ezer crossed his arms and leaned back in his chair.

"Because even in a place like this, the king has eyes and ears everywhere. I wouldn't want it getting back to the king that I was helping some girls who are trying to overthrow him."

"They aren't trying to overthrow anyone. They are just trying to set things right."

"You sound like a sympathizer. Is that why your family

ended up here? Were you rebels? Did you all bet on the wrong side?"

Ezer shook his head but didn't answer. He had nothing to say. He had no idea what his family had done to end up in Zaraneth. He only knew they had been there for several generations.

"Well," Osmond continued, "I'm a betting man. And I bet the king already thinks everything is 'right' just the way it is. Don't you? I, myself, like the way things are."

Ezer clenched his jaw as he stood up. "Did you even try to help them, Osmond?"

"Well, of course I did." His fake enthusiasm seeped out of his insincere smile.

Ezer turned away from the man. He could no longer stand to look at him. He walked toward the front door. Halfway there, he stopped and turned around to address the boss he loathed once more. "You didn't report them, did you?"

"Why would I have done that?"

"You're always making deals with people. These girls had nothing to offer you."

"My son"—Ezer cringed; he hated when Osmond called him that—"this is Zaraneth. We are all traitors of the king, or our families were at one point. Who would I have reported them to? And who would believe a simple, humble tavern owner from Zaraneth?"

He hadn't said no. But he had a point as well. Ezer had to hope for the best. More importantly, right now he had to find Gardeniyah, or it wouldn't matter whether Osmond had reported them or not.

CHAPTER THIRTY

Lorella was livid. They had wasted so much time at the tavern just to hit a dead end. *We could have been out looking for Methuselah ourselves instead of relying on that disappointing man.*

She was at that point of frustration beyond words or reason that we all get to at some time in our lives. For Lorella, unfortunately, it would occur quite frequently for the rest of her life due to her quick temper. However, this time it was rather justified and no one would argue otherwise.

She didn't know what to do with her frustration. She thought about tipping over the dresser in the room. But there wasn't anything on top of it or in it. So she wouldn't get the satisfaction of seeing everything fly across the room like she wanted. Besides that, her mind was still semirational, and she knew they couldn't afford to damage anything. After looking around the room once more, she gathered that it was not very conducive to her desire to display her rage.

It occurred to her then that perhaps that was, in fact, the reason behind the rather bland room. That or the despicable little man downstairs was just too cheap to splurge on anything to make the room better for guests. Both options she deemed equally likely.

Soon her eyes landed on a suitable victim. She walked over to the bed and started unpacking her satchel to unnecessarily refold and reposition her things. However, the surge of energy brought on by her immense anger made her feel like she had to do something or she would burst.

"Are you trying to rip your satchel?" Evanlee's voice came from the open doorway of their room.

"What?"

"You're shoving stuff in your bag so hard you're going to rip the strap."

Lorella didn't reply. She just set the satchel back on the bed and sat down next to it. She stared out the window to the chaotic streets below them. She did so just in time to see a man rush to the window in the building across from them and puke on the streets below.

Lorella's insides lurched. She whipped her head away from the window to the bed where Evanlee was now sitting. While she didn't usually like the sight of anyone when she was this upset, anything was better than witnessing the man's previous meal cascading down to the streets.

This place was despicable, and now they were stuck here. There was no way they would have enough resources to get to the Mountains of Man now, or even an outlying village. Worse, they didn't have enough money to restock. She had a hunch that a good job would be hard to come by in these parts. It didn't appear as though most people earned their money by honest means. So unless they discovered an alternate way to the North or they suddenly lost their morals, they were out of luck.

"It's going to be okay, right?" The voice came from her sister, who was still sitting beside her. Lorella turned to look at her again. It was evident by the fact that her face still had some semblance of color to it that she not seen the show that had taken place across the alley.

Lorella hated questions like that. How was she supposed to know if things would be all right? *Where's Gardeniyah? Comforting Evanlee is her thing,* Lorella fumed. *I told Gardeniyah that she needed to stop coddling her, and if she had listened to me, then Evanlee wouldn't be asking me this ridiculous question.*

Lorella decided right then and there that it was time to give the little girl a reality check. She couldn't be so naive out here. She needed to realize that things fell apart sometimes. And when they do, they can't always be fixed.

This was one of those times. They were at a dead end. That was the cold, harsh reality. *Evanlee needs to finally join us in the real world,* Lorella thought. *She needs to accept she's never going back to the East. Worse, we are most likely stuck here. And, of course, we would be stuck here. Because that's what life is like! That's how the world is, was and always will be: a dangerous and harsh place filled with disappointments!*

Lorella had accepted that life could be harsh before they'd even left the East. The longer Evanlee believed that one day everything would be okay, the worse off she would be. After all, the world is more disappointing when you expect it not to be.

Lorella was prepared to unload all of this on her little sister. But as she opened her mouth and looked at her, she saw that her eyes were filled with tears. They were clouded and dark—haunted by uncertainty. Lorella didn't like to see them like that.

So before she could talk herself out of it—really, before she even realized what she was doing—Lorella said the exact opposite of everything she had intended to say. The opposite of everything she believed.

"Yes, Evanlee. Everything is going to be okay."

"How?"

Lorella's thoughts raced. *Why does she think I have all the answers? I don't know how any of this is going to be okay. I don't know what we are going to do.* Lorella was growing more and more frustrated with her sister's questions.

Best-case scenario, Lorella thought, *any minute, if we are lucky, Gardeniyah will be up here to tell us we have to leave. Gardeniyah won't want us to stay here any longer than we have to. She will tell us that she has worked some miracle and that soon we will be on our way to the North. But how can I tell her that? That going North would be the best thing that could happen. Not only is that almost impossible, but she won't think that means everything is okay. Going to the North means we won't be going to the East. And going back to the East is the only thing that Evanlee wants. No. It doesn't matter what Evanlee wants. Nobody really gets what they want in life. Evanlee needs to know that! She needs to know that if we can even get to a decent city in the North, it will be a miracle. We have nothing and no one out here on our side. This is our new reality.*

Lorella breathed in deeply and then sighed. "I don't know, Evanlee, but it will be. We'll find him."

She was lying. She didn't believe that. *Why am I lying?* She had always prided herself on her blatant honesty. That's why her sister would now believe that everything was going to be okay. She would now think they would actually find the man because Lorella never lied to protect people's feelings. She said the things others wouldn't. Her sister needed to hear the truth. Lorella didn't need to shelter her. She had decided that just moments before. Now here she was saying the exact opposite of what she thought.

"Thank you, Lorella."

Evanlee's voice was weak and tired. Hearing it that way made Lorella realize why she had just lied. Whether she wanted to admit it or not, she was a big sister. She would go to her grave before she would ever admit it to either of them, but she would do her best to protect Evanlee. Right now, Evanlee needed reassurance, and Lorella gave it to her despite her better judgment.

Lorella got up without another word. She didn't trust herself to speak again. She wouldn't lie anymore.

She emptied her satchel onto the bed.

"What are you doing?" Evanlee asked. Lorella didn't reply. She threw the empty satchel across her and marched down the steps once more. When she reached the bottom, Ezer, Osmond, and Gardeniyah were gone. She was glad—no one was there to question her.

Lorella walked through the busy streets until she found a little store in the corner of one of the many forked roads. It was overly crowded. People were arguing over last pieces of fruit and dried leathery substances Lorella had never seen. There was hardly any space to move around.

Lorella smiled. It was perfect.

Lorella walked the aisles seemingly aimlessly. Whenever she came to an especially crowded aisle, she would push toward the target bin and lean over it as if trying to get out of the way. She would then swipe an item and stuff it into her satchel. Soon, her bag was as full as she dared to pack it. Too full, and anyone who had seen her come in would notice.

She grabbed the cheapest item she could find and walked to the counter. She paid for it and walked out. A few more trips like this, and she would have their food supply restocked.

It may not be what Evanlee considered as "okay," but Lorella would make her statement true. She would get them what they needed to get to somewhere besides the horrible place they were now.

CHAPTER THIRTY-ONE

Gardeniyah walked on and on in a vain attempt to try to clear her head. It wasn't working. Her whole body ached. Not from the walking—a girl who spent weeks walking across the world doesn't get tired from a little walking around the city.

No, this was the sort of ache in your bones and your muscles that comes from a deeper pain. The pain of confusion, disappointment, and heartbreak. The cause of the pain makes it far more crippling than sore muscles and achy bones. You see, your mind is normally strong enough, without you ever realizing it, to fight off the tiredness of your muscles. But when your mind is overcome with distress, as Gardeniyah's was now, your mind gives up as much as you.

So to say her mind was cloudy would be a gross injustice to her pain. It was a raging storm. Each thought flying into her mind at full speed. A new thought would begin fighting with the previous one for its place at the forefront of her mind. It made her head pound like the dwarves mining in the mountains of the East. With each step, she felt weaker.

Weaker in every sense of the word and in more ways than she had ever felt in her life.

Eventually, her body gave out, and she collapsed onto a rickety old bench on an unknown street in Zaraneth. It was grimy, and it creaked if you moved even an inch, but she didn't care. Truth be told, she never even noticed. She just sat begging her mind to slow down.

She was positive she needed her thoughts to ease more than she had ever needed anything before in her life. Gardeniyah needed to get up from the bench. She didn't trust staying still in this place. But she was frozen. Her body was unable to move in its overwhelmed state.

She couldn't see anything. Her eyes stung as if salt water from the Southern Sea was in them, and the pounding in her head sent flashes of light across her vision. She was vulnerable. So she had to keep moving. But she couldn't. Not even an inch. Her mind was ablaze with regrets, tormenting her.

You failed, Gardeniyah. You failed your sisters. You failed the East. You failed the world. A pain sprang into her pounding chest. She gripped her chest and hunched over. *What are you going to do now? You can't protect them. You think things will be different after a few lessons in self-defense from a stranger? Ha! You already nearly lost Evanlee once. You're a failure.* All the air left her lungs. She gasped for more air but, try as she might, she couldn't seem to take a full breath. *Did you really think you were up for this? Any of this? You thought you could save the world? You couldn't even save Evanlee. You couldn't even save yourself if you had to. You got lucky with the wolf. But a wolf is no man. You didn't even remember a heavier blanket to keep them warm in the North. You have failed.* She gripped the side of her head and tried to pull more air into her lungs. *You'll never see Mib again. Evanlee will never go home. Yet another way you failed her. Failure.* Her legs trembled and her arms shook as she pressed her hands deeper into her head in an attempt to stop the mind that was ablaze with self-torture. *Failure! That's all you are. You had one option. You trusted someone. You should have known better than to trust anyone. Man can't be trusted. You can't be trusted. You are human. You are no better. You think you are better than them, don't you? You aren't. You never will be. Failure.* Gardeniyah began to rock back and forth as her legs bounced, her body ached, her lungs fought for air, and her mind continued to assault her. *You are exactly like the ones you hate. Failure. Deep down, you are no better. You couldn't have saved the East, anyway, because you're just like the rest of man. The world is doomed now because of you. Failure. You just left your sisters alone because you are throwing a fit. Selfish. You left them alone in the tavern for hours. Greedy girl. Do you ever think anything through anymore? Clearly not. Failure. You are not who you thought you were. You will never be who you want to be. You don't even know who you want to be, do you? Surely a guardian of your sisters is not all you are. It better not be. You do a rather crummy job at it. Evanlee won't need you one day. Lorella barely likes you. Eventually no one will need you. You will be nothing. You already are nothing. Accept that you are nothing to anyone!*

Her eyes were on fire, as if tiny needles were prodding at them. She didn't realize that the stinging was due to the fact she was crying. She also didn't realize that a man had sat down next to her until he spoke. If she were in her right mind, she would have done a lot of things differently during the next few moments.

First, she would have noticed him sitting down next to her. She also would have noticed that he lingered. Normally, she would have gotten up quickly, but in such a way that he didn't notice her quickness was on purpose. She would have safely removed herself from his presence.

But she didn't. Her brain was too foggy. Her heart was too broken. Her body was too tired. So she sat, oblivious, as the man got comfortable.

"Tears are a good release, aren't they?" the man said.

Gardeniyah jerked herself up from her bent-over position. She removed her head from her hands and straightened out of the position of defeat she had succumbed to.

She was not one to surrender. But today she felt very much like giving up for good. What was the point? What was ever the point? Her life, from the day she was born to now, had been a series of dead ends. One start and abrupt stop after another.

She had known too many endings. Which, sure, meant she knew plenty of beginnings. But for her, and those of you like Gardeniyah, who have had more new beginnings than you would like, you begin to dread the beginnings more than the endings.

An ending you know how to handle. You process. You cope. You move on.

Then, right there, starts the new beginning. The scary part. Because no one can ever be sure, no matter how much they might think they can be, whether this new beginning will be better or worse than its predecessor.

For Gardeniyah, the only new beginning she had ever enjoyed was her arrival in the East. But it came with a clearly marked expiration date. So she had grown up hating the idea of "new beginnings." Now, she was faced with yet another.

And this time her body was wearier than ever before. Her ideals were broken. Her heart was a stone in her chest, and her mind was a disaster. It felt as though, no matter how much she tried to stay positive, to have hope and faith that everything would work out, she always ended up in the same spot. Alone. Contemplating every decision she had ever made. Torturing herself by trying to figure out what moments would have changed everything if she had only made a different choice.

She knew regret wouldn't help her. She knew over-thinking wouldn't help her. Yet, she couldn't stop feeling or doing either. No matter how hard she desperately tried. Nothing made her feel at peace in this turmoil.

You see, Gardeniyah was having one of life's rare moments. Perhaps you have experienced one. In this moment, you see all of the past flashing before you, and at the same time, you see all the visions of a future you wanted reeling through your mind. Yet, you can do nothing for either. You can't change the past. You can't control the future. And so she, and I'm sure many of you, have felt this way and this terrifying utter lack of control.

This kind of inability to govern anything eats at your every waking moment. It's the kind that shapes your view-point on the world forever. The kind that, no matter what you do, no matter how many avenues you mentally explore . . . you are still lost. Which is simply because no choice that matters is up to you. You can't do a thing about any of it. So you spend every minute you have mentally wrestling with your demon (which is exhausting, to say the absolute least), all the while still desperately clinging on to a promise that only you know about.

She'd fought hard. She'd fought gallantly. She'd fought for her old normal. But still, it was beginning to feel like it would always feel this way. No matter how much she fought it, she was starting to feel how Evanlee had felt in the wilderness of the North. She was stripped of what she lived for, the ability to take care of those she loved.

"Tears are a good release," the man said again.

"Pardon me?" she said as she attempted to wipe the tears from her eyes. She didn't even like her siblings to know when she was crying, let alone a perfect stranger. After blinking her eyes far too many times for any normal person not to notice she was upset, she could see a hazy outline of the man who was speaking to her. "I'm sorry. One more time. My mind is elsewhere, so I didn't hear you."

"I said tears are a good release. They are necessary sometimes so we can let the pain and anger out."

Gardeniyah blinked a few more times. Her eyes were now clear enough to see the elderly man beside her. Her heart had been racing when she'd heard a voice speak to her, but it suddenly began to slow down. Ezer had told her a lot about this place in the brief conversations she could get out of him the last few days. One thing he had made clear in their combat lessons was that if someone was nice to you randomly in the street, they were up to something.

Yet when she looked at this man, she didn't feel fearful. He had a presence that immediately pacified her.

His eyes were aged but cheery. His skin was dirty. His clothes were barely more than rags. He was a beggar. Ezer had also made it clear that most beggars would scam you here. But this man didn't seem to have an agenda. But in a place like this, calm was still skeptical.

She didn't like feeling skeptical of the man. She tried to ignore it. She felt she could trust him—though she didn't know why. She hoped and prayed she wasn't wrong. She had been wrong before when she ignored someone's warning, and it almost cost her sister her life.

But she had never been someone who immediately assumed the worst of another being. She had lost so much of herself in the short time she had been out of the East. She didn't want to lose that too. Trusting this man even slightly was a desperate and possibly reckless attempt to feel like her old self for even a moment.

"Yeah, I suppose it does help," she responded.

"What's it helping you with, dear one?" the old man inquired. "Is it disappointment or anger?"

"I think it's fair to say both." Gardeniyah sighed deeply and shook her head.

"Ah, those are the deepest sort of tears because that's the deepest sort of pain. What are you so disappointed and angry about?"

"A little personal, don't you think, sir?"

"Mm-hmm. Perhaps," he said, nodding. "But you never know who can help. We are often so wrapped up in not getting too personal that we miss the chance to help, or be helped by someone. Maybe I could help you? What have you got to lose? If you are this upset, I venture to say: not very much."

It went against every ounce of logic that Gardeniyah had to tell this man anything. Her sister had been right. She didn't need to keep telling people their story. Four people being aware right now was already more than she was comfortable with. Which is why when she opened her mouth to convey her thanks for his concern and then shut the conversation down as quickly as possible, she was utterly confused that this was not what came out.

"I'm looking for someone, a historian named Methuselah —he lives here. But I don't know the area. I'm not from here, and I went to the person who supposedly knows everyone, or at least knows someone who knows the person. Even he couldn't find him. It's so important that I find this man, and now I'm out of options. I'm going to let down everyone I care about. I'm going to let people I don't even know or care about down. I'm going to let everyone down."

"That's a mighty big burden you have there, dear one. Why are you carrying the weight of the world on your back? Who gave you such a load?"

"My mentor. My friend. My mother. My birth mother. The Omniscient. My home. My family. Seems like it's coming from everything and everyone I love." Gardeniyah had no idea why she was telling the man all of this. It neither matched her personality nor her common sense to open up to him like this. But it felt utterly magnificent all the same to tell someone how she was feeling.

"The Omniscient? That's a name I haven't heard from any man or woman in a very long time."

Gardeniyah nodded. She knew in these parts—and she guessed in all of the parts of the world inhabited by man—he was a legend, a phantom, a ghost of the past.

"Methuselah? You say?" the man continued. "Is that the name of the man you are looking for?"

Gardeniyah nodded again.

"I've heard that name before."

"You have? How?"

"We old men tend to know each other. Have to stick together to survive in a place like this. It's no wonder your connection couldn't find him. His safety depends on not being easily found. Even more than most in these parts. I can tell you where to find him. If you promise your intentions are pure."

"They are, I assure you!" Gardeniyah couldn't control the smile that overcame her face as she spoke. "I admire an old friend of his." The man only raised his eyebrows at her, so she continued. "I was sent to find him by a trusted companion to his closest friend. He is going to help us set right some things that are so terribly wrong."

At that, the elderly man smiled. It was not an attractive smile, but it was the best smile Gardeniyah had ever seen because it meant that her answer satisfied the old man. And so he began to tell her where to find Methuselah. When he finished, she thanked him and then for some reason unbeknownst to her, she leaned her head back and began to cry again.

"Ah. Tears of relief and joy. Believe it or not, those are

even more powerful. You are going to be okay, dear one. Just keep doing what you know to do until you know what to do next. You have more of the answers you seek than you know," the old man said.

Gardeniyah nodded and then began to wipe her eyes. "Thank you again for all your help. I don't know how to ever repay you," she said, rubbing her eyes so she could see clearly.

When she could see again, she saw nothing. The old man was gone. The street was nearly empty, as it had strangely been the whole time, and he was nowhere in sight.

"There you are!" the now familiar but still startlingly deep voice rang out through the air.

Gardeniyah turned around to see Ezer hustling toward her.

"You've been gone for hours! I've been looking for you everywhere! Do you know what could have happened to you? You could be dead. I could be finding you in an alley dead somewhere!" His eyes weren't angry; they were pleading with her. Gardeniyah felt a sting of guilt. She hadn't even been concerned with how the others might feel about the fact that she had disappeared. "I'm sorry, Ezer. I didn't mean to worry you."

"You all really aren't comprehending how dangerous this place is. I don't know how I am going to get you to under-stand. If you are going to make it here in Zaraneth now that you haven't found your historian, you need to start being smarter about how you handle yourself." A smile crept across Gardeniyah's face slowly as Ezer spoke. "I just— Why are you smiling like that? What, do you like seeing people worry about you? Was that your goal?"

"No, not at all!"

"Then why?"

"Because I know where he is."

CHAPTER THIRTY-TWO

Lorella and Evanlee didn't say much after Lorella returned. Evanlee hadn't even bothered to question her sister as to where she had been. Nor did she notice the now full satchel. The silence hung between them as they got lost in their thoughts. Lorella was lying on the bed staring at the barren ceiling. She was attempting to drown her mind in details instead of worries.

Forty-seven wooden panels. One hundred and thirty-three nails. Lorella wasn't sure if that was structurally sound. She wouldn't be surprised if it wasn't. Directly above her, she eyed five panels that had a much newer look to them. They were clearly replacements. They were on the top floor of the tavern, so it had been a leak. The leak explained the ever-present musty smell of the room. *I bet that sniveling man didn't even replace the mattress after the leak, even though the tavern would make enough in an hour to do so,* she thought. That made the twelfth reason she had found to despise that man. The numbers and the details helped to occupy her mind. She had figured out a couple of years before that obsessing over particulars, whatever they may be, helped her distract herself. Her fifteen-year-old sister, however, had apparently not yet found a coping mechanism.

Evanlee had been pacing their small room for the whole two hours Lorella had been back. Lorella was pretty sure since there weren't many options for paths in the tight space, there would be a permanent track on the rug because of it. Before she had begun counting the wooden panels of their room, Lorella had watched her sister. It had arisen out of annoyance and had grown to fascination.

The first five minutes Evanlee had wandered around the room, she had darted glances around the room as she did so. After five minutes of this, she seemed to find a path she liked. In the last nearly two hours, she had not deviated from that route.

Every time she turned, she sighed. Every twenty-third step, which equaled about every round and a half of her circular track, she ran her fingers through her hair. She started at her forehead and ran her hand to the back of her head. She would stop her hand there for a second. Then she would rustle her hair precisely three times. It was strange to see her do that because Gardeniyah had always done the same when she was frustrated. Then she closed her eyes and breathed in deeply. The same thing Gardeniyah did when she was overwhelmed. However, Evanlee was a little different. After she rustled her hair, she would then continue her hand down her head to her neck and rub the bottom of her neck twice. That was what Lorella always did when she was annoyed.

Noticing this made Lorella wonder: *How long has she been doing these things? Has she ever done them before? Or has she never been so frustrated and overwhelmed that she ever needed to? Why does she combine my mannerisms with Gardeniyah's?*

Though she had never noticed them before, her sister's quirks were now obvious. As were the floods of emotions evident by the different facial expression she wore with every lap. She was in a cycle of torment. Confusion to anger to pain to exasperation to fear to a brief moment of calm before it would all cycle through again.

She knew she should say something to Evanlee. But she didn't know what. The previous conversation went so far against her real beliefs on the matter. She didn't trust herself to keep up the charade if she continued to speak. So she let the stillness linger between them. The sounds came from the recently opened tavern. It had only been open an hour and wasn't very busy yet, which is why Lorella was able to hear the ruckus coming from downstairs as soon as it began as a faint, distant sound.

It didn't faze her as it grew louder and closer. She assumed it was something related to the tavern. Besides, both girls were very lost in their thoughts and so were visibly startled when someone came bursting through the door.

Lorella fell nearly completely out of the bed as the door swung open and someone came through it yelling with such enthusiasm she couldn't understand what was being said. She gripped the sheet, scrambling for balance as one foot hit the floor. In doing so, she managed to stop herself from fully crashing against the ground. She pulled herself back up onto the bed, pulling the sheets off the corners as she did so.

Evanlee did not react with any more grace. The incident only a few days earlier with the man in the street was still fresh in her mind. Evanlee whirled around and ran to the wall farthest away from the door. She crouched, shaking as she gripped onto the dresser that stood next to the wall.

"I found him!" the voice yelled again before the door had fully opened. Her exclamation was punctuated as the slammed door bouncing back and hitting the wall once more. This caused a loud thud that kept Lorella and Evanlee from hearing anything after the word "I."

Lorella had never been so glad to see her sister in all her life. She was also never happier that her sister had a rather obsessive personality that caused her to miss quite a lot when she was fixated on something. It was easy for Lorella to assume, based on that, and the fact that her sister wasn't laughing at what she knew had been a manically humorous sight, that she had missed their rather graceless reactions altogether.

"You what?" Lorella questioned as she cleared her throat and tried to act poised as she tucked the sheet back in on the corners of their mattress.

"I know! I could hardly believe it myself. I mean, there is a slight chance that it's not true or that the information is dated, but it's better than nothing."

Evanlee walked up behind Lorella and whispered in her ear, "What is she talking about?"

"I have no idea," Lorella whispered back.

"I'm a little conflicted," Gardeniyah continued in her flustered manner, not at all registering her audience's baffled faces. "I mean, I am so excited I want to just head over there tonight. Although, I guess that could be considered rude . . . Ezer discouraged that option, saying it was unsafe. So maybe we should wait until morning. What do you two think?"

Lorella's eyebrows were furrowed, and her eyes squinted. Evanlee's eyes were wider than normal and her mouth was slightly open. They both slowly looked at each other. Evanlee wasn't going to say anything, she never challenged Gardeniyah, and so Lorella spoke for them.

"Gardeniyah . . . What are you talking about?"

"What do you mean what am I talking about? I just told you. I found Methuselah."

With that, the girls, all three of them, started jumping up and down and hugging each other. They were laughing and crying and smiling.

It was one of those blissful moments that can only stem from prior pain. The special kind when you have lost all hope and then something brings a new chance at something you had thought impossible. It is one of the purest forms of joy.

The girls decided not to try to venture out that night. It had nothing to do with Ezer's warning of danger—although it should have. It also had nothing to do with the question of courtesy to the old man.

It had everything to do with the fact that they all wanted to cling on to that feeling for a little while longer. They knew that, as soon as they set out to find him, all of the doubt and the fear and the confusion would creep back in slowly and once again haunt their every moment. So instead, they stayed and reveled in the first feeling of happiness they had felt since they'd left the East.

CHAPTER THIRTY-THREE

The next morning, the girls woke early to the smell of breakfast filling the air. A strange smell for a tavern at any time of day but especially at a time when no one would be there but guests who had stayed the night. None of those guests could expect anything in the way of food. After all, a tavern isn't exactly a bed-and-breakfast. It was more akin to a "bed and good luck with the rest of your day—try not to get killed."

Lorella assumed it was one of the other guests taking it upon themselves to use the very limited kitchen in the tavern. A smart move on their end. While her sisters were still washing up, Lorella slipped downstairs to see if she could talk whoever was cooking into sharing with her.

It smelled even better downstairs, maple seeping into whatever was being baked. She was thrilled to smell real food. She had been eating canned food while on the road, and had eaten the absolute cheapest food since being here. To eat such food isn't a safe choice anywhere—but in a place like Zaraneth, it's pretty safe to assume nothing in what you are consuming is natural.

This, though, smelled like a morning with Mib back East. Whenever Mib had the day off, she always made the girls a big breakfast with maple everything because it was the girls' favorite.

Shock quickly replaced the pang of homesickness in Lorella's gut. The person walking out with a plate full of buns drizzled with maple syrup was Ezer. He stopped in his tracks. By the startled look on his face, Lorella wondered if this was some hobby he preferred to keep a secret and he had just forgotten they were there.

"I didn't hear you come down the steps." The statement explained the shock on his face—though Lorella would have preferred it if she'd happened upon a guilty pleasure. "Glad you're up, though. Figured we would need to get an early start this morning. It will most likely be a long day, so I made a few of these to eat now with maple and a few plain ones to take with us."

"Why?"

"Have you ever tried to carry a maple bun in your bag? It's as sticky as a three-year-old's fingers. It gets everywhere."

"What? No, I mean, why did you make food for us?"

"I just explained that. It will be a long day for us, and I was making myself food anyway, so I figured I'd save you from eating Morimer's Mush next door again. But, by all means, if you want so-called grain flavored with things I'm pretty sure no one should have before the afternoon, have at it."

"Nope! Maple buns sound great," Lorella said, grabbing one off the plate and sitting down in a booth right as her sisters came down the steps. "Ezer made food, and apparently he's coming with us," she yelled with a mouth full of sticky maple buns.

Gardeniyah always put so much effort into seeming put together. So Lorella always got a big kick out of seeing something throw her off. The look on her face almost made Lorella choke on the sticky maple bun in her mouth as she laughed. It was short lived, though, because it didn't take Gardeniyah long to recover.

"Choking is what you get. You shouldn't be talking with your mouth full," Gardeniyah said as she walked toward the booth where Lorella was sitting.

Lorella responded by sticking her tongue out, showcasing a newly chewed-up bit of maple bun. This was the absolute least mature way she could think of responding, which was exactly why she'd done it. Not because she wasn't mature enough to realize its childishness but because she knew the most juvenile response would be the one that got to her sister the most.

To Lorella's delight, it worked. Her sister let out an exasperated sigh and ran her hands through her hair and shook the roots twice as she sat down. Then she turned away from Lorella and moved on to address Ezer. Lorella beamed at her accomplishment.

"So you're coming with us?"

"Well, yeah. I've been telling you girls this place is too dangerous for you to be alone."

"Yeah! And we are starting to get annoyed by it, I might add!" Lorella called out in the middle of another bite. Gardeniyah frowned at her and Lorella smiled back. It was the sort of satisfied smile that lets one know that they have just given the antagonist exactly what they wanted by getting annoyed.

"Well, it's the truth. Look, I just figure I'll help you get to the guy safely, and then help you get safely out of the city. Then no matter how much I have annoyed you by then, you won't have to see me ever again, and I can go about my business knowing I didn't let three helpless girls get hurt."

"We aren't helpless," Evanlee chimed in while folding her

arms across her chest. "You taught us some stuff. We are tougher than you think!"

"Wow, you ladies like to gang up on a guy. If you don't want my help, then fine. I just know this city better than you. And admittedly, I'm curious about the guy—if he's alive, and what he will have to say about your little prophecy."

"Oh yeah, it's a prophecy that will undo hundreds of years of injustice if it's fulfilled, but sure, it's a 'little' prophecy . . ." Lorella snorted.

"You are some temperamental women this morning. I'll be glad once my conscience and my curiosity lets me be done with you and I can go back to my normal life."

"So will we . . ." Gardeniyah's reply to Ezer's comment was slightly out of character. It was the sort of thing her expression let you know on occasion, but not the sort of thing she ever said out loud. Lorella got almost as much amusement out of the eye roll Gardeniyah gave Ezer as her own antics earlier.

Ezer seemed to already know this was out of character for Gardeniyah, his eyebrows raised above his own irritated glance. Though it only lasted a moment before he gave in to a half-cocked smirk that he quickly hid as he cleared his throat to speak again.

"I say we leave in about an hour. That will get us in the streets at a good time of day. We won't stand out for being out and about too early. But the streets won't be so crowded that we might miss a threat."

Right as the group agreed on the plan, the doors to the tavern swung open. The girls were stunned to see a pig hop down from the handle it was hanging on to. He strolled into the tavern with his head held high and a bounce in his step. If they had never seen an animal with an arrogant attitude before, it might have been a shock to the sisters. But, of course, having grown up in the East, the girls were not fazed by the pompous animal—much to Ezer's surprise.

"So you must be the girls that this guy was talking so much about," the pig said as he cocked his head toward Ezer.

"I suppose so!" Evanlee said with the biggest smile Ezer had ever seen on her.

"Wait, so a talking pig doesn't faze you?" he said, his face scrunched in confusion.

"No. Why would it?" Evanlee said, looking equally as puzzled.

"Because most animals don't talk?"

Talking animals were mostly a thing of legends. It took a disturbingly short amount of time for mankind to rewrite history into a version that they were more comfortable with. The idea that they had displaced an entire civilization did not bode well with the average human's conscience—despite what many Easterners believed. And so most of mankind had managed to convince themselves that the animals they had taken the land from were never truly smart enough to appreciate it.

They ignored all signs that the beasts had their own civilizations. They turned a blind eye to the history accounts they otherwise trusted in every regard mentioning talking animals. An easy feat, as most talking animals had long ago been killed. And so the talking beasts who were left in any of the areas man now occupied had pretended they couldn't speak to the point that they'd forgotten how and didn't teach their offspring. Or they spoke to only those they fully trusted, as was the case with the pig and Ezer.

Even with Ezer's protection, the little pig was careful to play the part of the ignorant beast anytime he was in public. It was demeaning for him, and he was always in a foul mood afterward. But it was for the best. Talking beasts of any sort were all the rage in alleyway shows in Zaraneth and any festival in the land of man. Those gawking at the beasts would come up with every reason for how the animal could be talking: dark magic, an excellent puppeteer, an optical illusion, anything but the rather obvious fact that the beast was intelligent enough to be able to speak the language of man.

"What are you talking about? Of course animals can talk," Evanlee said. "If the monsters of the South, and the mystical creatures of the East, and us humans all talk, how would it be fair for the beasts to not?"

"I like her," the pig said, pointing his front right hoof at Evanlee.

"Well, maybe in the East, animals talk. But here, it's considered a myth that animals can, or used to, talk. All the ones that still live here and didn't flee to the East are just animals. No talking. No communities. They live, they eat, and they die."

"He always makes the lives of us animals feel so extravagant and captivating. Jealous, aren't you?" The pig leaned against the booth the girls were sitting in as he spoke.

Gardeniyah already liked the sassy animal. He was a plump little pig. He had a belt around his waist that held a sword a little too big and impractical for him. Half of one of his ears was missing, and he had a scar that ran from his snout up to his eye. Other than that, he was rather cute for a pig. However, by his attitude, it was obvious such a description would not bode well with the "gentleman."

"What's your name?" Gardeniyah asked.

"Hamlet, my lady," he said with a wave of his hoof and a bow. "After the late Lord Hamlet Worthington, the great human general of the rebellion against the invasion of the West . . . However, history aside, due to the unfortunate jokes"—he glared at Ezer—"I go by Letty."

"When I bought you, you were supposed to be dinner,"

Ezer said. "So the name 'Hamlet' was funny. A royal, regal, and honorable name—but, you know, funny for a pig. Plus, it also insinuated your supposed fate; it was perfect. Until you spoke and I became friends with my dinner. The rest, five years later, is history, Letty."

Lorella laughed as she looked around the room. Letty shook his head repeatedly as Ezer continued to try to defend himself to his small pink friend—who merely raised a hoof at him to illustrate he had no interest in hearing his justifications. Evanlee stared at the two of them gleefully. Gardeniyah was trying her best to hide the smile creeping across her face as she made eye contact with Lorella.

Gardeniyah was amused but wasn't finding it quite as funny as her younger sister. Though, she probably would have if she had been paying close attention to everyone's reactions. Her mind, however, was preoccupied with the historical reference the pig had made.

Gardeniyah knew her history well. She knew all about Lord Worthington. He was one of the last humans the East had respected. Even their stories still told of his bravery. They said he was the last human to fight against man's greed. He had rebelled against the king of man and what most of mankind had wanted. He had fought gallantly alongside the last king of the West, Ashton the Lion.

He was eventually captured. The East's records didn't know what happened to him. It was widely presumed he'd met a gruesome fate.

The story was a great one. One of Gardeniyah's favorites growing up. It had made her feel less horrible about being human. But she wondered why a man in the middle of Zaraneth knew that story. Surely, it wasn't a widely celebrated tale here. Yet, Ezer had said the name was an honorable one.

This man was proving more difficult to figure out than

she had initially assumed. However, now was not the time to overthink it. Letty would get offended if she didn't wipe the bewildered look off her face and recover.

"Well, Hamlet—uh, I mean, Letty—is an excellent name. I'm pleased to make your acquaintance, sir. Will you be joining us as well to find Methuselah?" Gardeniyah said, addressing the pig as if she were talking to a diplomat at one of Queen Ranosa's balls.

She could tell he was not used to being addressed in such a manner. His chest puffed out a bit. He stood up straighter, and his head tilted up. The way she'd spoken to him and the invitation she had just extended to the pig had made him feel very important.

"Yes, of course. This guy would be lost without me," he said, gesturing with his head toward Ezer.

Gardeniyah's mouth twitched quickly as she glanced over at Ezer. He shook his head at the pig's comment. However, Gardeniyah noticed he had a small grin. She lingered on it for a moment but quickly brought her attention back to their newest companion. Gardeniyah liked Letty and had been careful not to offend the pig, and she wanted to continue doing so, so she closed her eyes and nodded understandingly.

"I don't doubt he would be a complete mess without you," she said, flashing a smile at Ezer.

This was the first moment that either had addressed the other in a sincerely friendly way. Up until now, every inter-action they had had been factual or formal. Lorella always found it interesting to watch people interact. She especially enjoyed seeing moments when people's relationship shifted.

She pitied Ezer at that moment, though. Gardeniyah's smile could melt a brick wall. It had only lasted for a second, but that tall brick of a man clearly melted a bit too. He sucked his breath in, his eyes widened ever so slightly, and the fists Lorella hadn't even noticed he was clenching eased for a second. As soon as Gardeniyah's smile and gaze released him, he was back to the composed self that they had come to know.

Lorella doubted this would be the only time such an interaction would happen. Gardeniyah had a way with everyone; her only competition would be Evanlee one day. Lorella knew her demeanor was too intimidating to make her captivating like her sisters, and she honestly preferred it that way. She would rather be feared than loved any day.

"Well, if this is all of our party, then I suggest we quickly finish and head out," Ezer said, then cleared his throat. They all agreed, and before it hit midday, they were all out the tavern door and heading into the lawless city to search for a long-forgotten man.

CHAPTER THIRTY-FOUR

The five of them were an especially interesting sight in a Zaraneth. The four humans didn't say much as they ventured out through the streets, and for his safety, Letty did not say anything at all.

Ezer felt obligated to speak a few times to keep the silence from becoming an awkward thing. But it was mostly pointless small talk that didn't last long. After a while, he gave up his attempts altogether, for the mission seemed much too serious.

Gardeniyah was thoroughly glad when Ezer finally gave up on making conversation. She appreciated his effort, but there wasn't really anything she wanted to discuss.

She liked the streets even less than she had the first time they'd ventured through them. Though she had been thoroughly disgusted by them—she had been at least a little curious about it all. But now she felt nothing but loathing for this place, and everyone in it. Except for Letty, the man beside her, and the man she hoped to find.

Every time an overly large man passed, fear flooded her. However, she would feel calm once more when she saw Ezer tense up in preparation for any possible altercation. Though she had been annoyed with him earlier for inviting himself along, she was now glad to have him.

But it wasn't just the burly men who bothered her as they made their way through Zaraneth. She got a sick feeling she couldn't explain whenever certain people walked by. They wore dark-gray cloaks with a hood. They had black tattoo-marking around their eyes and intricate designs carved into their hands and arms. She was unfamiliar with it then, but those people dabbled in dark magic. And so they carried a heaviness with them that most people in Zaraneth were quite accustomed to. But an intuitive newcomer like Gardeniyah—especially one who had only ever been exposed to light magic—was momentarily haunted by their spirits as they passed by.

After they had been walking for about an hour, the temperature grew increasingly hot and the wind picked up. Ezer explained that a fire and tornado were somewhere near. He had said it so calmly she thought perhaps she needn't worry. But as the temperature rose, so did her level of anxiety.

For the first time, Gardeniyah started to envy the fairies' ability to only feel one emotion at a time. She had always thought it was their weakness. It could make them tempera-mental at times, and they held the strongest grudges. But at least they always, no matter what, had clear minds. They always knew exactly how they felt about a situation and could face anything with that assurance. She craved that much clarity, even for a moment.

Instead, she was a flood of anxiety, excitement, fear, joy, and at least seven other emotions she couldn't place. Her mind interrogated the situation with incessant questions. *What if he's not there? What if the old man had the wrong guy and it's not him? What if it is him and he's a crazy loon who doesn't remember anything? What if he's dead?* And perhaps the one that Gardeniyah feared the most: *What if he is stable and normal, but he just doesn't have any of the answers we need?*

The walk felt eternal as they passed through the different regions of Zaraneth to get to The Center. Zaraneth was broken up into regions like the rest of the lands. Though, unlike the rest of Tolatin, it wasn't segregated by weather. In one day, you could experience all four seasons.

If you were in an area that was closer to one border, you didn't have to deal with the constant change of climate; however, the worst of that region's afflictions culminated in those areas as well. Tropical storms hit the south region at least twice a week. Blizzards hit the north almost every day. The eastern region had almost constant rain, so the area was nearly always flooded and flash floods carried people away regularly into the Eastern Sea. The west dealt with tornados but otherwise would have been perhaps the most pleasant of anywhere in Zaraneth. But the constant fear of fire breaking out due to the dryness of everything didn't allow for that. Every day, at least one building burned to the ground.

Up until now, Gardeniyah and her sisters had only had to deal with the people of Zaraneth. However, upon entering the region of Zaraneth known as The Center (an altogether not very clever name, as it was just literally the center of the world), they could hardly see. The area was being beaten down by a blizzard. Which, because the girls had not yet endured a blizzard, would have been bad enough; however, it was exacerbated by the wind of a tornado currently hitting the western region.

Gardeniyah was freezing. By the time they got to Zaraneth, her list of things to buy had grown too long. To be as logical as possible, she had opted to buy nothing until she knew where the journey was going to take them next. But, right now, every inch of her regretted not purchasing heavier jackets at least. Or a hat. A hat would have been nicer than any crown in the four regions.

The cold wind flogging her and the snow disrupting her vision, so narrow she could only see an inch in front of her face, made her feel incredibly isolated. She couldn't see well enough to know where they were going. She couldn't see if her sisters were still with her. Her mind tormented her as it swirled with the possibilities of what this hazardous blizzard could bring. She panicked at the thought of someone yet again grabbing one of her sisters. She knew there was no way Ezer would be able to save them in this condition.

She worked herself up into quite the frenzy. The storm in her mind easily rivaled the one she was currently walking through when a hand grabbed her arm unexpectedly. The hand was far too big to belong to either of her sisters. Gardeniyah froze.

After a few moments, the face of the man whose hand was grasping onto hers came into view. Through the blinding snow, she could make out two familiar and intense bright-green eyes staring at her. The wind howling in her ears kept her from being able to hear what he was trying to say, but she didn't need to. She was surprised at how quickly it happened, but she realized as he tugged on her arm and she followed without hesitation how much she already trusted this man. Gardeniyah blindly swung her other hand around until she made contact with another arm. She grabbed firmly on to it, and hoped that whichever sister the arm belonged to would do the same to the other.

CHAPTER THIRTY-FIVE

E zer led them all into a small tavern. It was only big enough to hold thirty people, though not even ten were in there at the time. The place was called Machino's, according to the crooked and broken sign on the wall. It was nothing like Osmond's. Not only was it not even a fourth of the size, but it was much less crowded, which was a nice and unexpected change for all of them.

The four humans sat down at the table closest to the heater stove in the corner. Letty lay down in front of it to remain inconspicuous. Ezer eased into the quietness of the place. He liked the pace, the atmosphere, and he even liked its size. He had always assumed he'd hate to work in a place like this, that he would be suffocated by the tight quarters, but he found it very charming.

Ezer leaned down to Letty and whispered, "Maybe, once all this is over, I'll look for a new place to work. Find a quieter place like this."

Through gritted teeth, in hopes to not make it noticeable that the voice came from him, Letty replied, "If you're going to leave Osmond's and work in a little place like this, why not make it your own little place?"

"I couldn't do that." Ezer shook his head with a bit too much fervor for anyone to believe he really meant what he was saying.

"And why not, exactly? You have more than enough money saved up. We live like paupers despite the fact that you make more than the average man here. If you're looking to leave anyway, I don't see how it would hurt to try."

"I don't know. I'll think about it."

The little pig nodded once and then curled up on the rug. His breathing slowed as he gave way to sleep. He was used to napping while Ezer was at work. So he took full advantage of the opportunity to rest.

They didn't have to wait long before a woman approached them. She was dressed similarly to the woman the sisters had met on their first day in Zaraneth. The girls were no longer fazed by any sort of attire. It was just how people were and how they dressed here.

The woman wasn't quite as traditionally attractive as the other woman, due to the many scars on her face. One scar ran from the right corner of her forehead across her eye to the bottom of her nose. Another ran along the left side of her face through her left eyebrow to her cheekbone. Her nose was deformed from being broken several times. Her lip was swollen and broken open from a more recent encounter. This woman had obviously been a victim of the lowlifes of this neighborhood on more than one occasion. But she was pretty despite her scars—and intimidating due to them.

The Center was not only home to the worst weather but also the worst people. No one, including Ezer, was really sure why that was the case. It wasn't as if they were forced to live together. No one made those sorts of rules in Zaraneth—

in fact, no one made any regulations at all. It just seemed to be that they all enjoyed living in groups. The closer to the borders you lived, the tamer you were.

Which was precisely why, after finding out Methuselah lived in The Center, Ezer wasn't at all surprised. If you were a good man who needed to not be found, taking up residence in The Center made sense. No one would ever have looked for a good man there.

"Whatcha gonna have?" the woman asked without looking up from the pad she had been staring at the whole time she was walking toward them.

"Five spiced creams, please," Ezer replied.

It was at the word "please" that the woman's head shot up. She squinted at them and sized each of them up individually. Then she huffed, shook her head, and said, "Don't remember the last time I heard that word. You three ain't from The Center, that's for sure." Her voice was gruff, her accent a mixture of the one Zaraneth had created by mixing all the regions' dialects together and a faint Southern region accent. If the scars hadn't told Ezer that she had been living here a long time, her Southern accent being overpowered by the Zaranethian accent would have.

He liked that Zaraneth was so separate from the rest of the world. To the outside world, her accent would have just been Zaranethian. Actually, the men in the rest of the regions probably wouldn't have even acknowledged that people actually claim Zaraneth willingly or that they like that they have their own accent. People had built their own culture here. Sure, a lot of the residents were unsavory, but many had left other regions willingly. Other people, like Ezer, were just the product of a family banished long ago.

This woman was first generation; the slight Southern accent made that clear. He noticed as she wrote down their order that her hands were even more scarred than her face. Her wrists had still-forming bruises—fresher than her busted lip.

Ezer was a firm believer that people will tell more of their stories than they would like. If you only are listening for the details, they are silently screaming. This woman was a fighter. By her even temperament, he guessed she only retaliated when attacked and didn't provoke.

"Well, the blizzard was just too bad. It wasn't safe to keep going like that," Ezer said, his comment directed both at the woman and the three sisters sitting around him.

The woman nodded knowingly. "Yeah. But good for business. Ya order will be right out. We always start fixin' spiced creams as soon as a blizzard starts up. It's the only time anyone might order something not spiked. Course, most folks ask for it spiked too." She chuckled before continuing. "That the way you want it?"

"No. Without is fine."

"Yeah. Y'all ain't from here." The woman huffed as she walked away.

"How long will this last? Do you think we will still make it there by the time we planned?" Gardeniyah asked.

"Too hard to tell. I have seen Center storms that are brutal but last only a few minutes, and I have seen them last a couple days, and other problems join in too. A tornado from the East quadrant could be moving in. The wind was picking up pretty quickly."

"How do you all live like this? It's dreadful!" Evanlee whined, leaning back in her chair and flipping her head back with dramatic exasperation, a trait that Ezer was beginning to realize was as ingrained in Evanlee as her vocabulary.

"Well, the weather is not ideal, I'll admit. But it's home. Wasn't always like this, or at least, that's what everyone says. Has gotten worse as the years have gone by."

"Why is that?"

"No one really knows. Apparently, a long time ago when my family first got sent here, it was a pretty normal place to live. It still had storms in The Center that would hit when a storm from somewhere else was moving in, since this is where all the storms go before they fizzle out. But the storms used to be very few and far between. Not like today."

"You don't ever want to leave? Find somewhere less . . . less ruthless?" Evanlee sighed and put her chin in her hand as she rested her elbow on the table. It was as if the idea of this place was enough to wear the girl—but not her dramatics —out.

"Less ruthless in what way?" Ezer asked.

"In every way!"

Ezer shrugged and looked out the window. "No, not really. This place is all I know. I'm not sure that I would know what to do with something less 'ruthless,' as you put it. My family has been here so long that it's where we are from now."

"That's so sad," Evanlee said.

"I don't think so. Home is where you're comfortable, right? I've got a life here. I've got Letty, my job, a decent little place to sleep." The pig, who looked over at the sound of his name, grinned from the rug at his inclusion in the rather small list of things his friend found important in life. Then Letty tucked his snout under his front legs and resumed his nap. "All the other stuff people get all worked up about," Ezer said, flipping his hand in the air, "well, I just don't get it. Everywhere you live is going to have a downside."

"Yeah, but where you live, there are constant natural disasters, and everyone is an outlaw."

"Evanlee, not everyone here is an outlaw," Gardeniyah said as she subtly tried to nod in Ezer's direction. Ezer looked at her as she did so, and Gardeniyah quickly attempted to cover the motion up by addressing him. "From what I've overheard, most of the women aren't. Right, Ezer?"

"Yeah, a lot of them are just on the run from someone, not always the law. They are usually pretty good people."

"Well, people aside, the weather is still awful!" Evanlee said, crossing her arms and leaning back in her chair as she glanced at the window that was being assaulted by wind and snow.

"Yeah, so?" Ezer shrugged. "From what I hear, in the North, they have thick, foul air, and it's overpopulated. And in the South, it's hot and dry, and everyone is miserable all the time because food is so scarce there now. Everyone abandoned the West long ago when the region's resources ran dry. Going back there is giving up any sort of civilization. Man has cycled through all the regions and made them all terrible except the East. Now they are back in the North because they left it alone long enough and it had a chance to get a little better than when they left it, but not much. Seems to me that no matter where I go there will be something bad about it. So why not stay in the only place I know? At least I know what to expect here. I know how this place works. I know how to get out of any trouble I may find myself in. Even better, I know how to avoid getting into any in the first place."

No one responded to Ezer. There wasn't much for anyone to say to that. The woman had returned with their drinks, so they all just sat in silence listening to the storm beat against the building and sipping their spiced creams. Ezer absently watched people mill about the tavern. Lorella scratched at the table with a fingernail, scowling. Evanlee stared into her mug. Gardeniyah was looking out the window at the snow whipping and whirling around angrily.

Ezer could tell he had upset them. Though he wasn't sure

why. Surely, they knew what the world was like out there. After all, wasn't that why they were on this mission? He couldn't think of any other reason they would have taken on this quest.

CHAPTER THIRTY-SIX

Gardeniyah was, despite the appearance she was hoping to keep up, obsessing over what Ezer had said. Unlike Evanlee, Gardeniyah understood why he didn't want to leave the place he knew. That's how they all felt about the East. Ever since she found out about this quest, she had been so focused on finding a way to go back there that she hadn't thought about what it would mean for her family if they failed. If they truly failed.

What would happen if the historian was a dead end? Where would they go? Ezer had done a great job pointing out the grim reality that nowhere was decent anymore. The North would be cold and crowded. Plus, she resented humans, so the idea of living in some cramped apartment in a city filled with the people they blamed for their misery was sickening.

The West was desolate. They would like the lack of people better, but they would surely get lonely without contact with anyone but each other. It wasn't like they all got along well enough to be each other's only company anyway.

The journey here had showed how very poorly they did when forced to interact only with each other.

People still lived in the South, but it was hot and getting hotter all the time. What used to be a location that would rival any tropical paradise was now a grueling place. Man had done an exceptional job of destroying the South. They had taken far more pleasure in that region than in the West, as it was so far removed from where they had been told they had to stay. So man had successfully depleted the South of its glory. And then they had moved on. Now, only the poorest, those who did not have the funds to move, still lived there.

She had experienced the grief that comes with the feeling of failure before, but, in the past, it hadn't really been her fault. She hadn't been the one unable to locate Methuselah. Osmond had been the one to fail. But now she held the key. Now the journey was real. Now it was as if she could actually feel the adventure and the chance to fix things in her hand. None of her companions knew she had wavered in belief the very day that they would get the first significant lead they had since leaving the East.

The old man and his gift of information had given her new hope. But now the weight of her family's survival suddenly felt heavy all over again. Gardeniyah had been clinging to this possibility with dear life. The far-off dream was just that: a dream. It was something to work toward. A goal. Before, the possibility of failure had been a far-off thing; now it was right before her.

A dream itself is a great thing. It makes scary things in life worth facing. You have something to cling to when the world feels dark. The problem with chasing a dream is that, eventually, you get to the point where you must do *something* if you ever want it to happen.

And that's when it all changes. See, the closer you get to

fulfilling a dream, the less of a dream it becomes. Soon it becomes reality. That's when the thing that used to give you hope in the scary times becomes the thing you fear. There are few things in any world more terrifying than the reality that the basis of your hope can become the source of your distress.

It was in this state that Gardeniyah sat in the tiny tavern, wrestling with the fact that the very thing that had made her hopeful—the feeling she'd relied on to continue and to encourage her sisters—now absolutely terrified her. She no longer wished that blizzard would pass quickly. If it never ended, then they could stay in this tavern isolated from the rest of the world forever. And she would never have to face all the decisions and responsibilities that would come as soon as they walked back out that door.

Gardeniyah got her wish, to a degree. The storm did last an awfully long time. By the time it stopped, it was nightfall.

"We can't go to Methuselah's now." Gardeniyah huffed as the wind announced its wrath was finally over by whistling gently.

"Why not?" Lorella said, frowning.

"It would be rude," Gardeniyah replied.

"Who cares? It's not our fault the storm hit."

"I don't want to start out on the wrong foot with him."

"Surely, you don't think a man who stood up to a king and has lived in Zaraneth for the last who knows how long would be that petty, do you?"

"Lorella, it's disrespectful."

Evanlee, Letty, and Ezer sat silently watching the argument play out. None of them had any interest in becoming involved in the power struggle that was on display before them.

"Are they always like this?" Letty whispered to Evanlee.

"No, usually it's me and Lorella going at it," Evanlee

replied. "Lorella usually goes along with whatever Gardeniyah says."

Letty looked intrigued as he watched the rest of the disagreement unfold. Unbeknownst to Evanlee, the pig was rather fond of drama. The struggle of power and selfishness between man was a peculiar thing, and he loved it. So while Evanlee and Ezer were uncomfortable during the whole ordeal, Letty was fully enjoying the moment.

"Well, I think we should go tonight."

"I don't recall asking for your opinion." Gardeniyah's words were flat and matter-of-fact, but her eyes were flaming. Lorella's nostrils flared and her eye color grew darker.

The rest of the group was frozen. Letty and Ezer were staring wide-eyed at the girls. Neither of them knew the girls well enough to be sure what this sort of comment would do. Evanlee did, though. These sorts of arguments were few and far between—though they had become more frequent during this journey. They always shifted the balance of the relationships between the sisters.

Evanlee knew she should say something. But out of pure self-preservation, she didn't. She knew if she spoke up, she would become Lorella's new target.

Finally, Lorella's voice interrupted the tense silence.

"Funny, I don't remember needing your permission to speak my mind. I am an adult. That's the whole reason we got kicked out of the East. If I want to go tonight, then I will go."

"Fine. Then you'll go alone."

"Oh, so you speak for everyone now? Should I warn the Northern King about you? I think I should, since you think you're in control of things."

"I speak for her," Gardeniyah said, nodding toward Evanlee. "And I'm the only one who knows what the old man said. And he," Gardeniyah said, pointing at Ezer, "is the only one who knows how to get there. So we need each other. We don't need you. So go."

Gardeniyah knew she'd gone too far. She hated to get mad. It took her far too long, and far too many terrible things being said, before she could calm down.

The two of them just sat there glaring at each other for what seemed like an eternity to their audience. It was once again Lorella who broke the silence. Lorella only had two modes when she was mad: she either froze you out, or she told you exactly what she was thinking, although maybe not exactly, since much of what she said was sarcastic. But she was always sure her point was known.

"One day I'm going to take you up on that and you'll realize just how much you really do need me. But it will be too late."

"You're being such a child . . . Let's go, everyone. We need somewhere to spend the night." With that statement Gardeniyah and the rest of the group got up from the table.

"Whatever you say, Your Majesty," Lorella said, bowing as Gardeniyah walked past her and out the door. Just to prove her point, Lorella stayed bowed until the rest of the group had walked by as well. Then she followed behind them silently stewing.

The group wordlessly walked down to a place called Allen's Inn about a quarter mile from the tavern. It was the dingiest place any of them had ever been to. The floor was sticky, and paint was peeling off the wall every couple feet. Each peel was a different depth, revealing hidden layers beneath, making any one room at least seven different—but all equally hideous—colors.

"We will take two rooms, please," Ezer told the man at the front desk.

"Ha! Yous must not be from around here." The man

sneered. Ezer was beginning to get annoyed at hearing how much he didn't seem like he belonged here. Especially after just giving the girls a talk about how this place was home. "In this part of Zaraneth, we don't have those sorts of luxuries." The man slurred, struggling with every other syllable. "It's one room. Yous rent the bed, not the room. How many beds?"

Ezer looked to Gardeniyah. "How many? Letty likes fires and heaters, so he will sleep there if there's a rug."

"Yous gotta pays for a spot for the pig too!" the man practically growled.

"If that's the case," Gardeniyah responded, "we can make do with one for us."

"All right. We will take two beds and a spot for the pig."

"Fifty-seven shicklings."

"That's ridiculous! For this dump?" Lorella said.

"Now it's sixty-seven."

Ezer shook his head at the man. He would leave, but despite everyone's accusations, he was, in fact, from around here. He knew that all the places around here would be the same. So he paid the man and then they were escorted to the back room.

The room was not overly large. Considering the amount of beds, it should have been much larger. Instead, the twelve beds were pushed together as tightly as possible, making personal space nonexistent.

The sleeping chamber smelled of spilled drinks and body odor. The heater lamp was not big enough for the room. So it was either blistering hot next to it or extremely cold anywhere else. Covering up with blankets wasn't an option either. The "blankets" were pieces of thin fabric—pieces of old clothing, by the looks of it—which were stitched together in a single layer. The pillows were similar. There was no rhyme or reason to the size or shape—just patchwork fabric stitched together with what felt like more wadded-up fabric inside.

"This is terrible," Evanlee mumbled as she tried stacking multiple blankets on the bed to make it a little more comfortable. This worked momentarily until the man came through and ripped the extras of their bed, informing them that more blankets cost extra. None of them were willing to pay the greedy fellow.

"Well, at least it's indoors and some sort of bed," Gardeniyah said, trying to add some optimism. "Remember how miserable we were on the trip to Zaraneth? We would have given anything for this dump."

"Yeah, who would have thought somewhere could have made Osmond's look like a palace?" Lorella said, looking at Ezer teasingly. He did not give her the reaction she wanted. He simply shrugged and nodded knowingly. Gardeniyah frowned at the exchange between the two but said nothing.

The pep talk and the reminder of the awful conditions of their journey worked for a little while. The sisters all fell asleep slowly and huddled up next to each other both for warmth and due to the size of the bed. They had made peace with the awful place they were spending the night. That is until Evanlee let out a screech.

"Something just bit me!" she cried.

Suddenly everyone in the room was jumping out of bed and swatting bugs off of them. Night creepers were crawling out of the "pillows."

The girls stood and lit a lamp but immediately wished they hadn't. The place was crawling with bugs. The floor, the beds, and the walls. The five of them grabbed their things and rushed out of the inn.

They didn't care that it was the middle of the night. Or that an Eastern storm had moved in and it was now pouring down rain. They didn't care how much they had paid. They would not spend the night in that place. So, in the pouring rain, they walked down the road to yet another tavern.

They were miserable in the new tavern. They were wet and tired and it was extremely loud. Every time Ezer stepped away from the table, men came over to try to toy with the sisters. Lorella would quickly conjure up a response to their advances that would leave them embarrassed and retreating.

They hung out there until the place closed down. Which, thankfully, was only about an hour before daybreak. Luckily, a few eateries that served food to those who had been out all night participating in the nightlife were opening up as the taverns closed down. So they ventured to one of those establishments to pass the last few hours until it was socially acceptable to go to Methuselah's house.

When Gardeniyah had wished to postpone visiting him, she hadn't realized just how nagging the anxiety would be. It had gnawed at her all night long with not even sleep to occupy a few hours. Now, no matter what they found, or didn't find, she just wanted to get it over with so she could move on . . . Whatever that meant for them.

Their whole week in Zaraneth, actually their whole time since they'd left the East, felt like last night. A constant state of flux going from bad to worse to a little better to even worse than before. All the while filled with constant anxiety and uncertainty. She was ready for it to end. She could tell her sisters were too. As she gathered up their stuff once again and walked out the door of the eatery, she realized that her dream was about to either begin anew—or end.

CHAPTER THIRTY-SEVEN

Thankfully, they didn't have to interact with anyone outside of their group on the way to the historian—other than dodging the people around them who were acting foolishly and stumbling out of taverns and eateries intoxicated with the previous night's events and lack of sleep. Due to the uneventful nature of their walk, they arrived at Methuselah's rumored home midmorning.

The building was in the heart of The Center. It was on the top floor of a building that was long past its prime. Even though it was old, it was well maintained in comparison to the other buildings nearby. They climbed a flight of stairs that wrapped around from the front of the building to a door at the back. No numbers marked the homes, but the directions the mysterious old man had given Gardeniyah led directly to where he said the building would be.

After heading up the few steps to the door, Gardeniyah's hand felt like a ton of bricks as she reached up to knock. However, only a barely audible sound came from the contact of her hand and the door, making it very clear that it was far from a ton of anything hitting the door.

"Um. I could be wrong, but I think you are going to have to knock a bit harder than that," Letty whispered to Gardeniyah.

"That's an understatement," Lorella mumbled from behind her.

Gardeniyah's face flushed. She hated showing when she was nervous. She could feel Lorella's annoyed presence directly behind her. She cast a glance over her shoulder and caught sight of Ezer smiling ever so slightly, but very reassuringly, at her. She lifted her hand, forcing it to be steadier this time, and knocked again.

No answer came, not even after several minutes. Gardeniyah turned to face the group behind her with questioning eyes.

"Wasn't you that time," Ezer said, shaking his head, once more reassuring her.

She sighed deeply and nodded. She would have to try again. Knocking on a door had never seemed so intimidating. The last time she had stood before a door, her whole life had changed. This door was nowhere near as grand, but it held just as many questions behind it. Only, this time, she hoped it held some answers too.

Despite the more forceful knock, no answer came. Gardeniyah's heart felt like an anchor sinking to her toes, pulling her stomach down with it. This was what she had been dreading. The true dead end. To come this far and be out of options.

She knocked again. Over and over, this time, knocking harder and quicker with each second that went by. She didn't realize how frantically she was banging on the door until she felt Ezer's hand on her arm. She looked over her shoulder with her fists still on the door.

She scanned their faces and their eyes, hoping to find some sort of comfort. Right now, she didn't want to be the voice of reason. She didn't want to be the strong one. She wanted to get strength from someone else—anyone else. Evanlee had tears in her eyes. Lorella's eyes were distant. In Ezer's eyes, she saw the look she was hoping for.

"We should go," he said flatly in his deep voice, which contained a hint of sympathy.

She nodded as he released her arm, and she let her hands fall from the door. As they all turned around to walk down the steps, Letty stepped out of the way to let them past, putting his back to the railing so he was still facing the house. Lorella and Evanlee were already on the ground with Gardeniyah and Ezer not far behind them when Letty suddenly let out a cry.

"Hey! There's someone in there. I just saw someone in the window!"

The four of them rushed back up the steps toward the door. Lorella, who did not ever appreciate being ignored, was the first one to the door. She began to bang on the door with such force its weak infrastructure quaked beneath her fists.

"We saw you! You can't hide in there now! We aren't leaving until you let us in!" Lorella yelled.

Evanlee went for a different approach. "Please, sir, we don't mean any harm to you!"

Gardeniyah just stood back.

She felt too emotionally drained to try to coax the man into opening the door. Besides, she didn't need to lead everything. That sort of thought process was a new one for her; it was quite contrary to her argument with Lorella the night before. Despite what her pride may have wanted in this moment of weakness, stepping back felt like her only option.

It took her several minutes in that foggy state to notice that Ezer and Letty were no longer with them on the stairwell. She only noticed because the strong presence she had been finding some comfort in was now absent.

Gardeniyah didn't say anything to her sisters. They were still busy trying to get the man to answer the door. She didn't see any sense in interrupting them to ask if they had seen where the others had gone.

Now that it appeared as though the historian wasn't willing to speak to them, had Ezer and Letty just decided that there was no point in sticking around? After all, Ezer had said he was just curious about hearing what the man had to say and that they would be going separate ways after that. *Then there was all that he had said about Zaraneth being home*, Gardeniyah thought, a strange feeling of disappointment creeping up.

Right about the time she had convinced herself this was the case, she saw something move in the corner of her eye. Ezer and Letty were coming around the side of the building next door. Ezer was carrying a large crate, and Letty was attempting to keep up and push a medium-size one at the same time.

Gardeniyah was confused and almost called out to ask them what on earth they were doing—instead, she just watched.

Ezer pushed his crate against the wall directly below the window to the right of the door her sisters were banging on. He then walked a few feet to where Letty was still struggling to push the crate, and he picked it and the little pig up, one in each hand. He walked back to the wall, placing Letty on the ground—who was scowling at being rushed in such a manner. Ezer shook his head at the pig and then set Letty's crate on top of his own.

Gardeniyah scanned the house once again. She noticed that the windows were as old as the building itself. They were the same type that Osmond's Tavern had. More importantly, the same kind that the castle at Relis had.

A smile crept across her face. The windows, though tough to budge, didn't have locks. Just like the window to the library at the castle at Relis. Of course, many of the people who lived in the lower levels of the homes that were like this had boarded the windows up because of this lapse of security. However, many of the upper level owners had left theirs open. Luckily for them, Methuselah was one who had not boarded up his window.

Ezer climbed to the top of the crates and reached down to help Letty up. He then lifted the pig to stand on his broad shoulders. Once he was steady on top of Ezer's shoulder, Letty leaned all his weight against the window. Ezer put his hands on the wall of the building, holding himself in the push-up position he had made the girls practice—much to Evanlee's dismay—the whole week.

With the new angle, the little pig's weight had just the right amount of force. The window soon popped open quietly and ever so slightly. Letty scrambled up to the ledge, his hooves kicking in midair as his torso was balanced on the ledge attempting to get momentum to go through the window. After a few moments of this, Letty was successful and he disappeared through the window.

Ezer hopped down off the crates and pushed them back around the corner, then made his way back up the stairs. Gardeniyah turned around to give him a grateful smile.

"You saw us?" he whispered into her ear.

"Yes. Clever. Thank you," she whispered back.

"You three worked too hard to get here to be locked out. But don't thank me yet; let's see if the little pig will let us in," he said with a crooked smile that Gardeniyah had never seen him use but rather liked.

"You didn't tell them?" he said, nodding to the two girls

who were still relentlessly calling out and banging on the door.

"I thought about it, but I figured the distraction would make it easier for Letty to sneak in."

"Clever. Thank you," he said, imitating her words from before. This time, his smile was accompanied by a quick wink.

Gardeniyah quickly turned back toward the door. She could feel her face flushing in a way she was not familiar with and, unlike that smile of his, she didn't like. Though she hated to ever blush, it turned out to be excellent timing because, right as she turned around, she saw the door ease open with a pig hanging from the handle, much like the time they had first met Letty a couple days before.

"You have to be the best pig in the world!" Evanlee said, letting out a squeal that rivaled that of Letty, or any pig.

Letty grinned and stepped aside for the four of them to enter. The home was a small—very small. The front door opened to a short hallway with another door almost directly to the right that led into the room Letty had climbed into through the window. The door was still open, so as they walked by, Gardeniyah glanced in and saw that it was the bedroom. The room was so small that it would be rather difficult to maneuver around. The single bed took up most of the room, and so there was just a narrow path leading from the door to a closet.

They continued straight into the main living quarters. A sink and a lone counter beside a wood-burning stove stood off to the far-left corner. Along the same wall was a desk that faced out the window rather than into the room. A few chairs sat in the center of the room facing each other, a time-worn couch between them. They walked to the center of the room, looking around for the person who had peered through the window.

"Well, where is—?"

Just as Lorella began to ask the question on all their minds, a man popped out from behind a coatrack against the wall of the hallway that was now behind them. The man screamed as he swung a cane at them—shouting with each swing for them to leave his house. The girls ducked the slow attempted blows. The man kicked Letty, who returned the assault with a bite to the man's leg. After a very long minute of chaos, Ezer grabbed the cane midswing and yanked it from the man's surprisingly strong grip.

The old man stumbled and fell into one of the chairs, knocking it over, then scooted across the floor to the wall. He put his trembling hands in front of him, bracing himself for Ezer to start hitting him with the cane.

"I'm not going to hit you," Ezer said with a huff as he dropped the cane.

The man lowered his hands and began to rub where Letty had bitten him. Thankfully, he wasn't bleeding. The man squinted as he eyed them all but didn't move from his place on the ground. When his gaze fell on Letty, he glared at the pig. Letty snorted in response. Their distaste for each other was clearly mutual. Then the elderly man eyed Ezer.

Finally, his eyes made their way to the girls. He looked each one of them up and down in an equally suspicious manner. The girls stood, unmoving. They didn't want startle the man again.

"We just want to talk," Gardeniyah said gently.

The man looked puzzled. He looked at them once more—this time with less suspicion. His gaze was more mystified, as if they were a bizarre puzzle from another world.

After a moment, the man began to count on his hands. His eyes grew wide. He popped up swiftly, especially for his age, and began to hobble over to his desk. He was clearly having difficulty. Evanlee grabbed the man's cane and rushed to hand it to him. The movement spooked him, but only for a second. When he saw Evanlee's smile, he nodded, took the cane, and began to walk once more toward his desk.

He shuffled some papers around. He huffed and opened the single drawer to the left. The desk was ill made, and when he opened the drawer, the whole desk swayed and creaked. But the drawer contained the paper he was looking for. He scanned it once and then looked at the girls once more. He scanned it again. He placed the paper on the desk and grabbed a scrap piece of paper and scribbled down numbers Gardeniyah could barely make out. They were dates—that much was clear.

The girls all looked at each other, then back to the old man. A moment later, the man stopped what he was doing. He breathed in sharply. His eyes were now enormously big, like the pictures Gardeniyah had seen of a full moon during harvest in the West.

Gardeniyah was sure that if they got any bigger, they would pop out of his head. They didn't, though, and in an almost gasping way, his body tense, he said two words that rang through the air in such a way that it sounded louder than any bell they had ever heard.

It's peculiar how a few small words can change everything. The more unexpected they are, the more powerful they are. The queen's words about the quest had changed everything for them. And now this old man's words were about to change the way the girls and their new companions saw this journey. The way they saw their lives. More or less, they would change everything.

"It's you!"

CHAPTER THIRTY-EIGHT

"I can't believe it's you," the historian muttered, shaking his head. "I had given up that you were coming. You're a year late, you know," Methuselah said frantically as he paced around the room.

"Do you know this guy?" Letty whispered to Evanlee.

"No. We've never met him."

"He seems to know you."

"I know. Gardeniyah, what is he talking about?"

Gardeniyah was frozen. Her whole body was cold and numb. The words of the prophecy kept playing over and over in her mind like a song stuck in her head.

Her sisters hadn't read the prophecy. They just thought that meeting the historian was something Sanora wanted them to do. To them, it had been just a way to return home. It had never, to their knowledge, been an order from the Omniscient and a prophecy set in stone.

Gardeniyah had read the prophecy, and even she didn't realize that it was specifically about them. She thought it could have been any human—that they were just the East's best bet because they'd grown up there and loved it.

"Gardeniyah?" This time it was Lorella speaking. "Do you know what he's talking about?"

The man was now back at his desk shuffling through papers and muttering to himself some more. Gardeniyah almost opened her mouth to tell them. If she did, her burden, not just in this moment but since they'd left, might be eased. Her sisters hadn't been as adamant about this journey as she had. They would understand the importance if she told them. The weight of it would be shared. They'd know that if they failed, "the forthcoming end comes fast." They would carry those haunting words with them too.

"No. I have no idea."

She didn't want them to know. Not yet. She wasn't doing a great job at sheltering them as of late. They had to watch her nearly get killed, Evanlee had almost been kidnapped, and Lorella almost drowned. She hadn't protected them from the severe disappointments that kept happening, not to mention bugs attacking them and evil men's crude comments. Gardeniyah had been the direct cause of Lorella's pain the night before. If it hadn't been for Letty and Ezer, they wouldn't have made it in the door—and she would have failed them yet again.

She wouldn't fail them in this. Her strength would be enough. She wouldn't put that burden on them. She would protect them, at least for now. She had told herself that she would keep the secret about the prophecy until they were no longer all on board. For now, they still were. She would keep that promise to herself. She just needed the rambling old man to not say too much.

"Well, then, he needs to stop this nonsense and tell us! Hey, old man, what are you talking about?" Lorella said louder than necessary.

The man was not fazed by Lorella's yelling. He just continued to look through scraps of papers in various drawers. No one bothered to try again. They figured he would eventually address them again.

"Aha!" he called out as he grabbed a piece of paper and waved it in the air like a flag proclaiming his victory.

Gardeniyah's heart rose to her ears and began pounding intensely. She squinted as hard as she could to see if the writing looked like the letter in the library, but the man's joyful waving made it impossible to make anything out.

"I know you all don't know me. But I've been waiting on all of you! Well, not really you," he said, pointing to the pig that had bit him. "Or you, for that matter," he added, squinting at Ezer. "But you three, yes, yes, yes, I have been waiting on you," he said, shuffling toward them, his cane clicking rapidly on the creaky hardwood floor.

Gardeniyah studied the many deep wrinkles on the man's face. He had to be well over a hundred. His feeble walk as he reached from object to object, even with the assistance of his cane, was equal parts charming and heart wrenching. As he got closer to Gardeniyah, she started to feel her body get warm and her head get light.

It's a terrible feeling not being able to protect the ones you love. She could see how terribly this situation could go, and she wanted with all her might to stop it. She tore through her mind for a way to stop him from speaking. A way to make sure her sisters didn't get hurt. She didn't want this for them. No one wants pain for those they love. For people like Gardeniyah who take being a nurturer on as a personal responsibility, the moments before a truth comes out that can hurt the people you hold dearest are pure agony.

"Why have you been waiting for us, Methuselah?" Lorella's arms were folded and her eyes narrowed. It hadn't taken very long for Lorella to agree with everyone else in this city. People couldn't be trusted, not even the feeble old man before them.

"Please, call me Sulley."

"Okay, Sulley, why have you been waiting for us?"

"Why, because Sanora told me to!"

Gardeniyah had thought her heart couldn't race any faster. She was wrong. It could and it did. *There it is. He knows. He knows and he's going to tell them!* her mind was yelling, and her head was pounding as hard as her heart now.

"What do you mean Sanora told you?" Lorella asked.

"See, I knew you would ask that question! That's why I found this before I started trying to talk to you. Yes, yes, yes, that's why I found it first." He was holding up the piece of paper and waving it back and forth again as he sat down in one of the chairs in his living area. "Sit. Sit. Sit. We have much to discuss. Sit. Sit. Sit."

Gardeniyah was wobbly as she made her way to the couch to sit next to her sisters. She hadn't realized that the others had all moved farther into the room while she had remained frozen in place. Methuselah was dragging out telling them. And it felt as if he was dragging her heart along with him and his slow repetitive words.

"Would you like something to drink—maybe some tea? I don't have any spiced cream, though, on a cold day like this, I wish I did. Maybe some water? Are you hungry?"

"Will you please just explain how you know us?" Gardeniyah blurted out before she could stop herself. Though she didn't want him to say a word to her sisters about the prophecy, her mind was just too tired from the last few minutes of torture.

"I thought I already had? Sanora told me about you. I could have sworn I just said that." The man looked down and to the left as he said the words, shaking his head before he got up and walked toward his small kitchen. He began making himself some tea, pouring hot water out of the kettle on the stove.

"I'll take some," Evanlee piped up. When everyone looked at her with questioning faces, she defended herself quietly. "What? Seems important to him."

It obviously was, once they bothered to pay attention, because the eccentric man perked up and began to whistle as he got another cup down from the single shelf above his one counter next to his wood-burning stove. Gardeniyah was annoyed that her sister had made such an obvious observation that she had clearly missed. After he poured the tea, he handed Evanlee her cup, then sat down.

"As I was saying, I was starting to think you weren't coming. You're quite late. A year late, in fact."

"Well, we didn't know anyone was expecting us," Lorella said dryly.

"Mm-hmm, rather odd Queen Ranosa didn't tell you."

"Well, she wasn't even sure you were still alive," Evanlee added. She didn't usually talk this much to a stranger. But, from the way she was smiling and talking, she clearly didn't feel the same as Lorella. She'd liked the man instantly.

"Ha! Yes. Yes, yes. I suppose I have been around a while. Well, I am a Varkin, you know. I don't know how much you know about genealogy of the North, but Varkins, well, we live a long time usually. No one is quite sure why The Omniscient gave our clan such long lives but we typically live about a hundred and twenty-five years. But it made us good storytellers and good historians. But the fact that I am still alive, well, you—and I suppose I, as well—can thank Sanora for that," he said, waving his finger in the air wildly. "I was on my last leg before she left. My very last leg. The very last. I was old, even for a Varkin. She gave me a potion from the Omniscient himself, though. It gave me a little boost and kept me going to wait on you three."

"How old are you, exactly?" Ezer's face was clearly showing his skepticism.

"I will be one hundred and eighty-seven next week! Quite a life I've lived, quite a lot I've seen, yes, yes, yes, quite a lot."

"I have never heard of a human living that long," Ezer said, shaking his head.

"I just explained that. I had a potion." Sulley looked to Lorella and asked, "Where did you find this guy? He seems a little dense." Lorella erupted with deep laughter. Gardeniyah hadn't heard her laugh like that in quite some time. Even Evanlee laughed. Gardeniyah was still solemn, staring at her feet. Ezer realized this in the middle of rolling his eyes.

"You all right?" Ezer whispered to Gardeniyah.

"I'm fine."

"That's obviously a lie."

"Drop it."

Ezer didn't say another word. He put his hands up as if surrendering and leaned back against the chair he was sitting in.

"So what did Sanora say that tipped you off about us coming?" Lorella asked.

"She wrote me a letter that told me about a prophecy. It said that someone from the race of man—who is, of course, responsible for all of this madness—would come and fix everything, restore order. They just had to choose to. When a year passed after you would have been eighteen," he said, turning his attention to Gardeniyah, "I thought maybe you had chosen not to. That would be bad. Very bad. You're our only hope. It wasn't hard to figure out it would be you three."

Gardeniyah perked up; he had clearly been told about the same prophecy. If that was all he planned to say about it, though, then she was fine. He just had to leave out the part about the "forthcoming end."

"Oh. Wow. Well, we would have come last year if we'd known. They let us stay a year longer because they didn't want Gardeniyah to have to deal with taking care of all of us.

But now I think we could have handled it. And we would have tried if we had known you were waiting," Evanlee sweetly explained.

"Ranosa didn't tell you about the prophecy?"

"She knew?" Lorella eyes flashed with annoyance.

"Why, yes. Of course she did. Sanora left her a letter."

"Yeah, we know about the letter. Ranosa mentioned it before," Lorella said.

"Well, that letter explained the prophecy."

Lorella was fuming. Whether it was because she was mad they had lost a year and maybe this journey could be over already or because she didn't like having things kept from her, Gardeniyah couldn't tell. She figured that it was the latter of the two, though, which made her face grow red and hot with guilt.

However, she quickly recovered. Gardeniyah didn't have the energy to care about why that statement was upsetting her sister. This had been the most mentally draining few hours of her life.

She was exhausted. But she knew she needed to act like the older sister and leader of this group. She had to snap out of it and ask the questions they needed answered, and so she did.

"So, I guess since you have been expecting us, you won't mind sharing what you know? We were afraid that it might take some convincing."

"Oh, I would be happy to! Yes, yes, yes, very happy to! Did Ranosa tell you about the book?"

"Yes. She also said there was a good chance you would know some details about it. Like where it might be, or where she might be, or something."

"Yes, yes, yes. All in good time, I assure you. What's important is why you need to find the book."

"We know why," Gardeniyah said. "Ranosa told us it holds

some sort of spell. That the spell will help us put things right again. Restore order."

"Yes, good, good, good. That's correct. Now, I think to find the book we need to get inside Sanora's mind."

"We were kind of hoping you had already done that, to be honest," Lorella chimed back, rejoining the conversation. Her eyes were harder and more distant than they had been when they'd first arrived, but they weren't as angry as they had been moments before.

"Yeah, Ranosa told us that you were the one who knew her best and that you probably were already inside her mind in a way," Evanlee said, trying very hard to be a part of this conversation. Gardeniyah smiled at her. She seemed more grown up than ever.

"Well, I suppose that could be argued to be true. I have been searching my notes for years trying to find out where she might have put it. I think that we should all try. So, to do that, I think it's best you hear her own words."

Sulley began to read the paper in his hand aloud. It was the letter Sanora had written to him:

My dear friend,

I am sending you this letter because I will not be visiting again this year or for many years to come. The world is a hurting place right now. It has been for many human lifetimes. Your old age has let you see more of this hurt than I would have wished on you. However, I cannot let you leave our world and find true peace just yet. I know that your body is failing and that you have come to terms with the end. You have lived a good life. One that any person would be wise to be envious of. However, your work for our world is not yet done.

I told you when I visited with you last that I'd met with the Omniscient. It was the first time in five hundred years. I do not know why he stayed away for so long. At first, I was angry with him. I thought maybe if he hadn't been gone for so long, if he had intervened more, then man wouldn't have forgotten his power. Most don't even believe he exists anymore. I know that it was not the correct way to handle it. He always wanted us to keep things the way they were supposed to be because we wanted to keep the promises we made, not because he forced us.

He has explained to me that it is important that someone from the race of man be the one to fix it. I immediately hoped he was referring to you. He has specific people in mind, though. I think you will be able to figure out who they are by the prophecy I will leave you.

They will come to you when the time is right. When they do, they will be looking for me and the book. The book has directions on the fail-safe spell that the other Founders and I created. They will need to follow it exactly. First, though, they will need to find the book.

I have hidden my book. I needed it to be somewhere safe. If the wrong descendant of King Madeous got their hands on it, the world would be doomed. It holds too much power.

I have hidden it in a place that is representative of all of the Founders. The book has power because of each of us and, more importantly, because of the Omniscient. Therefore, it needed to be hidden accordingly.

Guide them, Sulley—they will need you. We all depend on it. I have faith in all of you.

Love and blessings now and on your future journey,

Sanora

CHAPTER THIRTY-NINE

"Well, that was not as helpful as I was hoping it would be," Lorella said after Sulley had finished reading Sanora's letter.

"I know that probably didn't have all the details you wanted, but I think if we all work together, we can come up with a few places to start looking."

With that, he got up and went over to the desk and picked out a few stacks of papers and divided them up between all of them.

"Look through these. They are notes about conversations I had with Sanora, and there are also letters she sent me and pieces of history I think will help."

"I don't see how you think we will be any help if you can't figure it out yourself. You actually knew her," Lorella said as she scanned the rather large stack of papers Sulley had given her.

"Well, four heads are better than one." He looked up at Letty and Ezer. "I mean, six heads. I keep forgetting you two are here."

They all fell silent and began to look through their stacks.

They read for hours and hours, taking notes and looking for any little clue they could find.

They worked individually for some time. But, as anyone knows who has pored over a tedious task for a very long time, the work eventually becomes mind numbing and even duller than you'd anticipated.

About two hours into the literary scavenger hunt, Lorella became quite sure that she would lose her mind at any moment. Her brain felt as if it had been turned to mush, liquefied by Sulley's rambling notes that were all but incoherent to her.

In desperation, the young woman, despite rather liking her solitude, suggested they all pair up to work. Gardeniyah and Ezer were already comparing notes they had made, and so they were a natural duo. Evanlee hopped up quickly and made her way over to Sulley. It looked as if Lorella would be by herself, but a moment later, Letty got up from in front of the stove where he had been napping and joined her.

"Now, Miss Lorella, I know I can't read, but I am a smart pig. I could be of some help if you were to read it out to me. My big ears make it easy for me to hear. You wouldn't have to be very loud."

Lorella saw the pleading look in the pig's big, round eyes. He desperately wanted to be needed. She knew that feeling all too well.

She smiled at him and said, "I couldn't think of a better partner. We need a beast's point of view." The little pig beamed, and Lorella felt the warmth of it in her heart. She returned the smile before clearing her throat and then explained the note she was currently holding.

"Okay, here's a note about a meeting of the kings and queens, dated a hundred years ago, but Sulley wrote this a while ago, and it's from Sanora's point of view, so it probably took place before then." The little pig nodded his agreement.

Lorella began to read Methuselah's note aloud: "'The King of Men only has one son. It is all they have every had. There has been but one exception and that was due to King Bramah's infidelity.'"

"Is there more?" Letty asked.

"No. It stops there."

"Peculiar place to end a story."

"He seems to be a peculiar man."

"Agreed. What does the next one say?"

"This is a letter directly from Sanora."

"Perhaps that will be more helpful."

"'I hate that things are the way they are now,'" Lorella began reading. "'The humans are growing tired of the South. They have used up almost all of their recourses there. I fear for what their next course of action will be. I long for the days where we all communed together yearly. Our meeting places were always lovely and the company better. A new king of man will be coming of age soon. I wonder what he will do with the future. It has been three hundred years since I last sat in the company of a king of man, and yet it still feels so strange not to know the man who leads the humans. I always looked forward to those meetings; it was a time of friendship and true diplomacy. Now I keep my borders and my heart shut to man.'"

"Doesn't this stuff just make you feel terrible about humans, Lorella?" Evanlee said from across the room.

"You should be focusing on your piles, Evanlee," Lorella said.

Evanlee scrunched her face and muttered, "Fine."

"It's not like we chose to be human or even did any of this." Lorella huffed.

"If we can figure all this out maybe we will be able to not feel crummy at all," Gardeniyah chimed in without looking up from her notes. She looked to be in her element among the piles of information. While Lorella and Evanlee already appeared exhausted, Gardeniyah looked as content as Sulley poring over the information.

∼

After several more hours, Gardeniyah suggested they stop for the day. The Lights of the Four Corners had set an hour before. And while Sulley had gathered all the candles he had, the room was still dimly lit. Gardeniyah's eyes were tired; she knew everyone else's were too. It had been a long day.

"Sulley, is it all right if we stay with you? We haven't had much luck at the inns around here," Gardeniyah asked.

"Of course, of course, of course. I wouldn't have it any other way."

With that, Sulley went into his bedroom. The girls, Ezer, and Letty found spaces around the living room to sleep. Everyone but Gardeniyah fell asleep easily and slept soundly that first night.

In the morning, they would wake up and feel refreshed despite sleeping in small chairs, on old lumpy couches, and on rugs by the fire. Gardeniyah would have no such luck.

She had been fortunate thus far to not have had another dream like the one she'd had back in the North. However, tonight her dreams were once again plagued with memories.

The air in her dream was hot and thick. The glowing flame of a campfire before her was as tall as she was—which wasn't saying a lot. She was only four in the dream.

She could hear Lorella's little voice humming from somewhere across the fire. Then it stopped. She walked around the fire and sat down next to their mother and said, "Mama, where are we going? Where's Father and Bai?"

Who's Bai? Gardeniyah wondered in her dream. She tried to ask her mother, but just like in her previous dream, anything she hadn't done in the past she couldn't do now. And the little version of herself knew who Bai was.

Her head turned to look at her mother, who was not looking at either of the older sisters but was looking down at tiny Evanlee in her arms. She was stroking the baby's face with her finger. As she rocked back and forth with Evanlee, a tear rolled down from her sad blue eyes. But then a small smile, one that a grown Gardeniyah would have easily spotted as fake, spread across her slim face.

"Why, darling, we are on an adventure. An adventure no boys are allowed on! That's why they are not here."

The answer satisfied Lorella and the conversation stopped. The last thing Gardeniyah heard was her mother's soft voice singing a song that, even in the dream state, Gardeniyah didn't remember the words to.

Gardeniyah woke up wide awake as the little version of herself closed her eyes. She felt more tired than ever after the scene that had played out before her. She tried hard to recall the details of the dream but found it was too difficult. She knew it was a memory. One she wanted to remember. But all she could recall of the dream was the name. "Bai."

She didn't know what the word meant because she couldn't remember the question Lorella had asked. She didn't even remember that it was a name. All the same, her mind replayed the word over and over as she fell back asleep. Her mind was begging her subconscious to share with her conscious mind the information it was withholding. But it refused, and so only the word remained.

Bai.

CHAPTER FORTY

It had been several days and Lorella was growing very tired of coming up empty-handed. She felt like she was seeing the same things over and over. No one else seemed to be finding any leads either. Whenever she overheard something someone else found, it sounded exactly like what she had just read. And none of it appeared to be what they needed.

She was tired of reading letters from this mysterious fairy Sanora. She was even more tired of reading accounts written down by Sulley, a man she deemed a borderline kook. He was repetitive. His descriptions contained details Lorella found completely unnecessary. She would never understand why he felt the need to spend an entire page describing a flame.

It wasn't just his writing that was irritating to her. Lorella was getting more annoyed by Sulley himself. He muttered underneath his breath constantly. A nuisance to anyone, but especially Lorella, who was immensely irritated by any noise she deemed unnecessary. Worse, he peppered each of them with personal questions at random times.

His most recent victim was Evanlee. Lorella listened as Sulley asked all sorts of things that Lorella felt either didn't matter or weren't his business. Sometimes both.

"So when you girls finish saving the world, what will you do, wee one?"

"I will go back to the East as quickly as I possibly can!" Evanlee said with a little giggle.

"Oh? No thought to it at all?"

"None."

Lorella rolled her eyes. Just like her sister. Openly admitting she had put no thought into something.

"Why so sure that's what you want? Perhaps you will like the North too? Who knows what all you will see on our way to get the book. Yes, yes, yes you might like a new area a lot."

"Nope! The East is where I want to go. It's the only reason I agreed to do this."

"Oh?"

"Well, that and because my sisters wanted to, of course."

"Why did they want to do it?"

"Well, Lorella wanted an adventure. She says life's not worth living without excitement. Though we disagree on what exactly excitement is. I like balls and parties. Lorella seemed to thoroughly enjoy when Gardeniyah got attacked by a wolf and she had to take charge."

Lorella cringed. She didn't like hearing someone say she had enjoyed her sister's attack. She had hoped it wasn't that obvious.

She also didn't like being talked about like she wasn't in the room. She almost said so. But she figured that would end the conversation altogether, and she wanted to hear where it would go. For a moment, she felt very much like the girl she was back East, eavesdropping on others' conversations to gain information.

It was strange for her to feel like that girl again. Lorella hadn't realized that she was no longer that version of herself. But, of course, this is no surprise. It's never until we feel like our old selves for a moment that we realize we aren't that person anymore.

"I see. I see. I see," the old man continued. "So Lorella wants to have an adventure. What about Gardeniyah? Why did she want to do it?"

"I don't really know, to be honest. I think because she wants to go home again like me. But maybe not. She's never really said. But I know I want to go back again. Brashen is waiting for me there. Or at least I hope he is . . ."

"Who's Brashen?"

"My dearest friend," she said with a smile that the old man knew, even at his age, and perhaps especially because of it, meant he was far more than a friend in Evanlee's heart.

"Ah, that explains it all," he said with a little smile and wink that accentuated every line on his wrinkled face. "I think I shall go lay down for a few minutes." And with that, Sulley got up and went to his room and closed the door. Evanlee, who did not like to be alone, came and sat down next to Lorella, who was on the floor by the fire pretending to read through her latest stack of papers.

"After we leave this house, whether we've found what we were looking for or we've given up, I will be happy to never see that crazy, annoying old man again," Lorella muttered, more to herself than to Evanlee.

But she realized it was a mistake the moment she said it. Evanlee looked at her, horrified—as if Lorella had just insulted their grandparent or father.

"How can you say that? He has been so kind to us. He's like family now!"

"Family?" Lorella could not believe what she was hearing, though she had guessed Evanlee felt that way by the look on her face. Actually hearing her say it was another matter. To

Lorella, it was beyond baffling or frustrating. It was infuriating.

"Evanlee, are you that desperate for love? I mean, come on! You, Gardeniyah, and I are family. Not him. We barely even know him."

"He has taken us in. Just like Mib did. She's family, right?"

"Mib stopped being family the moment we left. We went our way, and she stayed there." As soon as Lorella said the words, she regretted them as well. Her sister's large eyes squinted, her open jaw set firmly.

Truth be told, Lorella hadn't even acknowledged to herself that she felt that way. Now she had said it to the worst person possible. Evanlee was so young and the only mother she had ever known was Mib. So, to Evanlee, Lorella's comment was like saying she didn't consider her mother their mother.

"Ev, I—"

"Don't even bother saying you didn't mean that. You have said it time and time again: you don't apologize because you don't believe in regrets and you stand by what you say. You don't say things you don't mean. I just can't believe you think that."

Evanlee gathered up her things as she wiped a tear from her face. She took all the notes and letters she was in charge of over to the farthest possible corner from Lorella. Lorella saw Gardeniyah look up from her pile of papers and frown at the two of them. Lorella was grateful that Gardeniyah had been so intensely dedicated to this project for the last few days that she didn't tear away from the work to address the fight.

The rest of the day wore on. Lorella worked by herself the entirety of that time. Letty had grown very uncomfortable during Lorella's heated exchange with Evanlee and had retreated to his usual spot in front of the stove. After Sulley woke up from his nap, Evanlee partnered with the old man who had started the disagreement. She was sure to send Lorella a withering glare as she did so.

Lorella knew by the way Evanlee was acting that this wasn't a fight they would easily move past. This is not surprising, of course. It's a general rule of thumb in any world that when you insult someone's mother, whether biological or adopted, a line is crossed. And it is a hard thing for a relationship to bounce back from.

Lorella knew that before they had begun on this journey, Evanlee had secretly wanted to find their birth mother once they left the East. She had hinted about attempting it for months leading up to Lorella's birthday. But, she had given that up in their quest to find this book.

Evanlee was big on beauty, peace, and family. So in a time with no peace and in a place with no beauty, Lorella had managed to poke holes in the last thing she had.

The wedge between them would likely stay or even grow, this time. Eventually, Gardeniyah would take it upon herself to intervene. Lorella wouldn't admit it to anyone, but she actually relied on Gardeniyah playing the peacemaker because Lorella's pride didn't allow her to seek out her sister to apologize. And Lorella's intimidating temper always kept Evanlee from approaching her.

But to Lorella's surprise, even hours after their fight, Gardeniyah had remained uninvolved. Gardeniyah normally would have made them talk it out by now. Instead, she sat searching through her papers and writing notes as if there weren't a thick tension in the air between her two sisters. Lorella knew that lingering tension was something Gardeniyah hated even more than most. But right now, it didn't even seem to faze her.

The sisters were growing ever more isolated in their communal quest. They had each discovered pieces of information they deemed important. But what each found important was as vastly different as their personalities.

Evanlee found it crucial that the East was always described in such detail. She was sure this was a major clue. It wasn't. Sulley had just never seen the East and so wrote down everything Sanora said about it, asking his infamous probing questions to learn more. He would sit by the stove after she'd left and peruse the information leisurely over and over.

Lorella was sure that Sulley's details came only from his eccentric nature. She was sure that any valuable information would be stated plainly. And so, of course, she missed quite a lot of information that would have proved useful after all.

Gardeniyah was the most at home in the texts, but even she struggled. She felt sure that all information she needed would come from Sanora herself. So she often skipped any writings that were purely Sulley's and had nothing to do with Sanora. This was another unfortunate choice.

Ezer struggled to know what to look for at all. Everyone else knew at least a corner of the world they were reading about. Ezer knew only the center. So he often got so bogged down with trying to picture the world in the first place that he missed the point of his search entirely.

He wouldn't tell Gardeniyah, but he wasn't sure they would find Sanora or her book. It felt lucky that they had found Sulley. He knew they had already read all the information once to no avail. So, he focused on the human kings. If the sisters were going to restore order and peace despite the Northern King and his harsh rule and widespread power, they would have to come up with a plan.

Gardeniyah quickly dismissed Ezer every time he brought it up. It baffled him how much she hated a man she had never met. He wanted to know the man's background to try to figure out his motivation. Gardeniyah wanted to ignore his existence altogether. But she wouldn't be able to formulate a plan if she stayed ignorant.

Lorella was the first to call it quits that night, tired and disgruntled from another day of monotony and the fight with her sister. Then Sulley and Letty turned in. Ezer and Evanlee continued for some time after that. Gardeniyah was the last to stop, and she had no idea how much longer she stayed poring over everything because she didn't even notice when they all went to sleep.

CHAPTER FORTY-ONE

The next day carried on much the same way as the first few. They switched partners every so often to break up the monotony. Occasionally when one of the sisters voiced that they were especially tired of reading and needed a break, Ezer would also stop. Then the two would go out to the alleyway and work on their fighting techniques. It served as an excellent way for the girls to both learn to take care of themselves and also to let out their frustrations over not having any clearer idea of where to go next.

If you had asked any of them, they would have sworn to you that the piles of papers were getting bigger. This was not the case for most piles, except for Gardeniyah's. Whenever Lorella was sure no one was looking, she would add a piece or two to Gardeniyah's pile from her own. She was sure that these papers were the difference between stability and insanity for her. And she didn't feel bad. Gardeniyah still seemed thoroughly enthralled even several days into the whole ordeal.

The day passed with no luck. Gardeniyah could have kept going for hours more. However, everyone else in her group had once again grown tired and now were also extremely frustrated. So instead of continuing, Gardeniyah suggested they all try to get some sleep and begin again the next day. This turned out to be a bad idea. Everyone fell asleep right away except for Gardeniyah, whose mind would not slow down.

After what felt like an entire night of tossing and turning —but was really only about an hour—Gardeniyah got up. She was suffocating in the small room that was decreasing in size every minute she lay on the floor trying to sleep. She had seen the same four walls for what felt like weeks. *I just need some air,* she told herself. *That's all, just some fresh air.* She got up from her spot on the rug in the middle of the room and crept past Sulley's bedroom. She carefully eased out the front door and sat on the stairway stoop.

Her mind was reeling with possibilities of the future. This whole thing felt like a giant game—and they were losing. She knew the weight of it. But it was more than that. Even if she hadn't known the stakes, she wanted to succeed. She wanted it more than she had ever wanted anything.

But right now, she also wanted something else. She wanted the fresh air of the East. She closed her eyes and pictured being back home. When she couldn't sleep back then, sitting out in the night air had been one of her favorite things. Besides the sound of the nocturnal animals, the only noise would be wind rustling the grass and the trees. It was peaceful. It was as if a piece of her worry was blown away with every brush of the wind. The outdoors would lull her mind until her eyes were heavy and she would sneak back inside and back into bed finally able to sleep.

Not here, though. Here, the noise never stopped. In fact, the noise grew louder at night. Regardless of any responsibilities they may have had the next day, the citizens of Zaraneth never missed an opportunity to party the night away loudly.

Yes, she craved home like you crave your favorite dish before a holiday. She craved peace externally and internally.

Yet she didn't actually want to go home. Surprisingly, she desired this adventure more. She felt an unexplainable pull to this grand adventure.

Gardeniyah slumped against the railing of the steps. "I've read too many books." She tousled her hair. "I have my head filled with all these stories of greatness and adventure. That isn't life. This is life. One dead end after another."

She hadn't realized she'd said it out loud until she heard someone comment from the doorway behind her.

"That's a true statement, to a degree." The door behind her shut slowly. Sulley feebly eased himself down next to her.

"I'm sorry, did I wake you by coming out here?"

"Most things wake a man who spent years on the run from a king."

They sat in silence for a few minutes before Sulley finally spoke again.

"Your mind is busy, dear girl."

"You read minds too, Sulley?"

"No, but your body language, your breathing, and your eyes tell your story loudly enough." She didn't like that. She could usually hide her emotions from everyone. "That fella in there is worried about you. He looks at you with concern quite often."

"Great, someone else who can suddenly read me too well," she muttered.

"It's not a crime to show emotion, you know."

"I suppose, but it's rather difficult to retain someone's confidence in you if they see you shaken up or frustrated."

"Oh, that's nonsense," Sulley said, waving his hand dismissively. "People have to relate to you to like you. People tend to love and respect those who they can understand and empathize with. People who they can tell lead them with good hearts."

"That's one way to look at it."

"That's how Sanora led, and she had a successful empire for nearly a thousand years."

The silence lingered between them for a while.

"What are you so afraid of, Gardeniyah?"

"I'm not afraid."

"Yes, yes, yes, you are. Your eyes are strong when you are around your sisters, but right now they brim with fear."

"I don't know." She rubbed her face a few times and put her head in her hands.

"I've seen my share of people, Gardeniyah, and I can tell you are not one who doesn't know what you fear. You know your world, and you know yourself."

Gardeniyah huffed. "I used to."

"You used to what?"

"I used to know my world. I knew how to protect myself and, more importantly, my sisters." She leaned forward and rested her forearms on her thighs as she folded her hands. "Not here, though," she said as she looked around at the nightlife of Zaraneth carrying on all around her.

"Yes, yes, yes, that can be frustrating. That's obviously a part of what you fear. But, dear, you walk with the weight of the world on your shoulders."

"Well, do you blame me? This seems like a really important mission. What if we fail? What if we aren't up to the challenge?"

"Yes, yes, yes, so what if you do? I believe in prophecies. If you aren't successful, then you aren't the ones we are waiting on. Lucky me, I get to live however many years longer while I wait!"

He chuckled as he said those words. He meant them as a

joke, but, to Gardeniyah, they stung like alcohol on a wound. She felt her body stiffen.

She knew Sulley was right. She believed in prophecies too. Maybe there was someone else who could do what she thought they had to.

She wanted this to make her feel better. It didn't. Instead, her body felt cold and empty as the breath escaped her lungs.

"Ah. So we have found it," Sulley said in a knowing yet barely audible whisper.

"What?"

"We have found what you fear."

"Yeah, I told you. I don't want to fail everyone."

"Yes, yes, yes, but that's only part of the truth."

"What on earth are you talking about?" She could feel herself getting defensive.

"You fear failing. That much is true. But not because you think someone else won't save the day. In fact, that's what you fear more. You love this, don't you? The letters, the historical accounts I've written. You have loved poring through hundreds of years of history."

Gardeniyah nodded. "Yeah, I spent a lot of time studying history and reading books back in the East."

"Makes sense that learning about history fascinates you. It drives you to want more out of life. I understand that more than you know. Imagine my dismay when The Omniscient chose to pick another human—or three, in this case—to save the world and not the man who'd thrown his life away standing up to a king." Sulley chuckled the sort of way you chuckle when the joke you are saying is primarily truth. "You don't fear failing for the sake of failing, dear. You fear not being the one to succeed. You see, the people who study history spend their lives studying the people the world remembers. And that creates in them the fear of being forgotten. That, my dear, is what you fear the most. That you will die and the world will forget that you ever lived. No ordinary life will do for you. You want to better the world. You want history to remember your name. Someday, you want a girl like you to be reading about the past and find your name like you found the names of all the people you admire. You want your name on a list of people who inspired others, and you want to do it on a grand scale. So the idea of someone else doing this great deed, and that you haven't been chosen for some great destiny, breaks you apart. That's why you fear failing. You fear people forgetting you ever tried."

Gardeniyah didn't say anything to the old man. She couldn't find anything to say. She hated how often that had been happening lately. That wasn't like her. Or perhaps, in this world, it was exactly like her. She could add that to the list of things she didn't know these days. Her silence didn't stop Sulley from continuing on.

"Your fear, dear one, is why you will succeed. You won't let life slip you by. You won't let someone else take your story. You will fight for your chance to change this world. You won't find rest until you accept that this is why you are here. People who have these kinds of dreams and drives have them because they are meant to fulfill them. It's the desire of their heart in its purest form—that is why you won't fail. You need to accept that reality so that you can pursue it with a clear mind. Until you stop fearing your purpose, you will never fulfill it."

CHAPTER FORTY-TWO

Gardeniyah's mind was still swirling. But not in the way it had been before. This momentary mental chaos was the kind that brings with it distinct clarity. Like the moment when a storm that has been pounding down suddenly breaks and a single ray of light fights through the still-swaying tree limbs. The light is broken and jagged and everywhere, but it reaches the ground nonetheless, lighting up a surface that was previously dark and cold.

These moments of clarity are rare. Some unfortunately go through their whole lives not experiencing even one. But should you be fortunate enough to do so, they are life changing. They are pinnacle moments that are looked back on as the instant everything changed.

Everything in Gardeniyah's world started to feel like it was falling into place. The game she felt she had been losing now felt like a puzzle she could solve. She could suddenly reach out and grab the pieces and fit them together, instinctively knowing where they belonged. She felt euphoric despite the chaos of her thoughts.

Gardeniyah now knew Sulley was right. She hadn't felt

peace since she'd first found out about the prophecy. She had heard noise in the silence of the snow flurries of the barren North on their journey here, even when the wind was almost deadly still. She could find chaos anywhere these days.

She thought she had been craving the East. But truthfully, she knew she had always felt a longing for something more, even when she was living there. She assumed she was longing to fit in—for a place to belong in her world, a group of people that would call her their own.

But now she realized that longing wasn't really about where she was or wasn't from. Just as her current fear wasn't merely about failing. She longed for a purpose, to find it and to fulfill it.

She had never wanted something as badly as she wanted to succeed at this. Now she understood why. Though the pressure and seriousness of the situation remained, and nothing had changed, the weight of the prophecy was gone.

She had done the changing. She had accepted that her dream was now a reality and that she could bring it to life. She just needed to pursue it.

Now, finally, she knew what she had to do. She could stop thinking about what she would do if they hit a dead end. That was no longer an option. And she could stop thinking about what sort of life she would live if they failed and how she would spend her days. She could put aside the thoughts that made her wonder where they would live or what they would do.

Because there would be no life after failing at all. Gardeniyah decided that night, on a stairway stoop in the dead center of the world she was out to save, that she would never entertain those ideas again. Because Gardeniyah would succeed, or she would die trying.

CHAPTER FORTY-THREE

The next day, Gardeniyah woke up with a clearer state of mind. She was ready to take on this day of sifting through old papers and memories. Her body didn't feel as sluggish or achy either. Nothing had physically changed from the night before, but her new mentality made all the difference.

She woke up before all the others and decided to take advantage of this. Though no personal realizations had occurred for them the night before, she wanted their day to start out as refreshing as hers had. She knew that few things can start a day out on the right foot like a good breakfast. So she decided to give her companions just that.

She soon discovered the peculiar old man that she was growing increasingly fond of didn't have much besides ingredients for soup and tea. She crept over to her bag and pulled out a few shicklings. *Whatever I can buy with this is what I will make. They all deserve this breakfast, but I can't be too relaxed with our funds.* With that decision made, she eased out the door and down the steps into town.

It was a good distance to any merchants in this part of

town. When she came upon the closest shop, she passed it the first time, not realizing it was what she was looking for. The crowded store was a far cry from the market at Relis.

It wasn't just the physical appearance of the store here versus the markets she was familiar with that made this outing so bizarre to her; it was also the goods themselves. Back in the East, everything was made with love and with special attention to detail, whether it was a rocking chair or an apple. Easterners took pride in their work. This store smelled like spoiled meat and rotten fruit.

I don't see how Ezer can be satisfied to stay in this awful place. Maybe he will change his mind and decide to come with us. I hope he does. Gardeniyah was so startled by her own thought that she dropped the apple she had picked up back into the barrel. The apple bumped another on the way down, which caused a chain reaction and a brief landslide of apples.

She scurried to pick them up and looked around to find someone to apologize to, but no one seemed to care about the apple avalanche. If Gardeniyah had not picked them up, they would have stayed there all day until the store owner closed up or someone stole them off the ground—which was a far more likely scenario.

She decided after the whole ordeal that apples were not very appetizing anymore. She went on to purchase a few veggies to scramble up. *I can use some of Methuselah's soup spices. That will save us some money.*

Her day seemed even better after she'd purchased the goods. She was very proud of herself for not spending all the money she had budgeted while still being able to procure the ingredients to make her companions' morning better. As she headed toward the exit, Gardeniyah had a spring in her step that rivaled Evanlee's.

She was so busy mentally celebrating that she didn't notice at first that the gaze of the man behind the counter had lingered a little too long. By the time she did notice, he quickly looked away, so she had no idea how long he had been studying her face. The thought made her uneasy, so she quickly hurried out of the store. She wanted to keep her happy feeling. So she raced back to Sulley's home.

She did have the foresight to take a less direct route. However, she didn't know the area well enough to make it hard to be followed. *I don't even know that the man was watching me to see where I was going. There you go with the stories again. You must stop that. He was probably just being inappropriate.*

Despite her detour, everyone except for Sulley was still asleep when she returned. Sulley had most likely woken up when she'd left. He was sitting on his bed with the door open reading a letter from Sanora when she walked in.

She smiled at him and held up the sack of goods as she said, "I hope you haven't eaten." The smile he had already been returning grew bigger as he shook his head. He then went back to reading the letter as Gardeniyah eased into the kitchen and began to cook.

She liked the kitchen despite its small size. It was smaller than Mib's, but it reminded her of home all the same. Sulley's home was made of wood, not stone like the buildings in the first part of Zaraneth they had visited. And it felt nice to be cooking on the burner of a wood-burning stove again and not over an open flame. She loved the smell of the heated metal and the sound of the crackling embers hitting the sides of the pan and sizzling back down into the flames.

None of the noises, from cutting the food or scraping the pan as she cooked, woke the rest of her companions. Nor the loud creak the water pump made every time she pressed it down and water sloshed into the small sink below. What did finally wake them from their deep sleeps was the smell of a fresh, hot breakfast. One by one, their heads quickly perked up off their arms and cushions.

Ezer was the first to arrive in the kitchen. As he stepped closer to her and the pan of food, Gardeniyah felt her heart lurch. She was happy that this time, however, when something concerning Ezer caught her off guard, she didn't knock everything around her over. Instead, she appeared calm and collected.

Standing behind her, Ezer leaned closer, and Gardeniyah began to flush. She was annoyed at his forward manner. She was shocked that he felt the freedom to stand so close to her. Being that close was hardly necessary. She had just opened her mouth to correct him when he leaned not into her but past her, straight toward the pan.

"Smells great," he said and then quickly turned and walked away.

"Why's your mouth open like that?" Lorella questioned as she walked up to do the same. Gardeniyah shook her head.

She told herself she'd simply been confused because of the way men were around here. It would not happen again. She was not one of those childish women who assumed each man's every move was about her. She had been so annoyed when he was committing the action, yet now that she had realized she was wrong about his intentions, she felt something very much like disappointment.

Once they'd all grabbed a plate of food, they sat on the floor and the couch and ate together.

"So, has reading about all these places made you want to leave at all yet, Ezer?" Evanlee questioned.

Gardeniyah raised her eyes from her bowl and leaned forward a bit to hear better.

"Nope, can't say that it has. I mean, most of these accounts are old, anyhow, so I don't see how it would matter to me at all."

"You don't get bored here?" This time it was Lorella bugging the man about his life choices.

"Zaraneth is a lot of things—more specifically, a lot of unpleasant things. But a place where you can get bored is not one of them. I work in a tavern in the worst place in Tolatin. No two days are the same. Sometimes that's good, sometimes that's bad. But it's never boring."

"Well, you could do what you do here somewhere else. In the South or the North, perhaps?" Gardeniyah chimed in before she could stop herself.

"Why do it there when I can do it here? Look, if you ladies want me to come with you, you can just say so," he said with a wink and that smirk of his that Gardeniyah usually liked. But she did not like it now. Gardeniyah's face grew hot as she frowned her disapproval. She didn't understand why he waited until her question to bring up coming with them.

The comment hadn't annoyed her sisters. Lorella had even done an overtly obnoxious laugh, as if to say that was a ridiculous notion. But none of them were ready to let up on pestering the man either, especially now that he had challenged them.

"Well, what about a family of your own? Don't you want one? A wife and kids?" Evanlee asked.

"Well, sure, I guess."

"And you expect to find a wife here?" Evanlee put her hand over her heart as she asked the question.

"Of course. My father found my mother. He said she was a good woman; she was from here."

Gardeniyah suddenly felt an unfamiliar pang in her chest. She quickly dismissed the feeling, as she didn't like it very much. Besides, she had far more important things to do than wonder what that feeling had meant. She had heard enough, and he had probably had enough of talking himself.

"All right, Ev, leave him alone. It's his life. If he wants to

275

stay in Zaraneth or if he wants to spend his days swimming the dividing rivers, that's up to him and entirely his business." She hadn't meant for it to come out as callously as it had. She realized right as spoke that it sounded very much like she didn't care about the man at all. Lorella raised her eyebrows but said nothing. The air felt awkward for a few moments until Sulley saved them all from it.

"This breakfast is delicious, dear. I can't remember the last time I had anything but tea for breakfast. I try not to go out much. I'm sure you all were tired of soup for every meal. I know the men who hunted me are long since dead. But I don't know that a man who is on the run for his life ever truly relaxes. So I buy in bulk and go out as little as possible."

The others nodded in agreement, and they all started asking him questions about how he'd found the place and such. Gardeniyah, however, was busy recalling that morning when the man at the counter had stared at her face a little too long. Had she been followed? Had it been nothing? Regardless, she knew that it was best to follow Sulley's example from then on. They would go out only when necessary.

CHAPTER FORTY-FOUR

The next several days passed like the others before them. Everyone was busy sorting papers and thoughts from piles of papers and buzzing minds. Days were long and tedious, for the most part. But once they realized isolating their questions wasn't helping them, they began to work together more. Working together meant that relationships grew. The formation of the bonds during this time would prove to be very useful to the group.

The whole group, except for Lorella, continued to grow fonder of Sulley. And all three of the sisters thoroughly enjoyed having Ezer and Letty around. It was beginning to be hard for any of them to picture Ezer and Letty leaving them when they continued on their journey. The only relationship getting weaker was the one between Lorella and Evanlee.

Evanlee hadn't told Gardeniyah what Lorella had said about Mib or even what she had said about Sulley. Evanlee knew it would hurt her.

It was hard for Evanlee to imagine anyone loving Mib more than she did. But there was something about

Gardeniyah and Mib's relationship that Evanlee couldn't compete with. The best she could figure was that it came down to the dynamic of the relationships. Evanlee had Gardeniyah to look up to. Mib was her mother figure, but Gardeniyah was her role model. For Gardeniyah, Mib was both. Mib was also Gardeniyah's friend. That part of the relationship had grown exponentially over the last year after she turned eighteen.

Evanlee had never been old enough to have that sort of relationship with Mib. She hated that. But she would have it with Gardeniyah and maybe even Lorella one day, or at least she hoped, and both of them would always be around. But Gardeniyah's role model and best friend was gone. Gardeniyah certainly didn't need to hear that Lorella had dismissed that meaningful relationship as insignificant now.

Evanlee, however, was not very good at holding things in. She was the type of person who felt as if she would burst if she didn't talk to someone about what was on her mind. So she was especially grateful when Letty came to talk to her.

"Hello, Ev," he said as he placed his head on Evanlee leg.

"Hi, Letty." She patted his head and he looked up at her and smiled. When she didn't return the smile, he frowned and questioned her.

"What's the matter?"

"Oh . . . nothing." Her sigh did little to convince him.

"That's not true. You've been huffing like hog."

Evanlee giggled. "What's the difference between a hog and a pig?"

"Oh!" Letty said in surprise. "Well, quite nearly everything. Don't be ridiculous!"

"Why, of course. How silly of me. I'm sorry."

"It's fine. Common mistake." He waved a hoof in the air to dismiss her blunder. "Many don't realize how obtuse a hog is in every way and how very different we are. But anyway, what's been the matter with you the last little bit? You haven't been yourself."

With the repeated question, the weak gates holding back Evanlee's feelings gave way.

She glanced at Lorella before leaning in closely to whisper to Letty, "I got into a fight with Lorella—which normally wouldn't bother me, we used to do it a lot back home—but this one, this was different."

"How so?"

"Well, for starters, she said that Mib wasn't our mother."

"Who's Mib?"

"Our mother."

"Oh, quite right," he said with a quick nod as if he knew the information all along. "So why would she say a thing like that?"

"I don't know!"

"Ah. I see the problem now." Letty was nodding vigorously as if he fully understood the situation. He, in fact, did not. Not even slightly. But he felt very sure the girl needed him to understand and so he was trying very hard.

He wasn't sure how long he could pretend to grasp the whole ordeal and so was very glad when Ezer, who had been listening in on the conversation, came over to join them. Letty felt he needed to solidify his charade and so attempted to fill Ezer in on the situation. "Lorella said a strange thing. She said that their mother, Mit—"

"Mib," Evanlee corrected softly.

"Right! Mib. She said their mother Mib is not their mother—which has upset Evanlee a lot." With that, he nodded once more and then scurried away to sit next to Gardeniyah, who was too busy reading to involve him in any problems he might not understand.

There was an awkward moment or two between Evanlee and Ezer as they sat there both pretending to read the papers in front of them. Both were acutely aware, thanks to Letty's introduction of the conflict to Ezer, that social constructs obligated them to at least briefly address it.

"Look, we don't need to—" Evanlee began, but Ezer interrupted her.

"Yes, we do. But, look, um, let's not talk here." He glanced at Gardeniyah briefly. "Let's go outside and work on some self-defense. We will talk there." The two got up without another word and went out to the alleyway.

They were at the point where Ezer would not tell them in advance what they were working on. They would just begin sparring, and he would see what they could keep up with. He enjoyed seeing how far Evanlee had come. She was must stronger and more capable than when she'd started. She was borderline confident in her competence now. She seemed like a different girl than the one he had rescued that day.

After several minutes of sparring silently, they took a break. Ezer had used the time to gather his thoughts on how to address his concerns to the young girl. However, he had been unable to come up with anything but a direct way to restart the conversation, and so he took Evanlee back a bit when he abruptly interrupted the silence with: "I don't think you are as upset as you think you are about what Lorella said."

"What? What do you mean?"

"Of course you didn't like it. She's the woman who raised you and, by all important accounts, your mother." Evanlee nodded fervently in agreement. "But I don't think that's why it disturbed you so much."

"I still don't understand."

"Look, I overheard the argument. Lorella got upset when you called a man who you had just met family. She got more upset when you made him equal to Mib. Which I'm sure you can assume means she does actually hold Mib in high esteem and, more likely than not, sees her as a mother."

Evanlee looked down at the ground. His logic was sound. His logic was also very obvious. She felt embarrassed she hadn't realized that and that a man who barely knew her and her sisters could assess the situation better than she could. As if reading her mind, Ezer continued.

"I'm not saying you shouldn't have gotten upset by her saying that. Anyone would have. But I think you may need to deal with what's actually bothering you."

"That is what's bothering me."

"No, it's not."

"Yes, it is."

Ezer shook his head. "Look, you seem like a pretty rational girl."

Evanlee huffed. "Tell that to Lorella."

"If she ever asks me, I will." He smiled kindly. "But only if you admit this: it was a little strange for you, at the time— which was just a couple of days after you met him, remember —to compare Sulley to your mother, Mib."

Evanlee tucked a piece of hair behind her ear and began fidgeting with the end of it, all the while avoiding eye contact with Ezer. But, finally, she spoke. "Okay, you're right. It was. I'm a foolish and childish little girl just like Lorella always says."

"No. You're not."

"Yeah? Well, how else do you explain it, then?"

"You're scared."

"I am not!"

"You should be."

"Excuse me?"

"You heard me. You should be scared. Any normal person with a sane, rational, and mature mind would be, given what you've been through here."

Evanlee's breath caught as she flashed back to the first day they'd arrived. She could once again feel the hand over her mouth. It was difficult for her to take another breath as imaginary hands wrapped around her wrists. She felt it all over again nearly every night.

"Hey, hey!" Ezer said, grabbing her hand. "It's okay. See . . . you are scared. You are trying so hard not to be in front of them. And so it's coming out in strange ways. You felt safe with Mib, right?"

"Yes. Of course."

"So you wanted to feel that again. You knew you could trust Sulley because your queen back East told you that you could. So you created a safe environment for yourself by pretending this man was, so quickly, just like Mib. You weren't being childish, Evanlee, you were coping. Congratulations, you've developed your first coping mechanism. You're well on your way to being an adult now."

Evanlee and Ezer both let out a small huff of laughter. Then Evanlee sighed, and Ezer nodded toward Sulley's building and began to walk back to the staircase in front. After a moment he stopped and turned back to face Evanlee once more. "Look, I didn't say all this to get in your business. But it seemed to really be weighing you down, kid. And before you can forgive her and move on, you needed to realize why you were so mad. She didn't just insult your mom. She poked a hole in the way you were coping. Which is gonna happen, no matter how you try and cope. So you need to face the real problem. The fear. Or it's never gonna go away."

CHAPTER FORTY-FIVE

Time wore on for what felt like years, but it was really only a matter of weeks. Something unique occurs when people live and work together, especially in such close quarters. They learn mannerisms about one another that they may otherwise not have noticed as long as they lived.

Like that Sulley only went to the store on the same two days of the week, and it was always as early as possible. He would leave before the stores were even open and would return home just minutes after they had opened their doors. He always bought potatoes for their daily soup because they were cheap, and he bought a leafy green but varied which type. He claimed it changed the flavor, so he didn't feel like he was eating the same thing all the time. To the other five, it all tasted the same.

Ezer always had a coughing fit for exactly ten seconds every two hours while he slept. Letty snored for five minutes every night two hours after falling asleep. Lorella over-chewed her food, even if it was just the soggy vegetables in the ever-brewing soup. Evanlee whined every time a piece of paper had a stain. And Gardeniyah ruffled papers and rubbed her head with her hand exactly two times every time she got frustrated, which was about every three hours.

Of course, these simple things begin to grate on one's nerves after a while (especially if you are already annoyed with someone). Which was why, despite the fact that everyone was doing something to annoy Lorella lately, she only chastised Evanlee.

"Evanlee, why do you do that?"

"Do what?" she hissed. Though Ezer had helped her, she was still a little upset with Lorella and had no interest in being corrected or even spoken to by her unless absolutely necessary while she sorted out the rest of her feelings.

"The whine. It's annoying."

"What are you talking about? What whine?"

Sulley chimed in, trying to head off the brewing argument.

"Ah, noticed a quirk, have we? No need to bother vocalizing it. We all have one someone else is dealing with. Hush now and get back to work."

Lorella did not enjoy being corrected by the man. She liked even less that he told her to be quiet. But she didn't feel like having the others gang up on her, so she followed the others and did as he said.

The next ten days, as everyone became acutely aware of each other's many quirks, they all let them pass. So while they were all very sick of the letters and the notes and sometimes each other, they argued much less than anyone would guess six individuals in such a small place would.

That allowed them to focus on the task at hand. Which, despite their increasing knowledge of Sanora, was growing ever more challenging. In fact, it was because of their ever-developing knowledge that this frustration was occurring.

They now all knew a great deal about the humans and

their history—at least their recent history. There wasn't much in the papers about anything before man conquered the South. Lorella finally decided to question the historian about it.

"Hey, Sulley."

"Yes, Lorella?"

"I thought you were some great historian?"

"Lorella!" Gardeniyah called out, horrified at her sister's accusatory remark. Lorella ignored her, as did Sulley.

"I never claimed to be great."

"The East says you were. And yet, there's hardly anything here about our history before the South."

"There's plenty!" Evanlee said, attempting to defend her elderly friend.

"No, there isn't!" Lorella was initially just inquisitive albeit slightly annoyed. But she was now thoroughly angry at being teamed up against.

"No. No. No. She's right," Sulley said.

"See! He admits it. Here we are poring over all these notes, and for what? It's incomplete. We won't ever figure out where Sanora hid the book because we are missing history. He let us carry on with this wild-goose chase, even though he knows we can't figure it out! Logically, we need the information from when they invaded the West, or better yet, the days before. But aside from a few stories of Sanora's, there's none of that."

"Is that true? You really don't have it?' Evanlee's eyes pleaded with the old man to deny it.

"It's true."

"We need to stop this," Lorella said. "We are relying on a man who doesn't even have what he claims to have. We can't trust him."

"I never claimed to have a complete history."

"How can you say that? You claimed to be a historian!"

"And I am. But, as you know, I am also a Divine Order sympathizer."

"What does that have to do with anything?"

"Ha!" Sulley laughed for a moment, then grew very serious. "It has to do with everything! I am a historian. And I refuse to write false history."

"What do you mean?" Lorella folded her arms and scowled deeply.

"The men who win write the history books, dear. It's the job of the independent man to write exactly what happened. And at that time, we had no such man. I have no way of knowing exactly what happened then. And I will not make it up. Or else I risk destroying my credibility."

With that, he turned away from Lorella and her accusations and faced the rest of the group. They knew by his expression that he was no longer just defending himself against Lorella. He had something much bigger to tell them.

"Look, look, look. You three, no, no, no, all of you. I may not have been expecting you," he said, pointing at Ezer, "but you are a part of this too—I can feel it. You four have a special chance unlike any other I have ever seen. As I said, it is the independent man who writes and tells what actually happened. I cannot think of four more independent souls than you. You all have your stains. You are humans broken in more ways than one. You carry the weight of what your race has done, but you were not raised by them. You were raised in the East," he said, glancing at the sisters, "and in the worst place in our world," he said, looking intently at Ezer. "You are removed from them and their story while still being characters in it! It's why The Omniscient chose you. Yes, yes, yes, it's the job of the independent man to write what actually happened! Even if we cannot find this spell. Even if we fail. You still have a chance! You can still fix it all. You can fix it with the truth! It may not be in your generation or in your life. You may never see everyone, or even anyone, accept the true truth. But, no matter what, you must tell the truth anyway. Tell it with fervor, tell it with strength, and tell it until the day you die."

Sulley stood up and spoke with more power and clarity than the girls had ever witnessed from him before. "You must proclaim it to everyone who will listen, and even those who seem like they won't. Much of mankind will hate you for it. The king may very well hunt you down as he did me. But don't run scared like I did. Face it. I know that, one day, the fact that I ran away and hid from the king's men will be my downfall. But, you, you can make a different choice. Don't run. Eventually, men will wonder why you would risk dying for a lie. Then, and only then, will they realize that you wouldn't and, more importantly, that you didn't. You risked your life for the truth, and that, that's the moment when man will believe. When the Order will be restored."

Sulley turned back then to look at Lorella. "So, no, no, no, darling girl, I don't have all the answers. I may never live to find them all, and I may not have the answer you need. But we must try anyway. Because the world needs us. They need the truth, whatever that turns out to be. And they need us to tell it to them. So we must find the book, not just for the spell, but for the truth."

CHAPTER FORTY-SIX

The room fell silent for a while as they all thought about what Sulley had just said. They stared at their papers. Though it would have been quite obvious to any observer that none of them were really reading any of them. After some time, Sulley, who was the only one brave enough to break the silence, spoke again.

"I may not know everything, but one thing I do know is that humans used to be quite the asset to this world. Yes, yes, yes, quite the asset."

"Really? I assumed we had always just been a drain on the world," Gardeniyah said with a scowl.

"Oh no, no, no. The minds of man cannot be rivaled. It takes quite the mind to be greedy. To be able to picture a life more extravagant than the one you have. To imagine a life you never knew and see it with enough clarity to chase after it. Yes, those kinds of minds create wondrous things."

At the phrase "wondrous things," Evanlee perked up and left her spot by Letty and the stove to join Gardeniyah and the old historian, who were sitting on the furniture in the front of the room. "What kinds of things?" she said before she had even fully sat down on the floor beneath where her sister sat on the couch.

"Well, you see that stove?" he said, gesturing to the kitchen. "A man named Mormamur Hollingtous got fed up with cooking over a flame, and so he created it. They've created so many things up North to make their lives easier. Some of it is not so good for the health of our world, but it's incredible nonetheless that their minds knew how to do it."

Evanlee's face showed some disappointment. Stoves weren't a wondrous thing to her, but Sulley continued. "Oh, now, young one, don't worry, that's not all they have done." He brushed his thumb across her cheek and she smiled. "They can paint a picture of the world so real you feel you are there. They can tell stories in a way you feel you personally know the characters in them. They have plays, and shows, and music in everyday life that you would only expect of the king's court. Oh, and you should see the fashions, my dear, you would faint at the sight of the clothing. You would love it so much. Yes, yes, yes, you would love it so much."

"All of this is in the North?" Evanlee asked.

"Of course, of course, of course, young one, and in the South, and once upon a time in the West. Anywhere man touches, they leave their influence, for better or for worse. Truly, I am intrigued to see it all again when we go wherever this journey will take us."

Evanlee's eyes grew wider as he spoke. She lay down on the rug picturing all he had described.

"You can see it all, can't you?" Sulley asked the uncharacteristically quiet girl. "You can picture the parties, and the dancing, the music, the plays, the art, the inventions . . ." Evanlee nodded with a thin smile on her lips. "That mind. That ability to picture all the wonder. To picture the images of a life you've never known. That's your humanity."

"Sulley, you make it seem not so bad to be human some-times," Gardeniyah said with a slight chuckle.

"Well, because it isn't, dear. No, no, no, it isn't. You can be ashamed of the things we have done without being ashamed to be human."

Gardeniyah felt her body stiffen at the blow against her previous mentality about humankind. He was right. They could change—maybe it would take a spell, but they could do it. After all, she was different than the perception of man in the East.

She had been raised so that she was embarrassed to be a human. It made her feel like a lesser citizen because, as much as she hated to admit it, she was. That didn't make the Easterners bad beings, they were just scared, but they had let fear rule their lives. And just as it didn't make all East-erners bad for being afraid, it didn't make her corrupt because she was human. Yes, she could be all right with being human; she just would never be okay with what they had done.

"I like that mentality," Gardeniyah said.

"Good. You'll need it."

"Why's that?"

"Why's what?"

Sulley often lost his train of thought. But when you coaxed the thought back, it was always worth hearing.

"Why do I need to have the mentality that I can hate what they did but I don't have to hate all of man?"

"Oh! Well, it sort of makes it difficult to save people if you don't like them," he said, waving his hand flippantly. "So you need it to be dedicated to your cause."

"I'm not trying to save man; I'm trying to save Tolatin."

"Well, if you don't save them from themselves, won't the world just be back here a thousand years from now?"

"But it's so hard. I grew up being taught how awful they

are. I hate them. I can never imagine doing what they have done."

"Oh, dear one, that sort of thinking is a trap. The greatest lie we can ever tell ourselves is that we could never be what others have been. Instead, we must face the scars of our past and the humanity within us in order to not repeat the sin."

Gardeniyah's face fell. She knew he was right.

Lorella, though, challenged the man. "That's ridiculous. We could never do something so wrong."

"Rarely does a man set out to do something he believes is purely wrong. To some degree, he believes he is right."

"I don't think mankind ever believed it was in the right."

"You must not refuse to accept the truth. Turn a blind eye to history and your own humanity, and you will walk down a path that leaves you face-to-face with ghosts of the past reborn." He turned back to Gardeniyah. "You need to save the enemy in order to make sure they don't stay your enemy. If they remain your foe, you will just have to fight them again. And it will be sooner rather than later." He kept muttering as he got up to get himself more tea. "Yes, yes, yes, love your enemy. Save them from themselves to save the world. Hate what they have done, not that you are one."

It was only when he moved that Gardeniyah could see Lorella's face. When she made eye contact, her sister glanced toward the man and then rolled her eyes.

"Why are you rolling your eyes?" Gardeniyah asked.

"I don't know about you," Lorella said, "but I don't think half of what that man says makes any sense."

"Made sense to me."

"Really, now? Loving the people who have screwed every-thing up makes sense to you? If it weren't for them, we would have an open border policy and we could come and go in the East all we want. I mean, they probably wouldn't have even made us leave. I probably would have, because I want to see the rest of Tolatin. But you and Ev could have stayed. She wouldn't be away from the only home she's ever known because of the misplaced grudge all the Easterners have against us. They hold us three accountable for all the stupid things that those people did. If you ask me, the Easterners are petty for holding a grudge against us, and the humans are moronic for doing what they have done."

"So, what? You just hate everyone?" Gardeniyah asked.

"I don't really have much against the beasts or monsters. They seem okay. Never cared for wolves, though," Lorella said with a smile on her face, as if to kid around.

"Well, I personally don't want to spend all my energy hating the entire, or even half of, the world."

CHAPTER FORTY-SEVEN

Lorella was fuming at her sister's last remark. Just minutes before Sulley had spoken, if Lorella had said the same exact thing, she was positive Gardeniyah would have agreed with her. Now Gardeniyah was acting as if she was a fool for feeling the way she did.

"All of you have been brainwashed by this man. You all think he's this guru who knows everything." Lorella huffed.

"Well, he is the oldest man in the world, so I—" Gardeniyah began.

"How do we know that?" Lorella interrupted. "We have seen two places in Tolatin. We have accepted everything everyone tells us. Aren't you tired of reading other people's stories? Accepting other people's truths?"

"Yes and no. I want to live ours, sure. But I think this is how we do that. This quest, or whatever you want to call it. And to do this, we need other people's information because, you're right, Lorella, we have only seen two places in this world. So, yes, I want to read and learn from someone who has lived for more than a hundred years. Yes, I like him a lot as a person and as a mentor out here. What's so wrong with that?"

Evanlee was snapped out of the daydream she had been enjoying when she overheard the argument that was quickly escalating between her sisters. She stood up and joined them. She could only hear bits and pieces of it. She knew they were talking about Sulley, and she didn't want Lorella saying to Gardeniyah what she had said to her.

"I can't believe this. Next you're going to say the same ridiculous thing Evanlee did."

Evanlee had intended to enter the conversation as a peacekeeper. She so desperately wanted to be like Gardeniyah. She knew that if it were her and Lorella in a fight, then Gardeniyah would have helped resolve the argument. However, after she heard her sister's snide remark about her, that didn't end up going as planned.

"Oh yeah, I am so ridiculous?"

"Yes, you are! You are fifteen, and you think the world is all okay or will be after some spell."

"So do you!"

"Maybe I don't!"

"Then why are you even here?"

"Okay! Okay!" Gardeniyah stepped in between them.

"What? Now you're going to intervene yet again like you always do? Protect your precious idiotically naive little sister?"

"First of all, you are both my precious little sisters." The kind words did not match the tone Gardeniyah was using. Her voice was soft but laced with an angry warning. The kind that instantly makes you realize you pushed that person just a little too far. "And secondly, I'm not intervening. We are having the conversation that you two have needed to have for the last two weeks. We are just going to do it outside."

"Oh, of course, have to keep up appearances." She flashed an insincere smile at the rest of their companions.

"Just keep your mouth shut until we get out the door," Gardeniyah said, putting her hand on the back of Lorella's shoulder and giving it a little nudge toward the door. Lorella pulled her body away from her sister and led the way out the door.

Letty looked at Sulley, who was watching the whole thing from his bedroom. Then he glanced back at the door the girls had now walked out of. Without taking his gaze from the door, he leaned sideways toward Ezer and whispered, "Well, this is awkward."

"Yeah. Starting to really miss our bachelor pad," Ezer replied.

"Agreed. I say tomorrow we go back. We have given them a lot of time and help. You've probably lost your job at Osmond's."

"I don't really mind. I've given some thought to your idea of opening our own tavern, and it has grown on me. I think we should do it. But I don't know. Should we really leave them? They clearly need help."

"Sounds like they aren't even sure what they are going to do anymore. I say we leave them to decide. If they choose to go, they will have Sulley. He's more what they need than us."

Ezer huffed but didn't say anything.

"Why do you think they will need us out there? What good will we do? I mean, I suppose they are pretty helpless physically."

Ezer shook his head. "Maybe at one point they were. But that was only because no one had taught them. They have come a long way. Especially Lorella; she could protect them pretty well if need be. And I've been working with them every few days for weeks when they needed a break. They are much better off now."

"See! They will be okay. I mean, here it's pretty rough. So if they decide to stay, they may still need someone to look out for them. You could offer to help watch their backs. But if they go, well, out there isn't like here. Like I said, they will be fine."

"Maybe."

"Oh, I get it."

"Get what?"

"You heard Sulley say he thinks you are a part of all of this too."

"Yeah, but I don't know what he is basing that on."

"Well, regardless, I think you want to be, and that you want to go with them."

"Oh, do you?"

"Yep. But you're too scared to admit it."

"If I'm not scared of Zaraneth, then I'm not scared of the North, Letty."

The pig shook his head and got up from his spot on the rug. "I know that. I don't mean you're scared of the North. You're scared of her, you're scared of all of them."

"What?" Ezer scrunched his face into a very strange distortion. Letty was doing what Lorella had done to Evanlee. He was poking holes in his coping mechanism.

"You're scared to go because you're afraid of getting too close to them," Letty continued. "You're worried I'm wrong and that they won't be okay. And you don't want to be around to witness it if I am wrong." Ezer opened his mouth to protest, but Letty raised his hoof to stop him. "Look, you need to get over that. You can't shut everyone out just because you're scared to lose them. And you also need to figure out what you want. This whole time, you have been telling these girls you have no interest in being anywhere but in Zaraneth. Now you seem to be wanting to go."

"I—" Ezer started to say something but realized he had no idea what to say.

"Look, I'll be by your side no matter what. You know that. But you need to figure out what it is that you want before it's too late." The little pig didn't say anything else or give Ezer a chance to respond. He walked to the still open door of the old man's room and closed the door behind him.

It was strange when Letty was annoyed with Ezer. It didn't happen often. They hardly ever disagreed. *Must be the night for arguments,* Ezer thought. *But based on the sound of those voices, our disagreement is going better than theirs.*

CHAPTER FORTY-EIGHT

The air was still warm despite the Lights of the Four Corners setting in every direction. Evanlee had never been outside during the setting of the lights in Zaraneth. She didn't know you could see the beautiful colors of the Lights of the Four Corners all at once as they disappeared behind the horizons. During the day, it was just bright, and the buildings were too tall and the air too smoky or hazy to realize that you could see the four suns that kept the regions in their permanent weather at once. She was so lost in staring at the lovely view she missed when the argument started up again between her sisters.

"All three of you and Letty are so wrapped up in this, it's ridiculous!" Lorella said.

"What part are you referring to? Caring about someone, which you hate to do, or the quest itself?" Gardeniyah said.

"Both are ridiculous! Think about it, would you? You are bonding with an old man who is going to keel over and die any day, and what you are bonding over is a wild-goose chase!"

"You don't mean that."

Hearing Gardeniyah say that snapped Evanlee out of her trance and back into the argument.

"Oh, Lorella means everything she says, remember?" Evanlee said.

"Oh, shut up and go back to staring at the lights setting! That's more you than a fight anyhow," replied Lorella.

"Why are you acting like me staring at the setting is a crime?"

"Because look at where we are!" Lorella said, gesturing wildly in every direction. "We are held up in some hole-in-the-wall in this awful place all because you two won't realize that this man is a whack job with no useful information for us. You don't watch the setting in Zaraneth. It's not that sort of place. You watch the setting somewhere like the Sapphire Coast in the South. We could be there. We could be starting a life worth living."

"And what exactly is a 'life worth living' to you, Lorella?" Gardeniyah asked. "Because, personally, I think that working for the greater good is a pretty worthwhile way to spend your life. And I thought you felt the same way. You wanted to do this as much as I did."

"I don't know what that means to me," Lorella said. "How could I? We never got the chance to find out. We lived our lives knowing exactly when our lives in the East would end. Now we are spending our days chasing something we may never find. We went from one extreme to the other. We could have been in the South. Evanlee could have watched all the settings she wanted. You could have read as many books as your heart desired. Amazing ones like Sulley just talked about. I could have been figuring out what a life worth living means to me. Instead, we are here."

"We wouldn't have been in the South anyway!" Gardeniyah insisted.

"Why? Because humans are supposed to live in the

North? So we would have just obeyed some archaic rule that no one else follows?"

"Well, yes. That's kind of the whole reason we took on this quest."

"No, Gardeniyah. That's why you took this on." Lorella jabbed her sister's chest with her finger as she spoke. "I took on this quest so that she could go back to the East," Lorella said, pointing her other finger at Evanlee, "because, in the middle of a fight, that little girl stares at the lights setting!"

Lorella turned away from them after she said that. She was like that. She was hard, and she yelled and said things she wouldn't take back, even if she knew she should. She had venom in her words a majority of the time. She was bitter and angry, but she was a good person. She was doing this so her sister could have a good life.

Or at least that's what she was telling her sisters. And, of course, like every good lie (especially the ones we tell ourselves), it had truth to it. But if you could have seen her eyes, you would have been able to tell that she didn't believe the words she was saying. She wanted greatness and the chance to be a part of something bigger, just like Gardeniyah. But she was too scared to go after it.

Fear's cleverest trick is to mask itself as protection of loved ones. You fear your future not because you are afraid you will not get what you want. No, often what you fear most is what you know, deep down, you could become in order to obtain your desire.

So you hide your desires for the sake of your loved ones. You are, in fact, trying to protect them—that is part of the truth woven into the lie—but you aren't protecting them from what you say you are. Instead, you are protecting them from the self you are afraid will come out if that repressed part of you is ever given the chance.

You could swear before a thousand different moons that

you would never hurt the ones you love. No matter what. No matter the circumstance. And you could make wishes on a thousand suns that you are never tempted to do so. But, in reality, sometimes our desires are not so pure. And though you gallantly try to repress them every day, you fear you will one day fail. You don't trust yourself to be strong enough to not become what you hate. So you choose to never face it.

This was the state that Lorella was in. Afraid of herself more than anything in Zaraneth or in the whole world of Tolatin. She had felt a rush of power in the moments after her sisters' lives were in jeopardy. And she had liked it. She didn't trust herself with the power or the information the book contained. But she was in denial, lying to herself about why she wanted to end the mission. She didn't fear failing, like Gardeniyah did. She feared succeeding.

Of course, her sisters did not see Lorella clearly enough to catch her in her self-preservation-based lie. They were looking through the haze of an argument. And Lorella's lie was the perfect way to end one such as this.

Evanlee reached out and hugged Lorella. Who, of course, instantly pulled away from her. They all three stood there a little while longer in silence.

"You're right," Gardeniyah said after some time. "This isn't fair to you two."

Lorella sighed and then voiced her agreement. "Yeah, it's been long enough. We gave it a good shot. We have looked through everything he has. Twice, at least. I know I have read some of the letters at least three times. We can be done with this and move on with our lives."

"We are giving up?" Evanlee asked. By now, they were all sitting down on the small porch. They couldn't all fit, so Gardeniyah was sitting on the steps, which had become one of her favorite spots.

"It's not giving up, Ev. We gave it our best go. We've

reached a dead end. What else are we supposed to do?" Lorella said.

"Yeah, I suppose that's true," Evanlee replied.

"So are we all agreed?" Lorella asked. "Enough of this?" Lorella's sisters also missed at this moment how Lorella said this with just a little too much relief.

"Yeah, I suppose," Evanlee said, her voice quaking. "It doesn't feel right, though. We agreed to do it. We promised Ranosa and Vadeed we would do this. How are we supposed to let them know we had to stop?"

"Ev, that's exactly it, we can't let them know. If we keep going, we are going to spend our lives trying to save the beings that couldn't even bother to give us a pass to come back to give them updates."

"We aren't trying to save them," Gardeniyah said, the words Sulley had said earlier ringing through her head.

"What are you talking about?" Lorella asked. "That's who asked us to do this. That's who we are saving."

"No. That's who we are protecting."

"Okay? Isn't that what I said?"

"No. There's a difference in saving and protecting. We are saving us, the humans, from all the mistakes we have made. Just like Sulley said. And by doing that also protecting the East from those same mistakes."

"They need saving, and the East needs protecting," Lorella said, gesturing in each direction, "and we need to be living our lives. Not held up in this place for who knows how much longer trying to fix something that isn't our problem."

"I just don't see how it's not our problem." Gardeniyah shook her head as if tired and trying to stay awake, but her posture seemed more alert than ever. "It's the whole world's problem. Someone has to fix it."

"Look, I know you had your heart set on this thing, but just think about it. Okay?" Lorella urged.

"I am thinking about it, and I am thinking that you shouldn't have to do it anymore if you don't want to," Gardeniyah said. "However, that doesn't mean that I don't want to do it."

"Wait. Wait. Are you saying you would keep going with this?"

"Yes."

"So, you're saying we would separate?"

"I suppose so."

"What?" Evanlee screamed.

"I thought the whole reason they let us stay in the East another year was so that we could all be together?" Lorella looked at Gardeniyah in disbelief. Lorella couldn't believe what she was hearing. She would never have guessed Gardeniyah would ever even think about, let alone suggest, they separate.

"You're right, it was." Gardeniyah wasn't looking at them as she spoke. If she did so, she wouldn't have the strength to say what she knew she had to say. "I think, though, out here, we all want something different. I want to keep searching for the book and the spell. I won't be able to be happy living out my life, wherever that would be, if I quit. It wouldn't matter. I will always wonder and be tortured by what-ifs, and I can't live that way."

"I don't want to separate from you!" Evanlee reached out and wrapped her arms around her big sister, who leaned into her embrace. "If I were okay with parting from you, I would have stayed in the East another three years."

"I know, Evanlee, but Lorella is right. You hate this sort of thing. It's not who you are."

"I'm fifteen. I don't want to be separated from my big sisters. You two are all I have. I never thought I would say this, but I don't care if I never see the East again. I just don't want to lose you!"

"I don't want that either," Gardeniyah said sadly.

"Look," Lorella interjected, putting her hand out to stop the conversation and the decision that was looming before them. "We don't have to figure this out tonight. Let's just go back inside. It's getting cold. I think a blizzard is moving in. We can sleep on it and talk about it tomorrow."

They all nodded, and Lorella and Evanlee got up and began to go inside. Gardeniyah stayed sitting on the steps.

"Aren't you coming?" Evanlee asked.

"I'll be in in a few minutes."

Lorella and Evanlee went back inside. Gardeniyah stayed gazing out into the world at everything and nothing. She knew she had missed her moment to tell them about the prophecy.

Protecting them was no longer her main goal in life. But that didn't mean she didn't still want to protect them. She didn't know what she was getting into. She didn't know how dangerous it would be. The best way to keep them safe was to not have them go with her.

She would never have been able to leave Evanlee alone to fend for herself. So if it had just been her who wanted to give up, then she would have told them both about the prophecy. But Lorella wanted to stop searching too. Gardeniyah knew that Lorella was more than capable of looking after Evanlee. So Gardeniyah could continue the quest alone. There was no need to put them in danger.

After a few minutes, Sulley came outside and joined her.

"Quite a discussion you three had," he said as he sat down beside her.

"You heard all that? We went outside to avoid that."

"Unluckily for you, and luckily for me, I had just opened my bedroom window to let some air in a few moments before."

"Why is that lucky for you? You like eavesdropping that

much?" She felt guilty for the edge her voice still contained from the argument with her sisters.

"No. No. No. Not that. I like my own business. No. No. No. It's that I heard what I needed to hear."

"What are you talking about?"

"There's one, well, actually two, letters you haven't seen. That none of you have seen. I haven't even seen one of them, actually."

"I'm confused." She liked Sulley very much, but he often talked in circles that could feel very much like riddles.

"Let me explain . . . Sanora gave me three letters about the prophecy. One was the one I read you three when you arrived. The other two were a bit more sensitive in nature. One was for my eyes only. In that letter, she told me that the third letter was for one of the humans who would show up— but it was only for one of you. It was for the one who had the purest heart and most dedication for the mission. I was told to wait to give you the letter until I was sure which one of you it was. I've been asking questions for days, to the annoyance of your middle sister, I believe, trying to figure out which of you it was meant for. I've had the feeling it was you for a couple of days. Now, though, I'm positive it is. This letter is important to the quest, that I know. And I hope it will answer many questions."

The exchange between the two was full of questions as it continued and would be quite confusing to follow. Gardeniyah interrupted the old man often with questions, like anyone would, given the circumstances. Which, of course, threw the eccentric old man off and made him repeat himself even more than normal. So it's best for you to read the story as Gardeniyah came to know it.

CHAPTER FORTY-NINE

The air sent a chill down Sanora's spine. Never in history had the East been as cold as it was tonight. The moon was full, and the stars nearby had almost fully encircled it. Around the four nations, everyone would notice and find it astounding. Perhaps they would stare in wonder for a moment or two, but then they would move on with their night. Sanora, though, knew what it meant. Her brisk walk converted to a full-speed run as the stars finished circling the moon, creating a solid band of light.

Then, suddenly, that didn't feel fast enough. Right as she came to a clearing in the woods by a creek, she jumped into the air. The wings that lay flat against her back spread out wide and caught her ascension into the air. She had wanted to avoid flying, as the trees often made it difficult to maneuver, but the branches whipping her face were worth it if she could move faster.

She didn't know where she was going. She had never been told that, but she knew he would meet her where she was when the time was right. All she had to guide her was the prophecy that he had given her the last time he saw her.

"When a circle surrounds the ancient jewels
So starts the demise of recent fools
Seek out the word I will send
To prepare you for the beginning of the end"

The night was only growing colder as Sanora reached Serenity Falls, the highest point in all of the East. Here, she decided, would be good enough. No one would be anywhere near here at this time of night, whatever time that was. Very few even knew this place existed. She had no idea how long she had been running and flying. It had been close to five hundred years since she had been to the top of the falls, so she had long forgotten how long the journey took. In fact, she had been here the last time she had seen him. *Maybe that's why I ended up here,* she thought.

She took a seat on a rock near the water. The last time she was here, she'd sat in the same spot and allowed her feet to gently skim the water. It had been a calmer time—before the world was in chaos, like it was now. She had been here just enjoying the company of her dearest friends, the other rulers of the four regions; it wasn't their normal meeting place, but it had been a special occasion, which made the memory that much fonder. Like the years gone by, they were all long since gone.

But tonight was different. Had the weather been warmer and the circumstances less grave, she would not have been able to resist dipping her feet into the water as she had done before. But they weren't, so she refrained. She settled simply on closing her eyes to prepare herself for the meeting with the Omniscient.

After some time, the wind began to pick up, and leaves were swept off the branches. This went on for some time. The wind did not match the freezing temperatures she had been enduring. It was a warm wind that brought the heat back into Sanora's freezing body. She knew he was near.

She heard footsteps and looked up toward the top of the waterfall. There stood a figure glowing brighter than the moon itself. Sanora jumped off the rock and knelt down. By the time she looked up from kneeling, he was before her.

He had not toned down his aura as he usually did, and the light exuding from him was too much for Sanora to handle, so she simply remained looking at the ground. His hand reached out and touched her shoulder.

"Stand, dear one," the strong voice demanded. With that, the light around him dimmed considerably, and Sanora was able to look up into his face and do as he requested.

"Omniscient, what is going to happen?" Sanora said. She tried to control her voice, but she was not like the other fairies. The Omniscient had chosen her to preside over the fairies and because of that granted her two unique attributes. The first was the ability to feel more than one emotion. The other was the ability to wield all three gifts, war, mercy and healing. The first was why she was having a hard time controlling her voice, but both qualities were what made her the capable leader the East needed. Had she been controlled by any one emotion or gift, the history of Tolatin would not have been the same. A leader, for example, controlled by anger and with the war gift would have reacted vastly different to the humans' rebellion of the Divine Order than that of a leader controlled by fear and with the gift of mercy.

The Omniscient laughed the kind of laugh that erases all nerves and makes you feel comfortable. "That is the age-old question of all living things. To tell you that would be to set you above all other creations, and you already have enough of an advantage with all the wisdom you have."

"I understand." Sanora had now regained her composure and stood tall and dignified. "But why, then, my lord, have you summoned me tonight?"

"Walk with me, dear one." They began to walk to the top

of the waterfall where he had first appeared. The steps were steep and the ground slick and cold. Every so often, a step or two before anyone should know there was trouble coming, the Omniscient would reach out and steady Sanora. He didn't stop her from walking on the slick patch or guide her around the puddles, but he would make sure she didn't fall because of them. As they walked, he continued to speak. "I chose to bring you into this world first because you would not die unless killed. I made sure to grant you the unique ability to think clearly in any situation despite the weakness of your people. In recent years, you may have realized why . . ." His voice trailed off for a moment.

There's something especially disturbing about someone so strong and commanding seeming hurt or bothered by something. Sanora did not like to see this powerful, magical, all-knowing being this way, as none of us would. It made her stomach feel as though it was ripping apart from the inside. "The humans have violated the plan I created for Tolatin. Do you remember the day I brought you all together?"

"Yes, of course. I was placed here first. You put me in charge of the mystical creatures of the East. You then brought King Madeous into the world for the humans and put him in charge of the North. A little later, King Alexius the Lion arrived to rule over all the beasts of the West, and then King Torriel the Grateous for the Southern monsters."

"Very good, so your old age has not gotten the best of you," the Omniscient said with a wink. His playful comment eased the tension a bit.

"Oh, you should know it has not, my supreme; after all, you gave me and the rest of my people eternal youth." She was annoyed at herself at that moment for giving such a literal response when she knew full well he was attempting to lighten the situation.

"Yes, so I did," he said, laughing. Sanora wasn't sure if the laugh was because she had answered so literally or if it was because she had somehow managed to portray it as a joke. Now, of course, that was a ridiculous question. He knew her mind and so knew very well that she had been being frank. He was called the Omniscient, after all.

However, Sanora was so wrapped up in trying to interpret his laughter that she almost missed what he said next. If it had been anyone else, she probably would have. The Omniscient, though, wasn't the sort of being you could daydream around.

"Now, that day you all made a covenant with each other and with me at the spot where I brought all four of you together for the first time. Right when the world began. You were to rule your people and stay within your territories. I know I do not have to tell you that the humans of the North have long since voided that covenant by taking over the West and the South. I am thankful you have kept them from the East. You and your people did right by taking in the refugees of the other nations who were kicked out by man, but I have grown tired of man's greed. Enough is enough."

"I agree. What would you have me do?"

"Nothing. Your time is up."

"My lord, whatever do you mean?" Sanora said as she came to a halt. They were at the top of the waterfall. It was the highest point in the entire world.

"Look. What do you see?"

"I see the Lights of the Four Corners." At the edge of each corner of the world were the lights that burned that kept the regions in their seasons. They were miniature suns and gave light to the world at each corner.

"Does anything look strange to you?" the Omniscient questioned.

"They look dimmer than I remember."

"That is because they are. They are going out, Sanora,

and when they do, the world will become so uninhabitable, it will only be a matter of time before the entire population dies. The only way for the world to become right again is for all the damage man has done to be reversed. They did not just uproot entire civilizations; they destroyed each area they came in contact with. The West has lost most of its trees. Its food sources are nearly gone. The North's water has become polluted, and now the icebergs are melting and gray. The South has become less of a paradise and has been transformed almost entirely into a desert. Again, nearly all forms of natural life and most food sources are gone. The East is the only reservoir of hope left. Yet, even as bright at the East's sun still is, it is not enough to light the entire world. It is like all good things— once surrounded by corruption, soon its light, too, shall go out."

Sanora caught her breath. How could this happen? How could the East be punished? Her people had done nothing wrong; in fact, she had insisted to all the others that they not only take in the refugees from the other lands but treat them as equals. Her people, the mermaids, the nymphs, the Centaurs, and all the other native Easterners had gone above and beyond the call of duty, and now they would be wiped out along with mankind?

Sanora felt anger rising within her. As the heat from her anger rose to her face, the once warm and comforting wind turned into a vicious, icy, penetrating wind. Sanora's whole body let out a tremor as all the heat, including that which was caused by her temper, fled her body. She looked up to find a less-than-pleased look upon the Omniscient's face.

"So you find this is unfair, do you, Sanora? You want to know what will happen. Fine, look out again to the lights and tell me what you see."

Suddenly, the lights went out. All at once, the world was

dark in very corner. Then, from Zaraneth, a dark glow simmered and shone from the ground.

You might be curious about the term "dark glow," for it sounds like a bit of a contradiction—but, you see, there is no other word to describe what Sanora saw. The glow was so full of greed, shame, and hate that the evil welled up like it does in the most corrupt of humans, straight from the core. Like the anger that rose up inside of Sanora, the glow started giving off its own heat, which brought light back to the world. Only, this light cast a burgundy glow upon the earth. Then a stirring in the North caught Sanora's eye. A blizzard was forming, one stronger than the world had ever seen before. Then, on the ocean between the East and Zaraneth, a wall of water more than three hundred feet tall and two hundred feet wide crashed down upon the East. Sanora ran to the edge of the waterfall and saw a hurricane brewing on the Southern Sea and then start destroying everything. The West was set ablaze by a storm of lightning, and tornadoes ripped the trees from the ground. Sanora fell to her knees and watched as, minutes later, the disasters rotated clockwise, and each region was hit with what had just plagued the neighboring land. This continued until it had come full circle. After a while, Sanora could watch no longer. She was not crying, but her whole body was shaking, her face hidden in her hands.

When she no longer heard the howling of the winds and the phantom screams of those below her, she looked up and saw the profile of the Omniscient. His face was grave yet eerily calm. He looked down at Sanora and stretched out his hand to help her off the ground.

"My dear one, do not look at me with such confusion and pain. You wanted to know what would happen, and so I showed you. Perhaps now you will see why it is often best for us to not know the imminent future. This is not what I want for Tolatin. I do not want this utter destruction inflicted upon them. I will not, however, tolerate this obscene way of life mankind has created any longer. I will start anew if I must."

"There has to be something that I can do, Omniscient. I know I failed at keeping man in line. You warned us, telling not only me but the other three regions' leaders to warn their descendants on the ways of the wicked, and that if one should become corrupt to overthrow their leadership and put a new king or queen in place. It can't be too late, though. I can do that now!"

"Sanora, I am not angry with you for not doing so. I know you tried, but even you were not powerful enough. Man does not enjoy being informed of their wrongdoing by anything or anyone they find above them in any way. That is why they have convinced themselves I don't even exist. I create a sense of authority they don't want to answer to, as do you. They pay no heed to the instructions of a being they don't believe in or in one they don't believe is correct. The answer must come from within man. I could wait for every man's heart to change, but I would wait an eternity. I have chosen those who will bring the world back on the right path, or at least I have chosen those who will have the chance. You must not be available. You know too much, and you are too powerful. It would be too easy for them if you were right there beside them. Leave and go into hiding, tonight. They must find you in order to find me and find the answers they need to set everything right. I will tell you more when the time comes, but for now, take your book. Hide it, then hide yourself. Leave them with the prophecy I am about to give you, and we shall see what will come to be. If they fail to find me and you, the future I have shown you will come to pass."

CHAPTER FIFTY

Gardeniyah felt like she had been hit with a thousand stones at once. She thought she had wanted to know what the prophecy really meant. She had wondered every day about the words "the forthcoming end comes fast." Now that she knew, she regretted knowing, like Sanora had.

Up until now, Sanora had seemed like an almost mythical being. It had felt like chasing after a ghost. Now Gardeniyah knew that Sanora was someone who felt real emotions. More importantly, she felt all of them, like Gardeniyah. Sanora had been terrified by what she'd seen. She had wanted to fix things, like Gardeniyah did, and had been told no, even though she knew how to do it. Gardeniyah shuddered at the thought of how much more torturous the waiting must be for Sanora.

"All out of questions, dear?" Sulley asked.

"Yes." Gardeniyah stared blankly off into the night. The noise of the city was no longer as deafening to her as it once had been. "She was really real. She was flawed."

"Yes. Yes. Yes. She was flawed. But boy, was she wonderful."

"She was scared."

"She was the most scared individual I have ever seen."

Gardeniyah looked at the old man with eyes wide and the world swirling around them.

"Well, she was the most scared individual I had ever seen, until now, darling," Sulley said with a half-hearted chuckle as he pulled her in for a quick hug.

"Do you think the book could be at the waterfall?" she asked excitedly.

"I wondered that myself once. Sanora had told me about it. But, no, she said she hid it somewhere safe that was representative of all beings and regions. The waterfall is purely an Eastern treasure. Plus, it wouldn't be a very secure location to hide something."

Gardeniyah rested her head on the elderly man's bony shoulder. It was the single most uncomfortable shoulder ever to cry on. But she did so anyway.

"How are we ever going to find it?" she asked.

"We will."

"But how?"

"You found me, didn't you? I was a lost and forgotten man. So I suspect you'll find it the same way you found me."

"I got lucky."

"What do you mean? In my opinion, luck never has anything to do with it when someone is working hard for something. It's timing, my dear."

"Well, yes, I agree. I was at the right place at the right time."

"Ah, but you forget you have someone strong on your side. The Omniscient wants this done. There is no greater power working against you than the one who is working with you."

"I don't know. I've never even seen him. What makes you think he's helping us?"

"I have to believe he is. What are we fighting for, if we don't believe? That would mean we are fighting to correct a world for the sake of a being we don't believe could be bothered to help out. Now, I don't know much about him. Seems there is a lot of folklore these days. So I don't know how much he is helping; after all, we think he does want the race of man to be the one to fulfill the prophecy. So I by no means think he will make it easy on us. But that doesn't mean he won't ever help either. The being Sanora described, though scary and powerful, was good and kind. So I say we just have to try, and we have to think twice about calling anything chance or coincidence. I don't know the scope of his power or what he is capable of, so calling anything luck seems mighty brave to me. Yes, yes, yes, I wouldn't want to offend him."

Gardeniyah wanted the words to be more of a comfort to her than they were. Sulley was right. She was fighting to restore order for the Omniscient. Surely, he would help. But right now, she didn't know what to do. Or even where to go from here. They had read through everything. And she had read through everything twice. Now they had absorbed all of Sulley's knowledge, and they had come no closer to finding a clear answer. She was at a standstill, completely unsure where to go from here.

"It's going to be okay. It's all going to be okay," Sulley reassured her. "You can do this. You will do this. You are truly inside Sanora's mind now. You will figure her grand puzzle out."

Eventually, Gardeniyah stopped crying and they went inside. The others had all gone to bed, and Sulley and Gardeniyah followed their example. The weight of the world pressed down on Gardeniyah's eyelids until she fell asleep. Though, if she had known what was about to happen, she surely wouldn't have ever let them close.

～

Five hours later, a loud crash shook the whole house. Letty jumped about two feet off the ground at the sound. When he hit the floor, he immediately shifted on to his hind feet and grabbed his sword with his teeth. Ezer pulled a knife from his boot that no one had known he had. The girls scrambled to their feet. Lorella reached for her knife but saw it was across the room, so instead she lunged for a paperweight off the table near her. Evanlee, who was asleep in the kitchen, grabbed a pan off the counter. Gardeniyah picked up Sulley's cane from its spot next to the couch. Then they all waited.

The next thirteen seconds ticked by in slow motion. They would realize in exactly three of those thirteen seconds that the loud bang that had woken them all up was the front door being broken off its hinges. At second five, due to the excessive number of footsteps, they would realize that this wasn't some common Zaraneth-style break-in. At second eleven, when they heard the sounds of struggling, they would know something was terribly wrong. And finally, at the thirteenth second, when they saw six men dressed in matching uniforms standing tall with Sulley down on his knees in front of them with a knife to his throat, they would realize it was their worst nightmare.

They had been found.

CHAPTER FIFTY-ONE

"**D**rop your weapons, or I'll slit his throat!" the man holding the knife to Sulley's neck yelled.

They did as they were told. A man appeared from behind the soldiers. He was older but no taller than the rest, and his uniform was far more decorated than the other men in his company.

"Only two of those are actual weapons," he said with a chuckle that was as condescending as it was unattractive. "What, were you planning on taking over the world with a paperweight, a pan, and a cane, ladies?" The girls looked from one to another. To Gardeniyah, the man's words were muffled by the pounding of her heart in her ears. "By the looks on your faces, I'm guessing you thought we were here for the old man and not you?"

By now, one of the soldiers had turned on an oil lamp, and the girls could clearly see the group of intruders that stood before them. The man holding Sulley hostage was the largest. The man talking seemed the meanest, and the others seemed like emotionless beings staring at the girls, ready to strike without feeling.

"Well, we aren't here for the old man." The soldier bent down to Sulley's eye level and glared at the feeble old man. "The hunt for this historian was shut down long ago, despite my father's protests." He grabbed Sulley's jaw in his hand so tightly his fingertips were causing red and white marks on Sulley's skin. "He hated this man and his big mouth." He released his grip on Sulley and patted his cheek firmly three times before standing back up still facing the old man as he spoke. "But the king figured he had run away to hide in a hole like the rat he is, and they were naively satisfied with that. So he was living peacefully and hiding from people who weren't even looking for him anymore." Another of his sinister laughs seeped from his lips. Gardeniyah swallowed hard as the man whipped around to face them again. "That is"—he threw his hands up in mock astonishment—"until three girls showed up in Zaraneth and started asking around about a historian. They needed to save the world and apparently needed the man my father always knew would someday cause trouble again to do it."

"I don't know what you're talking about," Lorella said sternly.

"Neither do I," Gardeniyah said, glaring at the soldier. "You've got the wrong man right there. That's my grandfather. He's no historian. He's a former merchant."

"Oh, is that so?" The man waved his finger in a circular motion. Two of the guards began to rummage around the room. It didn't take long for them to find one of Sulley's journals. When they handed it to their leader, he began to read aloud from the pages.

"'In the year eight hundred and sixty-seven, the humans moved from the South to the West. King Clore wasted no time after his appointment to the throne to invade the South. All the beasts already resided in the East with their new counterparts. A similar fate was in store for the monsters of the South.'" With a flick of his hand, he shut the book and handed it back to the guard. "Sounds like an Order sympathizer's history book to me, doesn't it, men?"

The man then walked over to the stove and tossed the book into the fire. Sulley let out a cry, which caused the man holding the knife to his neck to dig it in harder. A drop of blood seeped past the blade and dripped down Sulley's wrinkled neck. The sinister leader watched the journal burn for a few seconds with a smile on his face before he turned back around. He then walked over to the girls and sneered in Gardeniyah's face.

"Any more lies, and I will have my man slice his neck open and make you clean it up." He turned away from her and walked to stand between Ezer and the girls. "So you wanted to save the world? Really? That's the story you are going with?" He laughed again. Gardeniyah had never hated any sound more quickly or so much. "It doesn't need saving; you are just power hungry. What, did you strike a deal with the East? They will let you control man's world if you start a rebellion?"

"No. We have no deal with the East. We have no desire to rule."

"I find that unlikely. Why else would you do this? And," the man hissed in Ezer's direction, "who are you?"

"A friend." His voice was as deep, steady, stern, and commanding as when Gardeniyah had first heard it in Osmond's Tavern. Then it had frightened her. Now it brought her comfort.

"Well, they didn't say anything about you. But if you are helping them, I suppose you need to come with us."

"What, you aren't going to kill us? That seems easiest. Everyone around here knows that's your style," Ezer challenged the man.

"Oh, if it were up to me, yes, I would. But the king wants

to question these three himself. You are obviously working with them, so I'll bring you along too. But this one," the soldier said, turning to walk back toward Sulley. "This one," he said again, this time grabbing Sulley by the nightshirt and pulling him to a standing position while all the while making sure the guard kept the knife pressed against his neck, "the king assumes is dead. He didn't think you would have found him. I think I'm going to make his assumption correct."

"No, don't!" Gardeniyah pleaded. "Like you said, he was living peacefully before we came. He wasn't rebelling. He wasn't hurting anyone! We will go with you peacefully. We won't struggle. We won't give you an ounce of trouble!"

The man rushed toward Gardeniyah. Gardeniyah saw Ezer flinch as he attempted to stand between her and the man before a guard reached out quickly and stopped him.

"Oh, do you really promise?" The soldier's fake enthusiasm rang through the air. He was now inches away from Gardeniyah's face. "I don't care about his rebellious mouth eighty years ago. I care that he was the only man my grandfather and father could never find. No one escaped my family. That's why we have always been in charge of the military. We could find anyone. Except for this man." He pointed so angrily at Sulley that Gardeniyah was surprised it didn't dislocate the man's shoulder. "It haunted my father until the day he died that he didn't give this rebellious scum what he deserved. But it tortured my grandfather until he went insane and killed himself over it. Then my father spent every day of his life when he wasn't on duty poring over notes trying to find this man and avenge his father."

"Please, don't!" Gardeniyah begged again. She knew it wouldn't work. She wished she could say more. But she couldn't.

The man turned around to face his comrades. "Did you hear that, fellas? She said please. Well, I guess I can't carry out my family's multigenerational vendetta now because she said please." He threw his hands up as if in defeat. Then, in one swift motion, he brought his hands down, grabbed his sword from its holster and thrust it into Sulley's stomach.

Time didn't slow this time. It stopped. Gardeniyah started rushing toward Sulley when she first saw the man reach for his sword. She was almost to him when the sword made contact. A soldier stepped out and grabbed her from behind. She tried to pull away, but she couldn't. The man was too strong.

"Gardeniyah. Save them," Sulley said as he locked eyes with the man holding the sword that was in his stomach.

Gardeniyah pushed all her weight against the soldier who was holding her. He had taken for granted that he had stopped her, and had eased his defense just enough for her to be able to break free. Gardeniyah reached Sulley. She put his head in her lap as she attempted to stop the bleeding with one hand. He coughed blood as he looked at his killer for a moment and then made eye contact with Gardeniyah once more and said, "Save them all." He coughed up more blood. "You can do this," Sulley said with his final breath, and then the old man who had lived longer than any man before him finally died.

CHAPTER FIFTY-TWO

C haos ensued as the leader commanded his men to seize them all. The sisters struggled and screamed, but it was no use. They were led out of the small house, and Sulley's body was left there. Ezer knew no one would think twice about the screaming in Zaraneth. Nor would they give a second thought to the murder of the old man or his dead body. Eventually, he would be removed, and the place would be rented out by whoever laid claim to it.

That was the sort of place Zaraneth was. However, the king's men were unaware of the fact that no one would have cared. So they took matters into their own hands and set the entire building ablaze.

Ezer looked over his shoulder as he heard the screams of the other residents of the building as they ran out. The whole building, Sulley's body, his life's work, any answers to the riddle the girls were trying to solve, were burning, giving way to the eventual lie that they'd never existed. The soldiers did not stop amid the screams of those whose homes they had just destroyed. Instead, they walked away calmly from the flames with their captives as if they hadn't created them —worse, as if they weren't even there.

Ezer knew who had ratted them out as soon as the man gave a few too many details. Osmond's Tavern wasn't so large just because of its popularity. Ezer had always suspected Osmond had an arrangement with the king. If Ezer had known how much he would end up liking the girls, he would have discouraged them from telling him a thing. But he hadn't known them, nor had he known for sure that Osmond would leak the information. And he had thought the girls needed Osmond to find Sulley.

Just thinking Sulley's name sent a pain to Ezer's gut. His mind was a tormenting reel. Images flashed in his mind over and over: Sulley's body. Jetta's body. Evanlee's ghostlike face as she stood in the room staring at Sulley and her sister before she collapsed to the ground. Lorella's screams as she fought. She had fought so well. Too well and so they had had to fight dirty to stop her. While she was fighting one, another soldier had come up behind her and hit her over the head with the blunt end of his sword. They both now lay motionless over the shoulder of a guard. The burning building. A bloody Gardeniyah being ripped away from her hunched-over position by Sulley's dead body. All of it played through his mind repeatedly.

They marched through the night and all through Zaraneth. After some time, Osmond's Tavern came into view. Ezer struggled against the grip of the chains bound to his wrists. He wanted to break down the door and tell Osmond what he had done. Make him pay for all of this.

But he couldn't get away. The largest man, the one who had held the knife to Sulley's neck, was holding the chain that bound Ezer's wrists. The guard raised his arm and whipped Ezer's back with the end of the chain for trying to get away. The pain sent Ezer to the ground. He rose to his hands and knees just as the guard lifted his arm to whip Ezer again. Ezer collapsed once more. His whole body shook as he felt warm fluid ooze down his back.

"Traitorous scum." The man sneered as he kicked Ezer's already limp body once in the stomach. Then he took a step back and kicked Ezer again, this time in the head, making contact with Ezer's eye and cheek. Ezer's vision blurred.

Through the haze, Ezer could see Gardeniyah struggling against her captor to get to him. She was kicking the man, not in a frantic way but in the deliberate way he had taught her. Ezer huffed weakly at the sight and laid his head back down on the muddy ground. He began to close his eyes until he saw the guard's retaliation for her desperate attempt to reach him. The man had her throat in his hands, her feet dangled inches from the ground. She clawed at his hands, still trying to kick the man. Her kicks were now desperate and frantic as she stared at Ezer.

She won't stop until I get up. I have to get up. He rose to his hands and knees with every ounce of strength he had. But mere seconds later, his vision went black and he fell to the ground once more.

When his eyes opened again, he could see a blurred face bent over him. He had to blink several times before he could make out the features. When he did, it took him a second to recognize Gardeniyah's now bloodied and bruised face. He closed his eyes hard. *Please let that not be right. Please don't let that be her. Please don't let her have been hurt because of me.* But as he begged for it not to be true, he heard the conversation between the soldiers and knew that it was.

"I told you the king wants them!"

"Sir, I didn't kill her."

"You would have if I hadn't stopped you! He wants them unharmed."

"Well, I would say then she resisted the arrest."

Ezer couldn't see the sinister smile on the man's face, but he could hear it in his voice.

"Well, I'm your commanding officer. I'm the one who has to answer to the king. So the next time you have the urge to leave a mark, clear it with me first. Or I will make sure the only thing you ever command is a mop."

Ezer opened his eye that wasn't swollen. She was still there. "I'm sorry," he whispered as he reached up and wiped the blood from her bleeding and swollen lip and looked at the hand marks around her neck.

"Don't be. No one would believe I came here if I had left Zaraneth without a mark."

His attempt at a laugh came out as a huff that sent pain through his abdomen.

"Hey, hey, hush. I think you have some broken ribs. Can you get up? I want to try and help you up, but I don't know how long they are going to let me stay here by you."

Ezer nodded and put his arm around her. He saw her wince in pain as his arm made contact with the bruises forming around her neck. He started to pull his arm away, but her hand shot up to his forearm and pressed it down onto her shoulder. They slowly stood.

When he was standing again, the guard holding Gardeniyah's chains yanked them hard, causing her to stumble. The jolt nearly caused Ezer, who was still using her for support, to fall again. Gardeniyah managed to steady him once more before easing out of the chained embrace they were in. She did so just in time, as the impatient guard whipped at her again.

When they finally reached the courtyard on the northern border of Zaraneth, it all sank in for Ezer. He was about to leave Zaraneth for the first time. He would be leaving the only place he had ever known, and it was not by choice. It wasn't supposed to be this way. Sulley was the one who was supposed to be going with them.

As he took one last look at his world, he saw all the people peering out from windows and cracked doors. He knew then that there had been people like this all along. Watching them being marched out by government officials and doing nothing.

It didn't matter if he ever got free—if they escaped or the king let him go. He could never come back to Zaraneth. Too many would remember his face. He had been captured in a land where everyone's primary mission in life was to not get caught. He would never have a chance at getting a job or doing business with anyone. No one would rent a home to him. He could never live in Zaraneth again.

He was now a part of all this—the journey to save the world. And his forced entry into it was right at the moment when it had become a lot more complicated. He hadn't planned on remaining a part of it, but here he was accused of trying to save a world he never even wanted to see.

He glanced around at his new permanent comrades. He had heard snippets of their conversation from earlier. They had discussed stopping all of this. Giving up to lead normal lives. He hadn't blamed them.

But now it was too late for that. For him or them. He was marked. They were all marked. They were now traitors to the crown, traitors of Tolatin. Traitors who had been caught.

He looked over at Gardeniyah. The expression in her eyes was like nothing he had seen in her before. There was a reason for that. Gardeniyah had never felt like this before.

CHAPTER FIFTY-THREE

Sulley was gone. Gardeniyah's mentor, her friend, was gone. Ripped from her to satisfy a vendetta. She hated mankind. She had always thought humans were evil and corrupt. Sulley had been the only one to ever try to persuade her to see things differently. He had told her there was good in man. She saw no good in any of these men. She hated them. She hated being one of them.

She felt broken. Torn apart. Every inch of her ached with the pain that was tormenting her soul. The weakness she felt in the presence of this pain was like nothing she had known before. She didn't just feel broken. At that moment, she was sure she was broken. She was even more sure, no matter what Sulley had said, that she couldn't do this anymore. It felt very much like man had won. Maybe she was never meant to succeed. She felt sure that it was over.

But then something happened. Gardeniyah got mad. Now, we are often under the false assumption that getting angry is only ever destructive and wrong. But sometimes that's not the case. Sometimes, it's the best thing we could do.

And in this instance, Gardeniyah's anger was exactly what needed to happen.

Until now, the hatred that had been building inside her toward mankind had been abstract. Her enemy had no face. Now it did. It had seven faces—and as soon as she met the king of man, it would have eight faces.

Yes, Gardeniyah got angry. She got so mad that she was sure there was a fire in her chest. Her chest burned fiercely, forging her broken heart back together, making it stronger than it had ever been.

With this steel heart, she yelled, "Hey, you!"

A soldier turned to her, his eyes flaming with anger at her audacity to address him.

"What, you traitorous scum?" he snarled.

Her heart sank. "I'm not a traitor."

Though she denied it, she knew that's how they saw her and her sisters. The soldiers had murdered Sulley like a traitor. They had captured them like traitors. But she had never wanted to hurt the king or his men.

When they busted down the door of Sulley's home, they hadn't found a group of traitors. She wasn't betraying them, because she had never stood with them. She felt no loyalty to them.

That night, soldiers had killed a man in cold blood. That night, they'd given a woman with a cause someone to avenge as well. That night, in a search brought on by their fear of a conspirator, they'd created the monster they feared.

The man walked over to her and spat in her face. "Yes"— he spit at her again—"you are." Then he reared his hand back and slapped her across the face. He hit her with so much force that her head flew to the side. She would feel the sting of his hand for hours. She slowly turned her head back and once more locked eyes with him.

Legends to this day speak of the moment she challenged

the enemy. When she, despite seeing what he was, rose up with power. Most agree it could not have been her own. Then she declared war on him and all his kind.

"Whatever you do, you won't win," she said. "None of you will win. Whatever you do to me, I will use it. I will use it to make me stronger. I will use whatever you do to me, to the ones I love, to this world, everything and anything you do, to destroy you. You will regret the day you made me your enemy."

He spat in her face for the third time. As she turned to face him once more, a slow smile spread across her face. It was the sincerest, most confident, and cockiest smile that the man had ever seen, especially given the circumstances. The memory of that smile would be burned in his brain for the rest of his life and haunt many nights of attempted sleep.

"Spoken like a traitor," he said.

"Well, then, maybe I am."

74473197R00200

Made in the USA
Columbia, SC
12 September 2019